BIRDS OF FLIGHT – BOOK FOUR

by J.M. Erickson

Falcon is the fourth book in the *Birds of Flight* series

Falcon: Birds of Flight - Book Four
All rights Reserved
Copyright 2014 J. M. Erickson
Edited: Suzanne M. Owen
Cover design: Cathy Helms, Avalon Graphics, LLC
http://www.avalongraphics.org

ISBN: 978-1-942708-00-1 (Soft Cover)
ISBN: 978-1-942708-01-8 (MOBI Format)
ISBN: 978-1-942708-02-5 (ePub Format)

Library of Congress Control Number: 2014922612

Action/Adventure Thrillers

Albatross: Birds of Flight - Book One (Revised)
Raven: Birds of Flight - Book Two
Eagle: Birds of Flight - Book Three
Flight of the Black Swan

Action/Adventure Science Fiction

Future Prometheus I: Emergence & Evolution - Novella I & II
Future Prometheus II: Revolution, Successions & Resurrections - Novellas III, IV & V
Intelligent Design: Revelations

"Turning and turning in the widening gyre
The falcon cannot hear the falconer;
Things fall apart; the centre cannot hold;
Mere anarchy is loosed upon the world,
The blood-dimmed tide is loosed, and everywhere
The ceremony of innocence is drowned;
The best lack all conviction, while the worst
Are full of passionate intensity.
Surely some revelation is at hand;
Surely the Second Coming is at hand..."

The Second Coming, William Butler Yeats, 1920

Prologue

"People who think honestly and deeply have a hostile attitude towards the public."

Johann Wolfgang von Goethe

September 11th 2001 - World Trade Center, New York.

"Are you okay, pal?" Alexander Burns was dazed, confused and exhausted. His eyes stung from his sweat and the noise from first responders and civilians running away from the World Trade Center made it impossible to get to anywhere near the towers. He knew when he hit the car it was a good thing the traffic wasn't moving at all, otherwise he would be dead. The young man helped him up. He felt his head and pulled it back to see blood on his scarred hands.

"My hands are scarred? Why are they scarred?" He touched his scalp and part of his face. The same burns he had for years were all in place. Friendly fire over Swat Valley, Pakistan.

Maxwell and Daniels's betrayal. A new life started.

"But that was May 2, 2011? How did I get here?"

The young man looked at him as if he were crazy.

"Hey dude, I got some news for you. It's September 11, 2001 and the two towers just got hit." As he spoke, he directed Burns to look at the New York skyline. The clear, crisp beautiful fall day was in stark contrast to marred World Trade Towers that had two gaping holes on the sixtieth and eightieth floor. Flames and smoke belching out, Burns had seen these events a million times over the years. London, France, San Francisco, Colorado – all those terrorists' plans were thwarted. All but the ones on the east coast. He immediately thought of Debbie Foley, the young logistics analyst caught in a firefight in Heathrow.

"Dude? You need help or what? I gotta go. National emergency," the young man said. He was still holding onto Burns's arm.

"I'm alright. Get going. I know where I'm going." Burns did his best to give a reassuring smile, something he was still not good at after all his years in the field. He looked down the chaotic street and saw he was just a couple of blocks away. He brushed his sweaty, bloody hand on his battlefield fatigues. His military t-shirt and web belt were soaked with sweat as if he had run a marathon.

I can't be here! I was in DC on September 11th. I was in the Pentagon with Daniels, not here in New York. Where am I going? Am I heading to the World Towers?

"How did I get here?" He looked back at his hands and arms to see that all of his scars from the helicopter crash and IED were there, ten years after September 11th. He looked back up at the two smoldering buildings. He turned back to see that the man was reluctant to go.

"No really, I'm okay. I was on my way to the hospital for supplies," Burns lied.

The man looked justifiably skeptical at him.

"Alright, pal," he said. The man got back in his car and moved it mere feet to the other parked cars on the curbs and sidewalks, and then left it like all the others. Burns kept watching the whole event. He moved against the tide of running civilians, approaching and waning sirens with sheer panic filling the air. Suddenly, Burns heard a burst of static break out near his neckline. He stopped to find that he had a wired ear phone attached to a radio. The ear bud was stuck under the t-shirt. It was the same transceiver radio he had used just days before on the Golden Gate Bridge. He followed the wire to the radio to make sure it was connected properly and then put the ear bud in his ear. The cacophony of voices were all over the place. He pinpointed Thomas Webber immediately by his shrill yelling and next he heard Anthony Maxwell's calm voice come over the wire, issuing instructions. With his intelligence and data-gathering hat on, Burns listened intently to find out how he was in New York on a date two decades before when he knew he was in DC instead. His scars came ten years after 9/11. The time, location and everything was all wrong, as if he were in a dream. The dream immediately turned into a nightmare. A voice from the grave crackled to life in his ear.

"This is *Falcon 7*. I've got Owen but Ramsey and Ellis are down. We are on the fortieth floor in the south tower. I couldn't get to the auxiliary control site on the sixtieth. Ramsey and Ellis got there and are KIA..."

"I need you to make sure that nothing's left of the auxiliary control room," he heard Webber say.

Burns closed his eyes and stood still in an effort to hear. He cupped his other ear and listened as he kept his gaze on the south tower less than two blocks away.

"Negative, *Falcon 7*, get the hell out of there. Webber! Get off the line and let the grownups deal with this," he heard Maxwell say.

"No way I can get back there, Webber," he heard *Falcon 7*, Debbie Foley say.

"But you died in Heathrow?" Burns said aloud.

"What!? I'm not dead yet, Burns! Some help would be nice! Where the hell are you?" Burns's confusion was still stymied by the facts of the events being completely jumbled. But hearing Debbie Foley's voice again spurred him on as if he were on a mission.

"Debbie, I'm two blocks away from your location. I'm on foot and will be there ASAP. I'll need a stairwell marker when you get the chance." Even as Burns picked up his pace and headed to the center of the storm, he heard Webber's voice come through much louder.

"*Falcon 5*! You are to stay in place with the VIP! You're not supposed to be near the World Trade Center! What are you doing, Burns!"

"Webber! Shut the hell up and leave us alone. Burns – get to Foley. She's not supposed to be there," Maxwell said.

"I know," was all Burns said. He was just about a block away when he heard a thunderous wall of steel, glass and concrete collapsing. Burns slowed at first as he watched in shock and awe.

The south tower fell first. It fell fifteen minutes after it was hit. He remembered the event. He saw it a million times. *But how can I be here, in real time? It can't be real!*

"Debbie! Get out of there! Now, Debbie! Run!" Burns yelled.

"What? I didn't get that. What was that noise? Is something happening? Owen's tired and we have to rest."

"No! Don't rest! Run Debbie!"

Burns was now in a full sprint. His body felt older, fatigued and exhausted. As he approached the falling tower, a wall of dark, heated dust and soot raced to meet him. The people, cars, fire trucks, and the entire world around him was engulfed in darkness and noise.

"Foley! Don't stop!"

"Burns? It's completely dark here..." The static's volume jumped just as his body's momentum was slowed by the shock wave of debris crashing into him and everything in its path. The roar of noise, screams, crushing sounds and heated darkness with metal and concrete pelted his body. No air, heat, filth and sweat filled his senses. He felt his head bolt up as if he had nodded awake from a horrible dream. He heard a car radio playing country music, and felt that his arms and feet were bound while he sat in a moving vehicle. It took him longer to orient himself as a result of being drugged.

Oh yeah. Daniels's men got me. Drugged me. Heading east. I wonder when it will be over.

He felt a wave of sleep coming over him. He was glad to wake up from the horrible nightmare even if it was drug-induced. Even before his head dipped back down he sensed another dream forming.

I wonder how bad this one will be?

#

May 2nd 2011 – Swat Valley, Pakistan

"I'm telling you I don't have a body! You think I'm out here sunning myself, Webber?! You might want to try coming out here and find out what a real mission's like," Anthony Maxwell said. He was annoyed at dumb suggestions. He was bent on one knee surveying the hot zone trying to focus on where things were and how things could play out as he listened to the voice on the other end of the radio cell phone. Just when he thought it couldn't get worse, he replayed the last suggestion Thomas "Steel" Webber offered.

"What?! Ask the embassy and local marines for help? We're not supposed to be here!"

He stood up straight to work out the stress from talking to his boss. The phone was crystal clear so to avoid any further discussion, he closed the line without waiting for a response. He tossed the phone to one of eight Foreign Intelligence Agency agents, and continued his abbreviated search of the crash site where the command chopper went down. Time was a luxury he did not have; he never did. The pilot was KIA and still in her seat, and the passenger seat, presumably the one Alexander Burns was sitting in, was empty. The blood trail went dry after several feet from the crash making a search by foot and overhead necessary.

"Damn him! Why can't he just be dead?"

Maxwell had known Burns for many years and they did not always agree, but he had to respect the man's abilities to survive the impossible.

Not much time before the curious and authorities show up asking a lot of questions, he thought as he looked at his watch and then looked toward the east horizon for any dust trails.

"Sir? Why is it so important that we find this Burns guy? I mean, he wasn't supposed to come in to check on our status; he was supposed to hang back and let us do our thing," a younger agent asked.

And just to aggravate me more, a dimwitted newbie agent to boot. Daniels must really hate me.

Maxwell closed his eyes. He hoped he could blot out the image of his boss and now the face of the new agent. Maxwell did his best to calm his voice and quell the impulse to simply slap the young newbie.

"Part of the mission was covert to Burns per Chairman Daniels's orders. Burns would have been key to selling Sudani's death to the White House. With him KIA at least we can say he died in the mission. With him MIA, we have a pretty big problem..."

Maxwell heard the young agent's voice cut him off in a huff as if he was the only agent on the field thinking.

"Yeah but if he's out there somewhere, MIA and shit, he'll probably get killed and our job is done, if you ask me," the young man interrupted. As predicted Maxwell felt the veins in his neck constrict along with the grip on his binoculars as he slowly turned around to look at the newbie.

Idiots...obviously you're a plant of Webber.

Maxwell was careful to take a few seconds to find the right words. It took less time than he expected to respond.

"No one's asking you, newbie! Unless we come back with Burns's body, he's a liability to this mission. He knows more shit about this mission and a whole lot of other missions that could be compromised. And if he thinks we screwed him, which we did, he won't let that go unanswered. With Burns killed in action, there's no retribution and it's a much better scenario; Burns missing in action is an unfolding nightmare that will bite us all in the ass some time in the future, on his schedule and terms. Do you want to be around when that shit happens, you moron?"

Maxwell had some satisfaction in seeing the young man's eyes grow wide and his mouth finally stop moving. The man was about to move off quickly until Maxwell stopped him.

"And don't ever interrupt me when I'm talking!"

"Yes, Sir! Sorry, Sir!" the young pale agent said as he tried to move quickly. Maxwell watched his rapid retreat as he marveled at both his arrogance and his pale skin. His anger subsided as he watched the pale agent take out a tube of something and started liberally applying whatever it was to his hands and skin.

Suntan lotion? Really? You think the sun's going to kill you? You'll be lucky if you live long enough to get cancer.

The irony was not lost on Maxwell. He shook his head in dismay at the incongruency of applying suntan lotion in a foreign land on an illegal assassination plot while looking for collateral damage. Once again he turned away to push the image out of his head. He looked back at the trail and felt another angry outburst emerging at the thought of losing Burns in the desert.

"Idiots! You pay peanuts and you get monkeys. And why the hell couldn't you just let it go, Burns? We needed Sudani alive. When did you get all patriotic and noble?"

The mission was launched in the early morning well before dawn. Right now, morning dawn was breaking faster than he wanted it to. As if on cue, his radio chirped. He knew what was going to follow.

"Recon 6 to CO: we've got two dust trails coming in – one from the east and the other from the south. ETA is ten minutes. Boss – we gotta move. This area will be filled with Pakistani troops, and we're not supposed to be here." He looked up in the sky and knew of the three helicopters above, it was the one furthest out that was reporting on the sudden change of events.

Just figures.

Maxwell focused on the mission and took his time answering. He felt his hand clench more on the radio before he responded. His assessment kept yielding the same results no matter how he changed the factors, premise and alternatives.

"Alright, have all squads report in for departure. Bring the pilot's body, and strip and torch the chopper. We evac in five minutes. And call Daniels and relay the following message – 'falcon has left falconer; his condition unknown.' Repeat: 'falcon has left falconer; his condition unknown.'" Maxwell said with great resignation.

This just sucks.

"'Falcon has left falconer; his condition unknown.' Got it. Heading back to you now," his radio said before it chirped off. Maxwell couldn't stop himself from scanning the horizon. He watched the two other helicopters break off their search and return to the crash site while the field agents on the ground returned quickly to the landing zone. Light of day was getting stronger. He sensed more than saw the charred remains of the downed helicopter burst into a contained fire. Even though the majority of the mission was a success, he felt uneasy not knowing whether his former friend and colleague was dead or alive.

"Damn it, Burns! Why couldn't you just go with the program?"

May 2nd, Five Years Later – Houston, Texas, USA

Damn, damn, damn. Do I have to do everything myself?

Chairman Eric Daniels knew he sounded calm as he directed Alica Wise to pursue a ghost while Denise Cratty returned to secure the crime scene at the Auxiliary Control, North Andover.

Acting. All acting.

Even as he managed to speak to Wise clearly, cogently and thoroughly, he knew it was taking all of his theatrical abilities and leadership skills from reaching out and slapping her to see the obvious and pursue the terrorist. With precious time slipping away and convinced that Wise knew the plan, he finally hung up. Daniels felt his heart pounding and rage exploding from his chest.

"God damn you, Burns!" Daniels yelled. He was now standing up in his home office in Houston, Texas. His chair rolled back violently crashing into another desk behind him as a result of his sudden movement. He stood with both fists clenched as he stared at his bank of eight monitors.

"How the hell did you do this!? How are you doing this? Who's helping you – the Israelis, you traitor!?"

Daniels tried to contain his fury. He grit his teeth to help with the anger. His hangover didn't help. To make matters worse, he felt his nose beginning to tingle as it sometimes did when it was about to erupt.

Damned blood pressure, he thought as he slowed down his breathing along with his pulse.

"It's all falling apart. Everything is just falling apart," he said at a lower volume. It was not in his makeup to be pessimistic or negative, especially in a crisis. He was always prepared. He looked at the series of monitors and images knowing that it had to be his missing former agent. But all his predictable actions were now different, very different, as if he were another person. And the timing, locations and situations couldn't have been from just one man, even from Burns.

You're a loner...not much into the team...and if there were other intelligence agencies helping, I would have known about it. But this is different. This is from the inside after years of absence. Why now? Why today? Why return from the dead or hiding? We thought you were dead and then you make it out of Pakistan a changed man. And just when we get you back, you disappear. What the hell?!

Daniels took a step back from his control center at home to get a different perspective, maybe clear his thoughts. He looked at the array of scenes and segments from Massachusetts. Even though he was still angry and wanted to hurl his chair into his computer station, he decided to verbally vent his anger at Cratty and Webber for their incompetence.

"Where the hell are you, Webber!?" Daniels yelled at no one. "At least Cratty is trying to do her job, however badly!"

And Burns, he thought, *I'm going to find you and rip your heart out, you bastard!*

It took all of Daniels's will to just stop and breathe while standing barefoot in his sweats and t-shirt. With his hands now moving to his head, he felt it really aching from the stress of waking up late from too much drinking. And when the phone calls started to come in, it was easy to piece together that his intelligence agency was nuked, America was under attack with all back-up systems off-line, a senior field agent dead, and his second-in-command missing in action.

All of this because a rogue field agent returns from the dead. What the hell else could go wrong? Do you have weapons of mass destruction too, Burns? You plan to bomb the White House?

It took longer than he wanted but Daniels finally controlled his breathing and felt ready to engage the problem. With a very deep sigh, Daniels turned suddenly to quickly retrieve his chair so he could sit and puzzle together what his former agent had done. But Daniels knew his questions were more "why and how" Burns did it.

With eight monitors attached to four powerful CPUs, Daniels took a swig of very cold coffee and returned to his panorama of split images on eight equal-sized screens.

"All right. Let's take another look," he said.

He turned to scrutinize the furthest screens where he saw various news updates and first-hand reports from first responders dealing with a range of "terrorists' attacks."

"All right...a condominium complex in flames across the street from a hospital. Bombs placed in both ER and maternity wards," he said as he shifted focus to another screen while continuing his monologue. "A truck filled with what looks like explosives in an industrial parking lot twenty minutes later. Almost an hour after that, a bomb is discovered in a public building next to an elementary school...and then FBI Boston Regional goes dark." He took another look at the array of screens, and then read the last piece of critical information he got before the Bureau shut down.

"Black knight in place. White knight on the move. Alpha out."
"Alpha, Charlie. White bishop on the move. Bravo out."
"White bishop secured transport. Black bishop, you are a go. Bravo out."
"Black bishop has delivered the package and is on the move. Heading to lair. Charlie out."
"White bishop to send package to our friends. Time for black bishop to move out. Bravo out." "Alpha and Bravo rendezvous complete.

Package exchanged. Alpha is on to prime objective, and Bravo to launch point two — out."
"Message received. Prepping for launch at primary location. ETA is 10:00 am. Charlie out."

Daniels sat back in his comfortable, leather chair for a moment He re-read the preliminary reports of the cyber attack, nodded, and then the rationale for the cyber attacks became clear. He shook his head in disbelief. He now had the final hard evidence it had to be Alexander Burns responsible for all this.

"Not only did you know the protocols for computer defenses and relocation, you knew where the firewalls were and their weakness, and you used the Trojan, you bastard."

He peered at the center screen for a long time to re-read the last message received by his intelligence agency's operations center before it joined the FBI's control center and went dark.

"I remember everything on May 2, 2011. Operation center, Foreign Intelligence Agency, all present foreign operations are compromised. Cyber attack imminent."

You remember everything because you were there. You were supposed to witness Sudani's death but you poked your nose into places you shouldn't and then got yourself shot down. I wished you were dead.

Daniels sat silently, recounting the reports of Burns's MIA status and no luck finding him.

"Screw you, Burns," he said at the screen as if he were talking to Burns himself. Visions of the *Four Horsemen of the Apocalypse* sprung into his head as he fully appreciated the damage his former employee was inflicting.

"So you're pissed about the Oman Sharif Sudani mission. And to prove your point, you used one of our cyber attack viruses meant for North Korea to shut down my agency," he said thoughtfully. Still sitting back in his chair, Daniels found himself confused.

But something is very different. Why warn us that our missions are in danger? When have you ever cared about collateral damage? You think you want that? Something is odd, missing.

Daniels turned his back on the monitors to look outside his windows to see bright sunlight trying to cut through the blinds. The act cleared his head of the images on the screens to see what was absent and "off" about the entire picture. The sun's rays reflected off his clean desk where he noticed that the rays appeared as individual beams of light hitting different parts of the glass desk top. The same sunlight but all with different beams.

"Where are the bodies, Burns? Usually you leave a lot of collateral damage along with your target...where are they? What are you doing?"

Daniels sat back up, turned back to his screens and searched for old, classified files backed up on external hard drives. Window after window of past reports and after-action summaries immediately surfaced. He scanned all the classified data before Burns's final mission. He also researched his disappearance from his therapist's office more than four years ago for the hundredth time. For a while he could see that Burns's methods still seemed to be the same, at first glance.

Wait a minute. He was seeing a therapist for post trauma...how could I have been so blind?

"The field agent watching him is killed in the parking garage, neck broken. The associate who was sent to clean up Caulfield went missing, and the other one was found dead in Littleton's hotel room," he mused.

Therapy for post trauma? Something else unleashed? He changed?

"But...Littleton and her sister were never found, and Caulfield's body was identified through personal items only," he said as he sat back again in his chair so as to take in the entire bank of monitors. It took Daniels a full minute to slowly re-think his premise before he was absolutely sure. He stood back up and walked away from the monitors as a means of consolidating his thinking. He then turned back to take in the array of attacks, walked back and sat down as the key thing missing made total sense.

"No bodies. All threats but no injuries or deaths. No civilians harmed to date and every first responder and law enforcement agency along the east coast scrambled...but Maxwell is dead," he said out loud. His conversation with Wise fifteen minutes ago flashed before him that the guards and Jillian Davis were attacked but, again, not killed.

You didn't kill them, or the civilians and we have no solid confirmations that Caulfield or the Littletons are dead...and you have four hard drives of five years of black ops...

Eyes narrowed and fists clenched, he stood up again and walked to the middle of his room. He stared back at the monitors as he took in the full breadth of his stupidity for not seeing the obvious until it was too late. Again images of the Four Horsemen flooded back as Daniels recalled the benefits of his classical education.

Different color horses with four riders...Conquest, War, Famine and Death...The Day of Judgment...end of days..the Apocalypse.

Cold realization settled in his bones.

"So...you're not a 'lone wolf' any more. They helped you. Caulfield and the Littletons aren't dead or missing. They're your team. These people, these civilians are your team, now. That's how you could be in three different places at the same time. That's how you could create all of these distractions, get into public buildings and launch the cyber attacks. That's why there are no bodies – you might have wanted to kill people but maybe they didn't. All this time you were missing, you weren't running dark and off-grid. You were training them and planning all this time for this day."

Closing his eyes, Daniels nodded in resignation as a man might after hearing he had less than a month to live.

"And they're a motivated group, too. What do they want? Revenge for killing Caulfield's wife? Do they want restitution for taking their lives? Do they want to make us all pay? I hate it when it's personal! Okay."

Daniels opened his eyes and returned to his chair to take

command of his bank of computers and agency.

"New behavioral patterns, configurations and parameters to consider: Burns has a team, they are trained and committed. Maybe they won't kill indiscriminately but they are committed to acts of treason to get what they want."

Daniels took a moment to review the new data and revised his thinking as the severity of the situation went deep.

Terrorists? No. Worse – vengeance. It is personal.

"They have classified data that could destabilize the government and the world, and it's clear that Burns won't just sell it and go dark. He could have done that before...it has to be for them...his team's benefit somehow," Daniels continued to talk aloud as he looked at all the raw data in front of him. The more he thought about the impossibility of Burns changing from a trained assassin to something completely different, the more the information made sense. Still, Daniels was puzzled as he looked at a small picture of a well-maintained home he knew was in a well-appointed, gated community in Missouri just opposite a dilapidated ruins of a building in the same neighborhood, worlds apart. He smiled since he knew his guest was safely in place, a nice home in Wisconsin while his own "bunker," the final fire front, was operational in St. Louis, if necessary.

No one knows where I am now, let alone my bunker. But still...if Burns can change, so can the entire situation.

He shifted his focus to the present and immediately opened a recently configured midnight blue smartphone he pulled from a pile of mobile electronics. It didn't take him long to search his short list of contacts on this "private" phone. He immediately found what he was looking for when the thought of Burns's return harbingered the possibility of his "tying up loose ends."

It only took two rings before his employee picked up.

He's high-maintenance and a pain in the ass but he's prompt to a fault.

"Carter? It's *Eagle* – move the VIP. Move him to the 'castle' near the bunker," Daniels said cryptically. A sudden news flash caught his attention. Local and national reports were calling the "Merrimack Valley Crisis" a joint domestic and foreign terrorist attack.

His focus was suddenly brought back by the man's complaining on the other end of the phone. Under other circumstance, if the world as he knew it wasn't coming to an end, he might have had the patience to deal with Timothy Carter. Instead, Daniels found his patience was strained at best.

"Tim! No one asked you what you thought! You've been on the bankroll for years and everything you have is because of me and the VIP. I don't care if you don't like how this looks for you. Do your job or I'll expose you and your cause for the sham it is! Got it?"

If there was a response, Daniels didn't hear it as he closed out the line before he could hear the response. Daniels took a moment to sit quietly, look at multiple screens of live streaming and new analysis before he threw his phone back into the pile. He now clutched his "work phone" with which he had spoken to Wise minutes ago.

"Who are you, Burns? What have you changed into? The 'Pale Rider?'"

Daniels would have considered the question more fully except his phone rang and the caller identification named "Cratty, D." came up.

As it rang, Daniels felt suddenly tired and almost groggy, as if he were asleep, while he reached over to pick the phone up.

Why is the phone so far away, he thought as it seemed to be taking him a long time to reach over and pick it up.

#

Present Day - Waltham, Massachusetts, USA

Daniels's hand finally landed on the alarm clock. He stirred in his bed at a low-end motel before finally sitting up in a stark, sparsely furnished room with all his belongings neatly stacked in the corner.

Daniels shook sleep from his head as he rubbed his eyes. Unlike so many years ago, Daniels's sleeping was sound as a result of drinking very little alcohol and exercise.

And the dreams. So detailed and so real, he thought as he realized that he woke up from a near-exact representation of what happened back on May 2nd when he was in Houston.

When Burns and his team destroyed everything.

"When the Four Horsemen rode into town," Daniels said softly after clearing his throat. He took his time and stepped out of bed. He immediately dropped to the floor for his standard morning sets of sit-ups and push-ups before hitting the shower. This routine helped move the slumbers and cobwebs of sleep from his head quickly.

Quicker than coffee ever did.

His mind fluttered from one subject to another as he did his sets of calisthenics which made it difficult for him to keep track.

Helms and Welch should be busy in either Colorado or Maine, or probably both. Littleton should be under surveillance and Murphy should be heading out to see her by now. Well, while not a minute-by-minute covered mission, they should be busy for a while so I can deal with Burns.

Liquids, fatigue and aches left his body at the final set. Daniels moved to the bathroom to take a shower before anything else.

Well, at least the water pressure is really good here, he thought to himself as he stood ready under the largest showerhead he had ever seen in such a low-end motel. As he felt the hot water hitting his body, he decided he would wear some lotion for a change after the shower since he planned to talk to his "guest" in a small, confined room.

At least one of us should smell good. God knows what you're going to smell like by the time you show up.

Of all the planning he had done, he was most concerned with how Colonel Carter's men were going to successfully rig the mine to explode, and if they could keep Burns properly medicated for interrogation.

When I had real professionals, it was never a question.

Buffoons, on the other hand, are what I got. I guess I should be happy they didn't just kill Burns.

Still, he was worried that without being able to remain in constant contact with his "field operatives," he had to rely on their abilities to read and understand directions, and to follow them.

"You know, it's like giving a monkey keys to a Mercedes," Daniels said sarcastically. He looked at the time, and started pulling his relatively small bundles of possessions together. Daniels focused on what he was going to have for breakfast as he waited for his ride to show up. Ticking off each potential scenario, Daniels figured that regardless, all the intrusive variables would be elsewhere and engaged while he could spend some time finally getting some answers he had been waiting years to get.

Finally. Judgment Day. After this, re-group at the bunker for a couple of months and then maybe head to Cuba.

He reviewed his recently acquired and updated green smartphone paired with a small computer tablet to make sure everything in the bunker was in place post mission. It took him longer to complete the simple task and then figure out the nuances of his phone. He was glad he had not had to bother with the usual passwords and encryption.

Later, after I finish with Burns. I'll have more than enough time then.

After a minute more he plugged more information into it and watched it sync up with his tablet. As Daniels came to the final list of objectives, variables and his exit strategy, he had a sudden thought of Jeffery Glenn, *another pissed off agent gone rogue.*

Still, Daniels dropped the thought as quickly as it arrived.

No, I don't have to worry about him. He's gone. He's more focused on his sister and niece than dealing with me.

Chapter 1

"Find the thing you want to do most intensely, make sure that's it, and do it with all your might. If you live, well and good. If you die, well and good. Your purpose is done."

H.G. Wells

Present Day – Andover, Massachusetts, USA

Jeffery Glenn watched six separate monitors in the unusually spacious communication van parked at the end of the street of his target's suspected rally point.

Nothing like an oversized moving van, one of many, to be hidden in plain sight. This never gets old.

He looked at a number of other vans, small to large, misshapen and newer ones, in addition to other commercial trucks traveling up and down the street from his target's projected location. With outstretched legs and arms, he sat in his chair and held the position for a long minute so as to fully appreciate the stretch before he returned to his sitting position. His hand immediately reached to his right cheek where he felt the constant thin line of newer skin. Its scar continued to make him smile. Ritual completed, he smiled before he returned to his bank of monitors.

"What are you smiling at?" Ruth asked as she cleaned her

assault rifle.

Jesus! Nothing gets by her. Are all Mossad agents like her? Hyper-vigilant. And the guns? Don't you have a hobby or something?

Glenn took his time answering her. His attention was focused on watching the progress on the projected staging areas, pending on whether he was accurate in his analysis and projections.

"Can't a man smile at his handiwork and appreciate how a plan is coming together so nicely?" Glenn asked innocently.

"He's smiling at his scar on his face. He thinks all the...belles femmes...beautiful women will find him attractive," John, Ruth's French counterpart, said. Similar to Ruth, he had been in the middle of doing something. Glenn was impressed with John's meticulous technique in reconfiguring the charges on packages of military-grade explosives.

Great. French Intelligence agents are not only observant but he's right. It's so nice working with real professionals again!

Glenn sighed before he turned around in his seat to take them both in: Ruth with her perpetually tanned skin and black hair, and John who was less tanned but had hair that was more red than the auburn he often claimed. Of all of them, Glenn was clearly the "whitest" and typically heard himself referenced by the other operatives as "Snowflake."

Still smiling though, he marveled at how months ago he was working with a group of unprofessional monkeys that botched a snatch-and-grab operation in Spain.

Now? I'm working with the Israeli's Mossad and French Intelligence. It really doesn't get better than this...well, maybe there was one time it was better.

Glenn was flooded with memories of his old agency; all the resources, power and clout the Foreign Intelligence Agency once possessed, the envy of all the other intelligence agencies domestically and abroad.

"Ruth? I liked it better when John spoke only French. Can he go back to that?" Glenn asked, deliberately ignoring the French man.

Ruth laughed and went on with cleaning her weapon as John shook his head and continued his own work uttering "stupide flocon de neige."

Ah yes... "flocon de neige"... "Snowflake", Glenn translated.

Glenn returned to his own task impressed with John's accurate assessment; he was impressed with his own scar. Granted, it was given to him by one of Cratty's women.

Ramsey? I think it was Ramsey. Yeah, it was Ramsey. Cratty threw punches and Ramsey used feet and knives.

Still more memories of his brief capture in Tangiers before his escape from the hospital. It was so simple to escape, he thought as he fingered his scar. Glenn was startled back into the present.

"I hope you are right about this location. If you are not, we have wasted a great deal of time and resources," Ruth said in perfect English. Without looking, Glenn reiterated his plan as if he had done it before. While typically surveillance vans, regardless of size, were always stinky as a result of poor ventilation, sun, sweat and heat from the equipment, Glenn was consistently surprised that there was no stench with either of his peers. In fact, Ruth consistently carried an odor of subtle scents such as vanilla, musk and at times lilac.

I know I'm obsessed with cleanliness but these two.

Once again, Glenn had to rein in his rapid thoughts and refocused on Ruth's last warning.

"I told you that Robert Wise would lead us to Daniels, and sure enough, he brought us here," Glenn started.

"But we have not seen any appearance of him. Just a couple of men that are poorly patrolling the area," John said.

Glenn closed his eyes at the misuse of "appearance" for "sign," and decided not to correct the Frenchman so as to keep him speaking English.

They may smell pretty good but they sure aren't trusting...

"I know. But Wise's showing up here with a group of the Daniels's men already at this site is more than enough to convince me. When we see Burns show up, Daniels will follow."

"If that does happen, it will take ninety minutes or longer to implement all of your objectives to ensure all authorities are engaged. He could leave before then," Ruth warned.

"No way," he said with conviction.

Burns burned down Daniels's empire. Everything was taken, gutted and left in ashes. No, Daniels is going to make Burns pay...I guess Maxwell was right back in the day – Burns did destroy everything on his own timetable and terms.

Glenn felt their gazes upon him. He knew both were staring at him trying to figure out how he was so sure. How would they know what motivates Daniels to do what he does?

"Daniels lost everything because of Burns. He's not going to simply kill him and walk away. He would have done that already. He's got to prove to Burns that he beat him. And the only way to do that is to bring Burns to him and have a chat. Stupid? Yes. But if I was in his shoes, I'd want to bleed Burns as slow as possible. Anyway, you two – Israeli and French, right? Aren't you guys known for melodrama, romance and vengeance?" Glenn asked.

"We French? Absolutely. But our Israeli colleague is less known for her patience and drama, and better known for her efficiency," John said with a knowing smile.

Oh yeah...you two have a history.

"I hope you are right. It took us eight hours to get resources and everything into place," Ruth said. By now she had moved from cleaning the assault rifle to cleaning her handgun. There was no smile or any facial expression, save for a determined look of a perfectionist cleaning her hardware.

"So...what do we do with Monsieur Burns?" John asked. Good question, Glenn thought as he watched his monitors, waiting for an answer to come to him. It wasn't long until he revealed what he had been thinking about the plan for a long time.

"I don't know."

"I see," John said. "Are we to let him go or eliminate him as a threat?"

"A threat?"

"I'm sure he's aware of your involvement with his friend's death in Spain. It will be easy for him to find recruits to assist – Cratty, Dillon, Ramsey, Davis, they all come to mind," Ruth added.

"Easy. Not difficult at all. I wish to kill you, often," John said. His red hair and smooth, tan skin made his smile glow.

"Your concerns are noted. Let's get Daniels first and see where the rest leads us."

"So you're not willing to commit to terminating Burns," Ruth said.

"Not at this point, no. Maybe later. Let's get problem number one first and deal with the collateral issues later," Glenn said.

"Sounds good to me." Glenn could tell that John was ticking off things on his to-do list at that point. The sound of a knife scraping across a sharpening stone was now punctuating the silent van indicating that Ruth was also done discussing the subject for now.

Glenn took time to focus on his monitors to see in clear black and white, high definition, how quickly his objectives were falling into place.

It's just a matter of time.

#

Lieutenant Steve Andersen stood just outside the double doors of the FBI control room. He knew that once he entered, he would be caught up in the multiple operations that were occurring simultaneously. He needed to finish his classified case summary simply known as the "Burns, Alexander, J" file. After years of living the story, seeing firsthand all the things that transpired with this one man, he found it so real, formal and almost foreboding to read it as a forensic, active operations file. Even seeing his own name and his best friend, Diane Welch, casually referenced as primary players was like hearing one's voice from a recording, or seeing a surveillance film of oneself – surreal. Still, he forced himself to jump to the brief summary bullet points if he didn't want to read about the present mission in the Boston Globe.

Relevant File Summary Points – Not to be duplicated or discussed outside of Federal Bureau of Investigation

> ➤ *Alexander J. Burns was seen in treatment for post traumatic stress disorder, and secondarily dissociative amnesia via head injury. Both conditions were a byproduct of friendly fire while on a mission in Pakistan to eliminate Oman Sharif Sudani. His psychiatric conditions were successfully treated by Dr. David Caulfield. "Successful" in that Mr. Burns recalled his memories prior to his head injury.*

> ➤ *The team charged with watching Mr. Burns was killed, presumably by him. Mr. Burns went MIA for four years. The following civilians associated with his care and/or related to the caretakers were MIA with him: Dr. David Caulfield, treating psychologist, Samantha Littleton, assigned nurse, Rebecca Littleton, sister, and Emma Littleton, niece.*

> ➤ *During this hiatus, it was reported by Dr. Caulfield during interrogation while in custody of Lt. Steve Andersen during "the Merrimack Crisis" that Mr. Burns had successfully trained him and the listed civilians to: a) launch a cyber attack against the Regional FBI office and the Foreign Intelligence Agency (FIA); b) distract potential obstacles to the plan – Diane Welch, Commandant, Massachusetts State Police, and Steve Andersen, Lieutenant, North Reading, Massachusetts; c) launch a series of fake attacks indicating a coordinated terrorist attack so as to confuse/disrupt law and military enforcement efforts to find real target; d) launch cyber attack to compromise all military and law enforcement efforts, and to compromise FIA's Operation Center and force them to relocate critical special operation mission hard drives to a lesser defended auxiliary control room; e) obtain mission hard drives for leverage/negotiate separate peace; f) relocate to predesignated safe zones; this*

safe zone was later discovered to be Kea, Greece."

"My God, you can't make this shit up. It all would have worked, too, if Webber and Daniels had let us do our job," Andersen said to himself. The memories came quickly - the failed meeting on March 15, the Ides of March, Davis being shot by Webber's men, and their killing Burns's lover, Samantha. He tried to push the sad images out of his head and looked for the last page of the summary. He didn't have to read about the final stand-off with Webber, and how Burns kept Jeffery Glenn and forty agents at bay as Rebecca Littleton took out Webber and shot down two helicopters. Sixteen FIA agents killed in Kea, Greece, several more killed by Burns in Government Center and outside Davis's house, and a sea of classified, top secret spec-op records released around the world – he remembered all that. Even with the number of agents killed, it was the breach that nearly wiped out all diplomatic alliances the US had built over the years. The top secret data sent via Internet made the Edward Snowden files pale in comparison, and was referred to as "the Great Flood." He scanned those sections briefly until he got to the part where David Caulfield was killed in Torrox, Spain along with half his personal protection team – Horowitz, Fitzgerald and Belben.

He reviewed how Janeson found the link between Emma Littleton, her half sister, Rosemarie Flores, and her paternal grandfather, John D. Murphy – known crime boss.

➢ *"Mr. Burns successfully rescued Ms. Rosemarie Flores and Mr. John Murphy from a crime syndicate rival, Angelo and Regina Panelli, siblings and crime boss linked to North End, Boston. Both were arrested for murder and conspiracy.*

➢ *Denise Cratty and Ana Ramsey located, subdued and detained Jeffery Glenn, former manager and colleague when all three worked at the FIA. Mr. Glenn was implicated in the murders of Dr. Caulfield and his protection detail. He was turned over to INTERPOL. Unfortunately, he escaped their custody and remains at large. Ms. Cratty and Ms. Ramsey successfully transported Ms. Rebecca Littleton and her ward, Emma, back to the United States. They were turned over to the Federal Marshals in the Witness Protection Program. Both Littletons and Ms. Flores are still in the program and location remains classified.*

➤ *Alica Wise, still under the command of Eric I. Daniels, former FIA Chairman, was located in proximity of Mr. Burns in Franconia, New Hampshire. Ms. Jillian Davis, Mr. Thomas "Nine" William, and Daniel "Ice" Maddox thwarted an attempt to kill Mr. Burns. She is now in the Federal Correction Institute, Danbury, Connecticut under charges of domestic terrorism. Agent Martin is already interrogating Ms. Wise for the location of her brother and potential location of Mr. Burns, presently MIA. "*

Andersen smiled as he remembered how wonderfully skilled Martin was in bluffing, acting and organizing operations.

"Not bad for a former bureau accountant and a part-time community theater actor," he said. Andersen rolled his shoulders as he read the final piece of the summary.

➤ *"Final assessment is that Eric I. Daniels arranged for Glenn, Jeffery to attack Dr. Caulfield, Rebecca and Emma Littleton in Spain, coordinated the Panelli siblings to capture, detain and/or kill Mr. Murphy and Ms. Flores, and directed Ms. Wise and her associates to capture and/or kill Mr. Burns — all this as a means for either revenge or restitution. Mr. Daniels is MIA and considered very dangerous. "*

There was a lot more in the indexes and more detail in the prior pages. He wanted to read more but he knew time was slipping by and as soon as he entered the control room, there would be no time for reading, just reacting. Andersen put the file down on the floor and made sure his suit matched as well as possible - navy or black, he could never tell. He re-tied his tie to be a little longer, re-tied his laced shoes, picked up the folder from the floor and took a deep breath before he pulled the door open.

Once more unto the breach.

Upon entering the darkened room, he took in the tense, electrified atmosphere of the FBI Regional Control Room. He watched the floor-to-ceiling screens split in two with Director John Helms on one side clearly situated in a car, as the other half held Diane Welch's image as she traveled in an airplane.

I wish we had had all this hardware and technology back in the day. It would have made all those cases so much easier. I don't think I would have ever left this place. Why leave when you have all this technology?

Andersen took his time and looked at the series of monitors manned by young men and women who were significantly younger than he but slightly older than his children. He felt comfortable with the familiar faces. Ana Ramsey and Christine Dillon, annoyed that they were grounded for the mission to see if Burns was out west, remained glued to their monitors for more intelligence on Colorado. Gilmore and Johnson were stationed beside Rachael Janeson while she juggled a series of tablets while giving her briefing.

How does she do that? How can she carry on a briefing while reading something else at the same time?

Andersen knew he was good at multitasking and his wife Laura was even better, but no one did multitasking like Janeson. He smiled at her as she stood perfectly erect looking at both hands in front of her as she reviewed her tablets. She reminded him more of a daughter and he found himself baffled at her striking beauty, focus to duty and a complete lack of understanding of social cues and etiquette.

Well, not complete lack of skills. They have been growing, Andersen revised. *Maybe too quickly, and not uniformly or the way we would like, but she is developing those skills.*

Drawn back to the conversation, Andersen finally heard Helms's long awaited request.

"Alright Janeson, let's do a recap of the events in the last five hours just so everyone is on the same page."

Poised, her pale skin in contrast with her dark clothes, she looked up from her tablets, strode to the front of the screens with Gilmore and Johnson in tow who were themselves directing others as they followed.

"Six hours ago, a CIA satellite picked up a faint GPS signal that was marked as an FBI transmitter that was attached to Alex Burns's tooth. A drone equipped with a calibrated transceiver in addition to its usual eavesdropping gear identified the signal's source. This is four days after thermal satellite images confirmed that Alex Burns was captured by four groupings of men and carried away to an overpass bridge where they were temporarily lost until eight vehicles emerged from underneath, heading in several different directions. One satellite went due east while two separate drones were scrambled to follow two other cars before we lost track of them. As a result of this maneuver, we lost track of five vehicles," she said as she handed one tablet to Johnson in exchange for another one from Gilmore.

She's just unbelievable, Andersen kept thinking as he stood in the background, rocking back and forth on his feet. He still held the large file in both hands behind his back and tried to ignore the pressure on the sides of his shoes.

I hate these new shoes. They're too tight and they squeak.

"The location of the signal is about one to two hundred feet below ground in an abandoned gold and mineral mine just outside Colorado Springs called Klondike Mine."

"You're kidding me, right?" Diane Welch said. She rubbed her eyes. "The mine's name is 'Klondike'?" she continued.

Andersen watched to see how Janeson would answer a simple question. As predicted, Janeson looked up to see why the name of the mine mattered.

"Yes. I am speculating that the mine was named after a person.

More likely, the person who first discovered some precious metal there, but that's not substantive to this briefing," Janeson said. Her response at best was abrupt and dismissive. She returned to looking at her tablets. While oblivious to Janeson, Andersen could easily see that he was not the only one surprised as both Helms and Welch picked up on Janeson's curtness, since it was very unusual for her to be all business at the expense of being curious.

Yeah...Helms and Welch are right. Something is wrong with her. Maybe she's developing faster than she can handle. This thing with Burns, maybe.

Andersen listened to Janeson talk evenly and without much emotion as was her typical mode of communication when she was in "research" and briefing mode.

"While the local police and rangers have secured the entrance and other potential exits, they have not ventured inside the mine as it is evident that there was recent activity, and the security of the mine compromised." Janeson stopped for a moment, where she appeared to sigh, and then carried on.

Tired? Fatigued? Not really her style.

"At the same time, there has been a significant increase in activity in Maine, near Mount Katahdin, where Secret Service Director, Robert Tombs, confirms that Colonel Timothy Carter of the Republican Citizens Army is presently located. With these activities occurring in both Colorado and Maine at the same time, it would appear that Alex Burns would be in one of those places," Janeson said.

Andersen found himself looking at Janeson who seemed engrossed in something she was reading. After another brief moment, Christine Dillon made eye contact with him and he raised his shoulders to convey he didn't know what was going on. As suddenly as Janeson had stopped, she started again.

"In regards to Mr. Carter, there are some other anomalies about his funding sources that require investigation later. Somehow there is a connection to Missouri. That doesn't make sense...but again, I digress." Janeson put one tablet down and retracted another from her own pocket.

Wow! She's distracted! That's not good either.

"Surveillance reports indicate that the two people of interest who identified themselves to Lt. Andersen as 'Ruth' and 'John,' remain missing even though the majority of their colleagues have clearly aligned with ours to unobtrusively observe as we move in on Colorado and Maine," Janeson said as she narrowed her eyes so as to better focus.

Of course, "Ruth" from Mossad and "John" from French Intelligence. It wouldn't be interesting if it was just a domestic issue. It's got to be international just to heighten the risk. Ruth sure is creepy.

"I take it you think there is more going on here?" Helms prodded.

It didn't take long for Janeson to nod her head affirmatively. The transition from reciting her briefing to speculating was smooth for her but still jarring for most who would be better in slowly transitioning from one mode of presenting to another.

"Yes. If past behaviors are any indication of future actions, I suspect that neither place is where they are holding Alex Burns. In keeping with Eric Daniels's pattern, there is more likely a third place or another series of actions that are occurring concurrently, and more likely hiding in plain sight."

For a moment, Andersen was sure she was done but then Janeson went on. As expected, her pause was not a social cue to ask questions or to join in, but rather a moment to organize her thoughts into something thoughtful, thorough, and logical.

"There may be another factor playing a role here that involves Ms. Littleton and her wards. While it is not a surprise that she and her family have disappeared into their own hiding upon Burns's capture and kidnap, the marshal that checked on her discovered that in addition to her disappearance, her home had been obviously gone through. While initially it was thought it was a coincidental robbery, nothing of value was stolen, and a message of 'we're not done, old man,' was scrawled on a wall," she said. As a visual aid, she added images of the apartment and writing flashed on a smaller screen.

"When I informed Mr. John Murphy of this, he instantly responded by informing me that those were the very words that Angelo Panelli said to him just prior to his and his granddaughter's rescue."

Just great. And of course an old vendetta just to make it all personal and heighten the risk. Laura is so right – I think once this Burns and Daniels matter is done, I'll go back to my quiet suburban neighborhood and do good old-fashioned detective work. Stick with DUI's, car accidents and identity fraud...all noble efforts to keep a policeman busy.

"Damn it," was Helms's response.

"Yes. Also, Mr. John Murphy has reportedly just left Massachusetts for 'vacation' as reported by Mr. Fitzpatrick. Additionally while we have confirmed that Regina Panelli is still in isolation at Danbury Federal Prison, Mr. Panelli remains among the missing, as does Robert Wise, brother of Alica Wise, who is also in isolation at Danbury."

Andersen watched Helms make some kind of connection with Alica Wise's name and seemed to jump at the opportunity to ask a question.

"By the way, Janeson, the warden and chief guard are complaining that 'Special Agent Martin' is interrogating Ms. Wise, but has yet to ask her a question. It's been about three days of this and they think this silent treatment is bordering on abuse."

"Oh please," Janeson said, too loud to be a whisper but not low enough to go unheard. While there were no emotions transmitted as she ostensibly continued reading, her response in and of itself was surprising. She continued to look down at her tablets while Andersen watched all eyes in the control room and on the screens focus on her with slackened jaws, sudden intake of air and total shock all over their faces. While still unaware that she was being stared at, Janeson continued her briefing as if nothing happened.

Jesus...what the hell is going on with you, Janeson, Andersen thought. Gilmore and Johnson, who had been by Janeson's side for years, even exchanged surprised looks while Dillon started to slowly approach her.

"As Agent Martin is notorious for unorthodox approaches that have yielded positive results, I am guessing that he is taking a less than direct approach to obtaining the data we need," she continued.

Everyone continued to look at her as she looked down at her tablets. It was evident that Helms planned to let the remark go and took another approach.

"And what is the data we need?" he asked.

Janeson looked up suddenly at Helms's image on the screen. Her facial features took on a deadly serious expression as she brought her tablets to her sides.

"The real location of Alex Burns," she said. After a pause, she elaborated on her prior statement. The control room fell silent except for a cough, the hum of warm monitors and some keyboard clicking.

"The signal at the mine is either a forgery or real, but Alex is not there. I suspect that Mr. Daniels has set up a trap so he can harm both Ms. Welch and her team, and to tie up resources away from the real target. Prior to the last three days, the whereabouts of Colonel Carter and his group were not confirmed but now they are making themselves more than visible. That said, Alex is not there either. It is another attempt to distract and tie up resources in Maine in addition to Colorado."

Andersen watched Janeson closely as he waited for her to continue. Finally, it was Welch that asked the obvious question.

"Then where is Burns?"

Andersen waited nervously as Janeson seemed to be frozen in place by the question. What little noise there was in the control room was not completely gone. Silence of twenty seconds dragged on as loud as an oncoming train.

"Unknown," she said softly at first but then she raised her tablets back up and her voice became stronger as she began to read again as she spoke next.

"However, that means we need to confirm that Alex Burns is not in Colorado nor Maine as soon as possible by investigating each place under the caveat that Mr. Daniels's desire is to cause us all great harm. This will spring the trap and force Mr. Daniels's hand to act. To push the issue, I would like to ask if Lt. Andersen would assist Agent Martin in his interrogation as it is well within Lt. Andersen's skill set. I would also want Ms. Ramsey and Ms. Dillon to be ready for rapid re-deployment should the relocation become evident and local."

"Why would he be in Massachusetts?" Helms asked.

"Because Mr. Daniels is ego-centric and narcissistic, and would want to show Alex Burns and us up by such a daring move," Janeson said for all to hear. But then, Andersen heard something he would have expected anyone else to say, except Janeson.

"He is an asshole, in short," she said. It was casually said as she read another tablet handed to her by a clearly surprised Gilmore. Again, unaware that she had shocked the entire team with her statements a third time, Helms asked what would have been seen to be an odd question except it was Janeson saying those impulsive, emotion-laden statements.

Janeson doesn't do "emotional" or "impulsive," Andersen thought as rubbed his head.

"Are you alright, Rachael?" Helms said. It was in a tone and volume that was caring, avuncular, and completely different from his typical "Drill Instructor" persona. Janeson peered above her tablets as if surprised. Still, consistent with Janeson's concrete logic, Andersen could see that she took a moment to review the question as an actual mental health status exam.

"Yes, I am fine. However, I find that I am more emotionally driven to find Alex Burns and to capture Mr. Daniels than I expected. I am also more irritable when I cannot find required information quickly, and I have no desire to eat, rest or sleep. I believe I am angry about how Mr. Daniels has turned the world upside down because he is being held accountable for his behaviors. It is both time-consuming and infuriating that he should act the way he does. As a result, I find I am focused on bringing his reign of terror to an end," she said. Again, there was no emotion, no breakdown of tears, no anger. Instead she stood motionless in the middle of the control room, apparently still thinking while two or three tablets filled hands behind her back.

Okay, so that's it?

For a room filled with thirty people, Andersen thoroughly understood why everyone was silent. Now, even the electronics were quiet, and Andersen was positive that the air conditioner was off.

"So, this is about Daniels and not about Burns?" Welch asked. It was easy to see that she was attempting to end the conversation and keep it focused on hunting Daniels. Everyone got that. Or rather, most people who were cued into verbal, nonverbal and subtle communication would have readily picked that up.

Finally, some closure that it's all about getting the asshole and not a personal thing she has for Burns, Andersen thought. It was wishful thinking.

"No. I have very strong feelings for Alex Burns which has exacerbated my condition," Janeson started.

Or it could be about how she loves Burns and wants to save him with little to do with Daniels. God! It's like a car accident, you just can't look away.

"I thought I would keep that matter private, though, I think I just made it public," Janeson said. Her eyes drifted down from the screen to the floor, clearly comprehending her failed logic and obvious error of explaining her feelings about Burns to a room full of people. Andersen found himself wanting to look away. It was voyeuristic, something illicit and private. He quickly scanned the room and saw everyone else doing the same thing-they focused on monitors, papers, sudden phone texts, dangerous untied shoes, everything but Janeson.

"Anything we can do about those symptoms, other than find Daniels and Burns?" Helms said. His approach was to go on as if there were no social mistake to be embarrassed about at all.

For a Marine, you're pretty sensitive and quick. Andersen peeked back at Janeson and watched as she took the question as seriously as she did everything.

"No. I think though after this mission is complete, I will take a vacation. Travel. For the present, I will take more breaks by taking the dog out for a walk. That might assist with these feelings," Janeson said as if she were explaining how she will get rid of a headache.

Andersen could see both Welch and Helms nodding approvingly.

"I think we'll all take a break after this, Janeson," Welch offered.

"Okay, Janeson. I like your plan. What do you think Steve?" Helms asked Andersen.

"I'll pack an overnight bag and see Agent Martin tonight. It would be nice to get involved in this case, after all." Andersen knew that Welch would pick up on the jab directed at her.

"No, no, no. No guilt trip, Steve. Last time I was stuck at the ranch while you people went in the field. It's my turn to go and your turn to keep the home fires burning."

"Me? Inspire guilt? Shocked. I'm shocked you would say that."

"Yes. Of course you're shocked."

Andersen started to laugh as Dillon chuckled.

"You sure you two aren't siblings? You act like it, you know," Helms said.

"You'd think that but no. She's a close friend of my sister, Darlene, but not a sibling, per se. Same town, though," Andersen said.

Helms nodded and took lead in ending the briefing.

"Alright people. We all have our jobs. Janeson? Keep us in the loop every thirty minutes once each mission starts."

"Done. All teams are on a rotating schedule for seventy-two hours' coverage."

"Good luck, everyone," Welch said as she leaned forward and turned off her screen.

"Ditto, people," Helms added. His image was next to flicker out.

Andersen still held the large file in his hand and was looking for an opportunity to turn it over to a lead agent in the control room before he departed. With the floor-to-ceiling monitors now dark, the main lights came on and everyone was back to work. Janeson looked back down at her tablets while Gilmore and Johnson conferred about something.

"You see what I mean," Dillon said under her breath."Janeson is not herself. Gilmore and Johnson wanted me to talk to her but then Burns was taken and we got all busy. Do you think I should talk to her now?" Dillon asked while she pretended to read a text.

Andersen handed the classified file to Dillon who took it without question, clearly aware that such a document needed to remain on FBI premises locked up. It took a moment to think before he came up with what he thought was the best strategy.

"No. She's made it clear that she is aware that she is emotionally vulnerable but focused to end this. I think if it were anyone else, I would worry about their ability to compartmentalize their feelings. But in Janeson's case, it may actually be a strong motivator rather than a distraction. What do you think?" Andersen asked to check his logic.

Dillon looked up and it was clear she was impressed with his logic.

"I guess that's why you're a lieutenant and I'm a grunt."

"A talented grunt."

"Maybe. But I'm not feeling the love. Me and Ramsey grounded in case the shit hits? Come on."

"Don't complain. I'm heading to Connecticut to support Martin. You know what that's like?"

"It will be entertaining, that's for sure."

"You've got a point there," Andersen said. He was now checking to see if he had his phone, wallet and keys for maybe the thirtieth time since 9:00 AM. Dillon nodded and walked away to the hub of the activity as Andersen started to walk out of the control room when he noticed that the floor-to-ceiling maps now held two separate images - both were topographical maps of target sites in Colorado and Maine. He turned to look at the maps closely and folded his arms across his chest. Similar to Janeson, he found himself more focused on finding Burns than finding Daniels.

That asshole will show up at some point. Assholes always do. I never thought I would say this but I'm not sure Burns is going to make it out of this one.

"Where are you, Burns?" Andersen said to no one in particular.

#

Present Day – Somewhere in USA

Alexander J. Burns took in a sudden breath of air as if he had been under water for several minutes. His head snapped up and both hands, still tied together, went to his head where he was positive he had been shot. After what seemed like a long moment, he felt exhausted but now oriented.

Wow. Now that's a dream I've never had. Mom was in it, too? They must have me on some serious psychedelics or hallucinogens to have that vivid a dream. Joshua? Why would she ever name me Joshua?

Burns took a moment to focus on his breathing. It was easy to tell that he was still between two people in some sort of cramped vehicle.

I wonder how this will end? Don't really need to think too hard about that. Burns kept thinking as he saw dim sunlight partially penetrating the dark blindfold covering his eyes. He could feel the warmth from the rising sun. While constantly dosing, he felt himself being held and led around with his hands and legs bound from one place to another. He could tell that he was often in a car or ground transport of some kind and spent days driving but as to how many days, he was clueless. So much for training, he thought, as he licked his chapped lips.

But then I was never drugged so much when I did this scenario.

Still, he could tell he was heading east as the sun was low on his face in the morning.

At least I think it's morning. Maybe it's the sun setting and we're heading west.

In addition to praying, he thought of Samantha, David and others he had known for really only a short time. His mind drifted in and out from the sedatives they were giving him constantly. At first he was able to keep track of time but after a while, the drugs and darkness clouded his mind. There were periods of time he would be sitting in one place for hours versus times when he would be up moving around. Burns was impressed with his capturers' ability to vacillate between a sack over his head to a blindfold, and to remain nearly silent for the whole trip with at least three men around him.

What do you talk about anyway when you have a prisoner for days? Well, I'm not too talkative anyway.

Burns still couldn't figure out why he was not more upset about the thought of his death. There were times when he thought that he deserved it for all the people, innocent and otherwise, he had killed over the years. Still, when he thought of them, he found himself feeling sad and seemed to instinctively ask for forgiveness. It was reflex now. Thoughts drifted to his dead friend, Dr. David Caulfield. Therapist, mentor, colleague, and friend he could think of in ease.

Well, David, I guess therapy worked. I'm feeling all the emotions. I don't think Dr. Cohen had much to do with this, though. I wonder what you would say about that? Redemption? Guilt?

The memories of David's assessment that he had changed from an efficient killing machine to a compassionate human being made more sense the older he got.

From a head injury, no less. At least before, I didn't feel pain or sadness...Samantha. Just to see her and David one last time. Well, I guess where I'm going next. I probably will see some people I know. In an effort to focus on past training, he focused on something else just so he wouldn't relive both Samantha's and David's deaths. It still felt as if it all was yesterday.

Maybe that's my punishment? To have her in my life to be happy and then taken away. To have a friendship with David and then he's taken away. Maybe that's my hell? To be shown happiness and then have it all taken away with no hope of ever seeing them again, no happiness, pain, struggling everyday to no avail. God, Burns! Enough with the reflection! Think!

Years ago, his only focus would have been on escaping. But now, after all he had been through, his resolve to live at all costs was gone.

So much for the survival instincts. Does it really matter now? Who was it that said that "man is the only creature who needs a reason to live"? Was it Nietzsche? You would know, David.

To distract himself again, Burns attempted to recount the facts just prior to his capture as a means of assessing time. Before he was subdued, he remembered talking to Rachael Janeson as he was surrounded by a group of men at his campsite, before the assault and loss of consciousness. There was an odd moment that he recounted not feeling himself as he woke up to see someone in his mouth. There was no pain, no fear but cold realization that they had found the transmitter in his tooth cavity.

Well, it was a long shot, he had thought. It was easy to see that there would be no help for him without a transmitter. His biggest regret, other than a life of carelessly taking lives without thinking, was that he had only experienced love, kindness and friendship for a short time.

Well, maybe I'll have better luck in the next life, he thought.

At least Roxie is with Rachael. She seems nice. She sure is smart, too.

Burns felt the corners of his mouth turn up as he thought about Janeson and Roxie. A surge of guilt flooded him and he tried to push his warm feeling aside.

Focus, Burns. You need to focus.

It was difficult to do: such an easy task to focus on one thing such as escape was now very difficult with so many drugs in his veins. Once again he drifted into sleep. Struggling to stay alert, Burns wondered why Daniels wanted him so sedated.

How are you going to gloat or interrogate me if I'm sleeping?
After a few more minutes, Burns had an academic thought in regards

to his situation.

I wonder if they'll ever find my body? I hope so. Becky will bury me with Samantha and David. She'll find a way to get me home.

Memories of the elaborate, well-maintained crypt in Rhode Island where Samantha and David were now resting crept into his thoughts.

I guess David was right. We'll be able to hang out together. Just like old times. We really can hang out together...just like you said, David.

As the recent dose of sedatives started to firmly take hold of his consciousness, Burns's mind leaped to another thought just as he fell asleep.

I wonder where they're looking for me now?

Chapter 2

"Life appears to me too short to be spent in nursing animosity or registering wrongs."

—*Charlotte Brontë, <u>Jane Eyre</u>*

Present Day - El Paso County, Colorado, USA

Jillian Davis kept obsessing over why her former boss, Eric Daniels, would bring Alexander Burns to an abandoned mine right off of Monument Valley Highway, El Paso County, just outside Colorado Springs. She was sitting comfortably in one of three large SUVs heading north on that same highway. She had trained for many hours for many days. She knew that the entire team had practiced for every scenario but one – an assault underground in an abandoned mine.

Why? Because he's brilliant...genius, evil, but a brilliant genius. I hate the man for that. Not only in plain sight just outside of Colorado Springs but just off the highway for easy access. Very convenient, almost as if he wanted us all to get here with ease and in force.

In fact, while it was just on the edge of Pulpit Rock Park, its notoriety was due to students from the University of Colorado getting drunk and high. With easy access off of Route 87, the Klondike Mine was located approximately two hundred plus feet underground of the park with a maze of tunnels and shafts that were closed off to the public. While once it had been a gold and mineral mine, after eighty years of service, it was closed and residential housing, highway and a park were built upon it.

So how the hell did Daniels find it? And why would he bring Burns there? And why not Wisconsin, California or Missouri, where all the evidence is pointing to some kind of base.

Davis kept thinking of why she was sure it was a trap as she fiddled with her necklace. After three days of silence, Burns's transmitter hidden in his tooth was signaling its location nearly halfway under the park. The signal was so weak that it took Gilmore and Johnson nearly an hour to realize the signal was underground via drones. Ten minutes after that, Janeson had located the abandoned mine followed by a list of park rangers, geologists, cartographers, excavators and historians that placed potential entrances and exits of the mine both near and in the park itself. Reportedly, even before they touched down at the military airport, the regional FBI, local police and State Rangers had locked down the area and had a number of specialists present as they confirmed entry and exit points. Davis turned away from her reflection in the window. She felt a pair of eyes on her, a familiar pair of a former rival now compatriot.

Maybe more friendly rivals than compatriot. Denise Cratty made it known that she was not happy with the surprise free fire zone location. Unable to avoid the clear, blue eyes, Cratty said the obvious question.

"How the hell did he do it? Find a place that would make a surprise attack or an assault impossible?" She didn't wait for an answer but rather fished around the pockets of her battlefield uniform for one of the many tablets she stowed away, along with lipstick, mascara and probably perfume. While it was clear that Davis was more the alpha male, it was not lost on her that Cratty was an alpha female with a strong dose of girly-girl. Regardless of presentation, attributes, sexual orientation, and dedication, Davis marveled at how they thought similarly, at the same time, about the same tactics and barriers.

You're like the sister I never had. It's hard to imagine we have anything in common, except we both wanted to kill Burns which changed to wanting to kill Webber and Daniels. How things change.

Once upon a time, Davis was positive that she could not work with Cratty because she was just too "girly." That all went away when Cratty saved the day, when Thomas Webber almost killed Burns. And then Cratty got Rebecca and Emma Littleton back safely to the States after more than half her team was killed in action. Much to Davis's surprise, she thought of Cratty as a sister.

A very opinionated, competitive sister that could be real bitchy at times, but nonetheless a sister.

"I don't know. And why did it take three days for the transmitter to come online?" Davis added as she continued to fiddle with her necklace. Cratty started to stretch her fingers and then handed Davis another tablet with more geological data and possible mine maps.

"Well, at least we're all on the same page. Welch is positive it's a trap and she's not taking any chances. Helms didn't need much convincing to go to Maine just to make sure Burns wasn't really there while we're here. It's classic Daniels misdirection, obfuscation and deception," Davis said. She looked over the data but then continued to sense that Cratty was staring at her.

"What?"

"That's an impressive string of words for you. I thought I was the brains and you were the muscle!"

"I'm expanding my horizons."

"Good timing, Davis. No time like the present to start using polysyllabic words. Right before we head into a trap."

"Yup. I'm complicated and multilayered."

Davis returned to her reading and smiled at their usual repartee. Much to her surprise, Cratty didn't continue the discussion. Instead she took a deep sigh, rubbed her eyes and continued to study elevations and depth readings while carrying on a conversation.

"Well it's perfect if you want to kill people you think are traitors. And with Burns as bait, I'm guessing that you, me and

Welch are at the top of the list."

"Absolutely."

"And he's not like Webber; he's not going to be sloppy, obnoxious, and overconfident."

"No. But he doesn't have the same talent he's used to. Second string players more focused on their own agendas. Limited options and nearly no resources. He may not be as invincible as he used to be," Davis said.

"And he may be tired. But he only has one objective. Kill Burns and maybe us. Then fade away."

Without looking up from the string of data crossing her own pad, Davis smiled.

"And that's his big mistake - Daniels should have just cut his losses and faded away. He's really doing something stupid with this vengeance thing. But still, he did hit the mark on the location."

By now, Davis stole a look at Cratty who was shifting uncomfortably in her plush leather seat between tablets, laptop, ammunition, two automatic handguns and two notebooks.

Just perfect. Trained for months for urban, rural, outside, inside, day and night scenarios, and Daniels picks the place where only bats and moles would fare well. Just perfect.

' No longer reading the tablet she was looking at, Davis placed it on her lap and returned to fiddling with her necklace while looking out the window.

I wonder if Burns still has the necklace I gave him?

The good news with this new development and "big break" was that no one suffered from any illusions that it was not a trap. The bad news, other than not training for this scenario, was that Welch was being very cautious to the point of insisting on having three separate SUVs to carry pairs of the fire team to ensure that if attacked, not all would be in one place as one big target. Further, she redeployed Christine Dillon and Ana Ramsey to remain at FBI Regional for rapid deployment elsewhere should the need arise.

Man, they were really pissed. I've never heard Dillon swear so much in one sentence. And when Ramsey's the cool one, then you know the shit is bad.

Even though Davis was worried about Janeson's emotional state, she found her plan of attack and assessment logical as always. Short on social skills but striking in looks and logical analysis, Davis marveled how Janeson could be so smart but still be drawn to Burns.

Burns? You got a thing for Burns? And Burns spent hours talking to just you? How the hell did that happen? How do two people that have nothing in common form some kind of virtual relationship like that?

It took a moment but Davis pulled herself out of her thoughts in an attempt to get tactical and focus on the new mission parameters. Davis found it safer to deal with the present than to speculate how any relationship might work between Janeson and Burns.

The world's most dangerous domestic terrorist gone rogue and the nation's smartest law enforcement agent together? Jesus. Maybe wind velocity's effects on a target two thousand yards away at dusk. Maybe that? That's almost as crazy as...as this trap we're walking into.

In an attempt to stop thinking about Janeson and Burns as a couple and how she and Cratty were polar opposites, Davis shook her head and focused on her last conversation with Welch just before they landed.

"If it's a trap, I don't want the entire team killed. I want people to find Daniels and bury him if we don't make it," Welch had said with a smile earlier that day.

I guess when you lose three-quarters of your team, you get kind of sensitive about safety, and assume the worst. Never mess with Marines – they never forget, never forgive, and will regroup in hell.

Davis looked back at Cratty as she studied her tablet intensely. Davis understood why Cratty was in full agreement with Welch's decision. As Davis looked at her, she lost track of how Cratty had gone from being so girly-girl years ago to steely and determined to find and kill Daniels.

I guess when you lose more than half your team, you're likely to do that too. Welch and Cratty are much more alike than I thought.

Cratty looked up and saw Davis looking at her.

"What?"

Davis snapped out of her daze and did her best to think of something to say.

"I was just thinking how shiny your hair looks in the early morning sun and was wondering what you do to make it glow like that?" Davis congratulated herself on the straight-face, totally serious presentation. To Cratty's credit, she allowed only her eyes to narrow before she returned to reading, completely ignoring her. Davis smiled and went back to looking out her window, fiddling with her necklace, again wondering how the day would end. Her mind drifted as she thought back to her father and the things he would say in moments of reflection. He was a sensitive soul. He was quiet and gentle but there was a strength about him that was palpable. Davis had been thinking more about him these days since talking to Nine and Ice about the dreams she would have from time to time. Her dreams always seemed to involve animals, nature and themes of good, evil, right and wrong. Just before they left the briefing, she had another dream. Reluctantly, she told Nine about it.

Just in case, she thought. After another moment of wracking her brain, it finally came to her. Her dad once told her that he had a distant relative that fought in the war who said "this day is a good day to die" or something like that. There was an obvious problem. While Davis had little information about her father's past, she was positive he did not serve in the armed forces. He never spoke of others that had, other than this relative and his cryptic sayings. Still, she found herself regretting not knowing more about her father and many of the things he would say.

So what war are we talking about? Maybe he's right. Maybe there is a good day to die rather than another. Maybe it has something to do with being prepared and at peace...or maybe it's a good day to die for the other person.

Davis fiddled more with her necklace as she thought more about the possible double meaning of her dad's phrase.

#

Thirty Seven Years Ago – Dorchester, Massachusetts, USA

Diane Welch approached the girls' bathroom with some trepidation. She did not like her new school and would have much preferred to have gone to the local school in her neighborhood than the "snotty-upper class" town. If it weren't for the fact that she hadn't peed all day, she would have just left. As she approached the bathroom door, she heard a whole lot of voices coming from the other side in addition to noting the strong smell of urine and chlorine.

That smell? That smell is so familiar...

She was about to turn away when she heard a familiar voice moaning "stop!" Rather than leave, Welch couldn't seem to walk away in good conscience. Seeing herself as a sixteen-year-old again, she knew that everything was familiar.

I know that voice! I've heard it, recently...

"No way" she said to herself. She clutched her heavy biology, philosophy and religion books to her chest with one hand and used the other to slowly open the door. While she might have been clad in Catholic uniform, her timid presentation was an experienced caution; she was going to look in before entering the lavatory. To get a clear look beyond the door, she had to walk through the archway beyond a small wall. As she approached the center of the bathroom, she saw a girl curled up in a fetal position protecting her head while a bigger girl was standing above her hitting her with hands and kicking her as well. The three other girls that stood watching had seen Welch show up but had then turned back to encourage the bigger girl. All the girls were in the same uniform, thin and blonde. The bigger girl stopped for a moment just to taunt the girl on the floor.

"You're not so smart when you're on the floor crying, are you, bitch? You think you can just come in here and use our room without asking permission? Are all you bitches from Southie that stupid?" the girl taunted.

It seems so real. Like yesterday!

Welch's vision turned blood red, just as it did then, when she heard her hometown being maligned. There was salt in her mouth, bile in her throat, and her bladder felt as if it were going to explode. Just like the last time she saw her friend from Southie on the floor, surrounded by blonde, snotty, know-it-all, rich bitches. As the pit in her stomach filled with hatred, she confirmed who the girl on the floor was.

What the hell? Darlene? Darlene Andersen? Steve's sister?

Welch's movements froze. Her body's sensations raged on. She felt heat rise in her skin and stomach as anger swelled. As she looked down at Darlene, she saw her hand move from covering her head to try to get her glasses that fell off of her. Welch knew they were glasses from welfare as the family periodically received free medical services and food stamps when times were tough. Just as Darlene looked as if she was going to snatch them up before they were broken, the bigger girl kicked them out of her reach and hit Darlene on the head as the other girls laughed.

What the hell!? Where am I? High school? St. Margaret?

"Hey! What are you? An asshole?" Welch heard herself yell before she knew what was saying. The bigger girl looked up for a moment at Welch and then made eye contact with one of the other girls. She was blonde.

I hate blondes! They think they're tough!

"Why don't you get lost?" the blonde girl said as the bigger girl was preparing for a new round of hitting and kicking Darlene. When Welch stepped closer, the blonde pushed her back. She felt herself freeze again. She always did before she went on the attack. It must have looked to the onlookers that she was scared then as it did now. They must have thought she was going to leave. But she remembered all the fights and roughhousing with her brothers and their friends who thought they were better than she was. The anger built as she felt the push back. And then the blonde made a very big mistake—she looked back to watch the abuse rather than keep an eye on her.

Okay. You want a piece of me?

Welch watched herself as she took that opportunity to kick the blonde girl in the stomach. She had been aiming for between the legs but she missed. The girl seemed to have a sudden exhale of air and doubled over to her knees while holding her stomach. Diane took her own hardback books with both hands and hurled them like missiles towards the other two girls watching. One of her textbooks hit one girl in the face. Her cry was cut short when she stumbled back and tripped over Darlene's body. Welch could hear and smell that the girl she had kicked full force in the stomach was now vomiting. Without any further hesitation, Welch watched herself barrel towards the bigger girl with all her force, catching her fully in the torso. Both went to the ground with force.

Just like football with the boys, she remembered. Welch heard the bigger girl's wind knocked out of her. In addition to great satisfaction, it also gave her a chance to straddle the girl's back. Once firmly on top of her, she began to hit her with closed fists, just as her father had taught her. As a former Marine himself, her dad showed her how to fight with closed fists and to never use the knuckles: "always use your fist like a hammer; you won't hurt your fingers but it will sure as shit hurt the other guy." As Welch began to pummel the bigger girl's head and back, she found herself yelling.

"Fuck you assholes! Fuck all of you's!"

Her breath felt shallow and she didn't know why.

Difficult to breathe...winded?

Suddenly, she felt her hair being pulled from behind such that she was forced off the girl. The one girl she did not hurt was now pulling her hair just out of reach of her grasp. Welch was convinced that she was about to be ganged up on but then she turned to see an unusual sight - she saw Darlene coming up from behind the girl and with her open hand, she slapped the girl right on her ear. The slap was so loud it startled both her and the intended victim. But the slap was nothing in comparison to the girl's blood-curdling scream that followed.

Crap! That had to hurt!

Welch could feel the girl's hand let go as she bent over and tried to soothe her stinging ear and head. But Darlene pushed the girl into the stall and then began kicking her. Welch turned in time to see the bigger girl starting to get up.

"Oh hell, no!" she uttered. Welch jumped back on the girl and proceeded to open hand slap the girl's face and arms.

So much for closed fists! Sorry Dad!

As everything seemed to slow down as if she were under water, the smell of urine from the toilets and freshly produced vomit intensified.

Jesus...the stench!

Her vision narrowed and focused on her target. But then she became aware of sudden movements from all around in the room. At first the blurs were just amorphous, black movements that seemed to flutter all around.

Like human-sized falcons or ravens...huge and strong.

With vise-like grips on her arms and with amazing force, she was lifted off the girl into the air with seemingly no effort.

Sweet Jesus! What is this? They're like claws or talons, or something.

It was one of those rare times when genuine fear invaded her entire body for the first time in this engagement. As she got her bearings, Welch realized that the birds of prey were the younger nuns, maybe under fifty years old, whom she had remembered from her childhood, and that even here, they had clearly heard the screams and investigated in force, as they would have done. Once Welch recognized that it was Sister Grace restraining her, she calmed down immediately.

From pitch battle to a sudden stop, Welch felt herself having difficulty breathing.

God, she's strong.

#

Present Day - El Paso County, Colorado, USA

"Ma'am? Are you alright?"

The strong, male voice startled her out of a deep sleep. Her head jerked up and it took her just a few seconds to get her bearings. To say that the dream was vivid was clearly an understatement. She realized that the dream was about thirty-seven years ago when she met Steve's sister in a fight at Saint Margaret's High School.

"You Okay, Ma'am?" Nine asked? "It looked like you were in the fight of your life." Welch took a moment to arch her back as best she could while sitting down and stretching her legs and arms. She couldn't fathom either the reason or the meaning of her vivid dream.

"Was it Swat Valley, Ma'am?"

Without hesitation, Welch regrouped with a painful revelation.

"Close - St. Margaret's High School. I just got in a fight. My friend was down and there were three of them. It looked good until the nuns showed up..."

Her friend, former subordinate and colleague looked confused but then his face hardened as if he knew too well what she experienced.

"Nuns? Say no more, Ma'am. We all got scars from them," Nine said.

Welch narrowed her eyes and looked deeply into Nine's eyes which were unusually revealing.

"Nine? Catholic school? Nuns?" Welch asked cautiously, painfully aware of how old wounds could be re-opened.

"Worse, Ma'am. Jesuits,"

"Jesus..." Welch said as she sat back. "Are you serious?"

"Yes, Ma'am. As serious as a heart attack. There was 'JUG' – 'Justice Under God,'" Nine said. He looked back out of the SUV's dark window. The pain was easy to see.

"Jesus Christ."

"Jesus Christ, the Holy Spirit and the Father Almighty had little to do with them, Ma'am."

"Sorry," she said softly as she tried to move quickly from the subject.

"We all got scars, Ma'am. Swat Valley. Saint Margaret's, the Jesuits."

"We sure do."

Welch pulled herself back into the present as she thought about how things were now. *Fifty-three years old and I'm still trying to get myself killed. You think I would have done it by now*, Welch thought as she sat with Thomas "Nine" Williams in one of three SUVs on Route 25 heading to Klondike Mine. Eight hours earlier, once she knew they were running into a trap, she knew she had to alter the entire plan.

Maybe that's what the dream was about?

If Daniels was consistent, this "break" was more likely a diversion and that meant concentrating all her resources would be foolish.

Much to Dillon's and Ramsey's chagrin, she re-deployed them to assist Janeson, Gilmore and Johnson back at FBI Regional in Boston while Director John Helms and Lt. Steve Andersen rounded up resources in Maine to cover areas just outside of Fort Kent near the Canadian border and further inland at Mount Katahdin.

I don't know how they're going to do that.

She completely understood why Dillon and Ramsey were pissed off about being "left at the ranch," but Welch was positive that somehow Daniels would pull something that would need to be addressed by trained professionals that were motivated.

Janeson is right. Daniels must have something else going. Dillon and Ramsey are both trained and motivated! Three of their friends killed by this asshole and Jeffery Glenn. Yeah, they're motivated for sure.

As the SUV sped to the abandoned mine, Welch found herself being both exhilarated and depressed at the same time. She was excited about having such a clear focus and the need to be back in the field pursuing "the bad guys," and at the same time wishing she and Joe were home watching grandchildren grow up.

I guess you're still not used to being a widow yet. Now, how many years has it been?

"Are you okay, ma'am?" she heard Nine say. She shifted her focus back to him. She arched her back again and moved her legs and was very appreciative that she was traveling with one of her men from her time in the service.

"Yeah. I'm just thinking that it's so obvious that this is a trap that it's hard to stay focused when you know the other shoe is going to fall somewhere else." Welch watched as Nine's calm, stoic presentation remained true to form as he surveyed the passing landscape through their speeding vehicle.

"Well, you've already re-deployed the teams as best you could to cover a broad area while keeping reserves in place in case of a surprise. Not much you can really do until you spring the trap which may give us an idea of what the real plan is. He's a slippery bastard, ma'am, but he's still human and is pissed. He's bound to make a mistake."

After a moment of silence, Nine added one more detail.

"Anyway, I know how this ends," he said casually as he looked out the window.

"What? You know how this ends?"

"Sure do."

Welch's eyes widened as she looked at Nine to explain further. Then her eyes narrowed as she figured out how it might be possible.

"Alright. Just tell me. What was Ice's dream about this time?" she said.

In the last mission, his dreams foretold the devastation that followed. Could this be a positive dream? It would be about time. Better than the one she just had.

It was rare that Nine smiled. He looked back at her and took a moment to form the right words before talking.

"Actually, ma'am, I got two dreams. Ice's dream was about three sly foxes that killed an eagle and freed a falcon from a box, while Davis dreamt about a couple falcons that overcame adversity in darkness as other angry falcons came across a grave and survived."

"Davis? Davis is having dreams now, too? When the hell did she get in touch with her inner spirits?"

"Yes, ma'am. She must have a little Native American in her somewhere."

"Davis? Jillian Davis? Am I the only one to hear about this last?"

"No, ma'am. She thinks her father might have been Native American. It never came up and he died when she was in her late teens. Heritage became important to her much later than that."

"But she has dreams like Ice?" Welch asked.

"Yes ma'am, and she's had them a lot. Same deal as Ice – she has a dream and somehow it's related to what happens next. I'm not saying it's right. It just seems to be the case," Nine said, scanning as always.

"So does my dream have any meaning?"

"No, ma'am," Nine answered confidently. "Your dream, while frightening, seems to be about your past. Like post trauma. I get those. Their dreams seem to be about signs and portents. Symbols that have meaning," he elaborated while looking out the window.

Blinking her eyes, Welch wondered how any of this could be good news.

Well, the last dream Ice had involved fire, death, destruction, black birds flying, and that's exactly what happened. She flashed back to holding Private Parks as he died in her arms, Swat Valley, Pakistan. She could smell the sand, blood and her own sweat. The grit of sand stuck to her neck and knees. Distant shots and screams. And just as suddenly, she was back in the air-conditioned SUV with Nine right across from her. The flashbacks were quite manageable now, lasting seconds but feeling longer.

At least there's only one death here.

"And this is good because..."

In yet another rare moment of raw emotion, Welch felt she witnessed an unusual event she was sure was only seen at the birth of a child or a grandchild; a warm smile emerged as Nine's eyes seemed to soften as he spoke.

"There's only one death, ma'am. I'd like to think it's Daniels."

Logical or hopeful? Welch could only nod and look back out the window as she spoke next.

"I hope you're right, Nine. But what makes you think we're the ones that make it?"

"Because falcons are known to be cunning creatures that figure out how to survive difficult situations. I think that describes us all pretty well." Initially she was at a loss for words until her standby Latin phrase, a common mantra of people like her that gave her strength, came to her lips.

"Semper Fi,"

"Oorah," Nine responded.

I really have to give Darlene a call when I get back home. It's been over a year since I saw her and the kids.

#

Boston Regional FBI Director, John Helms, did not like the idea of walking into a trap set by men like Eric Daniels or Timothy Carter.

But if it's a trap, I'd rather spring it than Janeson or the others. Much of law enforcement had a lot to do with things you just didn't want to do, and finding a kidnapped man took priority to what he wanted or liked.

"Where are you, Burns? Hanging out with Daniels? He doesn't strike me as good company," Helms said. While surrounded by a sea of blue law enforcement windbreakers similar to all agencies, he waited just outside the Republican Citizens Army's compound in Maine. With platoons of State Troopers, local FBI and local police behind him, Helms made sure that he had snipers and spotters in place long before he showed up, just in case Carter's people were dug in for a long fight. Drone and satellite coverage blanketed the area with everything from infrared, x-ray, ultraviolet to radar. When the data confirmed reports that the area was quiet with only a handful of men "in force" and none elsewhere, Helms really started to worry.

Hmm. For a Colonel of an army who might be holding a high-value asset, he's pretty sloppy about security. The dreaded federal government shows up at your compound and there are no cameras, news trucks and no "loyal, true Americans" holding the fort down? Nope-Burns is not here.

Helms stood outside the gate with only his protective vest, battlefield dress uniform, and windbreaker designating his agency. He waited weaponless until there was finally movement on the other side of the gate. A man close to his age walked casually to the gate with two armed men behind him. Helms was impressed that Colonel Carter at least looked like he was in shape, except for the cigar he was smoking. Carter came to a stop and motioned for the gate to open.

"I'm assuming you know this is private property," Carter said as he stuffed his hands in his pockets. The cigar stuck out of his mouth with red embers at the end and blue and white smoke escaping from his nostrils and corners of his mouth. Helms and everyone outside the compound had seen many pictures of Carter and his group, but seeing him in person was significantly different in one key area – the Colonel was about five foot five inches tall.

Not exactly imposing. Still, Janeson, Gilmore and Johnson are close to figuring out where and how you're getting your money. Who's bankrolling your operation? Daniels? I bet it's more than that.

"Sure do, Mr. Carter. That's why I have a court order to search the area." Helms handed Carter the documents to review through the now partially opened gate. Carter took another puff of his cigar, opened the documents to look at them briefly and then went on as he sized up Helms.

"That's 'Colonel Carter,' Mr.?"

"It's John," Helms said.

"And you know we have a right to be here, bear arms, protect ourselves against unlawful search and seizure?"

"Sure do. That's why I made sure to get a court order."

"I just need to have my lawyer look at it."

"Sure can. I did make sure to fax this document and supporting information to Ms. Jennifer Smith, Attorney at Law," Helms said.

Carter's eyes widened at first before they narrowed. Another man leaned in to tell him something. By the reaction, Helms figured he did not like it.

"So it seems my attorney's advice is to cooperate."

"That's great." Helms's response was near jovial though he spent a great deal of energy trying to keep his hands to his side. Carter was not amused by the levity. He signaled the gate to be opened and admitted Helms in.

"Follow me," Carter said brusquely. Helms fell in behind him with two of Carter's men on each side. Helms casually surveyed the area, noting the ill-placed security detail, the apparent size of the compound and the lack of expected resistance. Even though he was only twenty feet inside the compound, there was little by way of man and firepower.

Yeah. This isn't right. For end-of-days preparation, this place would be busy. Holding an important hostage would make it even more secure. Having the federal government show up en masse, still no resistance. Nothing.

"Alright, John. I'll have escorts bring you through the compound," Carter said. Helms stood still for a moment. While not looking at him at first, Helms really wanted to think of a different approach.

Hmm. No 1st Amendment speech? No resistance to search and seizure? No citing of the 2nd, 4th, 10th and 14th Amendments? For a guy focused on individual freedom, you're a bit too compliant about letting the government just walk in and look around.

"Thank you, Colonel Carter. But how about we just meet for a few minutes first before we start?"

Helms surprised himself with the suggestion. Just as surprised, Carter took another puff of his cigar and recovered quickly.

"Works for me. How about we meet in my office?" Carter suggested.

"Thank you. I just need to let my men know we'll meet first,"

Helms said with a smile. Without waiting for a response, Helms turned to ostensibly report in to the field commander. As he walked, he pretended to get a text. He made an effort to pretend he was reading it and then replied to the fictional message:

"Janeson. Carter's too easy. See if you can get any more heat signatures in camp. The drones have been too high. Have one or two of them come in real close. My guys are outside. Hurry."

As Helms approached the commander, he was quick to let him know that he was meeting with the Colonel first for reconnaissance. While the field commander was not happy at all with the plan, Helms allowed for one of his own people to accompany the sit-down. When Helms let Carter know, there was just another puff of his cigar and then a nod. After he crossed the yard and walked up a sloping incline, Helms was not surprised to see the main house was well fortified.

Still, no armed guards or sentries.

Helms had seen enough of these end-of-civilization preppers to know two things – they were always resistant to government types demanding to come in. And if they had to let them come in, there would be a grand display of force and firepower that typically exceeded that of the authorities. Helms felt like he overdressed for a pool party with all the people he brought to contain and search the place. Now sitting casually in his large leather chair behind a grand mahogany desk, Carter sat puffing on his cigar as he held court. Helms sat just opposite him and a FBI team member standing in the back of the room, clearly conscious of both men and the closed door.

"So, what do you want to talk about, John?" Carter asked.

Helms looked right at Carter and thought he would ask a genuine question as he stalled for time.

"Well, Colonel, I really want to know what your plan is if the US government really does collapse and there is a void. I mean, let's say it falls apart and there's chaos everywhere. What's your plan?"

Helms watched with some satisfaction as the surprise of the question registered on Carter's face.

"Are you bullshitting me?" Carter's tone was angry and his face was flush red.

Helms feigned surprise and gave Carter his best sincere look.

"Colonel? I may be a federal officer but I'm also a US citizen who has a vested interest in what happens if the unspeakable occurs."

Helms watched as Carter's features seemed to soften as he sat back and considered Helms's sincerity. After a long moment, Carter began to speak about the Minutemen, Paul Revere and the Revolutionary War.

Why do they always use the War of Independence when they promote running the world in their own image? And why do they always implicate "terrorists" when they cite end-of-days?

As forty minutes threatened to turn into forty-five minutes of Carter talking nonsense, Helms's phone vibrated indicating an incoming text.

"I'm sorry Colonel but I have to take this message," Helms said as he stood up to read.

"NSA satellite indicate fifteen heat signatures mostly in front of the compound; nothing in back. Two low-level drone fly-bys confirm NSA numbers. Just like last time. Not well positioned to hold off authorities or to keep a prisoner. Simply no movement elsewhere to tip their hand if AJB is there. What's next? RJ." Just as I thought.

He turned to see what Carter was doing. As his gaze fell to Carter's desk, he saw that the papers there were actually maps. As his eyes narrowed, he took a moment to formulate his next question.

"Colonel? Are those maps of the compound for us to use?" Helms asked.

Taking a puff as he sat back in his chair, Carter answered almost as if he were distracted thinking about something else.

"Yes."

We show up unannounced and you have maps ready to distribute to help us search your very large compound. That's pretty good foresight. Well, time for a bit of drama on a catastrophic level.

Helms texted Janeson back with a technologically difficult task.

"Janeson - block all cell transmissions in and out of this

compound and two miles around; have the NSA intercept and block all Internet transmissions, and tap hardline under Homeland Security Act; block all radio frequencies, even emergency bands, if the foreign intelligence surveillance court doesn't authorize, have Tombs sign off on it; contact field commander to change over to closed radio contact after compound is securely covered. Have one of my guys come get me when it's done; do it quick."

Helms turned to re-engage Carter and conjured up a lie he thought would appeal to him.

"I'm sorry about that. My son is having their first child and I'm waiting for news."

"Oh, congratulations! Do you know if it's a boy or a girl?" Carter asked enthusiastically.

"A boy."

"Good! Boys are the backbone of this country. Why we let our women join the armed forces is just beyond me..." Carter started.

Helms sat back in his chair and lamented that he had set Carter up for another long rant.

Please, Janeson. Make this fast!

Chapter 3

Present Day - El Paso County, Colorado, USA

If I wasn't here in the flesh, I'd never believe this shit!

Denise Cratty looked around in complete awe and frustration. In less than fifty-five square feet, she saw half a dozen different sets of uniforms for at least forty men and women walking and hulking around a locked chain link fence that stood in front of a wooden façade and an old door that led to a cave. With her eyes wide open and her bladder filling fast, she didn't even hear Robert "RC" Calandra come up from behind until he spoke.

"So much for the element of surprise," he said with a deadpan face.

"This is unbelievable."

"Yeah, the boss is going to be real pissed when she sees this FUBAR."

"This is fucked up beyond all recognition."

Cratty liked Calandra or "RC" for "Red Cross." Not only was he funny, he was an EMT, and one of Welch's fellow survivors of Webber's betrayal back in the Swat Valley, Pakistan.

A friend of Welch's is a friend of mine. And having an EMT on site might be a good plan if shit goes south or if Burns is hurt.

"Out of sight. I've seen a lot of operations FUBAR before but this is really messed up," Ice added.

"Son of a bitch. Welch is going to be pissed," she heard Davis say. Moments later their group fell silent as Welch and Nine joined them to see the circus. It was easy to see that Welch was not happy with what they were all seeing. It took about ten seconds for Welch to impress upon the persons in charge that she was not happy with the show of force, and that stealth was no longer an option due to their lack of discretion. After twenty minutes of re-deploying the different branches of local and state authorities, Welch emerged with two men and one woman. With gear already unpacked and ready to go, Cratty could see that her team was just biting to get the mission done. As they gathered around Welch and the new arrivals, she did a quick introduction of names and roles. Since Cratty was too hyper to remember details such as names, she assigned roles to the new people – the cartographer, Park Ranger and Sheriff.

"Alright, let's start this briefing with a map, a report of the mine itself, followed by a firsthand account of the mine and local law enforcement issues that are related," Welch said.

Cratty listened as she found herself looking around the entire area, scoping for possible vantage points and barriers. As each professional reported, it became evident that their training was going to be ineffective.

Great. Two hundred feet underground, old wood beams for support, old hand-rail system track for a trail in and out, questionable propane tanks with rotting gauges, and the locals stopped coming here to drink. And just for laughs and giggles there were a couple of close calls with cave-ins. Yeah, it's a trap.

"I hope you listed next of kin, Cratty. This looks like it's a one-way trip," RC said quietly.

"Aren't you supposed to be the medic, angel of hope and mercy?"

"Yup, I'm the optimist of the group."

"That's great."

Cratty's attention returned to Welch as she dismissed each specialist as each person finished his or her respective reports and left. Finally, it was just them. Alone, they formed a tight circle. All eyes turned to Welch for calling the plan. Cratty knew that it would be Davis and her going in. Part of her success in the field was her ability to size up the plan fast. She was sure Davis would come up with the same plan.

Ice and Nine could do it but their skill-set is long-range sniping. RC's a medic and will be pulled in if necessary, and Davis and I have more experience with close quarters combat and familiarity with the target. Sorry boys. Don't need sniping in a cave or a medic yet.

Before Welch could say anything, Davis jumped in with her own assessment.

"Well, I guess it's Cratty and me going in the hole?"

Can always count on you to get things started, Jillian, Cratty thought as she concealed a smile and readjusted her rifle sling.

"Ah, no," Nine said. As he spoke he shifted from scanning the area to looking directly at Davis.

"Should be me and Davis as team one with her on point and me further behind. Ice and Cratty should be team two," Nine concluded.

Cratty watched as Welch's eyes widened as she peered at Nine.

Okay...here we go.

"So, you think your skill set of long-range shooting in a mine will be critical to have for this fire zone?" Davis said directly to Nine and then turned to address Welch, leader of the operation.

"I couldn't have said it better," Cratty said.

"The mine gets a bit more narrow and has more turns and twists, not lending itself to a line-of-sight distance thing. Further, while Ice and Nine are strikingly handsome, they are large men that would need to fit in a small environment. Cratty is tiny and I am smaller than the guys."

"I'm average size, Jillian. I'm not 'tiny'," Cratty corrected.

"Are we back to first names again, Denise?" Davis looked

directly at her and made a face. Cratty watched the group smile for the first time since their arrival. The tension was still thick but at least they were not so tense they couldn't think out of the box. Welch spoke next. It was evident to Cratty that Welch had thought about this situation before they arrived once she had a visual of the mine; now that the landscape and actual hot zone were before them, it was clear that it was not going to be on good terms.

"My first choice would be for me to go in and do it myself but I already know that is a losing battle." There was a series of confirmations and assurances she was right.

"Well. Thanks for thinking about it," Welch said less seriously.

After a moment of silence, Welch gave the word.

"Alright - the State troopers are going to hold the perimeter with the Rangers keeping the curious away. Ice, I want you to take the sheriff and two of her deputies and find the east exit of this hole. All other exits are caved in. Nine, you go in seventy-five feet with RC as back-up. Davis and Cratty go all the way. Cratty's point. Oorah?"

"Oorah!" the Marines said in unison. Cratty was surprised at how loud and crisp their response were even knowing that the men did not like the idea of women going on point in a hostile environment, more likely a trap. As she and Davis started to get their gear in order, Welch joined them as she watched Nine and his team head out.

"Ladies, be careful. I like to think I'm not sexist but I agree with Davis's recommendations. Keeping in mind I think this is a fool's errand, watch yourselves, and take no unnecessary risks. Especially you, Cratty."

"Why are you calling me out? You let Davis go all gung-ho on Wise?"

"She had Nine and Ice as back-up and dwarfed Wise by two feet."

"Hey! She was armed, you know, and I had to make sure the civilians were not in harm's way," Davis said defensively.

"Yeah, whatever, Davis," Welch said as she locked onto

Cratty's eyes. Cratty smirked at Davis's jaw slackening.

"Why is everyone up my ass on this?"

"You want the short answer or the long one?"

"No, really? Why me? Why do you think I have to be more careful than Davis?" Without hesitation, Welch squared off with Cratty to be clear.

"Cratty, there's no mystery to everyone here that you have the most reason to kill Daniels. I get that. If Davis was just a bit smaller, I would have her take point..."

"Hey! I'm not a freak, you know? I'm bigger than average but not as big as Nine, you know?" Davis said.

"Whatever gets you through, Davis," Welch said without looking at her while still focusing on Cratty. Cratty did enjoy how Welch kept picking on Davis. Welch was clearly not done addressing her yet.

"That bastard killed half your team and right now he's still out there. The only reason we are here is the remote chance that Burns is there with Daniels. If he's not and it's a trap, I need you back to find Burns and terminate Daniels's command, once and for all."

Cratty said nothing as she looked back at Welch.

That rat bastard. I'll terminate his command.

Welch closed the gap between them and spoke in a low tone for only her to hear.

"Denise. I know what it's like to lose more than half your troops to some narcissistic asshole who thinks the world owes them. I get that." Cratty felt a bit guilty as she remembered that Welch lost fifteen of her men, along with women and children she wanted to protect.

"But you need to stay focused on the mission. Find Burns. Capture or kill Daniels. If he's not there, get the hell out so we can re-group and find him. Crystal?"

"Clear," Cratty said reflexively, remembering her time in the Army.

"I mean it, Denise. Don't make me regret this decision."

"You won't regret it."

"Alright. You're green to go," Welch said. After that, she turned to talk to another State Trooper who was talking to Nine as ten excavators were organizing several feet from the cave's entrance.

Cratty's responses to Welch were reminiscent of talking to her mother back when her mother was vibrant, commanding, and did not suffer fools well.

Hmm. Excavators. Just in case, I bet. She's always thinking.

Cratty stripped down her gear to water, rations, headset with video feed, ammunition and weapons. She felt Davis beside her more than heard her as Davis stripped down to the same gear.

"So my diminutive, little friend, it looks like you and I get to spend quality time in a cave. How nice," Davis said.

"'Diminutive' and 'tiny' are redundant, and I'm average, not little."

Cratty did yet another count of ammunition and looked for her water bottle to make sure it was full of water to reduce the sound in the cramped cave.

"Well, I was actually going to go with 'petite,' rather than 'little.' Petite has a more dainty quality that is more in line with your character."

Cratty was in the middle of adjusting her rifle sling and straps when she noticed that Davis finished with her own gear and was obviously waiting for her. Sighing while trying to move faster, she struggled with a response.

"I'm not petite." she finally.

"Whatever gets you through, Denise." A few seconds later Davis walked towards the cave entrance without her, apparently tired of waiting for her.

"Hey, slow down your pace. Your legs are twice the size of mine, Jillian." Cratty picked up her pace to follow her.

#

Burns found himself fighting to stay awake, slipping in and out of consciousness as his ride seemed to stop and start as if they might be in some traffic. At one point, he was sure that they had picked someone up but whoever it was, they were silent. There was a difference in the new occupant, though – they smelled as if they were recently showered and shaved.

Well, at least someone has taken time to take a shower. I hope the windows are tinted or closed. You'd think a car full of men with one of them blindfolded might be an indicator that something's wrong. Burns tried to test his restraints but found he simply had no energy to even try.

Why does Daniels want me so drugged? How will I even stay awake?

It had been that way for days. As soon as he would feel as if he were breaking out, he would slip again into another dream. The longer he was in transport, the dreams, visions and apparitions became more vivid. It was difficult to tell when one finished and another began. They were all remarkably different too, far from what he had feared and expected.

Maybe it's morphine or Valium? I bet it's the same blend I gave Maxwell. I guess it's better to be out of it than waiting to be killed by your own team.

Burns felt himself losing his fight to stay in the present and slipped into another dream. Of all the things he had done since his return from the dead back on May 2nd, being responsible for Maxwell's death weighed heavily on him. He tapped his fingers, moved his legs and took deep breaths as a way to stay awake. It was a losing battle. In the past, he had good reason to fear dreams. Either they were laden with silence, heaviness, and anger, or they were just blank. Burns had stayed away from all drugs for fear that all his dreams would be nightmares of past missions and all the people he killed. Instead this drug-induced sleep was of beautiful surroundings, mountains, rivers, oceans and other natural landscapes.

What is this?

#

Present Time and location - Unknown

Throughout the trip and even as he felt his body being moved, he still felt his eyes closed but could see everything. But then there was a sudden change after picking up the new passenger. First landscapes and open sky collapsed into a small cramped office. For just a moment he had wondered if he was just shot and his body tossed in a grave. He imagined he would have heard something like a gunshot, but there were no abrupt sounds. Just a swift change from open sky to a small office. The desk was well illuminated with a soft light. There were stacks of folders, a couple of computer tablets, cell phones and two net-books casually lying on the desk. Finally his gaze found an older man working on an ancient desktop computer. Based on the material in the office, this man seemed pretty busy like an analyst, and less like an executive with a corner office. Before he spoke, he looked to make sure he wasn't in a corner office. There were no windows or even a door in sight. The light was bright without being blinding but it only illuminated the desk and the man in front of him. Burns struggled with why the laws of physics didn't allow for light to travel wider than the desk. Even though his throat was parched, Burns did his best to speak.

"Where am I? Who are you?"

· Surprised that he was awake, the older man stopped his work to look right at him.

"Well, good morning, Alexander Burns. You have been out of it for quite a time. I'm glad you waited for me," the elder said cheerily. He moved to face Burns straight on with his large hands folded on the desk and his shoulders squared.

I waited for you. Burns looked down at his freed hands. He had no interest in leaving as much as he wanted to know what was going on.

"I waited for you?"

"You sure did."

"So I could have left anytime?"

"You could have left anytime, yes. You have quite a will to live but you've changed."

"Changed? How have I changed?" Burns asked. His scanning of the room revealed that it was empty except for them and what he could see. It's as if the world fell off just a few feet in all directions.

"Yes. You used to kill and fight to live for flag, country and yourself. You feared death. Now, you've changed. You will fight and even kill though it is with reservation of late. And it's your motivations that surprise us all. You do it for Emma, Becky, Rosemarie, you would die for them. There's no fear. Kind of a big thing around here."

"And here is?"

"A waiting room, of sorts. A place for you to hang out, catch up with friends and give us time to figure things out. You are one of those outliers, statistically speaking. I asked for your case," the older man said with one of the gentler, kinder smiles Burns had ever seen from a man. Nothing made sense but Burns was curious, a state and skill he acquired years ago when he first met David Caulfield. His mind was blank but the questions flowed quickly.

"My case file? You asked to be assigned to me?"

"Sure did. I asked to be assigned to you due to our common histories. Still, though, I hope you enjoyed the views before you arrived. An unusual choice, if you ask me. I never thought of you as a 'nature' guy."

Okay. What the hell? Did I just overdose or am I crazy?

Confused but feeling as if his faculties were returning, Burns lifted his arms to lean on the desk so he could look at the man's face. It was important to know if he knew him or not. His gentleness and calm voice didn't match his physique and presence. The man was "well worn" and in his late sixties. His strong features reminded Burns of people along the Mediterranean Sea. If it wasn't for the man's well-tailored shirt, tie and suit jacket casually resting on the back of the chair, Burns would have thought him some kind of tradesman. It was the calluses on his hands, the suntan on his face and strong arms that indicated he was a man who still worked long hours in the sun. And the man's chest was that of a well-built bodybuilder who clearly could bench-press him with ease. The man might have been in his sixties, but he was the most virile "old guy" Burns had ever met.

Contractor? Farmer? Builder or construction. Something manual.

The man's arm and chest muscles threatened to rip his tailored shirt. As Burns balanced all of the conflicting data, he took a deep breath as a means of clearing his head to help him organize his thinking.

Maybe I'm dead?

"You're not dead, Alexander," the man said as if he had read Burns's mind. Burns assumed that it was his facial expression that gave his thoughts away. He let it go in pursuit of another question.

"I'm sorry. I don't know who you are. And I have no idea where I am," Burns said.

The man sat back. He kept his hands and forearms on the table. It gave still more conflicting information in that the man's large chest tapered to a small waist as he gave a warm smile and his eyes seemed to radiate kindness.

"I'm sorry, Alexander. Where are my manners? My name is Paul. Think of me as 'your handler' from this point on," Paul said as he extended his hand. While still cautious, Burns extended his hand and shook it. To say that the grip was strong would be a profound understatement.

My God! His hand feels like heated iron. And the grip, it's like a vise or clamps. For a dream, this is pretty intense.

"It's more a waiting room but I can see why it would appear to you as a dream. Burns stopped and rewound what Paul had just said.

He smiled and retracted his hand. Hands free and seeing that he had the ability to move, Burns looked around the office for escape routes as he tried to figure out how Paul knew what he was thinking. With darkness just beyond the desk on all sides, Burns looked back to the man and smiled again. His immediate risk assessment and action plan surprised him.

I don't think I can take this guy. Either he is still active in the military or he's deadly serious about staying fit. I can't see beyond the table and chair on all sides. There could be a cliff there and I would never know it.

Burns took a sniff of the office air and took in the strong aromas of lilacs, roses and cinnamon. He extended both hands on the top of the desk just to see if it was actually made of thick oak as it looked to be a very heavy desk. That's when he noticed yet another very curious thing. He looked at his hands and arms and found no scars, burns or deep cuts. He rolled up his sleeves and there were still none. He moved his hands to explore his head, scalp and forehead repeatedly and again felt none of the scars he had become so accustomed to. He closed his eyes tightly and placed his hands back on the desk. He cleared his mind.

"You're not fading on me, are you, Alexander?"

"No," was all Burns said. He slowly opened his eyes to inspect his arms and head all over again. He had mixed feelings about their disappearance.

"Like I said, this place is more of a waiting area."

What the hell?

"No, that is an entirely different place. You'll find the absence of reason there," Paul explained.

"Ah, it's kind of like here. I was tied up in a cramped car being transported to my death high on drugs, and I also had quite a bit of scarring. Now I'm in a room with you, unbound, thinking clearly and without scars. That kind of sounds like lack of reasoning."

Burns sat still and focused on Paul to gauge his reaction.

His reaction was at first surprise but then it evolved into a broad smile. His eyes seemed to twinkle in addition to his face softening. The strong jawline and hard features seemed surprisingly gentle.

"Well, that was well put. When you put it like that, you make sense, Alexander. Like I said, you've changed quite a bit over the years."

Burns shifted gears to data collection and decided to ask some defining questions.

"You said I needed a handler?"

"Yes. A kind of case manager who will organize your files for extensive rapid review."

"So why do I need a handler?"

"We all need handlers here, especially the new arrivals," Paul started. He stopped when there was a faint green light shining on his keyboard and the CPU tower sounded as if it were starting up from inactivity. Burns was ready to ask another question to gather more information when Paul looked back at his computer screen and seemed engrossed in it. He raised his finger so he could either read something or review something.

What is going on? This is crazy.

Burns decided to give Paul a minute to review whatever it was that drew his attention. He began to get up but felt somehow constrained in his seat even though he didn't see any binds that were holding him. He looked at his freed arms and legs and was baffled as to why he could move but couldn't stand nor leave his spot.

Yet another odd thing here. I've never had a dream this real. I just don't understand...There's nothing binding me, and I can clearly move my feet. I just can't get up.

Burns repeatedly moved his hands from the desk to his lap freely, and then repeated a similar motion of moving his legs and feet just as easily. It was as if his butt were glued to the chair seat and the chair were bolted down to the floor. As he continued to figure out his dilemma, his attention was brought back to Paul who shifted his attention back to him.

"Ah yes. I'm sorry, Alexander, but I wanted to make sure I recalled your earlier case files. I have to tell you, ever since your helicopter crash and your friendship with David Caulfield, I have been following your work. While I think I might have made some different decisions, you have certainly struggled to change. I respect that."

David? Helicopter crash? Decisions? Is this a good thing?

"Okay," Burns said. He offered nothing more but found that he was simultaneously fatigued and thinking in overdrive. He focused on thinking things out for fear that the sudden flood of exhaustion would cloud his thinking and rationale for what was happening here. His arms and legs began to feel tired as his brain raced on. He needed more information and for that he would have to ask directly. His approach and the whole situation ran completely contrary to both his experience and training.

It's time for candor. How does he know about the helicopter crash? And how does he know about my "decisions?" And what particular decisions are we talking about? And why does he describe my relationship with David as "friendship?" I know it was to me, but who the hell is this guy? How would he know?

Pulling all of his waning strength together, Burns shifted from being asked questions to asking them.

"I'm sorry, Paul, but where do you come from? What agency do you work for? And more importantly, how do you know all of these things about me?"

Paul answered in a soothing voice as he casually folded his arms over his chest.

"I used to travel a lot but Damascus is my new home."

Burns knitted his brows and that small act drained him of more energy as fatigue encroached on all sides.

"Damascus as in Syria? Are you military or intelligence there? Or independent?"

What now? Why am I so exhausted all of a sudden?

Burns watched Paul tilt his head as if to notice that he was tired. He unfolded his arms and leaned forward to talk. His demeanor was that of a kind accountant who was easing someone into a tax audit. Burns was still struck by the rippling muscles and Paul's white executive shirt and conservative, stylish tie.

It's blue...the tie is blue with stars. Is that important?

"It's alright, Alexander. You should rest. I have to go see if I can find a couple of people before we conclude our business. I'll come get you when I'm ready. If for some reason I can't, I'll send my good friend Ananius but he likes to be called Andy. Deal?"

He was fading fast but was struck with Paul's continued use of his name.

My mother would say something similar.

Without warning, Paul looked at Burns as if he said something to him.

"No, she wouldn't," Paul said as he shook his head. "She called you by your real name – Joshua," he corrected.

Even though Burns slumped in his chair, his heart and mind sped up. It was his worst nightmare of being aware of danger and seeing it approaching, and not being able to run.

"What?"

How does he know that? I didn't even say it out loud!

"I know, Alexander. Like I said, I've been watching you for several years now and I'm sure my research is pretty solid. In regards to your earlier question of 'some of your decisions,' I was pleasantly surprised that you never told your mother you hated your middle name. Still, she did name you Joshua Alexander Burns. At the time, she would have been heartbroken since it was her father's and grandfather's name. I understand your not wanting to cause her pain. You know she would have forgiven you? Right?"

Burns's mouth slackened. It was the only strength he had left. His chest tightened and his limbs felt as heavy as stone.

No one knows about my name. I don't even think Daniels knows it. Who are you? Burns's field of vision narrowed to darkness and he felt lightheaded.

"My name is Paul. I'll be back in a few minutes. Don't worry."

But I never said anything.

#

Present Day – Andover, Massachusetts, USA

Burns felt his mind racing as he thought about how this person could know what he did. Remarkably, he felt some strength coming back to his limbs and a burning sensation in his right arm. He felt as if he could move his head, arms and legs. He tried to jolt himself to move which resulted in his jerking his body, but little more than that. He opened his eyes and found himself in a dark room with a table and a desk lamp illuminating the area between him and the man sitting across from him. The man's build and clothes were nothing like Paul's. While it was dark, he could make out walls outside the illumination.

There's nothing on the table. No folders or tablets? Just bare.

Burns shifted in his chair and felt his arms and legs bound. It took time but his eyes adjusted. While Paul was gone, he saw a familiar shape of a man in a room that looked very familiar though it was dark.

"So, Alex. You're finally back with us," the very familiar voice of Eric Daniels clearly announced. While still very drowsy and reeling from his dream, Burns looked at his arm to see the IV in it.

Oh. That's right. I was captured in Colorado, traveled for a couple of days, and now I'm...I'm...here with Eric? What a messed up dream. I wonder who Paul is? What was that all about?

Rather than feeling worried or concerned, Burns's mind traveled to how the room looked familiar and how Eric's voice had aged.

Now, how long has it been? And there's something about this room...the size or shape that's familiar.

Burns focused on clearing his head. A strong memory of Eric's full name made him smile broadly at the fact that he remembered something clearly.

"Eric Icarus Daniels. You look good!" Burns said with more zeal than he wanted and expected.

"What? What did you say?"

"You look like you lost weight."

It must be the Vicodin or whatever concoction they have in me.

Burns shook his head hoping that it might reset his thinking so that he could appreciate the danger he was in. He looked closely at Daniels, and noticed that the more he smiled, the more Daniels seemed to scowl. It was easy to see that Daniels's arms and legs were folded up and that he was staring intensely at him with enmity in his eyes.

"Burns, do you have any idea what you have done to me and

this country?" Daniels said in a low, firm voice.

"Yes. But I'm sure you and I have different viewpoints, so why don't you tell me your point of view and if you're interested, I could tell you mine." Burns's voice was cheery.

Wow! That doesn't even seem like me. What are you pumping into me? Who is Paul from Syria? Who do I know from Damascus?

In an attempt to see Daniels better, Burns narrowed his eyes and did his best to focus. It was easy to see that Daniels chose his words carefully as if he wanted to say much more but was restraining himself.

"That's the only reason you're alive. So I can tell you how much you have cost me and this country."

"Come on, Eric. You tried to kill me?"

"We needed that information and you wanted to kill Sudani!"

"He was a snake like Bin Laden. We needed to cut off its head."

"No, Burns! We needed to take him alive and get his entire network!"

"And why did you have to have Maxwell kill me?"

"You were compromised, damn it! You wanted to kill one of the biggest command and communication centers for terrorism on the planet. You weren't part of Seal Team Six, Burns! We're the smart ones! Burns!? Burns!"

He really looks pissed.

Burns found himself slipping off again. He tried to focus on what was happening and what Daniels was saying. Still feeling dizzy and having a hard time holding onto reality, Burns blurted out his next thought.

"Why did you kill Samantha? She was the only woman I loved. Why are you so angry?"

Burns watched Daniels's jaw slacken and his eyes blink feverishly.

It was easy to see that Daniels looked even angrier than he was a moment ago. But by then, darkness fell all around him and his body was weightless. He slipped into unconsciousness. He never heard Daniels's answer. He really wanted to.

I better get my head together or he'll just shoot me.

#

Present Day – Andover, Massachusetts, USA

"Now this is the part where you say *'Monsieur Glenn! Vous avez eu raison!'*" Glenn was at least quiet about it. He whispered it to John as they all watched Daniels and Burns arrive together. Ruth smiled as she shook her head more out of delight than surprise.

"I hate to admit it, Mr. Glenn, but you were right."

"Thank you Ruth. I have always been impressed with the people who can admit when they are wrong. A sign of strength, if you ask me."

"Well, I for one am glad you are right," Ruth said. She went right back to oiling her collapsible baton. Glenn moved back to his bank of monitors as he called back for John.

"Still though, it would sound so much better coming from my red-headed friend, John." Glenn didn't overtly gloat about his being right. Instead he aligned his tasks in order of implementation and pretended to be focused on them rather than patiently waiting for John to admit he was wrong. Not hearing anything, Glenn turned in time to see Ruth hitting John in the arm as John continued to look out the window. Glenn stood up again briefly to see Burns sluggishly moving into the building while Daniels waited impatiently. Smiling that he was on target and sure that John was simply in shock that he called it right, Glenn sat back down and waited.

"Say it," he heard Ruth say.

"*Non.*"

"*Faites-le,* John!" Ruth was insisting that he pull himself away from the window and deal with him.

"*Dois-je?*"

"*Oui.*"

John finally pulled himself from the small tinted window, and with great effort he looked at the van floor and started his admission.

"Monsieur Glenn..." John started with little enthusiasm.

"No, no, no," Glenn said as he looked at John. "In, English, *s'il vous plaît*, John."

John's eyes narrowed and his arms folded over his chest as he spoke. He was insulted and angry. Glenn watched with anticipation though it was difficult to keep a serious face with Ruth's tanned smiling face and bright white teeth shining right behind him.

"Mister Glenn. You were right all along," John said.

Glenn took in a deep breath as he enjoyed his face muscles relaxing into a small grin.

Now, that was very satisfying.

"'All along,' John? That was a nice addition," Glenn said as he turned back to his work.

Be the better man. Be gracious and don't gloat.

Glenn did his best to suppress a smile and forced his voice to be all business.

"All right, children. It's time to get to work," Ruth said as she moved closer to Glenn while John unpacked security uniforms.

"So, Mr. Glenn? Which of the chess pieces will you move first?"

With Ruth right beside him, he couldn't help but smell her.

Hmm. Vanilla bean? I really wouldn't have pegged you for a vanilla bean scent.

His thoughts jumped to chess pieces as he rapidly assessed various deployment strategies and settled on one.

The Rook. A very powerful though linear piece, but it will keep people focused.

He sat back in his chair to take in the view of the monitors as a way to digest the scope of the objectives. Ultimately Glenn chose to go with his original plan. Years of field training and experience at the Foreign Intelligence Agency and afterwards was now coming to bear. For the first time in his career, Glenn felt untethered, free to move as he wished and simply unstoppable.

I bet this is how Burns felt on May 2nd. All those years in command, I bet this is how Daniels felt. Now let's make sure I don't end up like them in an abandoned bank vault with final judgment outside their doorstep.

Glenn banished the thought of failure, leaned forward, and cued his citizen band radio band instead of military, encrypted bandwidth, the very thing federal agencies would be looking for. Citizen band? Not at all; literally they could communicate freely under the radar. While initially uncomfortable himself with using an open source of communication for risky tasks ahead, he had to remind himself and others that it was all part of the plan.

Obfuscation, subterfuge, misdirection and operating in plain sight. It just doesn't get any more classic than this.

"Fox Den to Fox One. Mobilize Trojan Horse and initiate plan alpha. Copy?

"Copy Fox Den. Fox One mobilizing. ETA, three minutes; completion in eight minutes."

"Copy. You are green."

Glenn sat back as he watched a small rental truck slowly drive away. He felt the corners of his mouth curl up again. He was happy to start the mission.

"You know, I think the scar does make you more handsome," Ruth said. John suddenly erupted into laughter. It made Glenn laugh himself for the second time in months.

Chapter 4

Present Day – Andover, Massachusetts, USA

Daniels found himself getting really pissed with every passing moment Burns sat in front of him drugged out of his mind. He was almost as pissed as when Welch baited him on the phone to triangulate his position. While he had nearly stopped the stream of drugs flowing into Burns, there was something wrong with how Burns seemed nearly unconscious.

What the hell did they do to you? You don't even sound like yourself!

He took a deep breath, centered himself and tried to figure out a way to engage Burns.

That's if you don't pass out again.

"Alex? Why didn't you just come in? Why did you have to go to war with me?" Daniels asked. It was easy to see that while Burns appeared conscious, he also seemed happy. Daniels patiently waited as Burns appeared to understand the questions.

"I...I didn't want to be that person any more. I wanted to leave but you went after David, Samantha and her sister, Emma..."

"When the hell did you ever care about collateral damage? You were the asshole who would leave bodies all over the place, and I would have to clean up your mess. They were civilians too! Why the hell are these people so different!?"

"Eric? Could you lower your voice? I have to say that I have a hell of a headache."

"What? You want me to what?"

"Headache, Eric. It would be great if you lowered your voice."

Eric was startled by Burns's casual response. He found himself speechless.

What? A headache? You destabilize our country's security, kill a slew of agents, release classified data on the World Wide Web, and you want me to lower my voice because you have a headache?!

"That would be great."

"Are you for real?" Daniels asked.

"I don't think it was a good idea to keep me so sedated. The...the dreams are real strange and I can't...stay awake," Burns said as he seemed to be nodding off.

"No, Burns! Why can't you fight it? I told them to give you the minimum amount!" Daniels yelled as he stood up in anger.

"I don't think they did. I'm sorry, Eric...I'm just so tired..." Burns said as his eyes seemed to glaze over and his head dropped into his chest.

"No! Damn it, Burns!"

There was no response. Daniels found himself standing, and staring at the man who destroyed everything of value to him as he slept.

Sleeping? Passed out? Dreams? What?

With a sudden urge to hit Burns, Daniels counted to twenty before he finally stood up and walked out of the vault. The plan was simple. He needed to talk to the men that transported him there. As Daniels stepped out onto the second floor foyer, he took a moment to take in the view. Four overweight, bearded men in camouflage sitting on chairs and the rest on the floor as they read the paper and magazines. With shotguns lying on the floor or on their laps, none of them looked up to even see what he might want.

So this is what I'm reduced to? You pay peanuts and you get monkeys. No, monkeys would be an upgrade in this case.

As Daniels stood looking at them, he was surprised but not shocked that they were not paying attention to either the access points or patrolling the empty building's grounds to make sure that no one was trying to get in.

Breathe, Eric. Welch and Helms are out of state looking for Burns and probably protecting Littleton and Murphy too. Just breathe.

After a few moments of doing just that, Daniels had to remember which one of the Republican Citizen Army members was the alleged leader of the group.

"Howard?" he said out loud. He was not surprised that it was the largest of the four men who responded. Somehow Daniels knew intuitively that the one who consumed the most calories and did the least was more like the boss of this troupe of apes.

"Ah, yes Mr. Daniels," Howard said. To his credit he tried to amble as quickly as he could. He used his hands and chair rail to help get up off the floor. Daniels waited patiently as he formulated his next series of questions that were short and monosyllabic so that they might yield the answers to what he needed to know. As the seconds ticked by, he closed his eyes so as to not witness the "team leader's" laborious efforts to get to him. He continued breathing until he felt the man bump into him as he finally stopped in front of him.

"Howard? Do you have that list of medication and times I gave you to give to Burns?"

"Ah yes, Mr. Daniels," he responded. He had to fish through his pockets. Daniels waited. Unfortunately Howard's efforts were slow which meant that Daniels had to wait and endure the smelly old body odor emanating from the man's armpits and elsewhere. Daniels suddenly blanched at the thought that he saw no toilet paper in the supplies Howard and his team managed to bring. Daniels pushed the thought out of his head and was then confronted with the observation that Howard's chin firmly held some calcified eggs and bacon remains in his beard.

Jesus, Burns! You should thank me for sedating you. Otherwise, it would have been more merciful to just kill you on the spot than to travel with these guys, conscious and aware. I'd have better luck with monkeys. I bet these guys toss their shit like chimps do!

Daniels's patience thinned while his disdain morphed into disgust with every passing second the man searched his pockets.

"Here it is," Howard said proudly as he produced a well-folded piece of gray paper. Daniels held the paper by the corners so as not to touch the stains on the page. After just a few seconds, Daniels closed his eyes as the mistake seemed clear to him.

"Howard? You gave Burns a mixture of Vicodin and valium. But I see here that you gave him four grams of Vicodin and I think this says four grams of valium? Right?" Daniels said as calmly as possible.

Howard took a moment to peer over and look at the paper Daniels was holding to confirm. As simple as the two sentences and one word were, he was sure that Howard needed time and the visual aid of the note to process it.

"Ah, yes. It was easy to remember because they were both 4 grams for both."

"Easy to remember?"

"Yes. The numbers four – four grams for Vicodin and four grams for valium. Simple.

"And that's how you remembered it? You only saw the number four and that was it for you?"

"Yes, Sir. Pretty simple, huh?"

Daniels stood looking at him for a moment deciding whether he should explain the problem or simply shoot them all and be done with them. While the idea of shooting him was pleasurable, the amount of time, effort and muscle power it would take to move and bury his corpulent body tarnished the idea immediately.

"Okay. I'm going to go back in with the prisoner. You might

want to check the perimeter just in case we have visitors."

"Sure thing, Mr. Daniels," he heard Howard say. Daniels walked away from the man quickly and shut the vault door behind him. He leaned against the vault door out of frustration and looked at the soiled paper again. After his third read, he made a sound of disgust as he walked over to Burns's arms and removed the IV as quickly as he could.

"Four grams of valium three times a day! Just great!" Daniels said, angry at himself. He had to take air in through his nose. He felt tingling there as if he was about to experience another major nosebleed. He walked back to his chair and sat back down to look at Burns who was sound asleep. Regardless, Daniels spoke to him as if he were awake.

"You see, Alex? You see what I'm working with here now? I wanted them to give you no more than four milligrams of valium, three times a day, and they give you four grams, four times a day because *four* for dosage and frequency was easy to remember. You see what you've reduced me to? I have to work with backwater, good old boys who can't manage polysyllabic words." Daniels complained to his unconscious guest.

"I should just walk away. These losers have 'voyage of the damned' written all over them. Better just to shoot you and walk away now before Helms and Welch get their shit together."

Daniels heard Burns snoring. It was insult to injury.

"You see, Alex. The monkeys out there gave you four thousand times the amount you needed, three times a day. I'm surprised you're alive."

Daniels watched Burns's eyes move under their closed lids.

Sitting back in his chair as he rubbed his temples to figure out what to do next, Daniels asked Burns another question.

"What are you dreaming about now?"

#

Andersen was surprised how quickly he found himself sitting in front of Alica Wise. She was far from the attractively dressed assassin he remembered. Fully conscious and with her eyes locked on Martin, she kept her arms folded over her bright orange jumpsuit and did nothing to change the scowl on her face. He had only been there five minutes and already had his jacket off and a pad of paper and pen resting on a cold dented steel table, all prepared for theater. Andersen looked right at Wise. He shook his head. He glanced over at Special Agent Martin. He was wearing a black funeral suit with a crisp white shirt and black tie. His hair was short with flecks of white. Martin was legendary in his new-found role as investigator and interrogator of difficult prisoners. Wise fit those criteria well. Upon his arrival and after clearing security, Andersen had literally only one minute to consult with Martin before Wise returned from a toilet break. The only strategy Martin gave was cryptic: "just go along with me when I start."

"So, Lieutenant Andersen. Are you going to at least talk?" Wise said with a sneer.

"What do you want to talk about?"

"You came to see me."

"I came to see Special Agent Martin, Ms. Wise."

"What do you want from me?"

She wore her frustration and hostility on her sleeve. Andersen had felt bad that Martin had effectively implemented the silent treatment. After this little outburst, he lost what little compassion he had for her.

"You know, Alica, I'm here to get answers. If you want to do it the hard way, that's fine," he said as he pushed himself away from the desk.

"So, you're not going to talk me either? Just the silent treatment?"

"No. Mr. Martin is far kinder than me. I'll just go," Andersen got up to put his jacket on, ostensibly to leave.

I hope this falls into your plan, Martin.

He pulled together his pad and pen and was putting his jacket back on. He watched Wise's eyes widen. She looked at Andersen then at Martin and then back at Andersen again. For a moment, Andersen was positive that Wise was going to say something.

"Shut up, Wise," Martin said in a low, smooth voice.

"I didn't say anything."

"You were. The less you say, the better for you."

"But I want to know what you want."

"You know what we want."

"No! No, I don't! You won't tell me!"

Martin sighed, pinched the bridge of his nose and sat silently.

Okay. Clearly he's softened her up.

Andersen continued with putting his jacket on. It was easy to see that Wise jumped at the chance to talk, and Martin was letting her stew. From the descriptions Andersen received from the Warden, sergeant, guards, and even the prison pastor, Martin had been sitting motionless and speechless in his black suit, starched white shirt and black tie for hours a day for three days straight. Unexpectedly, Martin turned to Andersen in the same calm position he was in when Andersen arrived. Martin asked Andersen what to observers would have seemed strange questions.

"Lieutenant? All the recordings here are off for the next ten minutes, right?"

Well, since he's asking me if it's off, I'll go with that, Andersen thought.

"For the next eight minutes, now," Andersen said as he looked at his watch for confirmation. *Sorry, Martin, I just had to improvise there.*

"Excellent. I have the documents here for you to sign and return to Director Tombs for the President's signature so we can move the prisoner to Guantanamo."

Martin was the epitome of calm as he extracted a perfectly white envelope from his jacket and handed it to him.

"Really? Gitmo?"

"She'll talk there."

"What if she wants to talk here, state-side?"

"I don't care."

Andersen opened the document while watched Wise's expression jump from panic to horror.

"They don't take women there," Wise started.

"And there are no female terrorists here at Danbury Federal Prison," Martin said serenely.

Beautiful. Under-played and well executed.

Andersen took his time to review the document. He was pleasantly surprised that in addition to acting, Martin's skills also included prop designs. The document looked more official than the real letter he received from the President a while ago. It took a moment for him to find the piece of fiction he found really interesting. He took out his glasses to get a better look and read the parts he thought might be good to say out loud to himself.

"Enemy combatants and terrorists will not be entitled to due process of private citizens, and fall under military courts..."

"I'm not a terrorist!" Wise yelled as she jumped up, slamming her fists on the steel desk.

Wow. That's got to hurt. I bet it'll leave a mark, too.

"Sit down and shut up, Wise," Martin said firmly. He made sure there was a clear tone of enmity in his voice. Still shaking, Wise slowly sat down. Martin turned to Andersen to continue the drama.

"Lieutenant? We have five minutes at the most before the recordings come on. Could you please sign it before you go? I have to be a witness."

How does he switch his voice like that – from deep-seated anger to calm and cool within seconds? Anderson thought as he took his pen out to sign.

"You really want to do this?"

"Yes. I've wasted enough time on her. She could have spoken to me, offered me anything, but she sat there like a sack of shit."

"Maybe she didn't know the specifics?"

"A former Foreign Intelligence Agency agent? Intimate Deep-cover specialist? No. She could have pieced it all together. She should have talked ten seconds after I arrived."

"Jesus, Martin. Is that why you got the Marshals here?"

"Yup. I don't have the time and don't want to waste the Bureau's or the Marines' resources. The Marshals were more than happy to get her out of here."

"I guess it's one less person they have to deal with, state-side," Andersen said. He looked back to the document for another few agonizing seconds. He then took out his pen and placed the document on the table as if he were going to sign it. Wise pulled her hands to her head and burst out in tears. As she sobbed, Martin casually got up to point out the signature lines of the documents.

"If you could sign right here, and initial here and here, and date here." Martin's tone, presentation and demeanor were those of a man signing out a rental car without the extra car insurance.

"What do you want from me?! You haven't even asked me any questions?! For three days, you just sat there and haven't asked me a thing! What do you want?" It was difficult to really hear what she was saying. She was sobbing into her hands.

Andersen looked at Martin who put up his index finger to indicate to wait one more minute. Time ticked by as Martin then gave the word.

"Damn it," Martin said in a low but annoyed voice.

Wise was barely able to look up at Martin as he spoke next.

"Lieutenant? Could you please sit down and put the document out of sight of the cameras? Wise? Miss. Alica Wise?" Still calm, cool and collected, Martin spoke with just a hint of urgency.

"Ms. Wise? I need you to be tear-free and to answer my questions in their entirety. Any deviations and I will turn to Lt. Andersen, and have him sign the documents, and leave while you and I wait for military transport. Do you understand?"

"I'm not a terrorist," Wise said, still tearing up.

"Look at me, Wise."

Andersen watched as Wise looked at Martin. His eyes were deep, dark and still, much like he imagined a shark might look right before he struck. And right now, those dangerous eyes stared into Wise's watery blue eyes.

"I don't care, Ms. Wise. I don't really care."

"But I have rights..."

"You had rights when you were a federal agent sworn to protect the Constitution. You had a chance to keep the rights, privileges and responsibilities of American citizenship."

"But I was following orders."

"You mean blindly following the direction of your leader, Eric Icarus Daniels? Do you know where you are? What year do you think this is, Wise? 1945? Nuremberg, Germany? This is America in the Twenty-first century."

"But I was given directions..."

"The excuse 'I was just following orders' hasn't worked for decades, Wise."

Wise was still tearing up, baffled and speechless. Andersen felt exhausted at the exchange. It was as if he were watching a well-scripted performance and was waiting for the next sentence. Martin let just a few seconds transpire before he filled the void.

"Right now there are two outcomes – one is you head out to Guantanamo or the other is some federal judge will actually hear your case. I would prefer to get back to my life and have you leave my country. So you need to make a choice and pull your shit together."

Martin's voice was low and emotionless. More time passed. There was a long two minutes before Andersen dared to say a word.

What are you going to do next?

"I don't want to go. I want to stay here." Wise's voice was weak and tired. Andersen looked askance at Martin to see what he was going to do next. It took another long sixty seconds for him to reluctantly move his hand to his breast pocket to take out a cell phone. Andersen looked at the phone. It was one of the newer phones that the FBI issued that had a powerful signal and tracking signals.

Ah, yes. The phone that's bugged.

Andersen wanted to smile. He wanted to stand up and applaud. He made a short list of the people he wanted to thank in accepting his Academy Award for supporting actor. He pushed all those thoughts out of his head and focused on the mission.

"Ah, you're right, Martin. The marshals are already here and I don't want this witch in my country," Andersen added as if he had just come to his senses. Wise shot a look of hatred and violence toward him. Andersen pulled the document towards him and looked for his pen. Martin put the cell phone in the middle of the steel desk.

"It's time for you, Ms. Wise, to call your brother and tell him the truth," Martin said. Wise looked confused. She kept brushing away tears from her cheeks and looked at the phone and Andersen while he ostensibly looked for his pen to sign the document for her transport.

Sorry, lady. I have no idea what's coming next. You're on your own.

Martin continued with his dramatic monologue. Ironically, Martin was instructing her to tell her brother the truth. Andersen's mind jumped to existential thoughts.

The truth? That has to be something difficult for you. So many layers of deception, webs and deep cover. Do you even know what the truth is anymore, Wise?

"It's time for you to tell him that you are here in a federal penitentiary, in isolation for your own safety. I want you to tell him that you are charged with an entire range of federal crimes. I want you to tell him that you are sitting with me and the Lieutenant. And let him know that his affiliation with Colonel Timothy Carter and his group has compounded your situation," Martin said calmly.

Well, if she does all that, she'll be talking with him for more time than we need.

Wise looked confused still as if it were a trick.

"Ms. Wise? It may be hard for you to believe but I want you to tell your brother the truth. You know? The truth – no deceptions, no secrets, the difference between fabrication and fact."

"That's all? Just let him know everything?" Wise appeared as if she was going to cry again.

"Please do not cry," Martin said.

"You want me to just tell him the truth?"

"Yes. Let him know that we are all in the same room trying to figure out what to do next with you. If at any point you want to put him on speakerphone, that's fine. If not, that's fine. Any way you look at it, it's time you let him know that in addition to your charges, he's not helping. His connection to Colonel Carter who's in bed with Eric Daniels makes things worse."

Wise still looked confused as she now stared at the cell phone in the middle of the table. A long minute seemed to pass as Andersen heard Martin sigh. A very low one but definitely a sigh.

"Or we can try when you get to your next destination," Martin said as he reached for the phone. Before Martin's hand was even close, Wise snatched the device up like a starving cobra finding its first meal in years. She jumped out of the chair and turned away as she huddled over the phone and furiously punched in numbers.

Here we go.

Andersen made eye contact with Martin. For his part, Martin was deep in character.

He's like a younger version of me, back in the day.

#

Becky Littleton took inventory as she looked around the mission launch area. Providence, Rhode Island was a place she had visited before, especially when she lived in Rhode Island for several years. But she never thought she would be running her own mission. She lost count of all the items she reviewed from her vantage point on the room's balcony. Once she finished, she took a look in the targeted fire zone and counted the number of tables and occupants several stories below her. After hours of waiting, she had time to think. Ever since she lost Samantha and David, she thought a lot more. She still couldn't quite comprehend how she became the person she is today. She sat quietly as if her stillness would reveal some answers. She had always desired to be more active in her life and moving from being a passive to an active participant in her life did make sense. Once Burns entered her life, bringing David into the fold, her world with Emma and Samantha was complete. Completely different, but nonetheless complete.

Yup. That's all you need - a death threat on your head from your own government and a trained assassin on your side to motivate you. The government wanted me dead? I don't even vote! I would have been just fine with David here minus the chaos, sabotage, killing and mayhem. I would have been happy with Samantha and David still being here.

Her gaze fell a bit lower from her inner mind's eye to the pictures at the base of the railing. She took long looks at her target's pictures. Thoughts of her girls' smiles immediately turned to determination. Her mood changed quickly from pain and despair to purpose and a will to live, for them to live, at all costs.

And if these assholes are connected to Daniels like Murphy and Burns say, then they just pissed off the wrong chick. Yeah, I've changed. You missed the memo, assholes! I'm the wolf, not the lamb!

Becky felt her jawline tighten. She flexed her fingers and shifted back into sentry mode. She narrowed her field of vision from the pictures and her full automatic assault rifle back to the plaza where she saw a family that all wore the same *Red Sox* clothing with corresponding shorts and baseball hats.

Tourists? Vacationers? You can go to Cape Cod, or Portsmouth or Maine but you come here?

She took another deep breath and continued her vigil on her fourth story terrace overlooking a closed street that was lined with shops, cafes and small restaurants. The five star hotel was the best one she knew that provided a perfect, unobstructed panoramic view of the street below that had only one point of entry that was also closed off to cars. With only pedestrian traffic and one place to enter and exit, Becky looked like many vacationers in Rhode Island. Though for early summer it was probably too soon for her to be wearing a bikini, but she wanted to look as dainty and fragile as possible. Chuckling to herself, she couldn't help but wonder who would want to vacation in Providence.

"What's so funny?" John Murphy said in her ear.

She forgot that her voice could be picked up from her ear phone. She had to constantly explain herself to him when she did things like that.

"Nothing. I'm just laughing at the fact I look like a vacationer and was wondering who would vacation in the thriving metropolis, historically laden city of Providence, Rhode Island," she said.

Becky held her breath as she froze in anticipation, fearing what might come next.

Now what were you thinking, you dope? This is Murphy. Retired Irish organized crime kingpin, doting grandfather and a New England buff of curious, unimportant, useless facts. I bet that was his weapon of choice back in the day - "sit down and let me tell you the entire history of Castle Island and South Boston's D Street Projects where I grew up..." Nice job!

"Actually, there are many good reasons to come to Providence," Murphy started.

Here you go, dumb-ass!

Becky closed her eyes knowing now that John Murphy, paternal grandfather of Emma and Rosemarie, was about to launch into a twenty-minute lecture of what Providence, Rhode Island had to offer, past, present and future. As he spoke, she scanned the area below. Becky kept her chair opposite the other terraces with the brick wall between her, while maintaining a view of her hotel door and the street below. She looked back at the hotel door and saw that a small bureau was in front of it to add to the triple lock.

Let's hope there's not a fire.

Becky reviewed her launch area again while Murphy droned on. She looked at her feet again to review pictures of potential targets Murphy sent to her, with her AR 15 with scope alongside them. With a cooler by her side, her anti-anxiety medicine not far from her reach, Becky did her best to adjust her blonde wig without being too obvious. Pretending to be something she wasn't, in this case, a blonde diva with long hair and short skirts, was not her strength but a talent she was developing.

God, Samantha, how did you do this all the time? I'm just glad I cut my hair short for this job. The wig would have killed me.

After years of having long hair, her short hair was an adjustment, especially for Emma who only knew her as her long-haired, thin mom. In addition to her cooler, medication and rifle, she had a large caliber, semi-automatic hand gun on the table beside her. Even with all the weapons, Becky was feeling nonetheless naked in her bikini set.

God, I hate this feeling. I feel naked in this outfit.

Still, she needed to blend in like all the other people sunning.

That is, those people sunning in early summer. Jesus Christ! Is Murphy done yet?

He was not. Becky found herself looking back over her target area and thought about how Cratty and everyone was doing. When Cratty texted her that Burns was taken four days ago, Becky immediately took the girls off-grid, and never returned to their apartment. Apart from their safety, she was worried about Burns.

Of the four, he and I are the last ones. The only person who knows me and what we had to go through. He can't die.

She pushed the thought out of her head and focused on her own mission. When Murphy told her that it was a good thing she left when she did because one of Murphy's rivals had tore her place apart, Becky got angry and focused. So angry, she felt something snap. Not in a crazy, impulsive, unpredictable way but in a cool, calm, low burn. It started with anger and then moved quickly to a plan. In keeping with Burns, she had a plan to go on the offensive when it was least expected.

These fucking people think they can screw with me and my kids? The government tried that a couple of times. You think you shitheads can?! Well, as David used to always say, "idle hands are the Devil's workshop."

At the time, she had been heading west on the open road. She shifted gears and turned around back east to link up with Murphy and formed a plan. It took Becky five minutes to hatch a plan that covered logistics, back-up and exit strategy. It would mean using Murphy as bait to draw in whoever was looking for her and the girls, having them walk into a dead-end street, and take them out.

I'm sure he won't mind being live bait.

Becky was a little vague though on the "take them out" part as she was not sure she could kill again. But she knew as soon as she shot her weapon, she would have to break it down in ninety seconds, dump her disguise and leave the room as is, with her clothes and gear in her backpack and completely vanish from the hotel in three minutes.

And a nice baseball hat just for extra cover.

Her immediate thought was that Murphy's rivals were looking for her and the girls which was somehow part of Daniels's plan. This just hardened Becky's resolve.

No more 'luck' and waiting for others to rescue us. It's old school. It's back to setting the stage, springing the trap, and evaporating into the night. And at least I won't be sitting around worrying about Burns.

As expected, Murphy was not happy with the plan at all, especially the part that left Rosemarie and Emma alone for days in a hotel on the state line.

"Rosemarie is seventeen, Murphy! She's going to go to college soon. Don't you think she should be able to handle her sister and herself for a couple of days for Christ's sake? Swimming pool, room service, arcades and cable – it's not a bad life they got going."

"There should be an adult with them. Come on, Becky. Do you really want to leave them alone?"

"No, but I really want to put these assholes to bed so we can be with the kids without looking over my shoulder all the time. I've done that. It's bullshit. Murphy? What's wrong with you?"

"I don't want to lose the girls, Becky. I've lost my son and lost Emma for years. Don't you understand?"

When she heard that, Becky was all confused and conflicted. Murphy's son killed her brother and put Emma in her life. Rosemarie was Emma's sister, making Becky her aunt. At times like these, she knew what to do.

"I get it, Murphy. I also know you want the best for the girls.

This is the best thing. We do this, they have more of a chance to live. If we just run, they'll always be in terror. I know you don't want that."

She knew when she had Murphy. He would be silent. Becky was still amazed at how overprotective Murphy was of his granddaughters.

I can understand that. But for a guy who used to run the Boston Irish mob, he's pretty much a candy-ass when it comes to his granddaughters.

She was pulled back into the present by her cell phone ringing. She could see from caller identification that it was Rosemarie. She smiled at both the call and a good reason to interrupt Murphy's dramatic monologue.

"Hey, Murphy? I have Rosemarie calling in. I'm going to keep you in my ear and talk to her so you have to be quiet. After we talk, I'll have her call you. Okay?"

"Great!" Murphy said enthusiastically.

Man. He always gets happy when they call. Kind of cute.

Becky put on her happy persona. Being "happy" required work and medication.

Fake it until you make it, David always said. Thank God for medication. You'd be so proud of how I act happy for them.

"Hello, Rosie," Becky said warmly.

"Becky!? Do you know what Emma did last night?" Rosemarie said before she was interrupted.

Oh boy...this opening sounds familiar.

"You started it! Be happy I didn't smother you as you slept!" she heard Emma yell back.

"Bite me! You started it!" Rosemarie said.

"No, I didn't, liar!" Emma yelled back.

"No, I'm not! You're the little liar!"

"No! You're the fat, snoring liar, bitch!"

With eyes knitted due the yelling, Becky heard the antithesis in her other ear.

"On second thought, I'll call them in about an hour," Murphy said quietly.

"You think it will be better then?"

"I can hope, can't I?"

"Is that what keeps you going? Hope?"

"After all the shit I've seen, that's all I have left. I'll call them in two hours."

"More hope for peace then?"

"Definitely."

Becky couldn't help but smile at Murphy's philosophy on life and the simultaneous banter back and forth from the girls. Her memories went right to Samantha and her when she was young.

Sisters should be together...even if they are pains in the asses.

Chapter 5

"...But when the blast of war blows in our ears,
Then imitate the action of the tiger..."

William Shakespeare, <u>Henry The Fifth</u>

Present Day – Klondike Mine, El Paso County, Colorado, USA

Welch stood nervously at a folding table that held two large laptops. She watched four personal combat video feeds segmented on each screen. With periodic starting and stopping of jerky movements, Welch was beginning to get used to the motion.

I still hate this part. The last time I saw this, sixteen agents were killed in Greece.

She focused on Davis's and Cratty's vision. She folded her arms, stood with legs a shoulder length apart and rocked slightly on her feet. For now her eyes were glued to the images.

The only good that came out of that was Webber's death and gutting that damned Operation Center.

Welch was appreciative that the excavator and cartographer were doing fairly well keeping their chatter down while giving her quick bytes of important data about the mine and direction. With Nine and RC's cameras relatively still about eighty feet into the mine, and Davis about thirty feet behind Cratty, Welch focused on

Cratty's point of view. At the beginning of the trail, the ground seemed more level though heavily littered with garbage from past college parties and other excursions. As they progressed deeper in, the garbage thinned out but old containers, large and small with old wood, rails, lumber and old discarded tanks increased while the trail narrowed. Even with night-vision goggles, the low light from old light bulbs spaced out too far in the mine was difficult to navigate, especially as the trail started to become more littered with yet larger rocks, debris and old timber.

Jesus. About a hundred plus feet to go. How are they going to get there with that shit everywhere.

She remembered her field experience in Afghanistan and was grateful it was in a more open setting as in a city, sand or valley. A mine? She was glad she never had to really deal with such cramped quarters. Even though Cratty and Davis could stand up and move relatively easily, it still looked difficult to walk, or in this case, crouch with fully-automatic assault rifles as they traversed obstacles. Welch's attention was drawn to Cratty's breathing becoming more labored. She covered her mouth piece to ask the excavator a question.

"Is it me or is it difficult to breathe in there?"

"It's difficult to walk with that stuff all around. Her shortness of breath is probably also a result of the darkness, still air and newness to the environment. More psychological than actual lack of air. Unless she's used to crawling into deep caves, she's bound to get edgy."

"I'm not edgy," Cratty said as her movement slowed down.

Welch and the excavator exchanged looks. She wondered how Cratty heard them talk until she saw that while she covered her microphone, the excavator did not cover his.

"Sorry," the man said. Welch nodded and was impressed with his knowledge of the situation without being macho. Even though he was a large, strong-looking man, she found his demeanor non-threatening as he watched the monitors closely. Even his apologizing so quickly made her smile.

What the hell is your problem, Welch?

Welch mentally slapped herself to focus on the mission and not the man.

"Nice timing," she said to herself, forgetting her live feed to everyone.

"I didn't think she was that funny," Davis jumped in.

"You never think I'm funny," Cratty said.

Welch closed her eyes at the mistake and jumped in quickly to redirect the team's focus on the mission.

"Cut the chatter, you two. Slow your pace, Davis. You're beginning to bump into Cratty."

"Confirmed."

"Copy."

Welch was appreciative of the rapid response. For a moment she felt as if she was being watched. She stole a glance at the excavator who was smiling. Heat seemed to burst out of her entire face and hands.

Are you kidding me!? A hot flash now? Right now? Or are you blushing? Ugh.

Welch pushed the thoughts out of her head to focus on the monitors. After another five minutes, Cratty's pace seemed to pick up again as she was closing in on what appeared to be light in an aperture to a larger chamber, forty feet ahead. Confused, Welch spoke into the microphone as she consulted the GPS and map.

"That chamber looks a lot closer than a hundred feet, and the signal seems to be much further down. Is there anything beyond that opening?" Welch asked the cartographer.

The young woman was about to say something when Welch heard a definite loud "click" as if a metal gauge was engaged. Cratty's motion froze while Nine, RC and Davis's motion slowed down.

"Everyone stop," Welch ordered. She was carefully looking at everyone's point of view.

Mine? Tripwire? Something.

"Welch. It's me," Cratty said.

"Crap," Davis said.

Welch found herself not moving as if she could possibly cause an explosion if she did.

"I felt something depress under my right foot and then I heard a snap like a switch," Cratty said softly.

As Cratty's camera angle slowly looked down, Welch could see that she had stepped on what looked like metal strapping. It was the same metal strapping that littered the mine's floor.

"Everyone. Look at your feet and see if you are near metal strapping," Welch said. It only took half a minute for the responses to flow in. Nine's deep voice came in first.

"Just a couple of small pieces. No large ones."

Davis spoke next as her camera angle got low to the ground for a better view.

"I got a lot of metal strapping but you can see most of the ends. They don't seem to be connected to anything." she said as she continued to look around.

Welch focused on Cratty's camera images. It was easy to see that her foot was squarely on the end of a strapping. As the vision held there, Cratty followed the strapping to some paper and cardboard that covered it. As she continued along the same trajectory, her camera eventually landed on an old style metal container that was hanging upside-down from a wire at the very top of the tunnel's ceiling. The container looked like a big bullet with the point going down. While Cratty's camera focused, the excavator was the first to talk.

"That's an old nitroglycerin canister that used to be dropped down a pipe to blow up rocks."

"How bad?"

"Depends," he said. By now he was staring at the object the way a surgeon would analyze an x-ray.

Welch was silent and waited. Seconds later, he stood back up and folded his arms over his chest.

"Blast radius could be as small as five feet or as big as twenty feet depending on the grade and amount of the nitroglycerin."

"Does it make a difference if this thing is going to fall on some plastic explosives?" Cratty asked. Her camera followed the point of the can to two neatly stacked brown packages.

Damn it!

The excavator bent back over to peer at the packages before standing up again, arms folded over his chest after just seconds.

"Yup. That's pretty high-grade military plastic explosives, for sure," he said. Welch shook her head at his casualness about it all.

"But that's not what I'm worried about," he said.

Welch found herself genuinely surprised.

Not worried about C4?

"We don't have to worry about high-grade explosives?"

"Nope. Not in this case."

Fortunately Davis asked the question everyone wanted to.

"Oh? Should we find something else more dangerous? You're not worried about the C4?"

"Now look who's edgy," Cratty chimed in.

"Are you two married? Cut the chatter."

"Affirmative."

"Copy."

"What do you mean?" Welch asked the excavator.

You're not going to kill anyone on my team, Daniels! Not this time. Not today.

The man tilted his head and looked back down at the camera. He then asked Cratty to look up at the ceiling as well as the others. After a minute of panning around the ceiling, the excavator stood back up and gave his assessment.

"The nitroglycerin is the only explosive you have to worry about for now. It's liquid and very volatile. But even if it hits point blank on the plastic explosives, the C4 won't react because you need a detonator or a blasting cap to make them explode. They're not there. Not even a wire to a detonator. Whoever thought this little scheme up thought the explosion of the nitroglycerin would ignite the C4. In an alternative universe maybe, but not here. It's really the nitroglycerin you need to be concerned about and the ceiling above these two," he added as he pointed to Cratty's and Davis's screens.

"Let me guess? Me and Davis," Cratty said.

"Figures," Davis chimed in.

Can you two ever shut up and stop commenting?

Welch sighed for a moment. She was about to address the situation when Davis asked a question.

"Ah, not that I want to ask for a reference and resume, but are you sure you know what you're talking about?"

The excavator chuckled for a moment before he answered.

"Excavation is more than a bulldozer and a shovel. We need explosives to get things done. That said, here's the deal," he started as he now addressed Welch.

Well. This is a pleasant surprise. A major problem and a specialist with a plan and crew.

"These amateurs got the nitroglycerin and trip right but the rest wrong. You need to pull these three out so I can get my guys in to about fifty feet of where she is. Once I'm in place with my team, I'm going to find something heavy to put in her place to keep the pressure on the trip wire, and then I'm going to either detonate it or see about disabling somehow. If we can't do that or something goes wrong, then she's going to have to leave everything behind because she's going to have to sprint as far and as fast as she can to not only get beyond a potential blast radius of twenty feet but to get as far away from the center of the cave-in as possible. Once she sees light, hit the ground, duck and cover. That's the worst-case scenario. The good news here is that if it was C4, there is no way you could outrun the blast. At least there's a chance to outrun the nitroglycerin blast especially if it's a small amount. It's the mine's roof I'm really worried about."

He said all of this in one breath as he took off his headphone, waved to two guys on his team, and made hand signals as he walked toward them.

Well...that's nice. At least there's a plan A and B. Not bad.

"Alright. Sounds like we got an expert and a plan. Cratty, drop your gear but keep your foot in one place. Everyone else, pull back.

Oorah?"

"Oorah," Nine and RC responded immediately as two less than enthusiastic "copy" responses filtered through.

As Welch listened to her teams moving out and Cratty slowly taking her gear off and carefully putting it on the floor, Welch spoke to Cratty directly.

"Are you a fast runner?"

"Well, I don't have huge legs like Davis but I'm fast when I'm motivated."

"I just hope this guy can find something as heavy as Cratty to secure the trip," Davis said.

"Nice, Davis."

"You started it."

"Are we done? What the hell, you two. This is why I prefer commanding men in the field." Welch took a moment to regroup before she went back on mission.

"It looks like you have some good motivation right now," Welch said as she watched the excavators getting into their own gear and walking to the mine's entrance. But then she found herself looking back at Cratty's screen as she heard what sounded like a hissing sound.

"Cratty? What's that noise?"

Other than a low hissing sound, there was silence. It took a moment for Cratty's camera to scan the area until she saw what looked like old scuba tanks. With so many discarded tanks and containers, it was difficult to see if it was the tanks or the wall beside the tanks that was spewing.

Without waiting for Cratty to respond, Welch yelled to the excavator as he was about to enter the mine.

"Hey! We got some kind of hissing sound coming from either a tank of some kind or the wall beside the tank!"

Even from her distance, she could see his eyes widen as he stepped towards her with her next question.

"Is it from the wall or tanks? Kind of important!"

It was obvious that Cratty heard the conversation as her

response was immediate.

"I really can't tell. I smell something though..."

"She smells something but she's not sure," Welch yelled back.

Suddenly, she saw three of his men race into the mine as the excavator looked like he was thinking, maybe doing some kind of calculation, before he looked up and spoke.

"She's got ten seconds to clear fifteen feet, right now!"

"Shit! Cratty? Run!"

Without another word, Welch could see from the camera angle that Cratty had obviously squatted down first and then her camera's image moved up and down rapidly. Welch held her breath and watched the jarring movements as she internally counted ten seconds. Then, as she hit eleven seconds, there was a flash of light followed by a violent sound. She could still see the camera's image moving but towards the ground.

Shit! Damn it all!

Welch felt her jaw clench shut and her hand ball up into fists.

#

Present Time and Place - Unknown

It was the warm breeze and the feel of the sun that woke Burns up. Still groggy and bleary-eyed, Burns took in the smell of cooked meat, lilac, clean laundry, and sea-salt air. He sat on a stoop at mid-day and rubbed his eyes so he could adjust to the light and look around. The sky was a deep blue with very puffy clouds and white birds flying everywhere. Once again, he looked at his hands and arms immediately and saw that his scars were no longer there. He felt his scalp and found only hair and nothing else. Standing and taking in the sights of crowing seagulls, Burns felt both good and curious.

My God. Where am I now?

He stretched his arms, legs and back, took in a deep breath and pulled in the smell of the ocean. He shifted his focus from the environment to the people. He watched them going about their business such as shopping, cleaning and eating.

I felt that, that stretch. The smell and sun. I feel all of it.

And the people, all animatedly talking, laughing and smiling.

While initially struck by how happy everyone looked, Burns thought the place looked familiar.

Hmm. This looks like Torrox Costa, Spain...this is where David, Becky and Emma lived. It's the same place but different somehow.

"Mr. Burns! Hey, Mr. Burns!"

It was a young voice that called him. Burns turned to see who it was. It was a young woman casually dressed in blue jeans, tank top, costume jewelry and a cell phone. He carefully looked at her and had no recollection of who she was. He struggled to even figure out how old she might be. He was never good with figuring out ages.

"I'm thirteen," she said as she approached and closed her phone.

Just as before when he met Paul, he was surprised that she knew what he was thinking. He wondered if his expressions were simply readable to everyone here...*wherever "here" is.*

While not smiling nor as positively disposed as Paul was, she was at least cordial, if not direct.

"I'm Claudia, Claudia Fitzgerald."

She stuck her hand out for a handshake. Burns smiled. He shook her hand as he wondered how Emma and Rosemarie were doing in their new lives.

"My sister wants me to bring you to her. Looks like she's found someone you know and she wants you to take a message back when you leave."

"Your sister?"

"Yup. She wants to meet you before you go back," she said quickly as she started to walk away. Confused, Burns caught up to her and tried to catch his breath as he blurted out a question.

"Who am I meeting? Where am I going back to?" Burns asked as he labored to keep up and catch his breath.

"Well, my sister for sure and some of her friends, and I guess someone you know."

"How do I know them?"

"I don't know."

"Where are they?"

"Where they always are."

It was obvious to Burns that she was becoming more annoyed with every passing question and second.

"Hey!" the young woman said. She suddenly stopped to put her hands on her hips and look Burns in the eyes.

"I'm 'annoyed' because I've been here for a long time, longer than Kelly and her girlfriends, and I'm still getting things for her. I got things to do here, you know."

Burns narrowed his eyes at the name Kelly and pieced it together with Fitzgerald.

"Oh boy."

"What?"

"And they say you're good at piecing things together? You're some kind of big spy? Geez!" Claudia turned abruptly and continued her high-speed walking.

Burns found himself confused until he remembered that he found the young woman had an attitude that annoyed him.

But I didn't say anything.

He picked up the pace as he kept an eye on the young woman. The people on the street continued to act very cordially to him as if he were a known guest. As an operative, he was much more comfortable blending into the background, being invisible. All the kind, warm attention was difficult to adjust to.

I don't get it. But I've never been here, wherever here is.

Still moving at a quick pace, he was approached by a woman in khakis, a light leather vest, strapped handgun and ammunition and wearing aviator glasses. She pulled her sunglasses off and smiled at him. She spoke in a very familiar voice.

"Well, I thought I would see you sooner, but I'm kind of glad you're just visiting. It's been a while, huh?"

The woman slowed her pace since she was going in the opposite direction. Burns came to a standstill and looked carefully at her, knowing that he knew her but the name eluded him.

"I never gave you my name, Burns. You just knew me as 'the pilot' and that was years ago. I'd love to stay but I got to get to work."

It was rare that Burns was at a loss for words. But this place, these people, his lack of scars, everything, was just too strange to articulate. The woman didn't give him long to figure it out.

She put her sunglasses back on and continued to her destination. He saw her wave to a group of men and women who were similarly dressed, smiling and looking pleased to see her. A sudden flash of recognition came to him.

Pilot? As in the one I went down with in Pakistan? The one Maxwell shot down? Why is she here? And what does she mean "I'm visiting?" Visiting where?

He suddenly realized he lost sight of the girl as he watched the pilot disappear in the crowd. He was truly baffled and dismayed at everything around him. As he rounded the corner of the street, Claudia was waving to him to come into a building.

How did she move so fast?

As he caught up, she pointed for him to go inside as she started to open her phone. Confused, Burns thought he would ask a question that hopefully would not draw the ire of the teenager.

"Aren't you going to come in?"

Claudia looked at Burns as if he had asked one of the more stupid questions possible.

"Ah...it's a bar? There's still rules here. I'm thirteen and you have to be twenty-one or older to get in."

Her expression was one of tamed disgust and she then walked away with her phone to her ear. He watched her leave. Burns found himself at odds of normally being able to figure out things fast but not having a clue as to what was happening to him now.

Maybe some drug-induced hallucinations? Maybe some kind of new drug Daniels is trying on me?

Burns's attention shifted back to see a bunch of girls swarm Claudia and start laughing.

"Unbelievable."

Burns moved to the front of the door, opened it and stepped into a dimly lit, tavern-like bar. He saw dust on the floor and heard low to moderate laughter and talking, with friendly shadows nodding to him as he walked through the room.

Well, the place seems friendly enough.

He felt unusually comfortable. He wondered if he should try a drink. Chuckling to himself, he had no idea why he would like to drink alcohol again. He heard a burst of laughter emanating from the back of the tavern where there were cards and game tables set up with a lot of military and security types hanging out, laughing, drinking and playing cards. He thought the rear of the bar was large, but when he cleared the people blocking his view, he realized that "large" was an understatement. From his perspective, he could see that the number of tables and people went on for miles, so many miles Burns couldn't see an end.

My God.

The view was spectacular. With all kinds of people of different races, nationalities, genders, sizes and shapes, Burns struggled with not only the scope and size, but the depth. It only took a minute to see patterns in the mass of humanity. Everyone in his field of vision was from some military or law enforcement branch of every nation he knew. They were all playing cards, games or something at each table with all their weapons close at hand. Burns held onto the irony of a sea of armed military personnel – enemies and allies – all enjoying each other's company. No enmity, no hostility, not even the threat of violence seemed possible. Further, while there were miles of people that appeared to be having fun playing, drinking, talking and even reading, the ambient noise level was far from overwhelming. In fact, while there were jubilant sounds of good cheer, the sound seemed to stay at a loud but easy-to-hear level. With several laws of physics broken in addition to very unlikely pairings of enemy combatants, Burns continued looking as he tried to summarize his impressions and calculate how it all could be possible. Only one answer could resolve his list of impossibilities.

The conclusion, while surprising, was obvious.

"I'm dead. Yup. Probably dead. They hear my thoughts. Physics don't apply here."

He immediately thought of his mother who told him often about the afterlife. While it was more of a warning, she had made it clear that the things he did on Earth would determine where he would go next.

"There's no phones where I'm going next," she had said long ago. "I can't tell you what it's like when I get there. You're going to have to make your peace here before you get there."

Burns had always assumed that there was no such thing, no heaven, no hell or purgatory or limbo. He thought about each place his mother described and the first thing that came to mind was that he was in heaven. He pushed that conclusion out of his head immediately based on his prior actions and what he recalled were the criteria to get in.

"Live a life of the Ten Commandments, live in peace and love one another. Well, I'm pretty sure I messed up in all of those areas," he said as he continued to take in the magnificent sight.

Burns wondered why he didn't feel upset.

I have to say, it's not what I expected. So, do I just stand here or look for an open seat and join in? Maybe I have to be invited or know someone? Who am I supposed to meet here?

Burns walked to the edge of the tables. He looked around to see if he might recognize anyone. Suddenly he saw someone who clearly recognized him and seemed pleasantly surprised that he was there.

"Hey! It's the 'Great Alexander Burns!'" The strong, cheerful voice came from a young woman in her mid to late twenties. She stood up from a game table and waved. With a cigar in her mouth and a beer in her hand she started towards him.

"Hey, Fitzy! What the hell? Are you in or out?" another woman said from the table. The young woman stopped abruptly, turned and threw some chips in the pot and turned over her cards to another woman.

"Play for me, will you, Witzy?" she asked in a very familiar way.

The other woman, Witzy, seemed all too familiar to Fitzy and the situation.

"Now, there's a surprise. That's the only reason I'm here, Fitzy. To be here with you," Witzy said sarcastically. Burns watched Fitzy approach while she carried on her conversation with ease.

"Come on, Witzy! This is a great place! Why do you complain so much about a great thing?"

"Nothing personal, Fitzy, but I thought I would be spending more time with my parents and stuff."

"I'm not holding you back."

Fitzy stopped to see Witzy's response. It was easy to see that she had no really good response. She shrugged, picked up Fitzy's cards and threw her own chips into the pot to continue the game.

"Just as I thought."

Fitzy was now right in front of Burns. Even though she held a beer and cigar and appeared pleasant, if not inebriated, it was clear she had something important to say.

"So, Burns, I want you to do me a favor when you get back," she started as she took another drag of her cigar.

Back where? When I go back where? Who are you? he kept thinking.

Turning as if surprised at the question Burns didn't say out loud, she started to say something but then her phone vibrated and rang at the same time. She looked down at it and frowned. She stuck her cigar back in her mouth and handed Burns her drink so she could get it.

"Do you mind?" she said as she surrendered her drink and looked at her smartphone to read a text. Burns felt the weighted glass in his hands. It was warm with small specks of melted ice in it. He took a sniff and realized that it wasn't beer but another mixed drink. The strong odor of gin and tonic was easy to identify. Breathing in the smells, Burns had just one thought – *it's been too long*.

Burns's attention came back to Fitzy who looked back at him

with a warm smile. She waved to her friends at the card table as she started talking.

"Why don't you finish my drink? I gotta run, duty calls. A couple of things though. When you get back and you see Denise, Christine and Ana, tell them we're okay. They don't have to worry about us. They should live and let live." Fitzy immediately stuck her hand out to catch a well equipped assault rifle thrown at her. Two of her friends, similarly armed, gathered around her. Feeling out of place and nearly speechless, Burns watched Fitzy check her weapon and then accept a protective vest and extra ammunition.

"Who are you?" was Burns's pervading question.

"Geez, I thought Burns was a quick study," Witzy said.

"Hey, cut him some slack. It took you some time to figure this place out."

"I'm Jewish! This place is not supposed to be here. Besides, I wasn't raised Christian, for Christ's sake."

"Obviously. You wouldn't be throwing Jesus's name around like that."

"Hey, Jesus Christ was Jewish! We're probably related," Witzy said.

Fitzy rolled her eyes and spoke to Burns again.

"I'm Kelly Fitzgerald, she's Cindy Belben and that's my best friend, Molly Horowitz. And the really cute, cuddly thirteen-year-old who brought you here is my sister, Claudia."

Burns processed the names in just a few seconds. By the time he reached his conclusion, they had all finished checking their gear. They were clearly prepared for a firefight. Burns was still frozen in place. He experienced a feeling he had never expected or experienced – *indecision.*

Fitzgerald, Kelly, Horowitz, Molly, and Belben, Cindy; all KIA in Torrox Costa, Spain while protecting David and Emma.

He felt sad. He might have stayed with that feeling but his attention was brought back to an argument.

"Why do I have to always protect Cratty? She's a lot of work! She's constantly taking risks and I have to go out of my way to really protect her ass," Belben complained.

After a very heavy sigh, Horowitz fielded the question, as it was evident that Fitzgerald was not going to. It was as if this were a long-standing discussion.

"Because Cindy, you're the youngest and most energetic. Anyway, if she doesn't make it there, great! That's one more player at the table," Horowitz said. Horowitz turned to Fitzgerald in an obvious effort to change the subject.

"So, do you want Ramsey or Dillon?"

What the hell? Cratty? Ramsey and Dillon? They're supposed to be looking for Daniels?

It took Fitzgerald a moment to think about the choice.

"Ramsey. I'm worried about her. I think she might be on the same track as Denise and she has a family to get back to. It's too early for her." The tone and words were thoughtful and filled with emotion. Horowitz agreed.

"You see? How come Fitzy gets a choice and I don't?" Belben complained.

"Give it a rest, will you, Cindy!"

By now, Horowitz was walking towards the front part of the tavern as Belben followed her in a further string of obvious inequities.

Stifling a yawn, Fitzgerald turned to Burns as she walked away with a short message.

"Burns, go through that door over there. There's a young woman waiting for you. She was here before us and made it clear that when you arrived, we were to direct you to her."

"Who? Who's waiting for me?" he asked. He still held Fitzgerald's gin and tonic in his hand.

"I don't know. I've been dealing with my own stuff here."

"So you didn't even get a name?"

Fitzgerald slowed her pace to a stop. She looked puzzled at first but then she smiled.

"Jesus, Burns! Don't be such a baby. Take a drink, soldier up and walk through the door like a man, will ya! Can you manage that?"

"Yes," was all Burns said. He felt the shame he was intended to feel. Fitzgerald turned to join her friends, picked up speed and left the tavern. Burns could still hear her yelling to the others to slow down. His eyes darted left and right. The shadows that surrounded him continued in their friendly way as he reviewed his assessment of the situation.

"Okay. So far, all the people I know that are here are dead."

As if to confirm he was right, he turned to look at the sea of people still having fun. He continued his line of thinking as he talked aloud to himself.

"That might mean that all these people might be dead. On the other side of the equation, all three of these women are going to...cover? protect...Dillon, Ramsey and Cratty who last I knew were alive. The young girl who brought me here was or is Fitzgerald's sister who, last I knew, is dead as well. A room filled with soldiers that goes on forever, and someone waiting for me on the other side of the door. Yeah. I must be dead too."

As he spoke aloud and heard his own voice, it still did nothing to make the situation more real. It sounded crazy. Burns shrugged his shoulders and decided to go through the door Fitzgerald pointed out. He walked to the door at the other end of the hallway. He still held Fitzgerald's drink.

"Really? What else am I going to do? Logic and reason don't work here. I just want to know if I'm dead or not."

He stood in front of the heavy wooden door. It looked like it was oak similar to the wooden bar and stools nearby. He took a big swig of the drink. It was warm and gentle, not biting as he expected. The alcohol flowed over his tongue and down his throat. He felt giddy as the taste of the gin and tonic was simply extraordinary. He took another sip, and then another until it was all gone. Feeling nothing short of great, Burns placed the empty glass on the bar and turned the doorknob to enter. He felt great but dizzy and intoxicated. He was curious about what was on the other side.

Chapter 6

"It filled him with a great unrest and strange desires. It caused him to feel a vague, sweet gladness, and he was aware of wild yearnings and stirrings for he knew not what."

Jack London, <u>The Call of the Wild</u>

Present Time Unknown...

It's black. I can't see a thing! When will this cloud end...it's so dark.

Davis felt the wind carry her higher and higher. Finally, the dark clouds broke and she saw old buildings, miles and miles of old vacant buildings in disarray and varying degrees of collapse. From her great height she could see empty fallowed fields, dead trees and miles of roads that were empty. There were patches of life, houses that might make good homes for humans but not for her kind. There were plenty of old buildings for her and the others to chose from. Circling, she could smell the warm air, and she could see from her great height a massive arch. Finally, she saw a fellow falcon on the roof of an old brick building. Alone and standing perfectly perched on a ledge, he was obviously looking at something in the distance.

What is this? I've seen him before. He chased the Eagle into the sun the last time we met. The Eagle's wings melted.

She circled the roof and then began her descent. With little effort, she was beside the falcon with a warm west wind at her back and sun low on the horizon. Not moving at all, she too looked in the same directions as her fellow raptor, wondering what was holding his focus so intently. In the distance were three foxes slowly approaching two unsuspecting vultures. They were too busy fighting over a rotting carcass to notice.

Those fools! Always fighting over food. Never helping each other. Never watching out for each other! Still, they are birds like us.

The foxes closed in on the unsuspecting vultures. Against her better judgment, she bolted to warn them, fellow raptors like herself. Not as noble nor as kind but still birds of flight. Her launch was cut short by a tether attached to her leg. She was pulled back to the roof, unable to fly to warn the vultures.

"What? What is this? Help me!" she crowed.

She turned quickly to her fellow falcon as she flapped into the air but was firmly attached to a weight holding her in place. She looked at the other falcon who remained motionless. Annoyed, angry and unable to help, she watched the foxes move in position to strike. In one final attempt to assist the vultures, she flew directly at her companion to jolt him into action.

"If you don't want to help them, then free me!"

There was a loud thud and dizziness and pain erupted on her head and shoulders. It happened when she struck the falcon with her body.

"What?" She waited for her head to stop moving and her eyes to clear. She stared at the falcon. Poised as a sentry, he looked impassively as the foxes devoured the vultures. She heard squawks and rustling wings.

He is as still as stone!

She pulled herself up from the perch. Still tethered, she moved closely to see why her falcon remained frozen. Her vision now perfect, she felt the heat of embarrassment as she discovered that her compatriot was in fact made of stone, not alive at all.

How could I miss this!? I'm not a Crow, frightened by sticks of hay!

Her discovery was disturbed by the high-pitched screeches of death. It was easy to see that the foxes were now feasting on the vultures. She took a breath and looked away. She felt winded as if she couldn't get enough air in her lungs even though she wasn't flying. She looked back at the scene and was saddened that she could do nothing. But then she had a curious thought: *I've never seen them act like a pack before. Wolves, even dogs, will act in packs. But foxes? This is new.*

As if they could read her mind, the three foxes stopped their feasting and stared directly at her from a distance. She felt her lungs come up short with air. The wind shifted and darkness enveloped her again as if a sandstorm with black ash had burst to life. A sharp intake of air and sudden breath struggled to fill her lungs...*dust? Dirt? Debris?*

#

Present Day...

Davis coughed out soot as she lay face down in the mine. Small amounts of dirt and small rocks were still falling while the smell of water and mold seemed to fill her nostrils.

That ain't good. Two dreams about birds in two days. It can't be good.

She focused more on her own body and moved her limbs slowly to make sure she was all in one piece. She did this as debris fell around her. As she tested her limbs and body, she played back the last thing she remembered. Bright light followed by an explosion. She was pretty sure the entire mine was going to collapse. Instinctively, she had dropped to the ground and covered her head. She remembered what she thought her last moments of life were going to be. Nothing classic. Nothing insightful or noteworthy. As always, she was embarrassed.

I'm going to die here? Mom always hated my job...afraid I'd get killed in a firefight. But no. I'm in a mine named "Klondike"? Kind of lame. No gun battle or fiery death...Out with a bang, at least. Crap! Anderson will make some kind of dumb ass joke about it. This sucks!

By now she was testing her torso.

Falcons, vultures and foxes...I bet Ice never had two right in a row.

After a deliberate inspection of her limbs, head and trunk, she sat up. Dust and dirt fell off of her as she looked around for her night-vision goggles. After a few tense seconds, she found them. While there still seemed to be low lighting, the goggles cleared up the vision ahead of her and it seemed clear. She finally stood up and found her footing among the loose ground and dirt.

"Well, 'clearer' is probably more accurate."

Her voice sounded hoarse. She coughed. There was not much of an echo. A thought popped into her head.

Cratty!

Davis took off to Cratty's last known position. She started to worry. She became more frantic the deeper she went. There were larger rocks, timber and debris the further she went in.

"Unbelievable" she said as she climbed over fallen wood beams and large stones in her path. There was more mold and dust still in the air. She took a moment to rest. Davis remembered that she had an earphone on and attempted to make contact with Welch. She only heard static. She took it out of her ear and saw that the device had broken in two.

"Must be solar flares."

Davis's attempt at humor to lighten the moment had little effect. She got back up and continued the slow trek. Her fear for Cratty's well-being was increasing with every step and every heavy piece of debris she came across that could easily crush a person. She pushed the negative thoughts out of her head and focused on carefully inspecting every three feet ahead of her. While still able to crouch, the limited light and littered mine floor made it difficult to navigate. She stopped for a moment to feel for her canteen. When she turned to look for it on her hip, she saw a mound that had a torso visible.

"Fuck!" Davis said.

She moved as fast as she could to the mound. Pushing fallen wood and some stones off, she saw Cratty lying in a near fetal position with hands still covering her head. She looked closely at her before she brought her ear close to Cratty's face. Her hope was to hear and feel breathing. It wasn't long for her to feel more than hear that Cratty was alive. Davis nodded to herself and sat on the ground just to enjoy a small rest now that she found Cratty alive.

"You are a tough little broad, my petite friend. You know that?"

The silence of the mine was nerve-wracking as Davis tried to rest.

"What? No quick retort? No smart-ass remark?" she said to Cratty as if she might be awake. It took longer than expected for Davis to catch her breath and feel as if she regained some strength. She got up to remove the debris that was on Cratty's lower quarters. At first, the lightweight wood could be brushed aside with ease, but then she saw two large strips of wood piercing Cratty's thigh.

"Shit! Nothing's ever simple with you."

Davis looked for something to slow the bleeding. She could only find her blouse as a viable piece of material that could be converted into a makeshift compress to slow the bleeding. Davis looked further down Cratty's leg to see that a large stone had also fallen on her just below the knee. It took a minute for Davis to figure out that in addition to wood piercing her, her leg was badly broken as evidenced by the wrong direction her foot was going.

"Ah, man...you really fucked up your leg, Cratty."

Davis applied pressure to the wound. She did not like the lack of noise except for periodic falling material and some skittering of rodents. As Davis continued to apply pressure on Cratty's leg, she started to guess how long they were into the mission so she might know when help might come. *If help is going to come.*

"Well, we were about forty-five minutes in when you decided to step into the trap. You know, when I said we should 'spring the trap' it was more hyperbole than literal. Though I have to say you do literal well."

As time ticked by, Davis decided to continue talking. She heard it was good for people who were unconscious or in comas, giving them something, anything to focus on.

Well? What do I talk about?

"You know, for a military brat, how come you're so girly? I mean, you train like a fiend, you can be a class A bitch when you want to be, and still you're all about frilly, girly shit. Do you have any idea how many guys are interested in you? Don't worry though, I set them straight, no pun intended. And that's when they need a shoulder to cry on about 'how come all the real cute ones are gay?' Before you know it, they're lasering in on me. Ah yes...timing is everything."

Davis took a moment to listen to make sure she didn't hear anything. As silence continued, she listened to Cratty's breathing which seemed deep but continuous. Upon closer inspection, Davis saw that there was a nasty cut and bruise on Cratty's head.

Oh great! Davis thought. *I need to focus.*

"What's that? Do I feel like I'm second fiddle?" Davis asked Cratty.

"I would, except most guys are real dumb and can't tell I'm manipulating them. It's all part of the plan. Andersen and Laura are still trying to set me up with a straight, smart guy. Kind of hard these days. Burns might have been a good choice but I'd be stepping on Rachael's toes. And he's a former terrorist who stole government property after he assaulted the shit out of me. I guess I still have issues with that. He does have a nice ass, though."

Davis stopped. For a moment she thought she heard something.

"You didn't hear? Rachael has this major crush on Burns. I know it's crazy. The weird part is, it's easy to see that he loves talking to her. Everything from the existential nature of man to the exact place to break a person's neck that would be considered humane. She kind of acts like a twelve-year-old when he's talking to her, and he's all curious and interested in her opinion. I mean, I want a smart guy too but come on! At some point, I need something more than intellectual foreplay."

Davis stopped as she heard Cratty moan and shift a little bit.

Not wanting her to make things worse, Davis held her in place.

"How about you just stay still for a moment," she said softly.

After more time elapsed and Cratty remained still, Davis started her conversation again.

"You know who's cute? Martin. He's a Special Agent now. From FBI accountant and part-time community actor to a field agent. Soft eyes, mocha-colored skin, big hands, solid chest, strong arms and a flat stomach. Do you have any idea how difficult it is to find a guy with abs who's straight?"

"Davis! Cratty!" she heard.

Thank you, Jesus Christ, Mary and Joseph!

"Sorry, Cratty. More on Martin later. Looks like help arrived," Davis said as she yelled out to RC.

"It's about time!" Davis shouted. Finally she saw beams of light piercing the darkness. They were getting closer.

#

Cratty knew she was feeling very ambivalent about finding Burns and Daniels. If she found him and killed Daniels, it was all over. If they missed, the shit would keep on happening.

What do I do after? What's next? Home? Where the hell is that?

Even on point as she checked corners and watched the shadows, she found herself feeling bad about the mission coming to an end.

Maybe if I'm lucky, it's a trap and they're not here.

"I better not say that out loud. Everyone wants to get home."

"What was that?" she heard Welch say. While the tunnel was cramped and the light poor, the transmitters were very clear.

"Nothing, Boss. Just thought about home."

"Do that after, Denise."

"Right."

Home. That's funny.

Cratty remembered how her small apartment in New York was

now downgraded to a furnished room she rented south of Boston, overlooking a pizza establishment and the highway.

But it's been rated the "Best in Boston..."

And that's when she heard the metal snap. From that point on, Cratty could only focus on one thing – *how the hell am I going to get out of this one...*

As she stripped off all her gear and then heard a hiss from the wall, her thoughts betrayed her: *Maybe you won't escape this one, Denise. Maybe it's your time to join Belben, Fitzy and Witzy...Focus, Cratty!*

Before Cratty could get her head around the new hissing sound, Welch told her to run, *now!*

Cratty followed orders, and she was off. After that, everything seemed confused until it was over. Cratty remembered sprinting with every drop of strength she had so as to put as much distance between her and the impact site. While she was not a mathematician or physics major, she knew she might have six seconds for the canister to drop ten feet.

Ten feet in ten seconds. Maybe twelve if I'm really lucky.

As ten seconds ticked by in her head, she saw the bright light illuminate the entire mine before the loud bang. While she was sure that she would not feel the force of the blast, she hurled herself to the mine floor to avoid any flying debris.

Run, drop and cover, she had heard the excavator say.

As she landed and skidded, she was sure she might have added two or three more feet to her distance from the center of the blast.

Cratty covered her head as she felt rocks and timber fall on her. Then she felt a sharp pain piercing her leg. She was about to cry out from the sharp pain but then she felt something enormous fall on her leg as well. The pain was so great that her scream was without sound as every nerve in her body was set on fire. And then, nothing. No pain, no sound, just the light feeling of her body. The sound, light and rumbling were all gone. Darkness was all around her for the shortest time before she heard someone talking. They were far away at first. The voice was familiar and friendly. Cratty felt as if she might be able to move, but someone was holding her in place.

Is that Belben? Cratty thought as she tried to keep her eyes open.

"How about you just stay still for a moment," she heard someone say softly.

Such a headache and my leg really hurts.

After that, she felt her body again. The she experienced pressure being lifted from her. And while that was fine, the sharp pain in her legs flooded her as she yelled out through gritted teeth.

"Shiiiittt!"

Her eyes finally opened. They were covered with film and it was difficult to focus. A minute or so later, keeping in time with the waves of pain, she finally identified the person next to her as Jillian T. Davis.

"And good morning to you," Davis said with a smile.

Actually, you're filthy...and where the hell is your blouse? Cratty tried to talk but her mouth was devoid of moisture. She also felt as if her body were moving in the air. She looked at her feet and saw RC holding the end of a litter with Davis right beside her. Then, as if she missed something important, Cratty looked back down at her right leg and saw two spikes of some sort jutting out.

"Oh, that's going to leave a mark," she croaked out. She leaned back and tried to moisten her mouth to speak. More pain ebbed but then returned in earnest.

"I'm amazed you're alive," a deep voice said from the front of the litter.

Who the hell is that? The voice is deeper than Nine's.

"Whoever filled the shell with the glycerin didn't do it the right way. And they especially had no idea how much to use. If they did, we wouldn't be having this conversation."

Finally Cratty had moisture to speak. She waited for the pain to pass. It was hard to focus when she kept waiting for the pain to crest.

"You're the excavator, right?" Davis asked on Cratty's behalf.

"Yup."

"You got a name?" RC asked. Just as Cratty thought the wave

of pain was about to break, it just kept going.

For the love of God! Can we forget the guy's name and get these spikes out of me?

"Peter." he said. His movement was at first odd but then he straightened out his angle and got back on track. Cratty started to laugh at Davis's expression of obviously waiting for more from the enigmatic "Peter." But then the shooting pain exceeded even her high pain threshold and it made her wince. The grimace drew RC's attention.

"Are you okay?" he asked as he motioned for Peter to slow down.

After a moment of a slight reprieve, she was able to find some air to help her talk.

Now, how do pregnant women do this? And why would they have more than one?

"I'm just hoping that none of you had to resuscitate me. And Davis...where's your shirt?"

"On your leg. It's my good one too. I have only four like it so you owe me a new one."

Cratty watched Davis as she looked at RC. It looked as if he had asked her something. Cratty watched RC motion to put the litter down and came around to her side as he dug into his EMT bag.

"She's not going into labor, is she?" Davis asked.

"Pregnant? She doesn't look pregnant," Peter said.

"It was a joke."

"I'm pretty sure her sexual preference doesn't rule it, though," RC added. He was looking at Davis.

"Don't look at me. She's not my type and I don't have the right equipment."

Cratty laughed for just a second until the pain leapt forward again.

"I swear I'll kill you for that. You're such a pain, Davis." Cratty's focus was on her and she was unaware that RC had a needle in his hand and had just injected her. She felt a warm, heated pinch in her upper thigh. Just as suddenly, she felt a wave of heat travel through her body, as just as the pain diminished, she suddenly felt very tired.

No pain. Just kind of great.

"Morphine. Moderate dose until we get you topside. Feel better?" RC asked. Cratty was not able to concentrate due to the bliss she was experiencing. She wasn't even sure she made sense.

"I feel warm and nice. What is this..." Cratty started to slur out but she was not sure if she would be awake to hear the answer. With her body feeling light and the pain nearly gone, she felt like she was the most relaxed she had ever been.

"Oh, boy. I thought I was bad on drugs," she thought she heard Davis say.

"Hey...I'm still tired...Why do you have five of the same kind of shirts..." Cratty said. She watched Davis look at her oddly and then she smiled. Next, she felt her face relaxing and smiling while she drifted into sleep.

God, I feel so great and warm...I hope I didn't pee myself. Ten seconds later she slipped off into a drug-induced sleep.

#

Welch wore three inches into the ground where she paced just ten feet from the opening of the mine. The excavators were clear that no one could come closer to where she was waiting. All the other responders, officers and now newscasters were twenty feet behind her. She was allowed to be there courtesy of Peter, the enigmatic excavator chief. She kept pacing. She was anxious to see her team, especially Cratty, come out in one piece. Welch was not sure what kept her from running into the mine. It was probably the clear message that everything was under control and that people needed to do their jobs that reminded her that team leaders often had to wait. Radio silence was a bitch. She kept pacing as she held onto her maps.

I'm getting too damn old for this shit.

It didn't take long for first reports to come back that there was a partial cave-in. It sounded worse than it really was but debris fell throughout the mine, including a big stone that hit Nine squarely on the head. Fortunately, since RC was with him, he was treated pretty quickly, but not happy about being ordered out of the mine.

He was twenty feet behind her. Bandaged up and scanning the area, always vigilant.

I get it, Nine. I sure as shit get it.

After ten minutes and some static communication, Welch got word there were injuries, but no fatalities. Cratty was done but not dead. Welch noticed that she started breathing again and only wanted to see them all out of the mine.

Nothing like Swat Valley.

Finally, she saw a couple of excavators, and then RC, Davis, Cratty on a stretcher and Peter taking up the rear. At last she felt relief. She watched as they came closer and could see that everyone was filthy, and that Cratty had spikes coming out of her thigh.

"That's gotta hurt."

While they were now in the open air, more activity started along with cheers and clapping. Welch nodded and waited for the noise to quiet down before she made her call. She hit speed dial to give her report to the Bureau. After only a minute, Janeson's voice came over the line.

"Ms. Welch? You are on speaker in the control room. Do you have an update?"

Sighing before she spoke, it took Welch only a minute to sum up what everyone already knew.

"It was a trap. Cratty's down but still alive. Other light injuries. Set by amateurs, though, I'm told."

After another moment, Welch said the obvious.

"It was a distraction. Burns and Daniels are not here."

After a moment of silence as Welch listed off in her head other alternatives, Janeson spoke.

"We did expect this, Ms. Welch, though similar to you, I am disappointed."

"It did seem hopeful. It's the kind of bullshit Daniels would do.

Find the only scenario we didn't train for."

"Yes, but subterfuge is his go-to tactic."

"Maybe Helms will have better luck."

"That does not seem likely based on preliminary scans but I appreciate the thought. Thank you. Janeson out."

It was classic Janeson. To the average observer, her response was without emotion, simply matter of fact. But after years of working with Janeson, Welch heard something else in her voice – disappointment. She waited as she saw movement at the mouth of the mine. More excavators were going in with high-grade explosives to collapse the hazard completely.

No deaths today. No deaths tomorrow. It's a good day.

#

Another hour of listening to Carter's ranting about how the real country's weakest link was not about the other country's "imperialism that threatened our way of life" but "the feminization of our boys" had passed. His voice was loud and his hand movements gestured all over the room as he elaborated in minute detail that asserting gender roles was key to America's future. Gender-based division of labor was just the beginning. By the time he got to how men should have a minimum of three younger wives, Helms broke out in praise and prayer as a firm knock rapped on the door. One of Carter's men let a very young female deputy enter, clearly on a mission. The irony wasn't lost on him.

"Director Helms?"

"Yes, Deputy."

Helms was on his feet. Carter remained sitting.

"All cell phone and hard lines are down, sir. They're saying it's something to do with solar flares and outages everywhere, but I'm not sure I buy that."

"Communication is down? Are we talking Merrimack Valley Crisis level or September 11?"

"Not sure, sir. It's some serious shit though. Land lines usually don't go down too easy," she said. Her hands were in her pocket, her windbreaker collar was up, and her serious expression stood in stark contrast to her small, compact frame. Helms looked at her name tag, Owen, S.

"So you think it's something more than solar flares, Deputy Owen?"

"Sorry, sir. I leave the thinking to the command structure and my boss. He thinks you should take command of the area. He said something about domestic terrorism being in your jurisdiction."

Helms was glad his back was turned to Carter. He struggled to keep a straight face at first and then finally pulled himself together. To the young deputy's credit, she stayed in perfect character. Stoic, impassive, and perfectly still. Helms made an effort to turn slowly, hopefully dramatically, to look at Carter. Fortunately the man was already sitting down. He was as white as a ghost. Carter immediately took out his cell phone and then checked his hardline. Likewise, Helms checked his cell only to hear a loud, continuous buzzing.

"Jesus! It's the end," Carter said.

Shaking his head as if angry, Helms looked at his FBI colleague and the deputy before he spoke. He did catch a smirk on the face of the FBI agent who also endured Carter's rants.

"Alright. I'm heading out with you. Colonel Carter? We will not start the search until we have this matter cleared up. Are you okay with that?"

Confused and baffled, Carter looked up at Helms and realized he was being addressed.

"Ah, yes. Sounds like a plan."

"Good. Alright team, let's find out what the hell is going on now."

Helms marched out with the deputy and agent hot on his trail. They walked through the camp to the gate as if he were facing a national crisis.

Thank you, Janeson, he thought as he approached the field commander.

"Alright, I would just contain the area and secure the perimeter to make sure no one leaves. I'm going to head out about two miles down the road and check in with the world and then come back with the next phase. Got it?"

"Sounds good to me."

"And whose idea was it to send that deputy in?"

"That was the sheriff's, sir. Apparently no one piles it on thicker and better than Deputy Sue Owen."

"She did a fine piece of work back there. I'll have Special Agent Martin give her a call."

"Don't bother, sir. His stunt in Boston City Hall back in the day is legendary up here. She and everyone under thirty knows his work."

The young FBI field commander turned back to do his work and directed a number of his teams to support the ones already in place.

Helms was impressed. He stood akimbo as he watched the redeployment. Suddenly, two jets flew low, cutting across the sky right over him and the entire compound. So loud and unexpected were the jets' engines that every head shot upwards to see what was going on. Helms looked at the young man and could tell that he had an answer for his unasked question.

"Just before the lines went dead, we got a call from the Air Force base in Concord, Massachusetts that they had scrambled two sets of fighter jets for fly-by's to add to the drama. Courtesy of the Secret Service, NSA and US Air Force," the young man told him as another set of fighter jets flew in from the west. Images of Janeson talking directly to the Commander in Chief came to mind.

"For God's sake, Janeson. I didn't say go to DEFCON 3!"

"I have to say, Sir, I like the back-up."

"Yeah. My second-in-command takes no prisoners."

"I like her style" he said before returning to his post on the perimeter. Helms walked back to his car. The roars of jets ebbed for a few minutes and then they were clearly returning for another fly-by.

Once in his car and finally driving, he was relieved to no longer be in the company of Colonel Carter but greatly disturbed about not knowing where Burns and Daniels were. As he drove, he kept tapping the wheel as he continued to think.

"This was a waste. They're not here. They're somewhere else."

Chapter 7

"...and I'll chase him round Good Hope, and round the Horn, and round the Norway Maelstrom, and round perdition's flames before I give him up. And this is what ye have shipped for, men!"

Herman Melville, <u>Moby Dick</u>

Present Time Unknown...

As soon as Burns entered the dimly lit room, he could tell it was another tavern-like place. It had a British pub feel to it. Similar to where he met Fitzgerald, Horowitz and Belben, it was filled with familiar looking patrons – men and women in either the armed forces or security. While not crowded, the pub was filled with what appeared to be thousands of people all talking, laughing and a couple of people actually making out.

Okay. Another place where the laws of physics don't apply. I have to be dead, drugged or in a coma. Ah, forget it, Burns. You're just dead. Pull up a chair and have another drink.

Burns felt a tap on his shoulder. As he turned, he saw a punch hurling towards his face. While he felt slow, he was able to move out of the way of the punch and then deflect another as the person seemed to transmit his strike very easily with his roundhouse punch.

"What are you? An asshole? Why would you get Becky

involved in your shit?" the attacker said as he missed yet again. By now, Burns had avoided three strikes and was preparing for another assault when the patrons suddenly swarmed the attacker. As they restrained the attacker, the bartender and three very large bouncers approached him as if he were a regular troublemaker.

"Littleton! What the fuck is your problem!? Every time someone you know gets here, you start throwing punches. You come from a troubled family or what?" the bartender yelled. The three bouncers took a hold of him with ease. Burns could see that he was not a large man but clearly a young man in his twenties wearing blue jeans and a t-shirt.

Littleton? Becky? What?

"Burns, you're such a dumb ass! Just make sure she doesn't kill anyone any more for vengeance. It will keep her out of here and I want to see her get here," he was yelling as he was being dragged away.

"You got some serious issues, Littleton!" the bartender yelled again.

"Tell her I love her!" he finished.

Confused, dazed and daunted by the attack and immediate suppression, Burns called after him.

"Who are you?"

While out of his line of sight, he could hear him yelling still.

"What are you? An idiot, too? I'm Tony Littleton, her brother! And the little girl's name was Emily! Who the fuck picked 'Emma'!? Was it you, you moron?"

Burns stood there, dumbfounded. He looked around to see that the patrons were chuckling and going back to what they were doing prior to the attack.

My God! What is this place? This is crazy.

"Sorry about that. Not everyone who gets here has worked out all their shit," the bartender offered as an apology. "You want a drink?"

"No thanks."

The bartender nodded and moved off. Burns felt as if he were being watched. Fearing another attack, Burns immediately stepped back with fists up to face an attacker from behind.

"You know, you really got a thing with people, don't you, Burns?"

The voice was feminine, familiar and young. It was a voice, tone and cadence he had not heard in years. It was a voice attached to a life he had thought was unquenchable. He was wrong then. He turned swiftly and zeroed in on a lone woman sitting at a table with a pixie smile, short cropped brunette hair and devilish twinkle in her eyes.

He dropped his hands while taking in a deep breath. A person he considered his first friend in his adult life after wreaking havoc, death and destruction in his career a lifetime ago was now before him. Burns closed his eyes and opened them again just to make sure he wasn't imagining it was Debbie Foley. Disbelief seized him and this time he kept his eyes closed. He heard her talking as if she were alive.

"Burns! Stop being dumb and open your eyes. I've been waiting for you and I don't have time for this bullshit," she said.

Okay. I guess I'm going to go with being dead. No dream or hallucination is this clear.

"For for the love of Christ," he heard her say. Next he heard her chair move and then he felt her pull his arm to the table to sit down. He opened his eyes wide. She was short, petite and smelled mildly of perfume. It was nice to see her after all these years.

He had always felt bad about her death at Heathrow Airport when she was caught in a firefight.

You never should have been out there. You were an analyst, not a field agent. I should have insisted.

"Just so you know, you're not dead. At least not yet. If you were, none of this would be necessary. And forget about what happened at Heathrow. It wasn't your decision."

Debbie pulled him to a waiting empty table with friendly patrons waiving to her as if she were a regular. After a moment of just taking a good look at her, Burns was happy he had a chance to see her. But instead of focusing on her, he decided to focus on the environment and just hear her talk.

I miss her voice. Rachael has a similar voice.

Mild confusion must have registered on his face as she didn't even wait for the question.

"If you were dead you wouldn't need these visual cues that are familiar to you to help you understand. You would just get it because you would be one of us," she explained. A waiter suddenly appeared to bring food that Burns never ordered.

"I took the liberty of ordering our dinner. I'm assuming you still like your steak medium rare, baked potatoes with sour cream, sautéed mushrooms, and rum and Coke?" she asked with an impish smile.

She remembered.

He felt saliva forming in his mouth at the sight and smell of the meal. He took note that she was sizing him up. Not in a sexual way but an assessment way.

"Kind of easy to remember since that's all you would eat. Though it looks like you've thinned out."

Burns tried to think of a question but found himself thoroughly drawn to the robust smell of his steak and potatoes. He almost forgot where he was.

Wherever here is.

"That's a good question but I'll leave that up to others to explain. I have a favor to ask, though."

It was easy to hear that Foley's tone and demeanor became serious and all business. Regardless, Burns found himself struggling with wanting to eat the steak but gather more intelligence. Again, as if she could read his mind, she answered his immediate concerns.

"For God's sake, Burns. Eat and I will talk. Just pay attention to what I'm saying."

Without hesitation, Burns picked up his fork and knife, and carved into his steak. He made sure he had a good helping of the sautéed onions and mushrooms draping it. As he took a bite, he felt himself spinning while savoring the taste. After two more bites, he truly thought there was a big mistake, and someone let him into heaven. To insure that he did not miss out on another texture and experience, he tried the potato and found it exquisite. Butter, chives, bacon bits, all perfectly balanced to enhance the potato and not overpower it. Thirsty, he was next drawn to his drink. He took it and sipped it, only to find that somehow it surpassed the taste of his meal. Burns was so focused on his meal that Foley's presence was an afterthought and then a distraction.

"Jesus, Burns. Don't let me keep you from eating. I've only been gone for about a decade or two, but eat up," she said sarcastically.

Suddenly aware of his actions, Burns was able to mumble out one word from his full, satiated mouth - "sorry."

"Yes, well," she said with her perpetual smile and humor that always drew Burns close to her. Thinking back, she reminded him of a sister he never had. *Definitely innocent.*

"Keep eating and I'll talk. You're just visiting, I think, and I want you to get a message to Eric Daniels."

Again her tone and demeanor was all seriousness. Burns's eyes widened at the mentioning of Daniels's name. It took a moment to clear his mouth so he could speak. He took another swig of his drink. For a moment he was caught up again in how refreshing and intoxicating both the food and the alcohol were. He took just a moment to find the right words.

"I don't know if you're keeping up on current events back home, but I think Daniels is about to torture me, kill me or both. Either way, I don't think he's in the mood to listen to me unless it's to beg for my life."

"I know, Alex," she said. Her expression was true sadness as she looked down at her food then up again to continue.

"He's not well, Alex. He needs to change his ways. If he could just admit that maybe he's wrong. Maybe he made some mistakes. That he can't control everything like my death or Maxwell's."

Burns felt a sudden twinge of guilt at her mentioning Anthony Maxwell's name.

"Debbie...I killed Anthony. I set him up," Burns confessed.

Looking at him in disbelief, Burns was sure she was going to hurl her food at him.

"Gee, Alex. Thanks for the update. I know. I saw. But this isn't about you. You have people, a bunch of people looking out for you here. Daniels has maybe me and his mother. He needs help and that someone is you, got it?"

Finally he was able to swallow his food. This gave him a chance to ask another question.

"Okay. What do you want me to do?"

"What?"

"What do you want me to do? You want me to help him? What can I do to do that?"

Debbie's look caught him off guard as if she were expecting more resistance.

"What? Did I say something wrong?"

Burns's attention shifted to his left. The waiter brought him another drink. He happily accepted and then looked back at Debbie to see that she was sitting back in her chair. She looked at him as if to take him into her field of vision. She smiled a soft smile that Burns saw maybe once when she was alive.

"You have changed. Daniels is about to torture you and maybe kill you, and you are willing to help him as a favor to me."

As she spoke, Burns could see her eyes brim with water. He felt sad that he might have hurt Debbie.

Jesus, Burns! What's wrong with you? You haven't seen Debbie in years and you make her cry. Nice job!

"No. You didn't do anything wrong. It's just nice to see that you have grown into someone who cares. That wasn't your strength when I knew you. You had faint glimmers of it. You've changed and I'm glad to see that."

Burns realized he drank the contents of the second drink too fast when the waiter appeared again with another drink. He also felt full from the food he had eaten so far. He sat back and put his refreshed drink down. He felt the alcohol dulling his senses.

Wow! Everything here is so good and strong, he thought as he felt his head getting heavy and fatigue coming on rapidly.

Smiling, Debbie got up and moved around to Burns to help him up.

"You still can't drink me under the table. You were such a wuss."

She was now coming around the table to guide him from the remains of his meal to a large leather chair with inviting large arms and a warm-looking blanket in a quiet corner of the pub.

Oh, this will be nice. Finally, a warm place to relax and sleep.

"You really don't relax, do you?" Foley said as she eased Burns into the chair.

"No, I don't." Burns said honestly. His eyesight blurred and he had a hard time seeing Foley. She helped him pull the blanket to his neck which reminded him of his mother tucking him in about a thousand years ago. He felt as if he was about to fall sound asleep. The ambient noise from the pub, sights and smell evaporated into darkness. Burns smiled as he sank into the chair. Falling, drifting, Burns was gone. Next destination unknown.

#

Present Day...

Glenn managed to keep his eyes on multiple monitors at the same time. As each part of the mission unfolded, he checked on the "breaking news coverage" that had been non-stop for well over an hour. During that ninety minutes, Glenn was able to launch a mobile attack on an elderly gated community with a rented truck that appeared to be filled with smoking explosives in North Reading, a car crash into an elementary school with two armed men that discharged their weapons and disappeared into the Reading neighborhood, a paint factory explosion and ensuing fires in Lawrence, three backpacks filled with explosives and timers discovered in Boston City Hall Plaza after a tip from a "concerned citizen," a freight train derailment in Andover causing traffic jams and cutting the town in two, and three separate medical containers clearly marked "radioactive-hazardous" left at three public high schools North Andover, Andover and Lawrence.

He smiled as he flexed his fingers. It was with great satisfaction that he turned from the missions to the television reports. He waited with great anticipation for someone to say that it all looked familiar. Finally, a very seasoned, serious news reporter, obviously the trusted member of the team in times of crisis and disaster, gave him what he wanted:

"Like lightening striking twice in the same place, it's not been since the Merrimack Valley Crisis that we've seen this systematic terrorist attack. The National Guard has been deployed and fighter jets are scrambled from the air force bases at Cape Cod and Concord. In a possible related situation, we understand that a squadron of jets has been deployed to a militia in Maine called the Republican Citizen Army, where their compound is already surrounded by local authorities and the FBI. All commercial flights are grounded. Presently, all law enforcement agencies, including academies, are deployed throughout the entire region. The major difference is the simultaneous attack in Boston's City Hall Plaza where Boston Police, Bomb Squad and ATF, local FBI are on the scene..."

Turning in his swivel chair, he looked at Ruth who was on her cell phone clearly listening to someone intently on the other end. After only one more minute, she said nothing as she hung up.

"Well?" Glenn asked. She was being quiet.

"Oh? Sorry. Reports from Colorado is that Welch's team is pulling out. The mine was a diversion. They have one injury but no fatalities," she said. He smile was warm. "Just like here," she continued as she now re-adjusted her uniform.

Hmm. Genuine warmth? She must be in a good mood.

John, who had been on his own headset and cell phones, turned suddenly to give his report.

"All teams have reported in and are all en route to leave the country. Primary exits will be through Canada. Minimal injuries to all civilians and no reported casualties on either side. And our ride is here," he concluded while still listening to his headset for updates.

"Ride?" Glenn asked. He expected some beat-up, old Crown Victoria sedan that would pass as a unmarked police car. He stopped in disbelief at what he heard next.

"Yes...a 2016 Charger with reinforced front bumpers and prepared to pass as an unmarked state police vehicle," he concluded casually.

Wow! Now, that is impressive!

Ruth, upon noticing he was unable to contain his appreciation for detail, gave her own opinion.

"Yes. John may be stressful at times but he is a perfectionist when it comes to details and logistics. Which reminds me, Jeffery - why did you have to replicate the same level of confusion that Mr. Burns did so many years ago? Is this a male thing?" she asked. Every time she spoke, she would readjust some weapon. This time she adjusted her knife back in its sheath. He looked at her askance and feigned innocence but then answered the question thoughtfully.

For a ruthless killing machine, Ruth does ask good questions.

"Yes and no," he started as he stood up to shake his legs awake while still watching the monitors for any changes in the teams exiting the area.

"What Burns did with two women, a blind man and a baby was impressive, ballsy and effective. It had the advantage of never being done before, hence taking the entire Northeast region off guard. Since then, the local and regional governments and law enforcement have made some impressive improvements in infrastructure and responsiveness. And after the Boston Marathon bombings, camera surveillance and civilian awareness increased exponentially. As a result, in order to create the same level of chaos, a coordinated effort that targeted soft targets, large groups and in multiple towns was required to achieve a complete and thorough diversion. All needing to be planned without phones, internet and texting so as to go undetected from the CIA and NSA."

"Yes. Your use of drones to transport explosives to the John Hancock and Prudential Building's Observatories for all the tourists to see was brilliant in its planning and execution."

"Yes. Yes it was. Now that's never been done before." Glenn was happy at that flash of genius.

"Yes, Jeffery. I understand that. But Boston? Why there as well? It was not part of the Merrimack Valley," Ruth asked. Now she re-checked her semi-automatic weapon for the tenth time.

Do you ever stop rechecking your weapons? You sleep with those things?

Focusing back on her question, Glenn continued.

"I am trying to work off of past fears and violence in the 2013 Marathon attack. Also, Boston fell in the mix so as to keep the FBI Regional Office, ATF and other federal agencies busy in their own back door just in case they regrouped from being distracted from Colorado and Maine, which appears to be the case," Glenn said. His genuine smile was fueled by passionate intensity of obtaining objectives.

I am just on fire today! Everything right! Nothing wrong!

He heard her sigh. Glenn waited for her own admission of his accuracy, planning and flawless execution. *I'm better than Burns.*

"Yes, Jeffery. Unlike John, I can admit when I am wrong. I am surprised that the FBI so quickly determined that the out-of-state scenes were theater. I did not expect them to be so nimble in their analysis and response. Our intelligence did indicate that the nexus of the team – Welch, Andersen, Helms, Davis, and Janeson – are far more able and adept than expected. Still, they were more swift than anticipated. We should move quickly. Wouldn't you agree?" Ruth asked. For the first time since the start of the mission, she finally stood still with her hands planted on her hips.

She's right. If they figured it out that fast, it won't take them long to figure out where Burns and Daniels are.

"Yes. John? When is the last of the teams out of state?"

"Ten minutes" was his rapid response.

He looked at his own watch, turned to Ruth, and gave the long-awaited answer.

"We go in at ten minutes."

#

Dillon watched Janeson standing in the middle of a quieter control room as she navigated one tablet after another with Johnson and Gilmore acting as near extensions of her limbs. With many of the team's control room staff and field agents now re-deployed to Boston City Hall, Janeson gave the order for minimal staff for the control room as "now it's a game of chess" she reported to Dillon. "No need for too many players – just me," she responded. It was classic Janeson - no emotion and never lifting her eyes off of the tablet. When Dillon suggested that she and Ramsey oversee the City Hall matter, Janeson's response was brief with no room for negotiation.

"No. I need you and Ms. Ramsey to be ready to mobilize as soon as we have confirmation of Daniels's location. He may be able to distract everyone. But not me. Not today."

"But what if nothing happens?"

Janeson's eyes lifted off the tablet and locked on Dillon's eyes. Her deep crystal blue eyes shone brilliantly against her pale skin and black hair in the darkened control room. Her intensity was hot and her emotions, strong and determined, spilled out all at once.

"It will. And when *it* happens, we'll be ready."

"Ready for what?"

"The unexpected. Something that seems so unusual and out of place until you think about it and it all of a sudden makes sense. It will be something logical and obvious upon reflection. But we'll figure it out first. We'll be fast. We won't miss. Not today."

Dillon felt as if she were assaulted. Janeson's eyes let her go and re-engaged another tablet. Dillon looked at Gilmore and Johnson who saw everything and waved her off.

They must have seen this before, this outbreak of emotions.

If Dillon didn't know Janeson any better, she would have thought that she was obsessed with finding Daniels, a personal vendetta almost as important as finding Burns.

The great white whale, Moby Dick, Dillon thought as she remembered Davis's story about Webber and Welch's feud.

"Jesus, Mary and Joseph. How long do we just sit here waiting for nothing to happen?" Ramsey said as she moved beside Dillon. She had missed the episode she had with Janeson. She had been glued to the floor-to-ceiling monitors displaying sites of interest – Maine and Colorado. Ramsey could easily see that she had missed something and motioned her head towards Janeson. Before Dillon said anything, she stepped away to ostensibly get some water.

"I don't know. I've never seen her this intense before. And she's always intense. Still, though, I bet she's right about this," Dillon said. Several feet away, she watched Janeson standing erect with the glow of monitors bathing her in an eerie electric blue light as she handed one tablet to Gilmore while Johnson gave her another one. Then from slightly below deck, Crepes broke the silence with an urgent response.

"Boss! I got phone communication from Martin's phone. It's a call placed to another cell!"

Still peering at her tablets, Janeson nodded before she responded.

"Put it on audio, please."

Dillon felt her heart begin to race as she waited for conversation.

God! I hope this is a break!

Alica Wise: "Bobby! It's me! Your sister? I'm at Danbury Prison in Connecticut. Where the hell are you?"

Bobby Wise: "Thank God! Are you alright? What the hell is going on!?"

Alica Wise: "Bobby, I'm sitting with the FBI and a police lieutenant. They're right here, okay?"

Bobby Wise: "What the fuck do they want? Are you okay? Jesus, Alica, I've been looking for you everywhere. I got nothing from Carter or that new guy. Just nothing!"

Alica Wise: "It's alright, Bobby. I'm in Connecticut. When can you get here?"

Bobby Wise: "Ahhh. I'm on Route 495 heading south to Route 90 I think. I can turn back and pick up...I think I can pick up Route 93 and head south from there..."

Dillon's attention was broken when the communication suddenly stopped as a result of Janeson, standing perfectly still and her hand raised and closed in a fist indicating silence. Whoever was manning the audio clearly knew the hand signal for stop and silence.

Wow. Helms's and Welch's Marine Corps signals have rubbed off on her. What did she hear? He was just giving her where he was?

It was an uncomfortable silence as Janeson stood still for a long moment. Dillon watched as Johnson and Gilmore made eye contact with each other but nonetheless remained just as still. Even from a distance, Dillon could see that Janeson's piercing blue eyes on her pale face shift from wide to narrow in seconds. And then the impossible happened.

"Daniels! You son of a bitch!" Janeson yelled out.

Holy shit! This is it! I don't know what it is, but this is it!

Janeson nodded her head in approval of something, and handed both of her tablets to Gilmore. Her posture and stance relaxed suddenly. She shoved her hands into her pocket and looked the least stressed that she had appeared in months. The only time she looked that way before was when she would talk to Burns for hours as he waited as bait.

"Crepes? See if you can confirm Robert Wise's location. Johnson? Put a map of the 495 Interstate Belt and add all locations of the last 90 minutes of attacks. Once done, highlight the towns they are in and the law enforcement resources presently deployed.

Gilmore? What end of communication have we been scanning and recording since the outbreak of attacks?"

Shaking his head in understanding the question, it took Gilmore just a moment to answer.

"Cellular, military and law enforcement bandwidths – federal, state and local, as well as microwave bands." He kept his eyes fixed on the panel as he spoke.

"Please shift to lower band and citizen's bandwidths, and review recordings that time index to five minutes prior to the first attack. The FCC should have those recordings," Janeson added.

"Yes, Ma'am."

What's going on, Janeson? What do you see? How did you figure it out?

A map of 495 appeared with the towns of Lawrence, Andover, North Andover, Reading, North Reading, and Boston which was further south than all the other towns.

"What's going on? I've never seen her like this before," Ramsey said in a hushed tone.

"I think our girl Janeson has figured out one of her biggest puzzles yet and is now finding corroborating data to back it up." Dillon watched the activity carefully for any clues. Looking at the map, she could easily tell that with the exception of the computer virus, *Albatross*, nearly all the towns mentioned looked like the same ones hit years ago on May 2nd by Burns and his team.

No way! No fucking way!

Dillon felt her heart accelerate and her breathing came up short. Janeson was so right. *It all made sense, in retrospect.*

Having caught Ramsey's attention, it was obvious that she was about to be asked a question.

"What? What is it, Dillon?" Ramsey asked.

"Of course" Dillon mumbled. She would have explained but a recording of an earlier transmission came through loud and clear over the speakers.

"Fox Den to Fox One. Mobilize Trojan horse phase and initiate

plan alpha. Copy?

"Copy Fox Den. Fox One mobilizing. ETA, three minutes; completion in eight minutes."

"Copy. You are green. Albatross Two is a go. Repeat – Albatross Two is a go."

"That was ninety-eight minutes ago," Gilmore said between transmissions. Dillon felt Ramsey grabbing her arm tightly as she leaned close into her.

"Dillon! That's Glenn! That white rat bastard, Glenn," Ramsey hissed out.

Dillon's voice boomed out catching her and the other staff by surprise.

"Janeson! Ramsey says one of them is Jeffery Glenn!"

"Which one? 'Fox Den' or 'Fox One?'" Janeson said calmly as she remained riveted to the large screen. She stood as still as a statue. Dillon was struck by her silenced gazing at the map.

As idle as a painted ship upon a painted ocean...

"I think he's 'Fox Den,'" Ramsey responded. Dillon refocused on the mission.

"Glenn. And the bastard has help."

"I bet it's our friends there from the Mossad. I knew they were watching us. I felt it."

"This is one time your paranoia was right, Ramsey."

"A broken clock is right twice a day," Janeson said as she remained transfixed. Ramsey and Dillon looked at each other first and once again, she saw Gilmore and Johnson give each other knowing looks as well.

Yeah. Our girl here is very different.

There was no time for interpretation or analysis. Another batch of cryptic communication came out of the speakers.

"Fox One to Den. Objectives completed. Fox Two en route to

final destination. Fox three on standby. Copy?"

"Confirmed, Fox One. Well done. Fox Den out."

"Fox Five to Den. Eagle and Falcon?"

"Oui. Merci. Sortir."

"That was definitely Snow White," Ramsey clarified.

Johnson turned at the mention of "Snow White" and appeared confused. Seeing the confusion, Dillon was going to explain but it was Janeson, the woman who could not read social cues and sarcasm, who responded.

"Glenn is very white. Hence, the name 'Snow White' as a sarcastic name to show contempt." And then a continuation of surprises: Janeson gave a full smile and turned back to the map.

"Yes. And the last transmission ended in French – 'oui, merci, sortir' – which I think means 'yes,' 'thank you' and 'move out.' I would guess that Mr. Glenn is aligned with both our French and Israeli counterparts and they are running this mission."

"But why? Why the hell would they cause so much damage and mayhem?" Dillon asked as she stood beside Janeson.

"They haven't," Johnson said from below. Dillon looked at Johnson who had his headset on as he continued.

"There have been no deaths and no real injuries as a direct result of these attacks. Two guys show up with assault rifles at a elementary school, shoot several rounds in the empty lobby and then walk out? A train is deliberately derailed but it's the only freight train that goes by once a week rather than the eighteen commuter trains filled with hundreds of people instead? A truck that appears filled with explosives shows up at a gated elderly community, is left open for all to see inside that it's filled with explosives but no explosion? Drones in Boston with devices that appear to be explosives. Boss, this is May 2nd all over again."

"Boston wasn't part of the Merrimack Crisis."

"Actually it was originally going to part of it - backpacks in City Hall I believe was the plan - but Burns had to improvise to cover and keep Andersen at bay," Janeson said calmly.

"Oh," Ramsey said. Dillon shrugged.

"Gilmore? Thoughts?" Janeson asked.

Dillon turned to Gilmore who had continued to listen in on the chatter as Johnson summed up his reports.

"I'm up to the fifth round of transmissions that correlate with these attacks time-wise. Some French is thrown in in some places. They are transmitting on citizen band – not the expected wavelength for a military operation. It's as if they wanted us to eventually find it. Like Colorado and Maine, it's a ruse," Gilmore said as he continued to listen.

"With one major difference. 'Eagle and Falcon' means that Daniels and Alex are together, and Glenn and his team are there, watching," Janeson said calmly.

Visibly angry, Dillon could appreciate the source and level of Ramsey's frustration.

"Okay, great! So where is the bastard?"

After a moment of silence, Janeson spoke as she took a step back as if to take in the floor to ceiling map in its entirety.

"They are at the site of the Foreign Intelligence Agency's auxiliary control room in Andover. The same site that Burns and his people hit on May 2nd. Unexpected and yet it all makes sense in retrospect."

Dillon felt her mouth drop as she turned to Ramsey who looked almost as bad as she felt. Janeson continued.

"Wise was heading south of Route 495 when he said he would have to turn back north to pick up Route 93. That means he was near the 495/93 intersection which, in turn, is right next to Andover where the auxiliary control room was once located."

"Boss! Another transmission you should hear. Index five minutes ago," Gilmore said urgently.

"Fox Den to litter mates. Continue exiting. Fox Den is going dark. Will be on line and en route in 20 minutes. Fox Den sees all. Out."

Shit! That means they're close to completing the mission.
Without hesitation, Janeson issued her orders.

"They're on the move. Gilmore! Contact Mrs. Welch and the Boss and give them our assumptions. Dillon? Ramsey? You are mobile to that location. Johnson? Give them the location and then re-deploy the rest of our team in the field to follow. Let's move, people!" Janeson said as she continued to look at the map.

"On it, Boss" Dillon heard Ramsey say along with a chorus of similar responses. After a long two minutes of armoring up, Dillon found that she and Ramsey had made it to the parking garage in record time. As they ran to their car, Dillon found herself smiling.

"What's up with you?" Ramsey asked as she took the driver's side of the car.

"I knew Janeson would find Burns," she said with great satisfaction.

"And there's a bonus. We get to get Daniels and Glenn!" Ramsey said as the car roared to life.

"Yeah, team!"

Chapter 8

"...We are not now that strength which in old days
Moved earth and heaven; that which we are, we are;
One equal temper of heroic hearts,
Made weak by time and fate, but strong in will
To strive, to seek, to find, and not to yield."

Alfred, Lord Tennyson, <u>Ulysses</u>

Present Day...

Helms sat quietly behind the wheel of his SUV taking in the beautiful Maine vista. He took a moment to take stock of all that had happened. While he was proud that Janeson and her people discovered the probable location of Burns and all persons of interest, he was genuinely pissed at being so far away from the fight. Even with the loaned helicopter from Maine's National Guard, he was still over an hour away at top speed.

"No point crying about it now," he said as he started his vehicle, rapidly launching onto the highway.

"I don't know. Maybe it's time to retire and let the young lions take over," he said to himself. Even though he and Welch suspected that they were on a wild goose chase, it still didn't soften the fact that they were so far from the action.

Jesus. Welch and Andersen are probably just as pissed.

Driving as fast as possible without endangering the public, Helms was trying to calculate the best possible ETA in Boston. After a number of best-case scenarios and guesses, Helms couldn't escape the fact that in the next hour, whatever was going to happen, would happen.

And I'll miss it. Just like Andersen and Welch. Shit.

"I hope you make it, Burns. I don't think Rachael will do well if you don't."

#

"Damn that asshole, Daniels! I should have known! Right in plain view, again! Son of a bitch!"

Welch made sure she ranted after she closed the line from Gilmore. She looked at Ice, RC and Nine which helped her regain some control from missing the fight.

Once again, these bastards pulled a fast one.

"Ma'am? What's the situation?" Nine asked respectfully.

Looking at Nine whose head was partially bandaged up from being hit, Welch took in a deep breath before she spoke again.

"Gentlemen. Once again, the enemy has outsmarted some of us. Janeson and the team back home have figured out that Glenn and probably Daniels and Burns are presently in Andover, Massachusetts while we are two thousand miles away at an abandoned mine."

Welch held her hands held behind her back, the same way she always did during briefings and after-action reports. It was so natural.

"But," she continued, "they did not, however, fool Janeson, Gilmore and Johnson. And even as we speak, Dillon and Ramsey are bringing the fight to them. Oorah?"

"Oorah!" they said in unison.

"RC? Do you want to go to the hospital and stay with Davis and Cratty?" Welch asked.

After a brief pause, RC gave his expected answer.

"No, Ma'am. They got a medical team there and Davis is with her. I'd rather saddle up and get back to the fight."

Sighing once again, Welch had to state the obvious.

"We're three plus hours away even on the G4 jet the Secret Service has for us," she said. She felt her shoulders slump a bit.

"No time to waste then, Ma'am," Nine said as he picked up his gear. The rest of her team got their gear together as she took in her last view of the Klondike Mine.

Well, Daniels. You didn't kill any of my people today, she thought.

I just hope Burns is alright.

#

"Unbelievable. Hiding right in plain view, again." Davis shook her head in resignation as she sat beside Cratty's gurney waiting to go in for surgery.

"What's unbelievable?" Cratty said with a slur.

Well, I thought I had a problem with medication.

Davis smiled as she stood up to look at Cratty. She was glad that Cratty was at least aware of things even though she was drugged up.

"I just got word from Welch that Janeson located where Daniels and Burns are. They're in Andover. You know, the old auxiliary control room."

After a long moment, it suddenly appeared that Cratty understood what Davis meant.

"Oh. Right in plain sight. Typical," she said as she looked around. Davis noticed that Cratty's gaze fell behind her to a chair that held clothes Davis had brought with her.

"Just some clothes. I thought I would change when you went in for surgery. I got some of your stuff but it's all FBI issue. Did you bring anything to change into? Something from home or civilian wear?"

Cratty made a small noise that sounded more like she was

annoyed than not understanding.

"Cratty? I can pick up some things or I can have Ramsey stop by your place to get you something."

"That's funny," Cratty said as she smiled and seemed to be falling asleep again. Confused, Davis asked what she thought was a simple enough question.

"What's funny? It won't be a problem. We can overnight it..." Davis suggested. With her eyes closed, Cratty muttered her barely audible response as she was feeling the effects of the sedatives.

"I don't have a home...storage and furnished room..." Cratty said as she drifted off. Davis found herself looking at Cratty as she slept, not sure what to think. Looking back on it, it all made sense.

She had a breakup and her mother died when she was in Waltham. She moved to New York and then took her team to Spain to protect Caulfield, Becky and Emma, and lost half her team, and then she came back here to hunt for Daniels. No time to make a house a home when you're on missions all the time. God knows keeping up with my house is a nightmare.

Davis sat down wondering what it must be like to have no anchor or roots.

"You'd think it would be great but I bet it sucks. What do you do between missions? Where do you go? Where do you hang out?" Davis said to a sleeping Cratty.

#

Andersen found himself moving as fast as he could to get to his car as he kept the phone glued to his ear. Ever since Gilmore brought him up to speed, he found that he was both relieved that Martin's strategy worked but frustrated to be more than two hours away even at top speed and siren blaring. Complicating things was his difficulty in getting a hold of any of his own team at North Reading Police Department with all hell breaking out around his town. With all the phone lines jammed, Andersen finally had to search his cell phone's "recent calls" to see if he recognized any numbers that might be his staff. After five long minutes of trial and error, Andersen thought he was lucky when a familiar voice came on the line.

"Honey! Not now! I'm in the middle of police business," he heard Officer Dempsey say just before he hung up. Andersen felt his jaw tighten. He stabbed at the phone button and remained poised to leap before Dempsey cut him off.

"Honey? I'm serious..."

"So am I, damn it! Dempsey? Wake the hell up and pay attention! Where the hell are you?" Andersen finally got to his car, started it and pulled up with a trail of dust pluming behind him.

"Boss?" Dempsey asked slowly.

Oh my God! Please help me!

"Dempsey! It's Andersen! I've got intelligence that Daniels and Burns are in Andover. I'm more than two hours away and you guys are a hell of a lot closer."

"But, Boss, we got the town on lockdown from the shootings, and there are radioactive bombs at the high school. The freight train accident is also making a mess. Everyone is out, Boss."

Of course they're all out. Every resource and everybody is tied up. Just like last time.

Frustrated, angry and tired of being ten feet behind the bad guys, Andersen simply hung up and drove faster as he thought of anyone he knew that was close enough to help. With seemingly no traffic and exceeding ninety miles per hour, Andersen's list of friends and colleagues were all occupied in their own messes as the entire Merrimack Valley and Boston was now on lockdown with every person in uniform on the street and every citizen sheltering in place..

Just perfect. I guess it's up to Janeson and whoever she has left. As he steadied his breathing and tried to release some of his grip from the steering wheel, Andersen realized that he was also concerned about another thing - *Burns.*

#

Present Time Unknown...

Even with his eyes still closed, Burns felt a light weight on his lap. He was unusually relaxed and comfortably sunk in a soft, warm chair. The weight and pressure were familiar: the feel of a woman sitting on your lap is never forgotten, no matter how long it has been. Eyes still shut, he felt her chest rise and fall as her breath fell on his forehead and closed eyes. The smell of clean skin with a touch of perfume - mocha - caressed his nostrils as smooth, warm skin cradled his head deep into her chest.

No. I won't open my eyes, he thought. *It's Sam. If I look, she will go. No...I won't look.*

"Don't be silly," Samantha said. Her voice was unusually warm, soft, and caring. It was a voice he only heard after their lovemaking or talking.

"We have to talk before you see David and Paul, and I have to go to work."

Work? What work?

Curiosity and anxiety forced him to slowly open his eyes and look up into Samantha's face. Here there were no wrinkles or creases, only her too-dark raven black hair and her different color eyes. Burns felt a smile emerge on his face as one did on hers. He never thought she could be so beautiful to see, again. Burns felt tears falling on his own cheeks, so uncharacteristic that he had no memory of ever crying before as an adult.

"Sam," he uttered. Even as he spoke, she pulled him in closer to her chest. While his breathing felt deep and his heart was racing, feeling her warm, gentle touch seemed to make all the pain go away. He was about to close his eyes again but as was typical with Samantha, she was not about to be ignored.

"Burns," she said as she gently shook his head to wake up. "What do I have to do to keep you awake? Start a mission briefing?"

Burns felt the corners of his mouth crinkle up. His eyes opened and smiled at how she seemed to be the same. He looked at her. She nodded to make sure he was awake, gently kissed him on the lips and sat back a little to take him in with her eyes. He had missed the sight of her full, curvy body, dark hair and different colored eyes. Her soft skin and smell were all familiar. He wanted to be there with her forever.

"You look like dog shit. And you smell real bad so I'm going to be brief," she said as she got up.

"I've been hearing that a lot since I've been here."

"You were looking like that before you got here. Ever since I've been gone." She was moving to get up when Burns held on to her suddenly for fear she might just disappear.

"I can't lose you again...I just can't."

Samantha stopped halfway, turned to cradle his face with both her soft hands and gave her very rare, reassuring look that penetrated Burns's eyes.

"Alex, I will never leave you. I have been with you ever since you said goodbye to me in Boston."

"But Sam..."

"I'm right here, Alex. I'm not going to vanish," she said as she stood up. As she moved away, she turned back to say something she had just thought of.

"You know, you were right about me getting here when the sun came out that day. It wasn't as painful as I thought it would be. I was glad Cougar and you were there, though. I don't know how people can die alone...it's so sad."

As she spoke, she was looking at some clothes on a bed that she was deciding on to wear. It was vintage Samantha to talk as she pulled her wardrobe and makeup together.

"It was hard to watch from so far away."

"You were right with me."

"I should have gone instead of you."

"Now you're thinking with your heart rather than your head. Anyway, if you did, Webber and Daniels would have won. Is that what you wanted?"

"No," Burns said immediately. As casual as the conversation was, he took a moment to look around his environs. He remembered exactly where he was; a hotel room many years ago. He remembered because the wallpaper was very distinctive with birds of all kinds. But it was the black swan among the white ones that reminded him of Samantha. It had the same look.

This is the hotel room where you got sick. It's the place you found out I thought you were cute.

"'Cute?' I'm many things but 'cute' is not really me. And it was 'attractive,' not 'cute' you said."

By now, the fact that everyone could read his mind was nonetheless annoying but it did save on time to talk. He watched her as she picked up an array of dresses, blouses, and carefully scrutinized the ensemble to her high heels. He cleared his throat to speak but he carefully chose his words as his headache seemed to retreat and some strength returned.

"Does everyone read minds here? And where is 'here'? Heaven?"

"Read minds? I never thought of it that way. More like hear thoughts. Not all the time, though."

"Not all the time?"

"If you're here for a long time, you can just chose not to listen to thoughts and wait for people to speak."

"Why would you do that?" Burns's curiosity was only matched by his observation of the room, the detail and all the clothes Samantha was looking through.

"Sometimes you want silence, privacy, quiet. Sometimes you want to be surprised and just go along."

Burns took another look at Samantha and realized she was clad in a white matching bra and panties with an actual garter belt that was attached to old-fashioned nylons.

Jesus...

Samantha turned to him and smiled. She turned to look at her own body in a strategically placed mirror before she went back to picking out her wardrobe.

"You are so sweet. I still have it, don't I?"

Burns felt heat burst from his face as blood rushed to his head in embarrassment. As if she had been aware of every thought and movement, Samantha turned back to him and smiled more.

"That's why I still love you, Alex. You're such an innocent sometimes. That's a very attractive quality about you."

"Thanks." Burns wished he could have thought of something more suave or brilliant. At the moment, Samantha was finally deciding on a striking, silver gray business suit with very thin, faint pinstripes. Burns was happy with the familiarity of it all. He found himself smiling as she continued talking as she picked out clothes, just as she always did when she was alive.

"So here's the deal. I'm not sure if this is heaven or not but I know that I like it here. I'm never hungry but when I eat, the food is great. I meet all kinds of people that are interesting and make me laugh. I can drink like a sailor but never seem to get drunk, though the buzz is really good without the hangover the next day. But I gotta say, it's the people I love talking to."

"Sounds like heaven to me."

"Kind of does when I put it all together. Still, there's something very human, very basic about the place."

"What do you mean?"

"I mean there's laughter, humor, sadness even but nothing like back home. I can't really remember being really angry at an asshole here or finding a real jerk."

"No jerks? No Webber, Daniels or any of my old buddies?"

"None that I could find. I doubt Webber will be here. I have some issues about him?"

"Yeah. Me too." Burns's thoughts went dark as he remembered how cavalier Thomas Webber was in telling David how he ordered Samantha's kill.

"Let it go, Alex. The hate won't get you far," Samantha warned. Now fully dressed, looking classy, sexy and just perfect, her expression made it clear that he should drop the thought.

"It's hard."

"Tell me about it. But I'm not shitting you. If I can let it go, I bet you can too, if you try. For me, Alex." Her expression softened until a sudden look of urgency came over her.

"What's wrong?" Burns said. Thoughts of Webber vanished as he was on his feet moving closer to her.

"Ah, yes. My watch." Burns smiled. He knew the expression was familiar. Samantha would have that look of dread when she knew she was missing a key accessory to an outfit.

To keep his thoughts on the present, Burns took a minute to re-group as he tried not to be distracted by Samantha's demeanor.

"How come everyone I see here is always on the move? You have a job?"

"Everyone has a job, Alex."

"I can tell."

Burns sat on the firm bed as he watched her brush out the wrinkles and some lint from her outfit.

Just the way it used to be. Some things never change.

"I know but even appearances here are important. At least to me."

Burns remained silent but still felt his face smiling.

"It's going to take me a while on the mind reading thing."

Samantha smiled at him as she started to look for shoes as she talked.

"Well, I guess there's a catch to everything. We all seem to have jobs of watching over people. My job is to watch over a couple of girls that are prostitutes and I got a couple of nurses that work ER that I keep an eye on." Her voice drifted off. She stood up quickly after looking under the bed for shoes as if she had heard something.

Again, Burns was back on his feet. This expression had nothing to do with clothing. He had seen this before. Usually it was about people she cared for, like Becky or Emma.

"Damn it! I knew I was running late," she said. It had to be obvious to her that his expression needed an answer.

"Vicky, a cute little eighteen-year-old hooker, is setting up a time with an incredible asshole, and she's definitely going to need some help." She dropped to her knees and found both a stylish pair of black pumps and a very menacing fixed, double-edge knife that was holstered.

"Vicky? Who's Vicky? And why the weapon?"

Burns's eyes narrowed as he looked at the dichotomy of the business-attire-clad Samantha he rarely saw and the all too familiar weapon of choice she always carried. At the moment, she was expertly securing the weapon carefully under her jacket.

"I mean, really? What's with you people? Except for the girl I first met, everyone is armed and mobilizing."

Completely dressed and armed, she looked perfect. Burns looked at her image in the full-length mirror and could see she was satisfied with her attire.

"Like I said, heaven or not, everyone has a job, a purpose. I like the work. Sometimes I can't help someone and that really sucks," she said as she seemed to look very sad for a moment. But then she sighed and talked again with some zeal as she took Burns's arm and led him out of the hotel room to the hallway. The hotel's corridor was very different from what he remembered. In this corridor, beautiful watercolor paintings hung on the wall, striking in vibrancy and complexity. The whole thing with art was a mystery to him before but seeing it here, as if for the first time, he wondered why he had never appreciated art before. In addition to the visual art, the softness of the floral rug was nothing he had experienced. Burns felt as if he were walking on air while there was a strong, persistent odor of cinnamon. Even as his mouth watered and his mind swam in sensations, he tried to stay focused on what Samantha was saying as she gently pulled him along.

Oh, yeah. She likes her work.

"But most of the time I do help. By the way, that prayer you said for me was not only beautiful but I think I found peace in it. I believed that a place like this could exist and then I was here."

Burns watched her beautiful face and her smile and felt her warm, embracing touch as she held his arm and pulled him along to the lobby. Her entire presence was more captivating than he recalled. Just as they turned the corner, they spilled into the front lobby. It was grand in size, luxury and accents. It was also alive and filled with people smiling, laughing and talking, sitting in comfortable-looking chairs and couches, as they ate and drank at the bar. As people passed him to check in at the front desk by the hotel's entrance, Burns was positive he heard an old 1970's song by the Eagles, which made him smile broadly at the irony of it all. Just before exiting the lobby, Samantha stopped Burns in mid step, turned to face him and with both hands cupped around his face, she kissed him. Burns felt his heart quake as his body shivered. She pulled back and held his face as she talked to him.

"Alex, I love you. I always will. But you need to let me go. You need to finish your work and help people. Emma needs you. Becky and Rosemarie need you," she said earnestly. Still holding his face, he knew she could see his confusion.

"I know it's confusing but you have made so many changes. Changes that are good but the more you hold on to me, the less likely you will come back here to see me. You won't heal if you don't let me go."

"I can't heal, Sam. I just can't with you gone..."

Samantha stopped him by putting a finger to his lips and took his arm again to head out into the street.

"You can and you will. And here's how you're going to do it. First of all, I'm not 'gone.' I'm right here where I can watch you...not in a creepy way but I'm there with you. Also, to get here, you need compassion, mercy, hope, and love. You're closing yourself off to hope and love."

"That's not true," Burns protested as he immediately thought of Emma and Becky. Before he could articulate his thoughts, he felt the strong pull of emotions to the left of the lobby's entrance. He looked to see what he thought were smaller framed pictures, but from his angle he couldn't see the images well.

"You know what I mean," he heard Samantha say. He slowed his pace down and felt her arm fall away as he swerved to take the steps needed to look at the portraits. Inches away from the main doors, Burns's attention was seized by the series of pictures that led to a large empty frame. While there were lovely images of natural beauty and man-made structures, including faces of all nationalities, Burns found they all led to a large vacant framed canvas with a plaque with no writing. He focused on the canvas. The more he focused, the more effort it took and the more fatigued he became. But the reward was an image forming at the center at first, and then it spiraled out into something he had never seen before. The image of soft green, blue pastels and a dark figure leaning heavily on a cane solidified. He was standing casually near the edge of a cliff that looked over an expansive sea. The blue and green pastels looked as if they might be sea mist. Beyond the mist and the solitary figure looking out, there was a range of mountains. The man, with his white, unkempt hair blowing in the breeze and his back turned, was transfixed, just as Burns was by the image.

"That's quite a picture. Do you know what it is?"

"No. I think I've seen it before but I'm not sure."

"It's Caspar David Friedrich's *Wanderer Above a Sea of Fog.* It's pretty famous. Some believe that the man stands for contemplation of the future, of things yet to come," he heard Samantha say with authority. Burns nodded and looked down at the plaque expecting to see the work's title and legend. Instead, there was a quote.

"His very existence was improbable, inexplicable, and altogether bewildering. He was an insoluble problem. It was inconceivable how he had existed, how he had succeeded in getting so far, how he had managed to remain -- why he did not instantly disappear."

"What? What is this?"

"The quote from Joseph Conrad's novella, *Heart of Darkness.* Coupled with this romantic scene from the early 1800's, I would say you're seeing something of yourself here. It's pretty deep."

Burns pulled away from the portrait and plaque to see how Samantha, a very smart, street-savvy survivor, was all of a sudden literate in classical art and literature. He had no idea of what he was looking at but she seemed to have an exact explanation. Before his shock wore off, she pulled him away from the scene and headed out the main doors as if she were in a rush. As he retreated from the wall of pictures, he looked back only to find that the image and words were gone, replaced by a large mirror and a polished name plate outside: "Hotel der Himmel".

"Another thing about this place is you know stuff, lots of stuff that's very interesting. That portrait and plaque are often a reflection of who you are. You only get one chance to see what's really in it and it's typically yourself in some form or other. You're not just a simple assassin just like I'm not just a pretty face."

Baffled, fatigued and truly disoriented, Burns slowed down in the middle of the congested sidewalk as Samantha raised her hand to wave down a taxi. He became suddenly aware of just how alive the city was with everyone going about their business. But unlike the thousands of cities he had been in with commuters and business people going to and fro, all of these people appeared as if they were all on vacation, laughing, hugging, and even some singing. And at the same time, the sun was bright but comfortable with puffy clouds and the deepest blue sky he had ever seen. The sidewalks seemed clean with grass and trees along the curbs and benches were filled with people eating. This mythical place was in sharp contrast to home, to his dream of Debbie Foley in the World Trade Center.

My God, this place is beautiful. Clean, not hot, no fears...wow.

Burns's attention turned back to Samantha as her efforts paid off and a cab approached.

"Your love for Becky and Emma is strong but that too will wane if you're not careful. I mean: be open to other people that love you. And I mean 'people' and not just Roxie. Though it's a shame her love doesn't count as much as I think it should. She adores you, you know? Every word and everything you do and say, she just loves you."

Oh yeah...I'm losing my ability to love. What? Roxie doesn't count? That's not right.

Burns smiled as he thought about his dog and wondered how she was doing. Then his mind thought about Rachael Janeson and if she was alright.

She seemed so worried. She wanted me to get away when the plan was to get caught. Funny.

Burns realized that he was distracted and looking away. He shook his head in the hope that it would clear his thoughts of Roxie, Janeson, Friedrich's portrait and Conrad's quote. With effort, he refocused to look at Samantha's face only to see she was smiling with her entire face and her eyes were sparkling.

An angel? Is she an angel?

"That's what I mean. That's who I mean. She's odd and wicked smart, but she has very strong feelings for you. I think she's had similar feelings for others but they are very strong for you. And I'm not an angel. Not even close."

Rachael? No way.

Embarrassed and guilty that he was caught thinking about another woman, Samantha's eyes narrowed sharply.

"Stop right there, Burns!" Samantha said in her contained, angry voice he remembered all too well.

"I mean it."

"I'm sorry."

"Don't be sorry, Alex" she said as she closed the distance between them so she could talk softly. "No more guilt and no more bullshit. I'm planning on being here for a while and I want you to join me. If you don't let me go, you won't come back. And that will really piss me off. Now get in the car. I can share a ride with you."

Startled, Burns was not surprised to see his "old" Samantha's attitude and no-nonsense approach finally revealed. It always did when she was serious about something. She nodded and pulled him to follow her into the waiting cab. Burns was already feeling as if he were fading fast. From the moment he focused on the canvas to when he was standing outside, he felt as if a wave of sleep or exhaustion was overcoming him. Whether it was the bending over to get in the cab or the shock of it all, Burns felt his fatigue change into dead tired. As if sensing his fatigue, Samantha reached over to pull him down onto her lap where she stroked his head as she talked.

"So just to recap, I'm not an angel. I'll be here waiting but take your time; I'm pretty busy. But don't just think you can 'yes' me and then do as you please. You've done a lot of shit in the past but you've also tried to change. Big change, and that's good. But open yourself up, Alex. And that image and quote? It means something. I just don't know what it means. Trust and love like you did with me. It will be different but then that's the way it's supposed to be," she said. His eyes had closed upon lying on her lap and her voice seemed to trail off as if he were falling into a very deep sleep. He could still feel her warm hand touching his head and the pressure of her lap on his face as his breathing seemed to become heavier as if he were on the edge of sleep.

"Please say hello to Becky and Emma, and give them my love. Let them know I've never been happier," she said as her voice seemed to be further.

"You should believe those words, Alex," he heard her say. "'For what shall it profit a man, if he shall gain the whole world and lose his soul.' I love you, Alex. I'll never leave you. Let me go." It was almost a whisper now. Her touch was gone and he felt his body float.

As he slipped off into unconsciousness, he heard Samantha's voice one last time and a bit stronger.

"And don't try to bullshit me either. You always sucked at it and I can see through you, for real this time. And make sure you get my necklace out from my tomb. I don't want anyone stealing it."

Taking in a deep breath, Burns smiled as he knew Samantha was really there.

"That's my Sam. She's the only one that knows where my necklace is," he said as he let go.

It's really her.

Chapter 9

"I have lost the faculty of enjoying their destruction, and I am too idle to destroy for nothing."

—*Emily Brontë, <u>Wuthering Heights</u>*

Present Day...

It'd actually be kind of nice to get a book, cup of coffee and sit at one of those tables like everyone else. What should I do? Not worry about getting in a firefight? Not my life, I guess.

It was less hot than it was only two hours ago. Unfortunately her blonde wig held more heat than it reflected. The irony was that now she felt hotter even though the temperature dropped and in spite of wearing next to nothing. Looking back over at her hotel door, and then back down at her weapon and pictures of potential targets, Becky finished obsessing about her immediate surroundings to survey the street area again. As she watched the entire dead-end street from her balcony terrace with ease, she found her mind wandering to how Burns and Cratty were doing. She was thinking about shooting Cratty a quick text when she saw something that just seemed to stick out of the ordinary.

"If something seems out of place, it probably is. If something just doesn't seem right, you're probably right," Burns would always

say.

She methodically looked down at her field of fire. Once she had a potential target, she took her eyes off the person of interest, and then returned to the person to confirm her suspicions. It was now easy to see that the man at a table had been on his phone a lot as he faced the stores and cafes with his back against the street.

While that in and of itself was not odd, it was the way he was dressed that threw her off. While everyone appeared to be either in vacation clothes and dressed casually, he appeared to be in less casual dress and he wore a wind breaker. While it had cooled, it was still an unusually warm day which made Becky's attire of a yellow bikini more appropriate than what the man below was wearing. Moreover, his shoes were shiny black dress shoes whereas everyone else wore very comfortable shoes.

You can tell a lot about a person from their shoes, Samantha used to say. Even if he was on break for work, the windbreaker is too much and the shoes don't fit the ensemble.

As she kept a close eye on him, she saw that he was back on the phone as a dark sedan pulled up and parked illegally in a handicapped parking space. She watched the whole interaction. It was the man putting his phone away as he stood up as two men exited the car that alarmed her. She looked at her AR15 with scope. It was out of view from below. She was on her earphone talking to Murphy as she closely watched the two men from the car close in on the man with the black shoes and windbreaker.

"Murphy? Your guys are out of view in the store, right?"

"Yes" was a quick response.

Becky looked at the pictures at her feet and there was one that looked like the guy she first spotted.

"Do you know anyone who looks stocky and kind of small? Well-dressed and kind of Mediterranean-looking?" It was easy to see the height difference in the men. The smaller guy was doing all the talking while the others just nodded.

"If you mean 'short, stocky Italian-looking guy who's perfectly dressed,' then it's Panelli. Angelo Panelli. He's the guy that left you

that note on your wall and almost killed me and Rosemarie."
Murphy made little effort to disguise his disgust. Becky looked
around her immediate area as well as adjoining buildings and any
other potential sniper positions that could make a shot at her if she
wasn't fast enough.

Okay. Here we go.

It was surreal. She was a citizen who not only was about to
shoot someone as if she were asking for two scoops of ice cream,
she felt completely at ease. She looked back at her rifle, and then at
her bikini and tried not to laugh at the incongruity of the image.

*It's like one of those bad spy movies. A blonde woman with an
automatic assault rifle clad only in a yellow bikini? Please!*

She broke from the ridiculous image to confirm that she was
not spotted as a potential problem. It was then she looked back down
at the three men to see that they were on the move.

"Alright, Murphy. This is it. Stay where you are and wait for
my signal," she said as she hoisted her weapon in her hands while
still watching and sitting.

"And that signal would be what?"

"That would be me firing a rifle. Now hold on, I got to make
another call," she said as she taped another button onto her ear set
that was preset for 911.

"This is 911. Please state the nature of your emergency," a less
than pleasant man asked.

Altering her voice into one that was meeker and weaker, Becky
spoke as she stood up, put her weapon into cheek-to-shoulder
position while she honed in on her targets with her scope.

"Please help. I'm at the Marriott Hotel in downtown
Providence, and I see three men with guns walking to a cafe. The
one where there's a dead end? I'm not sure."

Smiling still, Becky couldn't help but continue to think how
strange it would be if anyone was watching; *a blonde in a yellow
bikini holding a mean-looking rifle ready to shoot. Just awful.*

She found her targets' buttocks.

This is for Burns, she thought as she pulled the trigger twice.

"Oh my God. They're shooting," she said a bit more calmly than she should have. The man she had seen pointing towards Murphy's location grabbed his ass as he fell forward. Turning on the man she had first seen, she targeted the man's feet and legs with four shots.

"Please stay on the line. Help is coming," she heard 911 say urgently.

"I'm scared," Becky said quietly.

Funny, you don't sound scared. I better put some emotion in this call.

She re-adjusted her sights, turned to the third man to see him draw his weapon but pointed everywhere but upward. This left him totally open to three shots in his legs. As each shot rang out, there was corresponding screaming and people running.

"Oh my God! They're shooting at some old man! Oh my God, they're shooting!"

After her last shots, she closed the line. She clicked back to Murphy. She couldn't see him and barely heard him over the din of screams from people running. As she scanned the area, she saw another man exiting the illegally parked car with his gun drawn. Feeling almost guilty at how he, too, had not even looked up, she shot at his feet and legs four times and watched him fall to the ground.

"Jesus, Becky! What the hell! Is that your warning shot?" Murphy said as he was clearly rushing.

"Yup! You should see me when I'm serious."

"Thank you, no."

She looked back at the others on the ground and scanned her entire kill zone. Becky saw one of the men attempting to aim into the crowd.

"Dumb. Real dumb."

She squeezed off two more shots into his exposed ass. As she looked from left to right, she continued to keep the bad guys at bay until she heard sirens closing in.

"Are you gone, Murphy?"

"Yup. We're in the car. Need a ride?" he asked. "We can easily pick you up."

"Nope."

"Sure?"

"Yup." Becky was now moving at top precision speed to put the rifle down, duck back into her room to disassemble her weapon as she spoke.

"I don't think it would be a good idea for you to be anywhere near the weapon that just shot up a couple of bad guys."

"You got a point. I don't have many friends in this area."

"Kind of a long way from South Boston, Murphy."

"I got around in my past life."

She finished her breakdown and careful placement in her backpack.

"I'll call you when I get the girls. Out," she said, more out of practice than as a response to Murphy.

"Okay. Talk to you later?"

"In one hour." Becky's movement was swift and well practiced. She slid into her blue jeans, sneakers and light blouse, and pulled her blonde wig off her head. She felt instantaneously cooler with her short hair now exposed in the summer air.

"Okay. Thank you," Murphy said quietly.

"Yup" she said as she closed out the line so she could focus on cleaning the bureau of prints after she moved it from the door. As Becky looked quickly around the room to make sure she got everything, she stuffed the wig in her bag, happy to be sporting a much cooler, comfortable look. Suddenly thinking of Samantha's love of wigs and disguises, she also thought of Tony. As she carefully fitted everything in one backpack, she found herself suddenly taken with the irony of it all. She had just saved the father of the man that killed her brother.

"Wow. What the hell? Don't think, Becky. Do."

She returned to the task at hand – *escape and evasion. It's almost like shopping for dinner.* Everything packed in her backpack on her back and in her bag, she casually walked out into the hall with her short, dark hair and dark sunglasses. Rather than taking the elevator, Becky took her well rehearsed escape route down the stairwell that emptied out right onto the street on the opposite side of the plaza. As she opened the door, she saw three police cruisers driving by her as they closed in on the crime scene. She stood and watched like all of the onlookers. She didn't follow the crowd but instead walked in the opposite direction. After she walked three blocks, she turned into a public parking lot where she paid the attendant and found her car still in one piece. Without much fanfare, Becky pulled off her sunglasses when she was sure she was far away from the police and positive she was not being followed. After fifteen more minutes, Becky started to relax as she turned on the radio to find some music.

Finally. I can relax.

And for just one minute, she did relax until she started to listen to the breaking news reports from Massachusetts, Boston and the Merrimack Valley.

"What the fuck!?"

She pulled off into a store parking lot before she crashed. Her only response was to sit and listen. Other than the radio broadcast and her breathing, she listened to make sure she wasn't in some kind of time warp. She just couldn't believe she was hearing the same level of chaos she and Burns and all of them heard years ago.

Bombs, shootings, elderly and schools attacked, burning buildings – drones with bombs? And, no reported injuries! What is this?

Becky's fingers were frozen on the radio button as she leaned closer to the radio as if proximity would help her understand better what was happening. It was a throwback to May 2nd and a dissociation, as if she were watching a movie she had already seen before, plot ruined as a result.

I was in that movie. We did all that. Not the drones. That one's good. But we all made it out. All of us did.

"What the hell is going on!? Burns! Daniels?"

After a few more minutes of listening, Becky dug through her bag and found the emergency cell phone she and David had always kept on them when they were on the move. As she listened more to the radio, Becky revised her plan and called Murphy.

"Son of a bitch, Burns! What shit are you into now? You can't die! I'm not going to be the only one left!"

She found her other phone and hit speed dial to call Murphy.

"Murphy? New plan. I'm going to pick up the girls and I want you to meet me at the Mass./Rhode Island rest area. I need to get there in under one hour."

"I just heard what's happening in Merrimack Valley. Do you think it's Burns?" Murphy asked with worry in his voice.

"Are you kidding me? This is from our playbook! And I need you to take the girls while I go on reconnaissance. If this shit is happening there, that means Burns is close. Real close."

"Becky. I owe Burns. Tell me where the girls are and I'll get them and have them check in as soon as we are on the road. I'll take them to Florida and get you their location when we set up. Go get Burns. Okay?"

Becky felt bad leaving the girls. But Murphy was their grandfather and he allowed himself to be bait to protect them.

But he's right. If I continue, I could be up in the Andover area in less than an hour if there's no traffic.

"Alright. Just let them know I'm off to find uncle Alex."

"No problem. Make sure you find him, Becky. I'll have them call you as soon as they get in the car."

Nodding her head in approval, Becky gave him the address as she focused on her driving.

"See you on the other side," Murphy said.

Smiling, Becky couldn't help but notice the similarity of the phrase that Murphy used now which Burns used years ago when they had just about finished their first mission.

"See you there." She started the car for her trip. She turned the radio off so she could hear her thoughts.

"Unbelievable."

#

Andersen kept the phone on his lap as he sped towards the Connecticut border to get up to Andover as soon as possible when he got the call. Unable to see caller ID, Andersen answered very much at the same level he felt when he last spoke with Dempsey.

"What!"

"Lieutenant? This is Janeson. Rachael Janeson. You are on speaker. Do you have a moment?"

He wondered why she felt obligated to clarify which Janeson she was.

"You're the only Janeson I know. I'm driving so I'm not going anywhere." It took him mere seconds to register the irony in the statement. He hoped Janeson would not point it out and focus on why she called.

"Hmm."

"Of course I have a moment. I'm driving like a mad man with no assistance from my guys because of all the disasters Glenn, the Israelis, French and Daniels put in place."

"Yes. Well, there is another issue I need for you to help clarify. Could you please put your phone on speaker so you can hear a 911 call that came in from Rhode Island ten minutes ago?"

"Another issue?"

"Yes. It will become clear if you follow my direction."

"Okay," was all he said. The tone and direction were not lost on him. Janeson's clarity, direction and ability to read social situations were some of the many new developments over the last several days. Resigned to more bad news, Andersen gave a simple answer as he found the speaker button and announced he was ready.

"Go ahead." he said. After a moment of silence, he clearly heard the recording come in:

**911: "This is 911. Please state the nature of your emergency?"
Caller: "Please help. I'm at the Marriott Hotel in Downtown
Providence, and I see three men with guns walking to a cafe. The**

one where there's a dead end? I'm not sure...Oh my God.
They're shooting."

911: "Please stay on the line. Help is coming."

**Caller: "I'm scared...Oh my God! They're shooting at some old
man! Oh my God, they're shooting!"**

"Unbelievable. Just unbelievable. This is so crazy no one would
ever believe this!"

"Lieutenant? I think I know who it is but I would like
confirmation," Janeson said matter-of-factly.

Without hesitation, Andersen answered as if he were defeated
already.

"Rebecca Littleton. She's on the move. I'm guessing we know
who she shot was someone who deserved it for one reason or
another?"

"Preliminary reports indicate that Angelo Panelli and three of
his associates were shot down in broad daylight, and received non-
lethal wounds. Mr. Panelli was shot in the buttocks. Kind of funny, I
think."

Anderson was silent. While he wasn't shocked that Littleton
was on her own mission, creating her own kind of mayhem and
havoc, he was surprised at Janeson's response.

*Who are you, Janeson? Irony? Burns was shot in the ass by one
of Panelli's guys and you see the humor in Panelli getting shot in the
same place? You're not supposed to get humor! Who are you?*

"In the same ironic vein, you are the closest to Andover by car
than Director Helms by the helicopter and Mrs. Welch and her team
via the jet. That said, please hasten to join Ms. Ramsey and Dillon in
Andover as now Ms. Littleton undoubtedly has joined the fray."
Janeson's choice of words was more vintage as was her lack of
emotion in their expression.

"Hasten?" "Fray?" She has a unique vocabulary.

He smiled for the first time in hours.

"I will endeavor to hasten my progress. Please keep me advised if any more bomb shells drop," he said.

"Will do. Janeson out." The line closed off. Andersen tossed his phone on the passenger seat and debated the wisdom of pushing his aging car beyond 95 miles per hour.

"Some things never change. I should have seen this one coming."

#

Present Time Unknown...

When Burns finally awoke, he found himself lying on his side on a leather couch in an office waiting room. He sat up. His hair felt matted and his hands were tingling as if he had slept on them. He felt dried spit on the corners of his mouth, an obvious indicator that he more likely drooled as he slept. As he attempted to wipe it up with his sleeve, he looked around the empty waiting room and realized that he knew the place. He looked again at his arms and hands, and was pleased to see that his scars were still gone. He smiled as he remembered how he looked good on the outside but felt empty on the inside.

Hmm. Had to nearly get killed and disfigured to get to this place.

He shifted his gaze to figure out where he was and had a comforting feeling of familiarity. There was no logic for feeling comfortable. But then there was no logic or reason that applied to this place. Talking with dead people, interaction in environments that defy the laws of physics, experiencing sensations that bordered on ecstasy, everything was just perfect. Familiar and comforting even though he was the least likely to be in such a place.

Like everywhere I've been.

He slowly stood up to get his bearings, shake the stiffness out of his limbs and torso, and to take in the entire environment of Dr. David Caulfield's waiting room he remembered from so many years ago. Startled by David's door opening, he was surprised to see a middle-aged woman animatedly talking to a tall, middle-aged man who was bald and had sparkling eyes. As Burns watched the interaction, he realized he knew the woman. *Dr. Caulfield's wife, Jenny.*

As if transfixed by their discussion, Burns watched as they were leaving David's office and then noticed him.

"Alexander Burns! It's nice to meet you finally," she said as she grasped his hand.

Wow. Firm grip.

"You have no idea how much he's been looking forward to seeing you. And we are both glad you're just visiting," she continued.

"Yes...it's nice to meet you." Burns's mind went back to the time when he watched her get killed in a car bomb that he could not stop.

If I had only broken cover and warned you...

"Well, that would have gotten yourself killed and David would never have had a second chance. He never would have met Becky or Emma. That just wouldn't be right," she said.

Becky...Okay... Burns felt as if he knew more than he should. He found himself uncomfortable knowing that he was with David's first wife whom he knew David loved, but that there was another wife and family that David also loved.

"Oh, my God! Samantha's right. You are cute. Oh. I'm sorry. Where's my manners? Please meet Dr. Roberto Melendez, Dr. Caulfield's mentor, supervisor and friend."

As Burns took his hand, he found himself instantly liking him. It was more than the warm smile and strong handshake. It was the fact that he saw David in him, and that was comforting.

Smiling, Dr. Melendez smiled back.

"It's very nice to meet you, Mr. Burns. My biggest regret is that I never got a chance to consult on your case. Your recovery is impressive."

"Thank you," Burns said. He felt embarrassed and put his hands in his pocket.

"Changing wasn't easy, was it?"

Burns was surprised at how quickly the answer came.

"It was. I mean, the choice to be someone new and different was better than what I thought it was at the time."

"So there was no fear of the unknown?" Dr. Melendez asked.

"The only fear was backsliding. Going back to the way I was."

"No feeling? Just a commitment to flag, country. No sense of who you were inside? Was it worth it? It was easier before. Clarity. No feelings of loss or pain when others died?"

"No connection either. No sense of joy."

"Pretty insightful for a counter-terrorist specialist. It's easy to see why Dr. Caulfield is so impressed."

"Alright you two. I can see that you both could go on for hours," Jenny said. "Well, Alex. He's waiting for you and I have to see Dr. Melendez off to cover a shift with me at the hospital."

"I need to check in on my girls and wife first but I'll join you later," Dr. Melendez added as he looked at his watch.

"I'm guessing you'll look in on your grandson too, Jose?"

"Definitely. I'll talk to you later," he said with an even larger grin and sheen to his eyes.

"Deal then," Jenny said as she took his arm and started to walk away.

"Get going, Alex. He's on the phone, as always, trying to get answers. I'd go in and wait. He always pretended to be okay with people being late but that was all acting. He doesn't care for it at all."

Dr. Jenny Caulfield and Dr. Melendez were gone. Surprisingly, Burns found himself almost elated as he watched them go.

"This place is unbelievable. Dead or drug-induced, I wouldn't mind staying." He turned to face the door he walked through years ago that changed his life. He felt upbeat as he opened the door. As soon as the door opened, he saw David Caulfield sitting behind a desk with windows letting the sun shine through. Burns stopped at the door to take in the view just as he remembered years back. Like so many times before, there were closed files on his desk with books

littering the top. He had an old desktop computer with three
monitors juxtaposed against even more textbooks that were opened
to some odd neurological issues and brain scans. But instead of
David looking deep in thought while reading a case or something, he
was clearly in a heated argument with someone on the phone.

"Why do you people keep commenting on my middle name? So
what if it's 'Thomas.' It has nothing to do with what I'm asking...Hey!
I'm talking here, I'm talking here!"

Well, I guess I never saw this part.

"Look! All I'm asking is to get a couple of answers from
someone who knows something. Every time I try to get in touch
with the guy running the place or his managers, they're either too
busy or out of the office...We're all busy, Peter! We all have things
to do – you know – jobs."

Burns quietly walked to his old chair, enjoying the experience
of seeing his former therapist and friend "unleashed" to find the
truth.

"If I wanted to read people's thoughts, I would have...What do
you mean 'you're surprised I made it here!' You think I need that
guilt thrown at me?"

Who's he talking to?

"I know they said they were alright with it. It doesn't mean it's
right and it doesn't tell me any more about how this place works."
There was a brief moment of silence as it was clear David was
listening to a response.

"So how can I explain it if I keep getting the run-around from
you people? Some people like the old-fashioned way of
communicating, you know, like taking the time to organize thoughts
and then asking questions. You remember what that was like?"

David looked and was at first surprised to see him but then
produced a warm smile and then went back to listening. Burns sat
back in his old chair. He looked and saw that David had no scars on
his face.

"Look – my friend's here and I still got nothing of use from
you. So could you see if your boss can call me back. And I don't

want to hear anything about 'if I just used energy to read thoughts it would all make sense!' I like this way...Yeah...have a good day."

It was easy to see that David was fatigued by the person on the other end. He pushed the phone into its cradle a bit harder than needed.

"It was easier to get answers from the veteran's administration."

"So it's nice to see you're still at work," Burns said.

David was up and coming around to see him. He had a grin on his face that Burns had never seen before.

So this is what he was like before I changed his world.

"'Talk of the devil and he doth appear.' Though I bet there's some rule about using that phrase here too," David said as he casually shook Burns's hand just as he always did before each session. Feeling himself relax, Burns could sense tension leaving his shoulders and his chest open up without pressure.

"Finally. Someone who can give me some straight answers about this place," Burns said as he sat in his "usual" seat. Similarly, David went to his seat and sighed deeply as he looked carefully at Burns.

Anticipating the response, Burns thought he would start first.

"I know, David. I look like shit. Sam told me and I believe her. But right now I'm strung out on drugs, and Daniels is probably going to kill me so it would be nice to have some insights as to what is going on."

David smiled. "And I thought I was good at not showing my emotions."

Burns remembered that he would see that smile when David was with Becky and Emma. With eyes narrowed and jawline stiff, Burns had an urgent thought.

If David's first wife is here and they're together, what's going to happen to Becky?

David's smile seemed to become serious with concern.

"Alex? What's wrong? You look like you just thought of something." Burns' fear changed to total confusion.

He can't read my thoughts.

"Alex? You okay?" David said with a puzzled look.

"David? How come everyone here seems to know what's on my mind but you?"

Recognition seemed to register on David's face as if he realized something very basic.

"You're right. I get that a lot. I choose not to use that energy. Funny thing. As a therapist I used to wish I had the capacity to read my clients' thoughts. But here, I actually do better work going through the actual process of asking questions without knowing the answers."

"Logical."

"That was and still is my long suit."

Burns verbalized his thought faster than he wanted.

"So you chose to be blind here, in a sense?"

Taking in the thought, it was obvious that David had not lost his ability to be self-reflective and nodded in approval.

"I guess I got used to being blind in my second life. There is irony here. Anyway, I like to give people options for privacy, which seems to be something of a novelty around here. That said, what were you just thinking when you seemed to become unnerved as if being here was not enough to do that already?" David asked. He folded his hands and crossed his legs.

Yup. That sounds like David. Best interests of the client.

Clearing his thoughts, Burns tried to verbalize his concern about Becky and Emma.

"Well, David, I couldn't help but notice that Jenny, your first wife, was here. And while I bet she already knows about Becky and Emma, I'm not sure, ah, I'm not sure if your getting back with Jenny won't really hurt Becky," Burns stammered out. He watched David's eyes get bigger as if shocked that he would even mention it.

"I mean, it's your business and you have every right to choose who you want to be with but I'm worried that Becky will be hurt. She's lost a lot of people she loves and I'm not sure she's going to recover."

Burns did his best to be clear it was out of concern and not judgment.

God knows I'm in no position to judge, he thought.

After a moment of David just smiling and shaking his head, Burns was hit with yet another fear.

"Wait a minute. David, is Becky not going to come here?" he asked, almost panicked. Whatever this place was, people seemed genuinely happy, at peace but productive.

Damn it! I had her kill Webber and the people in the helicopter. Just great, Burns! You completely screwed it up for her.

He felt his face stiffen even more while his scalp and arms furiously itched and fists clenched for the first time since arriving. His eyes shot down to see that his scars had appeared on his arms and hands. He touched his scalp, and the familiar ridges of old scar tissue were afire with the guilt of having messed things up for his only living friend. It must have been easy for David to see his distress and urgency. David leaned forward to make eye contact with Burns to make sure he was listening.

"Alex. I'm not 'together' with anyone. It doesn't work that way. I love Jenny and we spend a lot of time together but we're not husband and wife. In fact, I spend more time with my mentor and just talk up a storm."

While confused, Alex still was concerned about Becky and it showed.

"As for Becky coming here, I think she will. She regrets her actions and in her own way, which is Becky, she tries to make it up. I don't think she'll ever kill again except to protect Emma and now, Rosemarie. Don't worry, Alex. I think she'll be fine. And when she does come here, hopefully not soon, she and I will hang out with Jenny, Samantha, Tony and everyone here."

David's words were reassuring. Just like a therapist should be.

It had the desired effect as Burns's itching seemed to subside and his face and hands relaxed.

"So did you get a chance to meet Rebecca's brother?"

The attempt at changing the subject worked.

"Oh yeah. Just missed me. He's a real charmer. I guess we got

Emma's name wrong."

"Emily is a nice name. I think she's more of an Emma, though. I'm probably not the most objective person."

"I guess you can see how he would be upset," Burns said.

He reflected on Emma for a moment and how it might be for Tony to not see her *in vivo*. Burns looked up to see that David took on a more concerned look.

"Anyway, I'm more worried about you. You've let this pain of losing Samantha and me eat you up and kill your future here if you don't stop it."

Frustrated and still puzzled, Burns sat back in his own chair and prioritized his list of questions.

Where to start? After a few moments, Burns found that he felt happy to be with David again.

He always let the silence sit. Still more moments passed until he finally had a rank order of questions.

"So, are you armed too?" Burns asked. With the sole exception of the teenager, he recalled everyone had a weapon at some point. Unless you count her mouth as a lethal weapon, he thought.

David smiled at the question.

"I think that all the people you met to date were probably well versed in weapons before arriving here. Anyway, my weapon of choice is words. You know that."

Too true.

"Okay. What is this place and why am I here?"

Burns watched as David's eyes seemed to narrow as he nodded his head to acknowledge he understood the depth of the questions.

"Yeah...about that. You might have heard the tail end of that conversation. I've been trying to get that specific answer for you and a couple of others since I got here. Since you can't read minds, it has to be weird. Similarly, since I don't either, trying to understand it in terms of language has been...restrictive and difficult," David said. He drifted off with the appearance of trying to find the right words. It took him a moment to find the words. Burns found himself smiling at the consistency and familiarity of his friend's habits. He felt comfortable settling back into his chair, just like old times.

"But let me give it a shot," David continued. "This place is a type of heaven, or at least our understanding of it. Think of our existence as energy in corporeal form when we are back home. Then when we die, our bodies release the energies contained within and it is no longer bound to earth."

"Souls, David?"

"That's probably the best interpretation of it. Still, our energies, or souls shall we say, still hold the essence of who we are. As a species, we are social creatures and tend to draw comfort from being with others. It's the same here. Our energies, souls, like to stay together, forming more energy. A greater energy that exceeds the sum of our mass at an exponential rate."

Burns felt a headache coming back on and rubbed his head in the hopes of relieving some pain. He looked up at David, nodded, and made a rotating movement with his hand to have David go on.

"You know, it's a good thing I'm a professor and love to hear my own lecture."

"Works for me. Please go on."

"So say this place is like heaven. A place where the sum of all energies that shared similarities on earth are now here. Kind people, smart people, compassionate people, caring people, all of these positive energies all in one place. Our essence is still human and we are tied to those we left behind. Not just loved ones but anyone that shows these qualities. They're not perfect. They're not special. Just people who are high on the kindness, compassion, hopeful scale. We want them here because the more we have here, the...happier? The more fulfilling it is here," David said as he searched for the right words. "So as to why you are here, I'm not sure. I'm guessing you are at a turning point where you are either about to die or you are in serious danger of squandering the positive energies you have achieved. I am guessing that Samantha has been keeping a close eye on you, as always, and probably made it her business to get you here so she could talk to you. She did, didn't she?" David asked.

Sighing and still rubbing his head, Burns felt a warmth and

calm flow over him as he thought of her.

"Yes. She told me I had to let her go. To be open to love. To be hopeful and share myself with loved ones."

David sat back as he seemed to take the time to articulate his thoughts.

"Ironic. Just like last time," he said.

Confused, Burns's look evidently spoke volumes.

No need to read minds with that expression, I'm sure.

"Samantha was the first person who went out of her way to get you help when you were in the hospital. Then she sent you to me to figure things out. The message is still the same – you need to let your past go to have a future. You know, cut the albatross from your neck and be free. I think this is about redemption and that you are in danger of losing all that you gained."

"So my coming here is more than a drug-induced hallucination?"

"Maybe yes. Maybe it's drug-induced but it's still about who you are. You could have hallucinated about anything but you chose this."

"This being the place to find old friends?"

"This being the place. It has meaning. What it is exactly, I have no idea."

"So no neat, clean answers, David?"

"When has a therapist given a client a neat, clean answer, especially about something so existential?"

Taking in a deep breath, Burns desperately tried to get his head around the whole thing.

So, even if this is an elaborate drug-induced hallucination, then it's real to me.

His headache increased and he started to feel dizzy.

"I've tried to stop hating. I don't mean to kill, I just don't know what to do," Burns said.

David leaned forward again and took his time explaining.

"Alex, whatever it is, live your life. Let guilt and anger go. You'll be much happier and everyone around you will too."

"You think guilt and anger are keeping me from moving on?"

"Guilt and anger always keep people from changing. They both lead to fear and fear hates change."

David's response was immediate as if he had had a lot of time and discussion about that very matter.

Listening to David, while comforting, still left Burns tired, dizzy and his head hurting. David clearly noticed as he got up and helped Burns lie on the couch. Burns was surprised that he didn't resist the help even though it was much appreciated.

"You look sick. Where are you? That is, when you're not here?" David asked as he lifted Burns's feet onto the couch and propped his head up with a cushion.

"Daniels is interrogating me. I think, though, he is not having too much luck because I'm pretty drugged up," he said with a weak smile. Burns watched David pull back almost in recognition of something far worse than Eric Daniels.

"You know he doesn't understand you, Alex. He remembers the old Alex Burns. He's not going to get you."

"Should I even try?"

"Yes. That's what the Alex Burns I know would do. He doesn't give up on people."

Burns felt his head spinning and his vision tunneling. He was moving again from a happy place to somewhere else. Since there was pain involved, he assumed he would be back with Daniels. He sighed. Well, I have to try, he thought.

"Deb Foley wants me to help him. How?"

"Probably by telling him to let go of the guilt. She died under his command?"

"Yeah. She shouldn't have been in the field. She wasn't a field agent."

"I'm guessing he feels guilt over that. And in the finest tradition of men, he's not letting it go. Holding onto guilt is a poison here."

"He'll never listen to me. But I did tell Foley I would try."

"Just try your best, Alex. Maybe he's listening," he heard David's calming voice say. But before David left, he had one more question.

"I don't understand why I have a chance to come here and he doesn't. I killed people. Even innocent bystanders. He protected a country. He saved lives."

"Yes, Alex. You killed people and I bet you've regretted every death, justified or not. Right?"

"Yes."

A disembodied voice from afar still held his attention.

"So I guess we're talking about redemption. Maybe you're ready for it. He's holding onto guilt with no redemption. Maybe Daniels should consider it?"

Maybe.

"You're not like him anymore, Alex. Let us go and live."

"Guilt and regret?"

"They are the darkness, the things that lead us to desperation, not here. He still thinks he fights evil when it's himself. 'Whoever fights monsters should see to it that in the process he does not become a monster. And when you look into an abyss, the abyss also looks into you.'"

Nietzsche. That's definitely Nietzsche. I wonder if he's here?

"He thinks he's right all the time. It's hubris, something you do not do well, fortunately," David's voice said as Burns drifted off again.

Chapter 10

Present Day...

Glenn took point upon entering the near-empty building. It was easy to navigate since the schematics were committed to memory. He knew all the activity would be on the second floor in or near the vault.

With only five men, including Daniels, Glenn was pretty sure that his insertion would just slip under the radar. As he came in through the locked rear, he had his automatic assault weapon with silencer ready to fire. He saw the first of four men sloppily patrolling the bottom floor while reading a magazine. He was a very large man both in height and girth. The camouflage attire did nothing to slim him down nor hide him in the environment. The scene reminded him of the time he worked with "monkeys" in Spain. He gave Ruth the signal to take him out without shooting. Ruth immediately put her rifle on her back and extracted her combat knife. She quietly approached the distracted man from behind. Glenn was impressed with not only how quiet Ruth was, but the fact that her target was easily one hundred pounds heavier than she and more than a foot taller made the whole picture - like a panther taking down a rhinoceros - all the more compelling.

It's almost unfair. He doesn't even have a chance.

Ruth lunged on his back with legs crossed and clamped over his stomach as her left hand clamped on his mouth. The pressure of her legs forced air out and her right hand drove her knife deep into the man's neck. Clearly hitting an artery, the man was shocked and unable to respond fast enough to even offer up much of a struggle as he slowly headed to the ground with Ruth quietly dismounting and guiding his fall. With her prey down, Glenn watched her wipe her knife on the dead man's shirt and re-sheathed her blade as she retrieved her assault rifle.

"You do that too well," Glenn said in passing as he took point again.

"Thank you," she said. She allowed John to pass her as she took up the rear.

Glad you're on my side. Yeah...if we were dating I'd hate to have to break up with you. I bet you're the one that ends relationships, not the guys.

He pushed her efficient lethality out of his mind and focused on the mission. He pulled up his mental picture of the bank and oriented himself as to the next steps. The small team turned the corner and quietly walked through the empty building. Glenn looked for any indication that they might be walking into a trap. It was easy to see that there were no traps, trips or surprises as they turned the corner to enter the bottom foyer. At the bottom of the stairs, he stopped to have John and Ruth catch up behind and listen. With his ears poised, he heard three men in a heated argument about which racial group was more of a threat when the government finally fell.

"If we had taken care of those black bastards back in the sixties and seventies like my dad always said, we would be able to send all those immigrant parasites back across the borders so they could live in their own shit holes rather than stealing our jobs and homes! They both will steal our country out from underneath us! My dad always said – 'send them all back to Africa!' Man, he was right!"

"Yeah, but the French are nothing like the Mexicans, are they?"

"They're worse! They think they know everything. At least the Mexicans and blacks know their place! We should even keep those Canadian fucks out of our country. Especially those French frogs from Quebec!"

It still amazed Glenn that after all his time in the field, he still hated ignorance. His eyes narrowed in anger and he felt embarrassed to be a US citizen. While initially he felt bad about killing misguided individuals caught up in Daniels's and Carter's insanity, it all fell by the wayside as he listened to more racial slurs and epithets hurled about people of Asian, Hispanic, Latin and African-American descent, all within sixty seconds. Glenn caught a glance of Ruth who looked as still as a stone.

Okay. This is bullshit!

Glenn made sure his safety on his assault rifle was in the "off" position. He heard his team do the same thing. John leaned into him and barely whispered: "We are doing your country a service by terminating these...pigs."

"You're not from Quebec, are you?"

"No. I have family there. Ruth's stepfather lives there too."

"Okay."

"Time for them to meet God."

Glenn was pleased to see that he and John were sharing more in common the longer they worked together.

"Agreed. I'll take lead in the middle. You take left; Ruth take right. We move when I'm on the top stair and cleared the wall. Ready?"

Both nodded as they checked their silenced weapons. After eye contact was made to confirm "ready", Glenn walked on the edges of the stairs as quickly and quietly as possible with John and Ruth hot on his trail. Upon cresting the second floor, Glenn saw the man in the middle had his back turned away from the stairwell while looking at two other men who were sitting in chairs. Seeing the man to the right look directly at him, Glenn unceremoniously shot the man in middle three times in the back just as he was about to get up. Before he could turn his sights on the one man standing with a shotgun, he watched his head snap back as he was clearly hit in the head by Ruth's single shot. The man on the left was in the middle of taking a bite of something as the man in the middle fell to the floor. While staring at his fallen brother, he was still chewing his food when Glenn watched three bullets hit him in the side, hurling him to the ground. The smell of discharged gunpowder and egg salad hung in the air. Glenn surveyed the area to see the carnage and to make sure there was no other danger.

"We just made your country stronger," John said quietly.

Wow. We agreed on two things within two minutes. We could be buds.

Glenn checked his weapon's clip more out of habit than necessity. He looked at the man who was shot by Ruth. It was a clean shot right between the eyes.

"Show off."

She nodded in agreement and looked at the vault door. It was closed. He gave a nod to Ruth who went to the left side while John took the right. Glenn moved out of view of the door until he had another thought. He put his weapon down. Ruth and John looked at him as if he were crazy but then they began to understand his reason for his next actions. Glenn was quick to rearrange the room, reset the chairs and place all three men back in their seats. He put the largest man's back in the middle, blocking the vault's door. Glenn took a seat just opposite the dead man blocking the vault's view with him facing both the dead man in front, and his two deceased partners on each side. He retrieved his weapon and sat calmly in the chair in front of the vault. With dead bodies as company, he felt confident that he would not be seen from the vault's point of view while Ruth and John flanked the vault entrance. Chessboard set, and the game in full motion. He just needed whoever was behind the vault to come out and make his move.

Now for the hard part. Sit and wait.

#

Daniels found himself becoming more impatient as he watched Burns's unresponsiveness to his efforts to wake him. Taking out his smartphone and tablet, Daniels checked the time as well as looked at his itinerary to head to Missouri, and eventually Cuba. He flipped through electronic folders and checked off the various money drops he had en route so he would have cash available since all his accounts were frozen.

They think I only had money in the account? They have no idea how much currency, bonds and shit I have!

He pulled up another window that itemized the amounts of bearer bonds, diamonds, rubies and other gems in addition to cash he had physically stored away. Once done and after placing his phone in his shirt pocket and tablet in his oversized pants pocket, Daniels sat with his legs crossed and arms folded. He felt curiously dissatisfied with his situation and his unresponsive prisoner.

They just ruined it! They drugged you so much you can't even stay awake. And I don't have all day to stay here.

"It was supposed to be dramatic," Daniels said as he reopened his phone for an incoming text.

"You know – a battle of will between us. David and Goliath, Cain and Abel, Achilles and Hector." Daniels's quiet complaining stopped so he could fully grasp the recent text.

"What the hell? 'nitro did not detonate C4!?' Of course it didn't! It can't! It doesn't work that way, you baboon!"

Even as his voice escalated with more contempt than hot anger, he stabbed at the keys to ask what happened.

The plan was so simple – the nitroglycerin is tripped causing panic - everyone goes into the mine and then you remotely trigger the explosives from above once Welch and all her people are in the mine. She and her minions are killed and we're even. What is so difficult about that?!

"That's why it's called a 'trap!'" he said loudly. He finally finished the text and pressed "send." He shook his head to clear it and then looked at Burns who now appeared to be in a less comatose state.

"What did I tell you? I'm surrounded by incompetence. Why the hell hasn't Carter called me? He missed his scheduled time. My God...how the mighty have fallen." Daniels re-crossed his legs and rubbed his eyes. He took a cleansing breath to settle his nerves and continued to hope that Burns might respond faster to hearing someone talking.

"You, one of the best field operatives and analysts I ever produced. And me? Well, now I have to rely on Howard out there who can't even keep his breakfast off his beard, and a self-proclaimed "Colonel" who can't tell time, dial, text or all of the above. Do you know who he's been handling all this time? An old friend of yours from back in the day," Daniels started until he heard a text back.

"Took long enough. Probably needed to find a first grader to help read and text." Daniels felt his heart jump in his mouth and his hands clutched the phone as he read the text. He blinked several times. Finally he gave a nervous laugh.

"So, Burns," he said as if he were awake, "check this out. Let me read to you what just came in.

Howard and the Colonel said the nitro could trip the C4 so we wouldn't have to be there. We heard from emergency police scanner that there was one injury and they're leaving. Does it really need to be triggered?

Daniels took yet another breath and re-read the text in the hopes that it somehow changed. He then focused on containing his blood pressure as he felt his nostril tingling as if it were about to blow a blood vessel.

"Okay. Put the phone away, Eric, and breathe."

Damn it! Welch has probably figured out we're not there. Even she can put that together! And that means they will be looking elsewhere, and here might be a good place to start.

Daniels became anxious that another key piece of the plan fell apart due to the idiocy of others.

Morons! Stupid morons!

He looked around as if the walls were closing in. He was about to revise his travel plans when his attention was drawn to Burns.

Frustrated, Daniels jumped out of his chair, came around and violently shook Burns as he sat slumped in his chair. Sensing that he might be waking, he shook him again as his anger grew. Burns's eyes fluttered open. Daniels looked at him closely to see if anything was registering.

"Burns! Are you awake? Can you hear me?"

He watched Burns blink and clear his vision and throat. Daniels became more hopeful as it was evident that Burns was trying to say something.

Finally. Something other than snoring!

Waiting but not hearing anything, Daniels pressed on with his questions.

Jesus Christ, Burns. I don't have all day!

"What is it, Burns? What do you want to say?"

Daniels waited with anticipation as Burns seemed determined and almost worried or concerned about something.

It's about time. You'd think you would be more fearful for your life by now.

He finally heard Burns speak.

"Eric? You have to let her go." Burns said.

Eyebrows knitted, Daniels stood erect, truly baffled by what Burns was saying.

"Let her go? Let who go?"

It was easy to see that Burns was fighting the drugs. He continued to wait as Burns seemed to get stronger in his resolve to talk.

"Foley. Deb Foley. It's not your fault. Not your fault at all. Not her death. Not Maxwell's. You can't keep blaming yourself."

Shocked, feeling exposed, Daniels felt a fury build up in him that took him by surprise. In anger, he struck Burns across the face with the back of his hand while he sat in his chair.

As Daniels watched Burns's head slowly return to look at him, he was surprised that Burns seemed more focused, and slowly moved his hands to feel his jaw.

"You have to let it go. The guilt. It's not your fault... 'when you look into an abyss, the abyss also looks into you,'" Burns said more clearly than before.

I've lost everything. My work and agency gutted. My legacy sullied. My respect reduced to working with ants. And now you have the balls to tell me to let go of my pain.

Daniels stared at Burns. He didn't know what to make of him.

"What do you know, Burns? What do you know about me? I made you! You're nothing. 'I am the vine; you are the branches...Apart from me you are nothing!'"

Flabbergasted, confused and not sure of what to do next, Daniels remained standing above Burns, waiting for him to recant and beg for his life.

What is this shit? Who are you? You can't judge me!

As Daniels waited, Burns looked into his eyes as he spoke next.

"Please, Eric. Let her go. She wants you to. You'll be happier if you do. You'll be free."

"Stop it! Who are you to tell me what to do? Who are you to tell me to let her go? I will never let her go! Never!"

Silence sat in the confined space for a minute before Daniels spoke next. A palpable feeling of calm came over him as if he made a decision.

"So be it. If you want to see Foley, Caulfield and your precious Samantha Littleton, I'll send you on your way."

Daniels walked away to open the vault door. He was done. There was no reward, no gratification, and no joy in his last encounter. Daniels coded in the key and pushed the heavy door open. The air smelled like gunpowder. He immediately assumed that one of the idiots probably shot a rat for dinner. Breathing heavily and committed to taking Howard's shotgun to splatter Burns all over the table, Daniels looked at the four men sitting down in front of the vault.

Just great. A know-it-all in there and idiots out here. I don't know which is worse.

Just as his rage subsided, he felt the beginnings of a bloody nose coming on.

Of course. A bloody nose is just what is needed right now.

He shook his head as he approached the quartet of camouflage. He found himself getting angrier at the fact that killing Burns was simply anticlimactic.

I could have had this done days ago. Nice job drugging him, you idiots. After I kill him, I'll take care of all of you, you morons!

Still focused on his anger, Daniels finally looked around at the group of men sitting in a circle.

What is this? A book group? Shouldn't you people be patrolling the perimeter? No one will mourn your loss. He pinched his nose to preempt bleeding. As he approached, he sensed something out of place. The smell of a bowel movement and egg salad was revolting but the four men were motionless. He stopped short of Howard and saw large bullet wounds in his back.

"Howard? What the hell happened to you?" Daniels said as he moved closer to the dead man's back.

"Howard had many problems but the one that killed him was being in the wrong place at the wrong time," a male voice answered in lieu of Howard.

That voice! I know that voice.

As Daniels's hand rested on Howard's back, the dead man fell forward revealing Jeffery Glenn sitting casually with an assault weapon on his lap.

Shit...Damn it...Shit.

Daniels felt his eyes widen, his jaw and neck set, and his legs weaken. He truly regretted his long-standing habit of not being armed when extracting information from a prisoner. He looked to the man on the left of Glenn and could see that he, too, was dead with his shotgun just three feet away from Daniels's grasp.

"You know, it's not me you should be worried about," Glenn said as he pointed behind him.

Daniels closed his eyes and sighed. He realized that Glenn

didn't even raise his weapon as there was obviously someone behind him.

Glenn doesn't have to protect himself. He has someone already covering me. Shit! Daniels's hope of snatching a weapon vanished. Opening his eyes again, he slowly turned around to see who had the drop on him. It was easy to spot the red hair and broad smile. Daniels knew the man was "John," French Intelligence.

"Bonjour," John said. By now, he stepped casually forward with an assault rifle leveled at his chest. Daniels looked to the other side of the vault to see a well-tanned, dark-haired woman he had known of for many years only as "Ruth" in the Mossad. Her various obscured surveillance pictures did not do her justice.

This is not good.

"Ruth," Daniels said quietly.

"Salut, Mr. Daniels," Ruth said. She leveled a semi-automatic handgun at him.

"Your pictures do not do you justice, Ruth,"

"Thank you."

Daniels felt his nose erupt. As a droplet of blood fell on the top of his lip, he sighed. The vision of killing Burns and living a life in first class exile vanished before his eyes.

"You should really have that looked at," Ruth commented as she pointed to his nose with her gun.

Shit. I really didn't plan on this.

"Goodbye, Eric," he heard Glenn say from behind.

"No! Wait! I have more money than God! I can..."

Instantly, Daniels felt very hot, sharp, stabbing pain hit his chest from two different sides. He felt his knees buckle and felt the ground rush up to him as he landed on the floor.

I wonder if I'll see Debbie again, he thought before he felt more sharp pain and then darkness.

#

Present Time Unknown...

Burns felt drowsy from lying down on David's couch when he noticed someone helping him to sit up. For just a moment, he thought he was back with Eric, but then he slipped away again. He struggled to open his eyes and found himself in the same office he first met Paul but now there was a different man in his place. Similarly dressed in a dark suit, pants, and crisp white shirt with a yellow tie, this man, while strong, seemed to have arms like cables, and long dark hair that framed his strong, chiseled, tanned face. Just above him was a large plaque he had missed before. It had official lettering but was in Latin. After years of memorizing certain scriptures in Latin, he knew the letters but there were times like this one where he couldn't figure them out. The man saw his gaze and spoke.

"'Rarus avis in terris nigroque simillima cygno.' It means 'a rare bird in the lands, and very like a black swan."

"I don't understand."

"It means Paul and I deal with people that are rare. You'd think they would be an easy read and easy to figure out but they zig when you expect them to zag."

"Sorry?"

"Black swans are rare. They typically are unexpected and are the harbinger of things to come. A change in the wind that leads to different, unexpected outcomes. That's who Paul and I deal with."

"Who are you?"

"Andrew. Good friend of Paul. He's tied up with another situation that will keep him busy. He wanted me to let you know you're heading back. It looks like you got a lot of people vouching that you're on the road to recovery so he wants to give you a try. Not surprising, considering your shared history," Andrew said. He stood up with hands now placed on his hips. Burns sat quietly for a moment and asked his question while still in a fugue.

"What do you mean, 'shared history?' I don't know Paul."

Andrew looked confused at first and then smiled as he seemed to realize that Burns may not know what he meant.

"Alexander J. Burns, known earlier in life for his crimes against humanity on behalf of President, flag and country, is struck down from the sky, crashes and suffers injuries of fire and head trauma. While not losing his sight, he does lose his memories of who and what he was. You're found by a, 'angel of mercy,' and then sent to a man for healing. Through the help of others, you change your entire life to help them, at the risk of your own life. And then there's the prayers. When Dr. Caulfield had you pick something to meditate on, you chose prayer. And then you prayed, morning, noon and night when it was expected. Whether by plan or accident you've made your case relentlessly for change and forgiveness. Alexander, even the changing of your name is similar to Paul. Or should I say, *Joshua*. But you know your bible. I'll let you figure it out."

While Andrew could have easily have passed as an executive on Wall Street, his smile was soft. Burns had a vague recollection of an apostle, a tax collector, struck down and blinded by God for sins against the Jewish people while on his way to Damascus.

*He pledges his life to God to change...he's directed to see...someone to have his sight returned...*Burns thought as he tried to recall the name.

"My name is Andrew, Joshua. But I went by another name back in the day, when I hung out in Damascus."

"No. It's all real? I was hopeful. Doubtful, but hopeful..."

"Ah yes, and that reminds me. I have to go visit Dr. Caulfield. I am impressed with his determination to get answers and to do it old school with limitations. He was pretty doubtful too about here, but then I should have expected it with his middle name, Thomas. Names do mean a lot, especially here as you can imagine."

*No way...*Burns kept thinking as he felt himself fading again. Looking directly at him, Burns watched as Andrew's pleasant, smiling face mutated into a scowling, angry face of Eric Daniels.

#

Present Day...

Still confused by the revelation, Burns's thoughts jumped back to Debbie Foley and the need to warn Eric before it was too late. He fought to find moisture in his mouth so he could talk.

"Let her go? Let who go?"

Burns could easily see from Daniels's expression that he was confused.

I have to focus. I have to make him understand.

"Foley. Deb Foley. It's not your fault. Not your fault at all. Not her death. Not Maxwell's. You can't keep blaming yourself."

A sharp pain registered on Burns's jaw as he heard the corresponding slap across his face.

I have to warn him. Debbie wants me to save him. David said he's turning into the very monster he's hunting.

"You have to let it go. The guilt. It's not your fault...'when you look into an abyss, the abyss also looks into you,'" Burns said more clearly than before.

"What do you know, Burns? What do you know about me? I made you! You're nothing. 'I am the vine; you are the branches... Apart from me you can do nothing!'"

That's John? I saw it written on the wall at mom's church...Why is he reciting John...He's so angry, so pissed.

"Please, Eric. Let her go. She wants you to. You'll be happier if you do. You'll be free." After a moment went by, Burns watched Daniels's face as it seemed to have calmed down.

Do you understand? Did I get through?

"So be it." Daniels walked out. Burns tried to turn to call him back but the drugs were still strong. He sat for a moment as he heard Daniels say something but he was too far out the door for Burns to make sense of what he said.

Damn it...I have to warn him.

After a moment more, he heard some voices just outside of the partially closed vault door.

Is that a woman's voice?

He moved his hands freely but found his feet were still bound.

"I've got to call Becky and tell her about Tony and Samantha...David too. She'll never believe it. Man, Rachael will never believe it either." He bent over to untie the rope at his feet. Unexpectedly, Burns took a whiff of what he thought was carbon discharge associated with gunpowder.

"But wouldn't I have heard the gun shots? Unless they're silenced. Eric?"

After a minute longer, he saw another pair of hands helping him untie his binds. He was relieved to have assistance as the dizziness from bending over returned. He sat up expecting Eric but instead saw a familiar though unexpected face.

"Glenn? Jeffery Glenn?" Burns stabilized himself in his chair.

"Burns. You look like shit."

"So I've heard. Where's Eric? He needs help."

"No. He's in a better place now. So Burns, listen up," Glenn said. Burns had a hard time focusing but he was getting his bearings and some strength back.

"What are you doing here? Eric will kill you. You better get out." It took Burns a minute to recognize Glenn's expression as confusion.

"You look pretty fucked up," Glenn said.

Several thoughts came to Burns as he fully registered he was back in the world and that Jeffrey Glenn was actually in the room with him.

"I really should kill you. You could have kept them from killing David. You killed Fitzgerald, Horowitz and Belben. You could have killed Emma..."

Burns watched Glenn's face become angry as he spoke firmly.

"Stop right there, Burns! I didn't mean for that to happen! Those monkeys got the jump on me and by the time I figured it all out, the damage was done. I killed them before they killed anyone else. I'm...I'm sorry."

"What?"

"I said I'm sorry. I wish I never got involved. I couldn't make it right but I fixed it as best I could."

Burns watched Glenn's pale expression move from anger to guilt to calm.

"You're sorry?"

"Yes. I made a bad mistake."

Burns sat quietly and looked at him. Glenn averted his look and stared at his pale hands.

He sounds pretty guilty for a stone killer.

"Burns. I'm letting you go free. Professional courtesy. Don't look for me and I won't look for you. We both have enough people pissed at us so we don't need to look out for each other. See ya!" Glenn said. He abruptly left as quickly as he had appeared. Unable to reach him fast enough to stop him, Burns knew he barely had the strength to walk, let alone wrestle him to the ground. After another few minutes, he stood up and carefully walked out of the small room. He looked around and he realized he was in the vault he had stolen the hard drives from years ago.

The auxiliary control room, Andover, Massachusetts. Now that's something I should have seen coming. Classic Eric.

Upon exiting, he saw that Eric, along with three other men, were all lying face down.

"Shit." Burns ambled to Daniels's body and felt for a pulse. Feeling none, Burns felt genuinely sad.

It was carbon I smelled. They used suppressors.

"Sorry, Eric. Sorry, Debbie. I don't think I got to him in time." Even though he was still dealing with the aftereffects of drugs, he still was a field agent in need of resources and intelligence. Burns felt through Daniels's pockets until he found a cell phone and a small computer tablet. As soon as he got the phone, he stood up again and walked carefully down the stairs. Halfway down, he heard a loud car crash with crunching of metal and then the squeal of wheels just outside the stairwell's lobby in the parking lot.

Okay. Sounds like a lot of activity in the front. I think I'll go out the back door.

He tried to pull up the building's design from years ago. Not even bothering to look out the window, Burns walked to the rear of the building to an exit he remembered. As he moved, he saw another dead body as he closed in on the door.

Will it ever end, he thought. He walked carefully out onto the sidewalk. With the heat of the sun bathing him, he smiled as he slowly walked. After what he counted as fifteen minutes, he was cognizant of there being very few people on the streets, but a lot of sirens, helicopters and cars speeding by. Confused by the level of activity and the lack of civilians, Burns felt conspicuous being the only person on the street, and clearly a disheveled one at that.

I think it's time to find a nice quiet dumpster and make a call. He saw an alleyway between two buildings he remembered that led to a back parking lot with a big recycling dumpster. After a minute of searching for a large enough opening and taking a look around, he pushed himself into the dumpster full of cardboard and bags filled with paper. He felt surprisingly comfortable inside. He opened up Daniels's cell phone and punched in a set of numbers he had known for years.

I wish Samantha or David would pick up.

After only two rings, he heard a familiar ring with an all too familiar tone.

"Burns?! Where the hell are you?!" he heard Becky say.

Chapter II

"...Let us learn the truth and spread it as far and wide as our circumstances allow. For the truth is the greatest weapon we have."

H.G. Wells

Present Day...

Dillon continued to look at her road map as the GPS continued to keep them on course to the former auxiliary control room in Andover.

Jesus, her voice is so annoying. I wonder if I could change the voice to South African or something.

Dillon listened and noted their location via the map and compared it to the GPS's estimated arrival. They would be there in thirty seconds. She flung the map into the back seat and felt for her shoulder holster where she kept her semi-automatic gun. She then picked up her semi-automatic rifle from between her legs to put a bullet in the chamber. Just as they were pulling into the driveway of the old private bank, Ramsey called out with excitement and anger in her voice.

"Mira! Look! It's Snow White!"

Looking straight ahead of their speeding car, Dillon watched in sheer delight as Glenn emerged from the entrance wearing a police uniform and his rifle slung on his back.

"Finally! Some good luck!" Dillon yelled. She was ready to jump out of her slowing car. While completely focused on Glenn, she was surprised to feel two hands on her shoulders and head pulling her down below the dashboard.

"Get down!" she heard Ramsey yell before pressing her whole body down on her.

What the hell! Who's driving if you're down here with me?

A fraction of a second later she felt an enormous crunch along the driver's rear side which sent the car and its occupants spinning for what seemed to be forever. After what was actually only a few seconds, Dillon heard the sound of several garbage barrels crunching, scraping metal, shattering glass and snapping wood from striking a tree. All of this noise seemed to continue even as the car rested firmly against a chain link fence that was now collapsed. While stunned, it was the sound of the car's engine racing coupled with a lack of movement that grounded her and kept her from falling unconscious. Unable to move, Dillon pushed Ramsey off who was conscious but clearly disoriented, bearing a gash on her head that might have been a result of coming into contact with the dashboard. And while the back seat and driver's side safety air bags deployed, the front bags did not.

"Ramsey? You okay?"

"Get Snow White, now," she uttered as she slowly moved to unclasp her safety belt. Without further hesitation, Dillon climbed out through the shattered windshield and pulled herself through as quickly as she could without severing her limbs on the shattered glass. She found her feet and pulled her gun out. She looked right in front of her only to see what looked like a state trooper's car fitted with high-grade bumpers. While the driver's side window was tinted, obscuring the driver, she had full view of the back window left open as the car launched at full speed out of the parking lot. The last image Dillon had was of a pale, white hand sticking out of the rear window and giving her the middle finger.

You son of a bitch!!

"Fuck you!" Dillon yelled as she chased the car out of the parking lot. She started shooting at it as it sped away. By the time she was in the middle of the road and had her second clip in her gun, the car turned the block out of sight. Standing in the middle of the road with her gun still pointed in the direction of the car, she felt anger, fury, hatred, enmity, and every other violent emotion she had experienced in a lifetime burst from her very core as she started yelling at the top of her lungs, the only way she could think of to release the bile.

"God damn it, Glenn! I'm gonna find you! I'm gonna find you and kill you, you son of a bitch!" Even as she yelled, she stamped her feet on the ground in fury.

"God! I hate you, Glenn!"

With some of the anger dispelled with her outburst, Dillon tried to pull herself together.

No time for this bullshit. Where's Ramsey? Burns?

Dillon turned back to the parking lot where she saw Ramsey wobbling out with her own gun ready. She shrugged off the last of the hate from her missed opportunity and ran to Ramsey before she nearly collapsed.

"Don't tell me we missed him," Ramsey said as she accepted Dillon's arm for support.

"Yeah. That white jack rabbit not only escaped but flipped me off." Dillon watched Ramsey's surprise mutate rapidly into anger as she took in the insult.

"He gave you the finger? That asshole," Ramsey said as she stabilized herself on her own two feet.

"Yeah," she answered as she scanned the smoking, wrecked car, and realized that they still had a mission to do.

"That pig!"

"I know. Ana, we better check inside," Dillon said. She pointed her head in the direction of the building.

"Yeah," Ramsey said.

"You up for this?"

"Yup. I'm from Chicago," she said as she made sure there was a bullet in the gun's chamber. "I bet we missed the party," Ramsey continued.

"You're probably right."

God. Just don't let Burns be dead. I can't be the one to tell Janeson.

As tired as she was, Dillon forced herself to move as quickly as she could. As she passed the car and the smashed tree, Dillon saw that her rifle had dislodged itself into a bush right beside the entrance.

Well I'll be damned.

Picking it up and looking closely at it, she saw that it still appeared to be in good working order, and put it to her cheek to take lead. The building was stone silent as she and Ramsey quietly went directly to the second floor where the vault was located. As they crested the second floor, it was easy to see four bodies of varying shapes and sizes dead on the floor. With all of them face down, Dillon decided to focus on clearing the floor and the whole building before checking their identities.

I'm not taking any chances of this being a trap, like that mine. Man, I hope Denise is alright.

She and Ramsey methodically checked the second floor foyer, vault and then downstairs, including the entire bank and exits. It was only after this sweep was completed that they both relaxed a bit and were about to speak when they both heard a door open.

"Federal officers!" Dillon yelled out in the direction of the sound.

"Come out with your hands up where I can see them!"

After a very brief moment, as sweat streamed down Dillon's face, she heard an all-too-familiar voice.

"Dillon? Ramsey? It's me, Andersen," the voice said as he showed both empty hands and then a smiling face from around the corner.

Shoulders dropping along with her rifle, Dillon felt her entire body relax as she finally had another person on her team present.

"Jesus, Andersen! Weren't you in Connecticut?" Dillon asked.

"Yeah. I probably broke every safety and speed limit to get here. My own men are too busy dealing with the theater all around us."

Andersen looked closely at Ramsey's head. He took out a handkerchief, handed it to her and asked his next question.

"I saw the body down back. Any others?"

Accepting the cloth, Ramsey appeared as if she were about to answer the question but ask something else.

"Who carries these things anymore?" she said holding the white cloth.

Dillon watched as Andersen closed his eyes as if annoyed but answered the question.

"I do. It's a gift from my daughter. Use it for your head, Ramsey, until the EMTs get here. What about upstairs?"

"Four dead bodies," Ramsey answered as she folded the handkerchief into a small, compact square and applied it to her gash.

"Let's see if we can identify them and get a report back to Janeson. Just so you know, Becky Littleton just shot a couple of Panelli's people in Rhode Island."

"Are you shitting me?!" Dillon said.

"Nope. I guess she got tired of the bullshit and decided to shake things up a little."

"I love that woman," Ramsey said. As they debriefed they walked to the second floor.

Well, looks like everyone Burns knows has been busy!

"Well, just so you know, Glenn was here too and escaped in a souped up state trooper vehicle," Dillon said. She left out her temper tantrum in the street.

"That bastard nearly killed us and then gave us the finger!"

As Dillon walked upstairs, she saw a smile coming on as Andersen gave Ramsey a look of shock.

"He flipped you off? What an asshole," he said as seriously as he could. Without turning around, she knew that Ramsey's eyes were probably slits at the very thought of a missed opportunity, an insult to injury.

"I hate him. I hate him so much," she said quietly as she looked at the first dead body's face.

"Take a number. We all hate him," Dillon said. She was about to take out her cell phone for pictures when she heard Ramsey mutter.

"Oh yeah? This is the third time I missed that piece of shit." By now, Ramsey was using her cell phone to ID the bodies. Dillon took a moment and began to understand how Glenn's getting away from her was only the first time around for her but for Ramsey, it was her third - the ambush in Spain, and then in Tangiers. This was the third time he slipped out.

Shit. That's right. I'd be really pissed too, if that was me.

"It sucks," she said, more to herself.

As she went back to snapping pictures of the dead men's faces to beam back to Janeson and her team for immediate facial recognition, she heard Andersen calling his people and the state troopers about the car that rammed her and Ramsey. There was one body she knew immediately. She was relived and sad at the same time. Dillon took a moment to look closely and carefully before she snapped his picture.

"Ana? Andersen? Looks like we found Daniels." She was surprised how anticlimactic and calm she was as she texted the picture to the control room. Andersen put his contact on hold to come around and see with Ramsey. Overall, though, Dillon felt a wave of relief.

"Well, one bad guy down."

"He's a pretty big fish. He was hit from two angles," Andersen commented as he pointed to two separate entrance wounds.

"Yeah, like he was ambushed. Kind of fitting if you ask me," Ramsey said, an obvious reference to the ambush in Spain.

"Can't say I'm sad to see him dead."

"Me neither." Dillon looked back at the empty vault.

Where are you, Burns?

#

Becky drove well within the town speed limits of Andover. She looked for the bank right off of Main Street that should be across from both the town library and old City Hall. Still reeling from the ongoing breaking news of chaos, mayhem and confusion, she found herself sympathetic with the citizens as she found being victim to it all was vastly different from being the one making the distraction.

Talk about a dose of your own medicine.

She drove more slowly than she needed so as not to miss her landmarks. She also noted that there were very few people on the road, making her car stand out. What made her route and travels more complicated was the appearance of mounted cameras and surveillance equipment installed in places she remembered being devoid of such devices.

"I guess things changed since the last time I was here creating havoc."

I've got to find Burns and get out of here. If I'm caught with my gear, it's going to be pretty hard to explain. Jesus...I have a flash guard and a thirty ammo clip – all pretty illegal in Massachusetts. Let alone, it was used in a crime across state lines. Actually...it would truly be ironic, she thought as she smiled at what David would have probably said.

"'You weren't responsible for this mess, but they could blame you for it anyway, and you would still be ahead,'" she said to herself.

At least I don't have four top-secret hard drives with me.

Her mind wandered as she remembered David's smile and his warm embrace. *God, I miss him.*

Becky recognized the landmarks and slowly turned the corner down the street making sure to use her blinkers. The parking lot looked empty. At the far end, she saw a very large recycling dumpster. She pulled her car right beside the dumpster, got out and opened the back door before she went looking for Burns. She scanned the rooftops and service poles. She was happy to see she was out of their primary field of vision, obscuring her task of collecting her package. Becky opened the large panel and saw Burns for the first time in months.

"Holy shit! You look like crap!"

She leaned in to pull him closer. He finally opened his eyes and gave her a weak smile. He crawled closer to her and then up through the panel. Becky couldn't help but wave her hands by her own nose to dissipate the smell as Burns approached. She was truly impressed with both Burns's degree of body odor and dishevelment.

"Jesus, Burns. Did they torture you and then throw you in a cesspool or something?" she said as she firmly got a hold of him.

It was strange to see him take his time. The normally hyper-vigilant Burns was drugged and completely not himself. It took him a long moment to look at her first before he spoke.

"Drugged for three days. Daniels is dead and I think Glenn killed him. I just need to sleep for a couple of days and have this shit work its way out." He crawled into the back seat. Becky felt her mind go blank as he uttered the words "Daniels is dead."

Finally. The man who killed David and my sister is dead...nothing. No joy. They're still gone.

She turned to help him get comfortable. He turned on his back and then she saw a strange expression come over his face.

"Burns? You alright?"

"Yes."

"What's wrong? What are you looking at?"

After what seemed like an eternity to her, he uttered his next full thought.

"I like your haircut. Makes you look younger." He then rolled over to his side to ostensibly sleep. Stunned more than surprised, Becky had to repeat to herself what she thought she heard.

"Great. Thanks, Burns."

She closed the door, climbed back into the driver's side, and took her cell phone to make a quick call. She put it on speakerphone as she started the car.

Last thing I need is to be pulled over for talking on the phone while driving. God, this state is restrictive! Didn't the Revolution start here? Tea Party and shit?

Buckling herself in, she started her long trek out of Andover with the plan of taking back roads only.

"Becky?" the voice said from the speaker.

"Murphy. I got the package. Will be off-grid for at least a week. He's been drugged and is pretty fucked up. Tell the girls he's fine though and we'll be back then," she said. She immediately thought of a quiet place just over the border in Rhode Island.

"Sounds good. I think I'll take the girls to Florida. You okay with that?"

Funny. He's an ex-mob boss asking for permission. Didn't we go over this already?

"Yes. But don't let Emma eat chocolate. Her face breaks out. And don't let Rosemarie have pineapple, she's allergic," Becky warned.

"What? She loves pineapple. How do you know?"

"Her throat and her mouth get itchy and she sneezes. Those are the first symptoms. Just don't let her have pineapple and she will be fine," Becky said. She tried to focus on driving and looking for a route out of Andover.

"Wait a minute. Is that just pineapple or all citrus fruit like oranges or apples?"

Are you kidding me? Do we have to do this now?

She looked at the phone as if it could understand her look of sarcasm. She shook her head to focus on getting Murphy off the phone.

"Murphy! I can either do or teach but I can't do both. Right now I have to 'do.' I'm trying to drive here. I've had a full day and I'm beginning to get cranky. Just don't let her have pineapple. Okay? I'll call you later once I'm settled. Okay?"

"Oh, yeah. Right. Call me when you're ready. Do you want to talk to the girls now or later?"

Are you trying to piss me off?

She took a deep breath, and took David's long-standing advice when dealing with people.

Pretend. Just breathe and pretend you're happy.

She cleared her throat and composed her next words that would hopefully end the conversation.

"Maybe later. Let them know I love them both and I will see them in a couple of days. I will call tonight to say goodnight. Thanks."

"Sounds good," Murphy said cheerfully.

Thanks be to Jesus Christ, our Lord and Savior.

"Thanks Murphy," she said as she closed the line.

Becky kept the radio off and she could hear Burns's snoring. She found herself actually relieved to get a break from the girls and Murphy.

"Do other terrorists have to do this? Really? It's like my work is never done." Becky waited patiently for the light to change.

#

Helms entered the near-empty cavern that was his control room. With only Janeson, Johnson, Gilmore and Crepes, Helms found himself wondering if it was the end of the world.

"I take it that you have deployed everyone to fight fires everywhere while you four hold down the fort," Helms said. He kept his windbreaker and sidearm on in case he needed to re-deploy. Janeson stood at full attention while looking at the floor-to-ceiling screen. She turned to address him with her hands behind her back.

"Boss? How was your flight?"

Helms was very surprised at the casual nature of the question. He decided to just answer the question and get an update rather than check on her mental status.

I'll get to that later.

He closed the gap between him and the small group. With the exception of Janeson, Helms could see they were all busy working at various monitors and stations.

"So what's the deal, Janeson?" Helms asked as he looked at the map of Rhode Island.

Now, what the hell is going on there?

"Well, Boss, while you are already aware that Ms. Littleton's shooting spree in Providence, Rhode Island resulted in Angelo Panelli getting shot, both Christine Dillon and Ana Ramsey confirm that they witnessed Jeffery Glenn at the crime scene where they also confirmed Eric Daniels's body. He and others apparently were shot. Facial recognition scan also confirms that it is his body. But as we are talking Eric Daniels, I plan to obtain a DNA sample as well."

Helms nodded his head in approval. He was pleased.

"Daniels is dead and Panelli is in the hospital while his sister and Alica Wise are in jail. Looks like a good day for the most part. Except Glenn."

"Yes. The nature of his escape and his parting hand gesture have already spread throughout the ranks."

"How did Glenn get away?" Helms asked.

"It appears that as Ms. Ramsey and Dillon were bearing down on him, they were struck by what appears to be a reinforced state trooper cruiser with ramming bumpers. I suspect that, based on the coordination of all these events and the transmissions of French at key points, Mr. Glenn obtained more than assistance from the French and most likely the Mossad."

Logical. Now for the million-dollar question.

"No sign of Burns?" Helms asked almost quietly. Because of Janeson's odd behavior and disposition towards moodiness of late, he was surprised with her immediate response. Based on her prickliness about Burns over the last couple of days, he was not sure what he was going to get.

"No signs or indications that he was at the site. No hard evidence of him being alive or dead."

Wait for it.

"But," Janeson continued, "I am convinced he is alive based on more circumstantial evidence obtained via cell phone transmissions forty-two minutes after Mr. Glenn's escape, courtesy of the NSA. Mr. Johnson? Please put on the transmission we obtained."

"Will do, Boss."

Helms found himself smiling at Johnson's use of the title "Boss" in responding to Janeson.

Maybe it is time to pass the torch. The Mrs. sure would be happy. Time to go to the tropics.

Helms snapped out of his daydreaming and focused on a somewhat static phone conversation.

Male: "Becky?"

Female: "Murphy. I got the package. Will be off-grid for at least a week. He's been drugged and is pretty fucked up. Tell the girls he's fine though and we'll be back then."

Male: "Sounds good. I think I'll take the girls to Florida. You okay with that?"

Female: "Yes. But don't let Emma eat chocolate. Her face breaks out. And don't let Rosemarie have pineapple, she's allergic."

Male: "What? She loves pineapple. How do you know?"

Female: "Her throat and her mouth get itchy and she sneezes. Those are the first symptoms. Just don't let her have pineapple and she will be fine."

Male: "Wait a minute. Is that just pineapple or all citrus fruit like oranges or apples?"

Female: "Murphy! I can either do or teach, but I can't do both. Right know I have to 'do.' I'm trying to drive here. I've had a full day and I'm beginning to get cranky. Just don't let her have pineapple, okay. I'll call you later once I'm settled. Okay?"

Male: "Oh, yeah. Right. Call me when you're ready. Do you want to talk to the girls now or later?"

Female: "Maybe later. Let them know I love them both and I will see them in a couple of days. I will call tonight to say goodnight. Thanks."

Male: "Sounds good."

Female: "Thanks Murphy,"

Smiling at the interchange, Helms could immediately tell that it was Becky Littleton talking to John Murphy.

"Somehow it all sounds normal – a parent telling the grandparent about some medical information about the children and the grandparent asking too many refining questions. Even these two have some normal qualities...a former mobster king and a trained assassin, former terrorist."

"Yes. Not the typical conversation one would expect," Janeson added.

"Well, both Ms. Littleton and Mr. Murphy get around. From a shoot-out in Providence to a pick-up in Andover, it looks like they have everything pretty well tied up."

Helms continued to look at the map of Rhode Island, but then he noticed that the map was more on the Rhode Island/Massachusetts border rather than Providence where the shootings were earlier.

"How come you're looking at the borders rather than the crisis and crime scenes?"

"Because, Boss, what usually happens next is Alex Burns disappears into thin air. And we know what's happening at the borders. It's Alex's and Ms. Littleton's location that remains unknown. And based on my earlier studies and research, I am convinced that I can narrow down where they will be in about a week, based on Ms. Littleton's last transmission regarding time, their proximity and the need to get out of sight quickly, and both of their needs to pay tribute to their loved ones."

Helms stood quietly for a moment so as to fully appreciate Janeson's work before he spoke.

Well, well, well. All those months of talking to Burns, reading, reviewing, and studying his files, hours of collecting poems...it's all paid off.

"You've found where Samantha Littleton's and Dr. Caulfield's bodies are buried," he said.

"Close, Director. Very close," Janeson said with the unusual addition of a smile. Helms looked back at the screen of the borders again.

Man, these kids have skills. Maybe it is time to pass the torch.

"So what are you going to do when you find it?"

Helms focused on the various towns near the borders away from big cities, especially the points indicating cemeteries and burial sites, active and inactive.

"I'm not sure," Janeson said as she stood behind him. "I guess just knowing where he is and what he is doing is better than not knowing," Janeson continued.

"You have an excellent point," he said.

You are so right.

Chapter 12

"'You don't talk with that man—you listen to him.'"

Joseph Conrad, <u>Heart of Darkness</u>

Five Days Later...

Welch rolled the tension out of her shoulders and waited patiently for Robert Tombs, Secret Service Director, to finish his dramatic monologue about how Daniels's death has finally taken America off the "shit list of the world." It was a phrase he said far too often. Not even Helms's comfortable leather chair with lumbar support could ease her backache. Ten days after their wild goose chase in Colorado, Welch was feeling the side effects of months of training with no rest, only to follow a lead to a dead end, and then miss all the action by three hours.

I knew it was a trap but it still sucks missing the fight.

She listened to ascertain if Tombs was still going through his list of international intelligence agencies that were now on speaking terms with the US again, and how the Mossad and French intelligence communities were "thanking" the US for "allowing them to complete their mission within US borders."

That is such bullshit! We're going to need wings stay above this crap they're flinging! Steve was so pissed that he missed getting Ruth and John. Even though there's no confirmation that they were there, he's positive that Glenn had their help.

Welch focused on what Tombs was saying just in case he was close to finishing. She heard what seemed to be a summary of key people positively affected by Daniels's death and Burns's "retirement."

At last. He might be close to done!

"Finally Liang of China and Vladimir of Russia are returning my calls. At least they believe we no longer mean to kill them all. I'm glad Helms secured DNA testing in conjunction with the pictures. Sey-yeon of North Korea is still on the outs but then again she liked it when the world simply hated the US."

Yeah. He still has a little bit more time to go.

Welch zoned out again. She cradled the phone to her ear with her neck so she could clean her nails a bit. She decided to put Tombs on speakerphone so she could find a nail file and do it right. Putting the phone down to find the phone manual, it only took her two minutes to find the right button before the speaker came to life, freeing her to multitask on the business of grooming.

"And lastly, there is one more piece of business I want to mention," Tombs said.

Thank God!

She had found a nail clipper with a file in her purse and was done at the same time he seemed to finish.

"Now that you're going to be a free agent after months of screwing around looking for Daniels..."

"Hey! I almost lost a soldier there, you know. And Ice took a nasty hit to the head," Welch protested as she leaned forward to address the speaker.

"Well, what do you think is going to happen when you charge into an abandoned mine? Anyway, Ice has a hard head and I'm sure it did little harm. But seriously Welch, what about Allied Federation International, Inc.? The Board of Directors there want a more seasoned, 'hands on' CEO that has some clout and integrity. After all this and your support from the President on down, you would be a perfect fit."

Tombs had been telling Welch about this defense company for a while. While headquartered in Washington D.C. with offices in Boston, Texas, California, Frankfurt and London, he had been selling her the position of running a defense company that supported the US Armed Forces and private agencies in everything from data collection to personal protection of VIP's to military transports. It was a huge job, and Welch was able to avoid the discussion while she searched for Daniels and finish the Senate Hearings on the defunct Foreign Intelligence Agency.

"I don't know, Bob. Don't you have someone else to hound?" Welch asked.

There was a long moment of silence, so long that Welch thought she might have dropped the call.

"Welch. It is a powerful company that needs a strong leader that can handle the power and make good, ethical decisions. I am going to assume that because you're a woman, you are second-guessing yourself when you are more than qualified. If you were a guy, I wouldn't have to convince you of anything, except that maybe you weren't God. But that's a gender thing. It's also not lost on me that the Foreign Intelligence Agency's Operation Center started out this way but as you can see, 'absolute power corrupts absolutely.' I need...no, *we all* need someone who has not just the tenacity and experience, but a person we can all trust. You would get to create your own leadership team, reconfigure the goals and missions, and restructure the company so that it serves not just US interests but the interests of our allies, new and old, and even some of our enemies out there."

Welch was struck by Tombs's sincerity and clarity of what he was asking.

You can always depend on Tombs to be blunt and to the point. The hard sell is not his strong suit unless he believes in it.

After another moment of silence, Welch found herself feeling the same way she did when the Marine recruiter came to her college. The day she saw the Twin Towers fall.

I can do this with the right people. People of integrity. Independent thinkers. And there is still one man who is yet to be found... Oman Sharif Sudani. Where are you? None of us would have been in the Swat Valley if it wasn't for you, and your friend Bin Laden.

"I can make my own team?" Welch asked. She started to feel a bit more excited about embarking on a new mission. She always felt that way and it showed.

"Yes. You can hire and recruit anyone you think is up for the job. Even Nine and Ice, though I suspect that you already thought of them. Someone has to man the front desk, I suppose."

"Hey! I owe them!" Welch said as she heard Tombs laughing but then return to being serious again.

"You are so easy to bust, you know?"

"I'm working on it, Tombs. I haven't said yes, yet."

Quite a range of emotion today.

"But also, word on the street is that Helms is retiring in a month. I bet he would be interested in consulting at least during start-up."

Still thinking about a new opportunity, Welch had already put together her short list and long list of whom she would ask. Helms and Andersen were near the apex while "the girls", as she was fond of saying, were also at the top of the list.

"I would have to do due diligence. Probably three to four months. Is that too long?"

"Are you kidding? The present CEO was planning on it taking a year to get a short list together let alone months of review. So are you in or out?" Tombs asked.

It took Welch a little longer than anticipated to finally answer him but when she did, it was short.

"I'm in."

As more silence passed, Welch could hear Tombs strumming his fingers on his own desk.

I guess I was on speakerphone too. I wonder if he heard my clipping?

"Okay. I'll let the CEO and the President know. I'm going to have the Board of Director's President set things up for you to take a look at things at their headquarters and their offices. How long do you have with the Bureau?"

Taking in a sigh though still smiling, Welch had to remember what day it was before she could answer. Just as she was about to answer, she saw Helms peeking into his own office to see if she was done. Waving him, Welch gave the short answer.

"About three weeks. If there are no pending issues, then the contract is up." After another brief moment, Welch could hear Tombs shifting papers before he signed off.

"Great. Welch? You're not going to regret this. I promise."

"I hope not," Welch responded as she hit the button to close the line.

Welch leaned back behind Helms's desk while he sat on the other side. She was about to get up to give him back his seat when he waived for her to remain sitting as he asked his question.

"So I take it you are seriously considering the CEO position of that defense company," he said as he folded his hands above his chest. Welch felt a bit of calm wash over her as she envisioned the future project. With the end of her career with the State Troopers and now with her role ending with both the investigation and hunt for Eric Daniels, she felt some relief that she might have something more to do than to stalk her boys and her grandchildren in Florida.

Ugh! I hate Florida. Old men and women playing shuffle board. Slow death's waiting room.

She pushed the image out of her head and re-focused on Helms's question.

"Yeah. It beats the alternatives of retiring, reading books and playing board games."

"Not likely. Sounds like retirement."

"Marines never retire, unless we're re-grouping in hell, oorah?

"Oorah."

Welch found herself suddenly focusing on Helms's smiling with an accompanying sparkle in his eyes.

"What's up with you?"

He shrugged his shoulders as he stood up. His smile seemed to broaden as he turned towards the office door as he spoke.

"Nothing. I was just wondering how much money you're going to make as CEO. But before I forget, there's a call for you on line two. He's been waiting for ten minutes and said he would wait, 'for as long as it takes,' I think he said."

Who the hell? Well it's clearly not Darlene, she thought as she was about to hit the speakerphone.

"Ah no, Diane. I wouldn't put it on speakerphone. We did do a quick background check on him, as is customary with people in your position."

"What? "People in my position?" What the hell?"

He didn't answer. Speechless, Welch made what she knew was her classic look of confusion with raised eyebrows and arms. While exiting the office door, Helms continued speaking.

"Ah yes. His name is Peter. He says you know him as 'the excavator.' He apparently has some follow-up on the devices used to try to kill you and your team in Colorado. And just so you know, he's a volunteer firefighter, teaches geology in high school, divorced thirteen years ago and is on good terms with his ex-wife. He also spends a lot of time with his two girls' and two boys' families and children. And he's 51 years young." Helms didn't wait for a response as the door shut. Still stunned by the new business opportunity, Welch felt truly out of her element as she looked at the blinking light.

Okay.

Startled at her own confusion for just a second, she started to smile as she felt her chest release tension, and she picked up the phone to connect the call.

#

God, I hate it when the parents fight.

Ramsey sat quietly in the front seat while Davis drove and

Cratty awkwardly sat in the back seat.

"I just don't understand why we're heading north of the airport when I live south of Boston," Cratty complained. It was easy to tell that Cratty shifted in her seat to get comfortable in her cast.

Oh man. She's not going to like this one at all. The last time Davis did something like this, Cratty was thrown out of a bar.

Ramsey looked out the window as innocently as she could. Being an accomplice with Davis did not sit well with her as she knew she was terrible at lying, especially to her boss. She watched the passing cars and made note of every souped-up charger she saw as memories of her being rammed ten days earlier were still fresh in her head.

That pale, white bastard! Next time I see you, you won't get away, you slick sack of shit. She felt her own healing scar on her head. Smirking for only a moment, she saw the irony of her giving him a scar several months ago, and now her nursing one as a result.

You think this is a mother fucking game? We're not even! You killed my friends. I'm going to find you and the first thing I'm going to do is cut off that middle finger and shove it...

"Ramsey!" she heard Cratty say loudly.

"What!?"

"Where were you? Still thinking about that rat bastard?"

"Yeah. I was just twenty feet away from making him my hood ornament when the little white rat had his friends take us out."

Even as she spoke, she felt her stitches.

"Don't worry about it. You and Dillon got at least three more months left in your contract to find him. I'm guessing he will make some mistake and you'll get him," Cratty said reassuringly.

Cratty's voice sounded somber. Ramsey turned to look at her and could see that she looked sad.

Man. It's got to suck being sidelined. Six months of rehab? Shit!

"How are you doing, Boss?"

Clearly changing the subject, Ramsey could see that Cratty looked for something else to discuss instead of her physical therapy and rehabilitation to come.

"I would be fine if I knew what deranged logic possessed Davis to drive to her own home when she could have dropped me off from the airport when I was just ten minutes away," Cratty kvetched.

Davis looked as if she was going to ignore her but then she clearly decided to take another approach.

"Denise, my tiny, abbreviated friend. Why are you in such a rush to return to that second-floor, poorly furnished though very tidy room you call a home? How were you going to get up to the second floor above the pizza shop anyway? The only good news with that place, other than the rent, delivery from downstairs would have been easy."

Ramsey turned to look out the window and tried to shrink in her seat. Davis slowed her speed to under the speed limit and drove as if she didn't have a care in the world.

Shit! What are you doing? She's going to know that you were at her place! Or worse – like last time, she's going to figure I was there. It's like the Purple Sierras all over again.

Ramsey did not want to witness the explosion. An eerie silence fell over the car as Ramsey felt her teeth grind and her eyes wince. She was sure Cratty was going to somehow lean forward and strangle Davis. It was quiet. Too quiet. For just a moment, Ramsey thought maybe she didn't hear. That was until she heard the deadly tone underneath Cratty's words.

"Jillian. Am I to assume that you have already been to my apartment? Or worse, sent someone I trust to spy on me...again?"

The tone was both icy and volatile at the same time. Ramsey felt her eyes peering through her as if they were lasers.

"Well, 'apartment' is more of an overstatement for that room. But unfortunately, when I checked to see if it was handicapped accessible, I discovered there were no public records of it being a legitimate apartment, as in on the books with the town and all. And even though it's a furnished room for rent, it appears that the landlord did not disclose his profits to the IRS. The good news here is that he is very appreciative of your service to our country, so much so that he refunded three of the last six months of rent while you were in the field, since you weren't even there. The bad news is, and I agree, since there is no easy way in or out for you, you need another place to live. And that, my little, petite friend is where your pal, me, comes in." Her speech was delivered cheerily as she pulled slowly up to her own home. Ramsey had watched Davis as she spoke. It was as if she believed she had done Cratty a great service. Getting rid of Cratty's apartment was as big a favor as getting her thrown out of a bar and slapped by her date.

Okay. Well, it was nice knowing you, Davis. I'll ask Janeson to find and notify any next of kin once they identify your body.

Ramsey did not dare to look back. She felt the pit of her stomach press upon her bladder and stared forward for fear Cratty would kill her next.

She's just like my mother. Small but dangerous! I'm not here, I'm not here...

"Ana Bastante Marie Ramsey? Were you a part of this? No mientas."

The question was delivered in the same deadly tone she gave Davis.

Oh, God. Shit no. How does she know my full name...

"Now Denise! What did I tell you about pulling the kids into our arguments when you're angry?"

By now, Davis put the car in park, turned off the engine, smiled at Cratty and then exited the car. Ramsey jumped out of the car as if it were about to explode. She moved quickly to the back of the car where Davis was opening the trunk. Ramsey pulled Davis closer so Cratty wouldn't hear.

"Davis?! Are you crazy? Is that your problem? She's going to kill you. Not now but when you're sleeping! You know she can do it too! You're crazy to have her stay with you! Now I'm going to have to help her get rid of your body. I feel bad but I'll do it!"

"What? I think she's handling it quite well," Davis said.

"She's just taking your size and measurements for your grave!"

"Aren't you overreacting, Ana? I mean, really?"

Suddenly, a blood-curdling scream erupted from the back seat of the car and the only intelligible words Ramsey could figure out were "fuck" and "Davis." After seconds of banging on the door to get out, Ramsey ran around to open it before Cratty started shattering the car windows with her crutches.

"Ah, let me get that, boss," Ramsey said as she opened the car door that was being hammered. Cratty pulled herself out of the car while banging her foot-to-hip cast and her crutches in the process. She winced in pain. Ramsey was glad Cratty wasn't armed. That is until she saw that the crutches themselves looked as if they could be easily wielded. Cratty brushed by her in a rage. Ramsey counted her blessings and got her cell phone ready to call 911. It was a toss-up as to whether to get the police or an ambulance there first.

"Damn it, Jillian! What is your problem? That was my home..." Cratty started.

"Denise? Please. That was a fourteen-by-fifteen way-station until the next mission. But there's not going to be one for a while. And there was no way you were going to be able to get in and out of the building, let alone your room. You got several months of rehab and then physical therapy. How were you going to do all that from there?" Davis handed Ramsey Cratty's personal belongings from the apartment which were easily contained in one suitcase. Cratty noted the exchange and continued.

"I could have managed."

"Oh and if there was a fire? I mean, if your place wasn't above a pizza parlor with its ovens, I would have played the odds."

"The *best* pizza in Boston. And I had personal stuff. You went through all my stuff?"

"Technically, no. We found all six drawers, a bare medicine cabinet, and threw out the old, rotted food from the refrigerator and cabinets. We just dumped the clothes in the suitcase. Not much in the way of variety of clothes. Undergarments, however, I must say you either have high hopes or you plan ahead where it counts." Davis looked as if she were finished. She had been fishing through her pockets to find her keys.

Cratty remained unusually silent. She looked at Davis as if she were going to argue. With eyes narrowed and knuckles turning white from clutching the rungs of her crutches, Ramsey was surprised by Cratty's response.

"Two weeks, Davis. Two weeks and if it doesn't work, you have to help me find another place to live," she sneered out. Cratty ambled to the front door. Ramsey remembered to take a breath and looked at Davis who gave her the thumbs up for success. She followed Davis to the house.

"Madre de Dios!"

Once at the door, she was hoping to simply drop off the suitcase and run back to the office. Instead, the hits just kept coming. She watched Davis turn the key in the lock and give Cratty a heads up as to what was on the other side of the door.

It's got to be better than out here, Ramsey thought. The view of the fallow lawn, dead trees and burnt flowers and bushes did not inspire hope.

"So just so you know, I haven't been home for several days and I turned off the air conditioner before I left."

As she opened the door, Cratty rolled her eyes at what Ramsey originally thought was Davis's excuse for the unseen mess. After a moment, even she could feel the heat with accompanying garbage smell wafting out of the house.

"And I might have forgotten to take the garbage out for a while. Just give me a moment," Davis said. She disappeared into the house leaving Ramsey alone with Cratty. Standing quietly, staring at Ramsey, Cratty uttered in a low, menacing voice what was on her mind.

"First, it was the Purple Sierras and now it's Davis's home for two weeks. Don't think for one second I forgot your role in this, Ana. Not now, not tomorrow, maybe not even next month, but at some point, I am going to make you pay for this."

Ramsey squinted her eyes and raised her shoulders as if she were about to be hit. She gave a weak smile before looking back at the ground to avoid eye contact. In life, the one person she feared without reservation was her mother, Sophia. That is, until she felt—

more than heard — Cratty's threat.

Okay. Time to go inside and get out of this hellhole.

The door opened and the heat and stench rushed out. Ramsey didn't wait for Davis to return and moved quickly into the house.

I swear she's worse than my mother – she makes me feel so guilty, too! It would be easier if I were innocent.

The heat enveloped her as she walked in. She tried to not hold her nose. All the rumors about Davis's Spartan apartment were understated. The front room had only one large reclining chair with a couple of small tables, a television, and unfinished wall repairs around the windows. Fighting the urge to run, Ramsey watched Davis enter the room and apparently caught some kind of face that Cratty had made.

"Okay, Denise. How about this. You give it two weeks and if you hate it, I'll help you find an apartment that is close to the rehab facility," she offered.

"I don't know, Davis. It's summer and I bet I can get some homeless shelter to take in a former, disabled veteran..." Cratty trailed off. It was easy to see she was looking all around her. Ramsey couldn't tell if she was thinking or if she was too shocked for words.

"Alright. How about this. If you stop complaining, I will decorate your room any way you want," Davis threw in.

"You decorate?" Ramsey pointed her head towards the front room.

"Well, obviously I would have your assistance."

"Obviously. You own this?"

"Sure do. Mortgage free and no bills."

Ramsey turned to see that Cratty was looking into the guest room and did not seem too hopeful about its future.

"I don't know. It's going to take a lot of money to get this room to look inhabitable, let alone presentable," Cratty said as she shook her head.

"Oh my God! You're such a girly-girl. What are you going to need? You just sleep in it, right?" Davis's question looked genuine.

"Cracks need to be sealed, sanded and then primed and painted. Preferably oil-base paint. The rug needs to be pulled up. God knows how much mold and mildew is under there. I bet there is some salvageable hardwood floor. You know what, Davis, since you saved my life, I'll pay for any renovating needed for this room," she countered.

"How about this," Davis proposed, "If you stop complaining, I will split the cost and let you stay here as long as you need."

"Oh...joy," Cratty said. She took another look around and then ambled to the kitchen.

This just can't work. They're totally opposite. Oh, man! Why do I ever listen to Davis and her stupid ideas?

"You see, Ramsey? You worry too much. Cratty's going to be fine," Davis said.

"Who's your next of kin, Davis? They'll be getting a new house once Cratty is finished with you."

"My God, woman. Such melodrama. Denise will be fine."

"Well, the stove is absolutely spotless from lack of use. I guess there's a silver lining to every cloud," Cratty yelled from the kitchen.

"You cook, Cratty?" Davis said as she went to the kitchen to join her. Ramsey took in a deep breath, thinking that maybe their rooming together might possibly work as she put Cratty's suitcase down.

Then again, maybe this could work.

"Jesus, Davis! This refrigerator is early 1930s. What do you spend your money on? It's obviously not for keeping up the house, appliances or lawn care!"

"Shooting. Ammunition mostly." Ramsey heard Davis respond casually.

Or maybe not.

Chapter 13

"I have a very old and very faithful attachment for dogs. I like them because they always forgive."

Albert Camus, <u>The Fall</u>

Ten Days Later...

Burns continued to go back and forth on whether he wanted to go back to using his middle name as his first again or to just keep things the way they are. After ten days of detoxing, cleaning himself up and writing down everything he remembered from his hallucinations, visions or revelations, or whatever they were, Burns found he was genuinely split on what to do. When he asked Becky what she thought, she laughed and said, "it doesn't matter to me, Burns. I use your last name anyway." For now, he had to make a quick visit, pick up his keepsake and start an extended search for a hidden bunker.

Burns put the car into park and exited the driver's seat to allow Becky to take over the driving.

"Are you sure you don't want to come in and visit? There's no one here at this time."

Becky shook her head no, adjusted her seat and mirror as she spoke.

"I came here two days ago to spend some time. I'm good for a while. Are you sure you don't want me to wait around? No bother, really."

"No. I'm going to be off-grid for a while but I'll keep you in the loop as things develop."

"You're on the hunt, aren't you, Burns?"

"Long hunt, big game, final solution."

"So you don't need a ride to start with, rather than public transportation?" Becky asked.

Pulling his backpack out of the back seat, Burns adjusted his light vest and found his cash and express bus schedule.

"No. I'm good. Becky?"

Becky looked at him as she put on her sunglasses.

"Thank you. Thank you for saving my life and helping me get through this last bout."

Cocking her head to the side, Becky gave Burns what he thought was one of her warmer smiles.

"That's what family does," she said.

Funny. That's what David would often say.

"Anyway, based on what you told me, if I keep doing all these good things, I might become like that 'Good Samaritan' guy and be rewarded in heaven," Becky said. She shifted the car into drive, pulled slowly away and gave Burns a wave.

"Give my love to Emma and Rosemarie."

Becky gave him the thumbs up as she drove away.

Burns reflected on how she just didn't seem to be comfortable with strong emotions.

Just like Sam. Just like David, too.

He pulled himself and gear together and walked to see Samantha and David. Burns felt great, the best he had felt in days, maybe years. He walked slowly in his new clothes and shoes as dusk fell. He calculated he had about two hours to spend before he needed to catch the 9:00PM express bus to Boston for a connecting bus that would take him to California. He touched the tablet he took from Daniels in his pocket. He made sure it was securely affixed to him. There was a lot of data to mine.

So many secrets and yet you have no passwords on it. Must have thought you'd never need to.

As Burns reached the top of the small hill where the mausoleum sat, he knew that the caretakers would be leaving the grounds entirely in just forty-five minutes. Though it was early September, it was warm. A breeze picked up that made the environs look and feel more desolate. He looked up at the red sky as night approached. While he felt good, he also felt alone and tired. The last time he was there was right before he allowed himself to be captured. He had spent the night sound asleep in the crypt with Samantha, and with David's body soon to arrive. As he read the inscription in German, he noticed that the crypt's door was as expected - solidly in place. He rolled his shoulders before he applied pressure to pull the heavy door open and then he felt a wave of sadness.

David has to be here by now.

Firmly closing the door behind him, he slowly walked to the center of the crypt, smelling incense. At first there was a faint smell of lilac as he approached but then a much stronger, persistent odor of cinnamon.

Hmm. Just like my time with Sam in the hotel lobby.

Sighing, he saw Samantha's smiling face at first, and then he saw that indeed David's picture was in place and his placement more settled than he imagined.

Just like old times. Hanging out together in Rhode Island. I guess you were right, David.

He felt sadness fall upon him but to his surprise, his scars remained still, no burning or itching to speak of. He walked to the back of Samantha's crypt. He bent down and focused on retrieving his necklace which he had hid for safekeeping before he allowed himself to be captured.

I hope it's still there. I'd hate for Samantha to be pissed about that.

He turned to extend his hand. As he bent over, he saw what appeared to be a picture set in the frame by his assigned crypt.

Okay. Since I'm not dead, this could be a problem.

He stopped instinctively and moved to the picture set to see a series of pictures of Roxie with a sealed envelope that held a bulge. He carefully looked at the pictures first. He could see that they were taken by a digital camera rather than a zoom scope that might be on a sniper rifle.

Alright. So far pictures of a dog. Just so happens to be candid pictures of my dog that Janeson is watching. Ergo...

It was easy to see that the background setting was the FBI regional office in Boston. Extracting a pair of disposable gloves from his backpack, he looked closely at the envelope in one hand and with a spring-assisted knife in the other, he prepared for a careful operation. After he was sure it was not laced with some chemical agent, he surgically cut the top off and tipped out an old cell phone. He narrowed his eyes as he looked at the cell phone first. He sighed.

"Burns...you must be getting old, senile or just plain sloppy." Suddenly, the phone vibrated with an incoming call.

"Of course," he said to himself. He looked around the vault for any new items that might be in the room.

"Hello," he said as he focused in on two new icons that were carefully placed to observe the door and the middle of the room. He surveyed the larger wall area and also found a small, well-lit framed picture of Caspar David Friedrich's *Wandered above the Sea Fog* portrait. He was amazed that such a conspicuously placed portrait was so readily overlooked.

Now this is like déjà vu all over again.

"Alex. It is very nice to hear your voice."

The voice was a very welcoming, familiar one. He moved closer to inspect the portrait to confirm it was the same one he saw when he was in and out of the world ten days ago. The portrait's and icons' frames were replaced with a thicker wood with an additional two new pots of flowers that helped balance out the entire room filled with hidden cameras. He guessed there would be more than six to cover the entire vault area under complete surveillance.

Nice placements. Solid coverage. I bet she has sound here, too.

"Well, Rachael, if anyone was going to find it, I thought it would be you."

He pushed out the defeat of being caught and moved right into a new focus. He calmly cradled the old-style FBI cell phone with his shoulder to his ear and went back to retrieving his necklace.

"While Ms. Littleton is very good at subterfuge and evasion, she does not have your level of expertise. I believe she was also compromised by her emotions when she made arrangements for Dr. Caulfield. Did you find all the cameras?"

Burns held his necklace in his hand. He smiled as he thought of Samantha's smiling, warm image he remembered from his time with Daniels.

Real or hallucinations? I'd like to think it was all real. Regardless, your necklace is safe with me, Sam.

"I found six for sure but I might have missed some. Did I?"

He asked as he placed the chain and cross around his neck.

It's been too long.

It comfortably fell on his chest.

"Actually there are eight inside and three outside, with one at the main entrance. Still, I am impressed with your rapid assessment of the situation and your preparedness with latex gloves. The cell phone is not bugged should you wish to take it. I recommend you use it to call me at a later date at the office, should you want to contact us," Janeson said quietly.

Hmm. Is that a bit of sadness?

"Was there anything else that gave the site away?" Burns asked with genuine professional interest.

"Yes. If it wasn't for the inscription on the mausoleum, referencing the "Albatross Family" in German, I might have passed by it. Observing Ms. Littleton's arrival two days ago confirmed I was right. How you managed to remove this site off the visitor's map while keeping it on the groundskeepers' roster for maintenance is still a mystery I am hoping you will reveal at some point."

"You know German?"

"Yes."

"And your choice of Friedrich's work. Was it yours?"

"I have always loved Mary Shelley's work. Especially her modern Prometheus piece that sported that picture as a cover."

"*Frankenstein*? And the portrait synonymous with the romantic period?" Burns said.

"You're familiar with it, I see."

"Sure am."

"And I suppose you're trying to keep from answering how you managed to keep this crypt on the maintenance rotation but off the map in addition to gaining insight as to my preferences?"

As they spoke, Burns had been going through his backpack to rearrange a few items as he spoke.

"Sorry Rachael, but the groundskeeping and map thing are both secret. Actually I am glad you called. Would you be able to take care of Roxie for a while? I have to go back into the field to tie up a major loose end from a couple of years back. I would greatly appreciate it."

He located maps of California, Wisconsin and Missouri. He took a moment to feel his pockets and made sure that he had Daniels's smartphone and tablet in his possession.

There's a lot there. A lot of secrets. I know he had a place, but where?

It was Janeson's voice that reminded him of where he was. Initially quiet, Burns was happy to hear the tenor in her voice lighten as if she were happier.

"I would be happy to take care of her," she said.

He also heard what he thought was surprise in her voice. As there was no initial resistance, he went on with his thoughts.

"I would like to remain in contact, the way we did when I was in Colorado except I would like to schedule it out, and if possible, visit from time to time, in person, if that would be alright with you?" He listened and hoped he wasn't too blunt for her.

"Yes. I would very much like that," she said. He remembered all the times they had spoken before and could tell by her thoughtful response and watching Roxie that staying in contact was not an imposition. He felt his mouth and eyes crinkling upward. Burns took her response as positive and looked at the pictures of his dog. He took two of them and carefully folded them, and then went to both Samantha's and David's frames to take a picture of each that he liked.

"So, can you tell me what the mission is or is that on a need-to-know?" Janeson asked.

Nodding with approval of his choice of pictures, he placed them all in his backpack and then pulled it on his back to prepare to leave.

"Need-to-know, Rachael. Sorry. But let Welch know I'll be calling her. Looks like Daniels had her phone number on speed dial. I think she'll appreciate the mission I'm on, if I'm right."

"Is there a security issue?"

"I don't think so. It's more of a treasure hunt."

"Anything associated with Daniels is not to be trifled with."

"Trust me. I'm sure that if there is a treasure, it's booby-trapped and set for self-destruct. Daniels and his specter are never without surprises."

Burns had pulled all his gear together and was ready to move out. He turned to each crypt, made the Eastern Orthodox sign of the cross three times in rapid succession before returning to the phone conversation.

Your memories will be eternal.

He looked closely at the phone contacts of the calls and committed Janeson's to memory before he spoke again.

"So, Rachael, I gotta go now. I have the number but I can't take the phone. I'm still working on my trust issues and while I trust you, between the Panellis, Carter and the Wise siblings, I want to make sure there is no chance of a trace. Still, I am impressed with your detective work. I will call you in two days' time during work hours. How's 3:00 PM?"

"I'll be working the second shift. How about 10:15 PM Eastern time?" Burns could tell by her expression that she was excited.

"You got it. Say hello to everyone and will talk to you in two days," he said.

"Alex? Be careful," she whispered.

"Will do," he said. He closed the line, dropped the phone on the floor and casually saluted goodbye at the cameras. He took his time and walked out of the mausoleum and backtracked his steps.

Shaking his head as he reviewed how he had essentially walked into a trap, it was easy to guess what David and Samantha might have said.

"You must be getting old."

Hm. No itching. Nothing. Well, Sam? Is this what you meant about letting go?

Chapter 14

"...Horror he had adjusted to. But monotony was the greater obstacle, and he realized it now, understood it at long last. And understanding it seemed to give him a sort of quiet peace,..."

Richard Matheson, *I am Legend and Other Stories*

Four Months Later...

Andersen took the long way to work. He drove through the tree-lined side streets of North Reading, with sunglasses and windows open in his late-model Crown Victoria sedan. He felt an easy, almost blatant smile on his face as he casually drove to work. With Daniels's case closed, Burns MIA and Murphy reportedly on vacation visiting his granddaughters, he predicted having time to focus on his real job of local police work. As the sun shone brightly, Andersen drove into the "Police Only" parking lot of the station. He stepped out of his car, stretched his back, took out his jacket and finally retrieved his coffee.

Ahh. No briefcase, all caught up at work, and only need to conduct a few interviews and make calls. It doesn't get any better than this. And it only took a couple of months to get back to normal. He felt so comfortable that he ambled towards the entrance rather than his quick, "on police business" march he typically used. With no more international intrigue and an end to domestic terrorism, Andersen began to feel more hopeful that he might be able to spend more time with Laura and the kids. As he thought about Laura, the kids and his financial future, his mind turned to the serious subject of Diane Welch's offer to join her new venture.

If I wasn't so close to retirement and getting the kids ready for college, I would take the job in a second. Maybe a high-paying "consultant" position might be possible.

His thoughts suddenly froze in place as he came across an all-too-familiar sight.

No way. She's got pretty big balls coming here!

From easy-going to police alert, he picked up his pace as his jawline hardened. Andersen moved in quickly on the two people waiting outside the staff door entrance. Just like last time, both looked as if they were trying to tone down their hypervigilant posture and presentation and blend in.

"Well, well, well. Ruth. You should be happy I haven't found any evidence to tie you into that crisis you created and Daniels's death. Ramming federal agents and fleeing a crime scene are minor in comparison to murder of US citizens. And the chaos you created? I'm going to find a way to get the evidence and when I do, I will find a way to make the charges stick. And where's your friend, John?"

Ruth stood up straight from leaning against the wall and gave a remarkably brilliant smile as she looked Andersen straight in the eyes as she spoke.

"Lieutenant. I believe I was not in your country four months ago but I understand that while the crisis in this area appeared serious, I believe there were no injuries sustained from the chaos, except, of course, I do hear that Mr. Daniels was killed. Were there others?"

Yeah. Nice innocent look. Not really convincing, though.

Andersen tried to release his clenching fists. He decided to disengage from a losing argument.

"Hmm. So who is this?" Andersen pointed to Ruth's dark-haired, tall friend with piercing blue eyes. Without extending his hand, the tall man spoke in a language that sounded Italian.

"Ciao. James," he said with a brief nod. While he made eye contact for just a moment, he went back to scanning the area for danger.

Just great! The French and Israelis aren't enough! Did anyone get the memo that Daniels is dead and the case is closed?

"Yes, Lieutenant. His name is James. He is less talkative than my French friend, John. John is on assignment. James is from the Italian Military Intelligence. While Mr. Daniels's demise is welcomed, there are some missing files and data that we would all like to make sure never see the light of day," Ruth said calmly.

"Tell me about it. Last time his files came to light, my country fell in the cross-hairs of the world."

"Yes. It was not good for you Americans."

"No, it was not. So there is more shit out there?"

No way! More shit? Please, God, make this end! And how do the Italians fit it?

"The information I'm talking about would make the prior release look like...how do you Americans say...'a walk in the park,'" she said.

"Are you shitting me? Worse? And the Italians are involved too? Now I have to worry about the Italian intelligence community in addition to the Mossad? Now what do you people want?"

Andersen knew that his frustration was evident. He continued as any thought of peace in his time slipped away.

"And what are these files and data she's talking about? More secrets to set the planet on fire again? Worse than last time?"

"Lieutenant, I am here only as a courtesy. Why would you be so angry at me when we are trying to collaborate with our US friends and allies? Our only purpose is to maintain the proper world order," Ruth said with almost a convincing pout.

Ugh...just great. "Proper world order?" What the hell is that?

Not at all convinced of the sincerity, Andersen decided to remain focused and blunt.

"What is it, Ruth?"

Smiling again, it appeared as if Ruth were going to simply state what was happening.

"Well, as you know, while your Alica Wise and her brother are at large in your country, we have taken an interest in our own national security."

"Really? Alica Wise poses a danger to the Israelis and the Italians?"

"No," Ruth corrected. "The Wise siblings in conjunction with Colonel Timothy Carter pose a danger. This is the same Carter that Mr. Tombs and Mr. Helms are concerned with, justifiably so. Mr. Carter's alliance with an unlikely enemy of the state is concerning, but again, I digress."

"Who is Carter associated with?"

"That will become evident at some point, I am sure," she said. While Andersen was surprised that Ruth knew the week-old data, he was surprised at the depth of their surveillance.

Well, I won't get an answer to that, for sure.

"A federal judge gave her a pass on most of the charges and she is reportedly not able to leave the country until further questioning."

"Yes," Ruth said immediately. "And while the FBI had been able to keep up with her for some time, she is presently missing. But of more pressing concern, Mr. Angelo Panelli has been in constant communication with some key crime bosses in Italy. This concerns both us and our Italian friends." She spoke with less than a positive tone and no smile on her face. For the first time since their meeting, James was now fully engrossed in the conversation.

That is disturbing. Wise missing. Carter underground and has some connection to a bad guy, and Panelli building up resources. Daniels's missing files...just great!

"While all important, they are all secondary to the mission your Mr. Alexander Burns has embarked upon. We are confident that he will be successful," she said calmly.

Burns? A mission? What mission? What now?

Still in thought and completely confused by this new revelation, Andersen was jolted out of his thinking when Ruth closed the distance between them.

Jesus! I hate when you do that!

"Once again, we offer our services. I believe you still have my card?" she asked sweetly.

"Okay. That's just creepy," he said as he backed up. To his surprise, Ruth did not take offense. She didn't move but still smiled.

"But you still have my card?"

"Yes," Andersen said quickly so as to get her away from him as soon as possible.

"Good," she said. She suddenly turned and walked away with James closely in tow.

With eyes narrowed, still clutching his coffee, Andersen forced himself to talk.

"Thank you."

Without turning back, Ruth waved back to him as both remarkably fit specimens kept walking.

"Yes. Thank you for the new set of headaches, trouble and a whole lot of problems on the horizon. Just great. Time to let the troops know...and what the hell is she talking about Burns?" Coffee cold and peace of mind shattered, Andersen found his cell phone.

#

Welch was pleased that she didn't have to rely on GPS to find Davis's house in Wakefield. The directions that she gave her were just perfect, as was her timing. She pulled in by the curb while Davis pulled into her own driveway. As Welch gathered her portfolio of papers together and put away her glasses, she caught sight of Davis juggling her gun case and a bag of groceries out of the trunk.

I knew I should have waited until morning. It's dinner time and people have lives. But this is really a good idea. With this talent and our connections, this could really fly.

After four months of Daniels's case being closed and most of the loose ends tied up, Welch was focused on taking over a security consulting and protection firm for the last month. After talking to

Helms and Andersen about her idea and outlining how a firm might run and find funding, Welch had to pull in key players she could trust to make it work.

But it was Tombs who once again opened a door to the future.

Now to recruit all the players.

Her mind immediately jumped to Davis and Cratty. She did think of Steve Andersen but knew he was in a tight spot.

He could make a lot more money if he joined us but he's only three years from full retirement, and a lifetime of health care and pension is pretty hard to let go when your kids are still at home. She did feel bad about leaving her friend out of the loop of her new agenda item which was a new mission with Alexander J. Burns. Her conversation with Burns was brief but it had sweeping ramifications. Something about tying up loose ends "in a big way," and it was related to a hidden site. This mission was so important, Welch devised a two-tiered plan. Operations fell immediately into place but that meant keeping just a few in the know while sparing the others, until maybe the very end.

Anyway, he'll make some good money as a consultant if it's not a conflict of interest.

As Welch looked at Davis's house, she was hopeful that since she and Cratty were not yet employed, they might be open to a new venture.

How far should I bring them in? They certainly can do it. Maybe we should bring the Mossad in after all?

When she talked to Davis on the phone earlier about it and her plans to involve Cratty, Dillon and Ramsey if they were interested, Davis suggested that they all get together for beers and a barbeque to talk it over. While initially reluctant to impose on their off-time, the friendly environment sounded like a good launch point.

What's the worst that can happen? I guess an argument could break out.

Davis's and Cratty's bickering was the stuff lore was made of.

As she walked over to Davis, she could see her smile broadening which made coming over to dinner a good idea. There was something about Davis that looked different. She couldn't put her finger on it but Davis definitely seemed to look physically different.

Maybe her hair? Something.

Andersen and Helms had warned her to expect a Spartan home with little décor and a gym-like odor to it. But as she approached the home, she couldn't help but notice that the lawn seemed well manicured, watered and that there were several beds of beautiful flowers that were well maintained and flourishing.

"Are you sure I'm not imposing? We could do this tomorrow."

"Absolutely no bother at all. Ana and Christine will be here in an hour and we'll be ready to eat then."

"That's great." Welch followed her hostess on the re-pointed walkway to a recently painted entrance door. She was surprised with the exterior of the home as Helms and Andersen had painted a dumpy picture of a bachelor pad rather than a home. It made perfect sense to her that Davis's home would be in disrepair and disarray as she spent nearly all her time in the field and was rarely at home.

Still though, something's different about her. Clothes? No...still shades of black, brown, tan and olive green...

As soon as Welch stepped into the house, her senses were blown away. Cooling conditioned air embraced her body, while the smell of fresh bread and seasoned meat invaded her olfactory sense. Visually, her eyes took in artistically and tastefully chosen furniture carefully arranged in the living room, dining room and the small adjoining hallway. As if to ensure all senses were engaged, low background jazz music was playing and somewhere there were chimes ringing. Welch was struck by elegantly color-coordinated wall paint and prints, as well as fresh flowers placed at key positions to accentuate each corner and centerpiece of the rooms. Stunned and baffled, Welch could utter only one word.

"Wow."

"Yeah, I know. It's all Cratty. I hate to say it but she has some serious interior decorating skills. She sees it, orders it, I pick it up, paint and done. She's also an absolute gem in the kitchen."

"She cooks, too? Really?"

"You have no idea, Diane. I wish I was gay or at least bi. I'd marry her in a second."

"I'd fake it if I were you," Welch said. Her mouth worked faster than her screening.

"Trust me. I thought of it."

Davis walked to the kitchen where Welch could hear someone cooking.

"Denise? I'm home. And Diane's here. I asked her to come early so we could talk before Ana and Christine came."

Welch was still taking in the entire scene when Cratty entered the room, barefoot with a leg brace going from heel to hip, and a tight pink t-shirt and sweatpants that clearly indicated that she had obviously been cleaning and cooking.

"Oh, thanks for the heads up," Cratty said with a bit of an edge.

Well, the edge sounds familiar but everything else...pink?

"You could have given me a little warning so I could at least have cleaned up before we had guests," Cratty said as she snatched one of the bags from Davis.

"You look fine, Denise. And Welch isn't a 'guest', she's a friend, for God sakes."

"Does she live here or work here?"

"No."

"Then she's a guest, Jillian." Cratty rolled her eyes and addressed Welch as she inspected the bag of groceries.

"You see what I'm dealing with here, Diane? I try to make things right for our friends and she can't even give me a courtesy call," she said. Welch was still at a loss for words as she watched Davis close her eyes as if this conversation were a regular event.

I swear I've seen this happen with Laura and Steve.

Suddenly, Welch saw Cratty's eyes narrow as she took out a pint of cream.

"Light cream? Light cream, Jillian?"

"What now, Denise? What's wrong with the cream? You said get cream and I got cream."

"No. I said get heavy cream. Light cream is what you use when you want to ruin your coffee. I made a point to tell you get 'not light but heavy cream' so I can make *real* whipped cream for the lemon meringue pie for dessert tonight," Cratty corrected.

If Davis was annoyed, she didn't show it even as there was a sudden shift in her presentation at the mentioning of dessert.

"You're making lemon meringue pie? Damn it, Denise! If you told me that little tidbit I would have made sure I got it!"

Davis turned to Welch, pulled out her keys and handed Cratty the second bag.

"Welch? Want to go for a ride? It'll take just five minutes."

Still stunned by all she was taking in, Welch found it difficult to respond. But as it turned out, she didn't have to.

"Oh forget it, Jill. I'll make this work. You did get the barbeque sauce, right?" Cratty asked.

Jill? Who the hell is "Jill?" You mean "Davis?"

Returning to a calmer state, Davis seemed to be herself.

"Absolutely," she said with authority.

Welch kept looking back and forth between the two. She was still wondering who the hell "Jill" was. *And when did they get married? Twelve years ago?*

Cratty expertly maneuvered with her leg brace and took the bags into the kitchen as she yelled back at Davis. As Cratty moved away,

Welch couldn't help but notice that she seemed more petite than she remembered. Not small, frail or weak but rather curvy and petite. As a result of her smaller frame, Welch found herself completely off balance.

That's why her boobs seemed so much larger. What the hell is going on here?

"Why don't you get Diane a beer, and I have chips and salsa already out in the front room," Cratty said as she disappeared.

"Excellent," Davis said. She followed Cratty into the kitchen to ostensibly get cold beers. Still standing in the middle of the room holding onto Davis's gun case and her portfolio, Welch had no idea what to do next. She looked at the floor and noticed that the area rugs looked new and the hardwood floors seemed recently waxed. She looked at the door and saw that there was obviously a shoe mat she missed. As she saw Davis return with two ice-cold beers and no shoes, Welch did her best to take her shoes off, hoping that Cratty wouldn't notice.

"So Diane, have a seat."

Davis smiled as she put her own beer down on a coaster, took her gun case and handed Welch her own beer.

"Thanks for having me," Welch said instinctively.

Now the last time I said that I was definitely with the Andersen's.

"Are you kidding? We should do this more," Davis said as she retreated to another room to put the gun away. Welch watched her walk away. It finally hit her what was different about her on the outside.

She's gained weight. Davis? You gained some weight. Your cheeks seem fuller and your ass is bigger. Jesus...

Welch sat back to see how the entire home hung so well together. The muted pastel wall paint, the accented window treatments, and the early American and Mission furnishing. She was drawn to all the small accents as well. On a glass table in front of the middle bay window sat a series of glass bird figurines. All were refracting the light in a beautiful rainbow of colors. It was easy to see which were birds of prey, and which ones were birds of color. There was one opaque figurine that had the shape of a full adult swan. It was the only glass one that held color, as if making its statement. Welch's attention shifted back to Davis who returned to sit down and retrieve her beer. Welch took a closer look at her face to see that Davis's cheeks were in fact fuller. Then she realized that over the past year, she had seen Cratty and Davis training for war. And now, it was over. They could relax.

I guess you do gain weight when you're happy. Kind of catty, don't you think, Diane?

She took a big gulp of her beer and wondered what Joe would

think if he saw this.

My God! What will Peter think if he ever comes up again? While Peter was open to many things, she was still feeling him out over gay rights, saving whales and social security, all of which appeared consistent with her own beliefs.

"So, what's this idea about you becoming CEO and taking over a security firm?" Davis asked as she settled back in a tastefully upholstered Mission-style chair. Welch took a deep breath and organized her thoughts for the millionth time.

"Now that Burns has 'retired' and Daniels has been neutralized, the world is still a dangerous place. Based on our experience and talents, I think we can offer people, companies and our government a niche skill set that could be useful and profitable." She opened her portfolio and removed a couple of color-coded files. Davis put her hand up and asked her a question.

"Before we start with details, if you want Ana and Christine, will we be able to dedicate some time and resources to bring Glenn in for prosecution?"

"Prosecution? Or do you mean execution?"

"I think they see it as the same."

It was not lost on either of them that both Dillon and especially Ramsey were not done in their pursuit. It was one thing for Glenn to play a part and ambush their friends, but quite another to escape from their very grasp, again.

And he gave them both the finger. What balls! I wonder if I should recruit him? I bet the Mossad could find him.

Davis shook her head in agreement.

"I know it's personal. It's personal for me and Cratty too. But for Christine and Ana, they won't rest unless it happens."

Without hesitation, and rapidly recalling her own obsession with killing Webber, Welch shook her head positively.

Webber and Daniels are dead...that just leaves one guy we've missed almost completely...almost. Deep in thought with visions of Parks in her arms, the smell of recently discharged gun powder and sand sticking to her face, Welch felt her phone vibrate. She glanced down at the number and saw that it was Andersen.

Hmm. I wonder what's up.

She had missed his call earlier that morning and tried to talk to him that afternoon but he didn't answer.

"I get it. And I think we can do that if they don't obsess about it."

After each woman took a sip of beer, they both started to go through their own prepared files.

"I think this is the start of something big, Diane."

"I think so too."

Welch heard Cratty yelling from the kitchen. Her voice, while loud, seemed somehow very *feminine?*

"Jill? Can you come in and get a plate for me and then bring the hors d'oeuvres out?"

Welch felt her eyes widen along with Davis's but the meaning behind each set was obviously different. While hers was surprise at how both women seemed to be acting as a married couple, Davis demonstrated she had an entirely different understanding for her own expression.

"Oh, Diane! If she made what I think she made, you're in for a real treat. I'll be right back."

No one will ever believe this! I don't even believe it.

Remembering that she had a text from Andersen, Welch took the moment to return to the Earth she knew and read it. While not taking long to read, it took her a minute to digest.

"Well...looks like we'll be getting this party started sooner than later. Ruth and the Italians. Just great." Her thinking was interrupted by shouting from the kitchen.

"Jillian! Stop eating those! They're not ready!" After a moment, she heard an explosion of laughter from both of them, like teenaged girls about to get in trouble.

"Denise! You're one sick bitch, you know that?"

Welch's only regret was that she had not recorded everything since she arrived.

No one will ever believe this.

#

I'm going to miss this place. Now, how many years have I been here?

Dillon walked with Ana Ramsey to the FBI parking lot carrying her personal effects in a plastic box. With eyes still glistening from saying goodbye to Gilmore, Johnson, Crepes, Martin, and all the guys, she knew she would especially miss Janeson. Still, Dillon was glad to see that Janeson was taking more time off to talk to her "boy friend" and her dog rather than working 24/7.

I just can't believe that she and Burns are together. All that talking on the phone? I wonder if they ever physically get together or is it some weird virtual relationship?

She turned to look at her friend. It was easy to see that Ramsey was far more upset as her nose was red and her eyes were a complete mess with running mascara. Doing a double take, Dillon felt a little better at her ability to control her feelings.

"Jesus, Ramsey. You look like Alice Cooper in the early days! You know, they have waterproof mascara. You might want to invest in a couple of tubes."

"Shut up, Dillon."

"No, I mean, really. It's not that much more. And did you have to park so far away? You knew our contract ended today and we'd be leaving, right?"

"You know, they say you can lose a lot of weight if you park further away than right by the elevator," Ramsey said.

"Oh, that's real nice. Too bad your reflexes aren't as fast as your mouth. You might have been able to avoid losing Glenn last time."

"Now, were you born a bitch or was there a school you went to to get the finishing touches?"

"Fuck you, Ana."

"No problem, Christine."

After a minute, they reached the car, put their belongings in the truck, then both entered the front seats and buckled in.

"So, we need to find a place to live, you know. If we relocate to Texas or California." Ramsey said.

"Yup, until we figure that out, you can stay with me. I've got a second room and it's much better than the hostel you're staying at."

"Thanks. So, what's this thing we're going to? Welch's been working on something and she wants to see us tonight at Davis's place to go over the specifics? I already know that if we're state-side she wants us located in Texas or California."

"'Davis's place?' Or do you mean 'Cratty and Davis's place," Dillon corrected.

It's like they're married. Still, Cratty does know how to cook!

"I'm telling you, it's not that way. Cratty really likes being the girl in the relationship and she really likes 'girly girls,' and Davis is not that."

"Now, how do you know this?"

"It's easy to see. All the ones she picks to hang out with are always pretty, young and nubile."

"So Cratty's two weeks there is now four months. She and Davis spent a whole lot of money, time and energy that's gone into renovating Davis's dump, and you're telling me it's just a 'roommate' thing?" Dillon asked.

Poor thing. She's almost as naïve as Belben.

"Yup. Anyway, Cratty just started seeing her physical therapist, Linda, who is a looker, and I guess is gay."

"No way! Are you sure or did you lose something in translation? English as a second language can be tricky sometimes," she said, proud of her own ability to slip in a shot at Ramsey.

"Nice. Real nice. Cracking on my accent. A new low for you, you know."

"No. I can get much worse but I like you," she said.

Ramsey explained again as if she never heard Dillon's response.

"Anyway, the scuttlebutt is that Davis and Martin have been seeing a lot of each other. You know, going to the gun range for an hour reservation and a half-hour lunch, and then thirty minutes to get back to the office. And since Cratty has made Davis's house more presentable, I think it's a win for Davis to have a nice place to bring her victims. And Cratty has both a place to live, recuperate and do the same. Like I said, Linda is a looker. It's a win for both. You see? They're a team."

Dillon's eyes narrowed as she looked for an on-ramp to the highway to head to Davis's place.

Damn. Ramsey has all the dirt on everyone. How does she do that?

"Anyway, Davis is not Cratty's type," Ramsey said with a laugh.

Dillon smiled at that one. It was legendary that Cratty would often say that to Davis just to bust her ass. Just as it was legend that Davis got Cratty thrown out of a gay bar by pretending to be her jilted, cheated wife.

"You can't make this shit up. And this is really good shit, too." The next ten minutes were silent as Dillon drove until Ramsey spoke next.

"So if Mrs. Welch's plan sounds good, will you join or no?"

Dillon had thought long and hard about this. Nine and Ice had told her that Welch was pulling together people to create a leadership team for a security firm. She and Ramsey were on the short list to be recruited. Since their contracts with the Bureau were up, and they had about six months' vacation and accrued time, the timing and idea were tempting.

"Only if we can go after Glenn," Dillon responded.

That bastard. The pale pig-bastard. She clenched the steering wheel at the image of a pale middle finger jutting out at her.

"Blanco bastard," Ramsey said with palpable vehemence.

"Next time I see him, I'm going to cut more than just his pretty face," she continued.

"Yeah, I'll hold the sack of shit and you can cut him. Quietly." Dillon tried to focus on her driving and not see the faces of her friends.

Belben, Fitzy, Witzy. I'm sorry I wasn't there.

She and Ramsey drove in silence to Davis's house.

#

Alica Wise sat in a darkened living room further away from the television and couch. It was hours of sitting in a recessed part of the room that allowed her eyes to easily adjust to the television's electric blue light. It took longer to adjust to its loud volume and the faint smell of a bowel movement. All these things assaulted her senses as she sat in the darkened apartment. It was close to 4:30 PM.

Hmm. She should be finished with her shift by now. Unless she has new playmates. She always liked to have her asshole licked.

Wise looked at her expensive gold-plated wristwatch. Her jawline hardened and fist clenched so tightly that she needed to force herself to stretch them out within her flesh-colored gloves. It was easy to force herself to relax. She had done this before. Wise looked around the room to take in the pictures of parents and some children.

Could be her family. They have the same eyes and chin.

Scanning the room, she laid her sights on the couch where a middle-aged man's body lay motionless with a light blanket over his body, partially obscuring his face as if he were asleep. She smiled. Wise continued to be amazed at how stupid men were.

Not all men are stupid. Special Agent Martin was pretty smart. And of course, Alex Burns is pretty smart, too. Even Jeff Glenn shows promise.

Wise was still thinking about men in general when she saw a cat slowly inching its way into the room. Motionless, Wise carefully restricted her movement to allow the cat to see her, and then to continue into the room without assault.

"That's alright, kitty. I won't hurt you," she said quietly. Seeing the cat and using the word "kitty" reminded her of Davis.

Ah, yes. Then there's Jill Davis. At some point, I should pay you a visit. If it wasn't for you, I would have killed Burns and been done with all of this shit. Daniels would have made it, too. I was supposed to kill him, fucking bitch!

Suddenly, Wise heard and then saw the door open allowing a

corpulent woman dressed in a prison uniform to come in holding shopping bags in one hand and her keys in the other. From the deliberate movement and her throwing the keys at the body on the couch, it was easy to see she was pissed as she turned the television off while still clutching a six-pack of beer.

And speaking of bitch.

She watched Officer Tate turn her attention to the couch, oblivious to her presence.

"Danny! What the fuck is wrong with you?! You deaf?" she yelled. She didn't wait for an answer. Tate left the room to go to what Wise figured was the kitchen. She heard the refrigerator door open and then close violently while Officer Tate continued a one-sided conversation.

"Danny! I hope to hell you got a lead on a job and weren't sleeping all day."

"I'm sorry, honey. I'd like to answer you except a pretty little girl I was hoping to screw shot me, put my sorry-ass body on the couch, covered me with a blanket with the television still on. I think she's going to kill you, dear. I wish I could warn you, but I'm dead. Been dead for a while. Can't you smell me?" Wise said quietly.

A moment later, Wise heard another door at the other end of the apartment close. She looked at her large-caliber revolver with silencer. Wise patiently waited as the cat looked at her from her position at the top of the couch.

Maybe the 9mm would have been a better choice? No. This one looks more imposing. And there's nothing like watching the barrel turn.

Her choice of weapon had been the subject of an hour's debate ever since she pulled the trigger on Danny. She shifted her attention to the man's body. It was easy to get inside the apartment hours before. Smoothing out her black short skirt with matching stiletto heels, he nearly threw the door open when she told him she was from a church and wanted to talk to him about God and his soul.

Wow! His eyes were as big as saucers when I pulled the trigger.

Finally. Wise heard the toilet flush and the door open.

What? Didn't you wash your hands? Now, that's just gross!

"Danny? Can't you at least get off your ass and talk to me?" Tate said. With the cabinets banging in the kitchen, it was obvious Tate was still looking for food.

Wise got up and turned the television back on to a moderate noise level.

"What are you!? An asshole? You can't come in and talk to your wife for just a few minutes?" she said in an angry tone.

I wonder what you two talk about? Do you tell him about all the fun you have at work or do you leave out some details? I bet you do keep some secrets, don't you?

Wise sat back down in her chair, and patiently waited for Tate to come into the room. After ten more minutes of plates moving, cabinet doors closing and bags crinkling, Tate finally came in with what looked to Wise like a plate of microwaved left-over chicken and some yellow macaroni and cheese in one hand and a beer in the other.

Chicken, mac and cheese? Not really good for your heart. That explains why you are so heavy. No wonder you sweat so much whenever you'd walk upstairs.

Wise watched Tate take a seat by the man's feet as she watched the news that was on.

For law enforcement, you suck in picking up details. Sitting at the feet of a dead man, with a jittery cat on the couch and a killer in the corner. You are a sad sack of shit, Officer Tate.

Wise couldn't help but smile from the dark corner with only the flickering of light from the news report. She truly wondered how long it was going to take for Tate to finally turn on the light and realize she wasn't alone.

Still, at least you'll have a last meal. Would you have picked something else if you knew it was? I wonder what?

Even as she sat feet away from Tate, Wise was sure to keep her grip firm and revolver trained on her, even as Tate devoured her meal and finally sat back to finish her beer. Nodding at some of the news discussed, Wise watched as Tate commented on various reports.

Wow. Do you always come home to have him not talk to you? Not much of a relationship. You should have seen someone about that. Probably be a better use of your time than abusing prisoners, wouldn't you say?

Suddenly, Wise saw that Tate took in a whiff of the obvious bowel movement that she had had to sit with for at least two hours.

Finally, you noticed.

"Jesus, Danny! What the hell is wrong with you?"

It was easy to see in the electric blue light that Tate was pissed off. She put her beer down forcefully, leaned over and snatched the blanket off his face. Wise watched with satisfaction as Tate seemed to freeze for a moment, and then got up quickly to find the switch for the overhead lights in the darkened room. With years of covert training, Wise's eyes adjusted far faster than Tate's vision. Tate's realization that she had been eating and having a beer with her dead husband for at least twenty minutes was priceless.

Ah, yes. It doesn't get better than this. But wait, Tate! There's still more!

"Oh my God! Danny!? Oh my God?" she yelled. Her hand went to her mouth in shock as she took a step back, bumping into a chair.

"Officer Tate," Wise said enthusiastically from the far corner of the room.

Tate jumped back and clutched her chest. She gave a short cry in surprise as if sitting near a dead man was not enough to be shocking.

It took time for her to regroup while still holding her chest. Wise watched her stand motionless and frozen as she tried to remember who Wise was.

"How soon we forget. I'm Convict 38· from Danbury Federal Prison, Isolation Max Wing. Remember?"

Wise stood up. She looked completely out of place in the cramped, disheveled, cluttered apartment as she stood with her petite, athletic body clad in a black fitted dress, black-red plaid jacket over a tight red top. She held her gun on Tate. Still savoring the moment, Wise reflected on how difficult it was finding the right shoes and the black sheer pantyhose to match the dress.

"You used to love that thing I used to do. You know. Lick your ass and pussy until you came. And then, just for fun, you'd especially liked to watch me and Convict 22 go down on each other and then you. Which reminds me."

Wise produced a smartphone in her left hand and snapped a picture of Tate, clearly in shock standing beside her husband's body while confronted by an ex-convict with a gun.

"Gina wanted a picture of you before you died," Wise said as she squeezed the trigger which sent a large-caliber bullet into Tate's left knee.

"Oh my God!" Tate yelled out as she dropped to the floor knocking over a small table that had her plate and beer.

Man! I love the sound of a suppressed gun shot. Just loud enough to give a satisfying pop without alerting the world, she thought.

Wise watched Tate gripping her knee and writhing in pain as she tried to push herself away from her dead husband, whose face was obliterated by being shot point blank. Wise stepped in front of Tate and snapped another picture. Wise found herself feeling calm and without stress.

"Why do people make such a big thing about killing someone?"

"Please...please don't kill...kill me."

"Just a couple more pictures, Tate. You don't mind, do you?" Not waiting for an answer, Wise shot Tate's other knee and then her shoulder at close range.

"Please...no more...I'm sorry. Please don't kill me. I have children and grandchildren," Tate said through tears of agony.

Still snapping pictures as she squatted over Tate less than a foot from her face, Wise seemed to take a moment to consider that fact.

She then heard the cat's meow as it hid behind a chair. Wise smiled at the creature and looked back at Tate who looked like she was going to pass out from the shock and blood loss.

"And you have a cat, too," Wise said quietly. She felt sad all of a sudden. Tate's face became even paler but Wise was not sure if it was because she killed her husband or if Tate was losing so much blood.

Probably loss of blood. You don't strike me as a person who gets too far beyond yourself.

"So that might be the last bullet so I should be done," Wise said as turned the gun on Tate's stomach and pulled the trigger that sent another bullet into Tate. She was sure that Tate would have bled out but in her line of work, being sure was not as good as a confirmed kill. Her last shot needed to be lethal.

"Oh, I'm sorry," Wise feigned surprise and shock. "I used only one bullet on your husband's face. My bad. Sorry."

Wise took another picture as she stood up. After she stretched her back, she slipped the cell phone into a small pocket, smoothed out her dress and jacket again and looked at her shoes. All of which had flecks of blood on them from the close proximity of the shots. From a distance she was sure the dark red would not stand out though she regretted the need to get rid of the clothes. She took the time to look closely at her clothes again. She realized she had a new spot remover she was planning on trying.

Maybe I'll try it tonight on these. What? You're still holding on? You're much more of a survivor than I thought you were.

Wise turned her attention back on Tate. She was becoming impatient with the process.

"Well, it's been nice," Wise said as she covered Tate's mouth and nose with gloved hand. It took only a minute until she saw Tate's eyes glaze over as she struggled weakly to breathe.

"Good night, Sweetie" she said with a smile. She continued to suffocate Tate while she looked around the apartment. She wondered where the cat had gone. Sensing that she was motionless and no longer breathing, Wise removed her hand, casually stood up and walked around the house to find the heat and air conditioner's controls. While warmer than usual outside for September, Wise made sure the heat was off entirely and turned the air conditioner up high.

"That should keep the smell down for a day or two longer," she said as she put her gun in her oversized purse she left on the chair.

Looking at the two dead bodies all around her, Wise shook her head, appreciating her work.

Hearing the cat again and then seeing her run away, Wise realized it could be several days before the bodies would be found.

"Yeah...that might not be good," she said aloud.

Perplexed, Wise stood for a moment as she decided if her next actions were worth her time. Her decision was clear within seconds.

"It's worth it. They are always worth it."

She walked to the kitchen and found it in disarray from Tate's cooking and recent grocery shopping.

"Well. I guess cleaning is not what you do, either," she said as she stood beside the cluttered kitchen table in front of a filled sink. Even though she had to contend with the mess, she enjoyed hearing her stiletto heels click on the floor as she approached the cabinets to start her search. After a minute, she found both the dry cat food and kitty litter she was looking for. She put them on the floor and searched under the sink until she found a fresh garbage bag to put the old kitty litter in. Using primarily her nose, Wise traced the litter box to the apartment's bathroom.

You know, people are just gross! You'd think they would empty this once in a while. Wise carefully transported the over-used kitty litter box. Retrieving and emptying it in a new bag in the kitchen, she refilled it with clean litter and tightly wrapped both the old litter bag and the half-filled kitchen garbage bag. Satisfied that all the garbage and soiled kitty litter were closed in the bags, Wise took both of the cat's bowls to rinse out before drying and refilling with fresh water and dry food. It was obvious they had not been cleaned in a while. This just made Wise angry. This was more difficult to do as she had to navigate cleaning and drying with her tight-fitting, flesh-colored gloves still on.

"If I had known you mistreated this cat earlier, I would have killed you much sooner. Bacteria and all kinds of things can kill a cat, you know." After she was sure the bowls were clean, she filled them with food and clean water. She stood looking at the amount she gave her.

"Hmm. That won't be enough if it's a week or so."

She went back to the cabinets to find another bowl.

"Ah, yes! This will work," she said as she found two soup bowls.

She tipped the cat food bag until it filled the bowl up to the rim and next she filled the other bowl with extra water. Finally, Wise was satisfied with the amount and put them both on the floor beside the other bowls. Next, she opened the refrigerator and found deli meat that was only a day old.

"Oh? This is still fresh, surprisingly."

She took it out of its wrapper and cut it up into pieces on a plate. Putting the meat plate beside the cat bowls, Wise grabbed the kitty litter box and put it back in the bathroom. She returned to the kitchen, grabbed the two garbage bags and shut the lights off. As she headed to the bedroom, she saw the cat scampering quickly into the darkened kitchen. At the bedroom door, she flung the two garbage bags into the bedroom, and closed the door firmly. She made sure all the lights were off except for a small night light where the bodies were. Wise took another look to inspect her work while she picked up her purse from the chair. She was truly relieved that the cat would be fine as she stood in the room of bodies. She took another moment to adjust her little dress and check her shoes. She felt the corners of her mouth turn up knowing that the cat would be alright for at least a week.

"What a day," she said as she headed to the front door. With the smell of chicken, mac and cheese still lingering in the air, Wise realized that she was hungry. As if to agree, she heard her stomach grumble.

You know, I think I'll do drive-through and get a burrito. I bet they have real good hot sauce in this neighborhood, real authentic. Wise opened the door and walked out to the fading day. She heard the apartment front door lock behind her as she took in the warm air. If anyone was watching they would have wondered was who the attractive young woman walking quietly to her parked car across the street.

"Now, where can I find a Mexican place?"

Wise turned the key to the ignition, put the car in gear and drove away.

Chapter 15

"When the long winter nights come on and the wolves follow their meat into the lower valleys, he may be seen running at the head of the pack through the pale moonlight or glimmering borealis, leaping gigantic above his fellows,..."

Jack London, <u>The Call of the Wild</u>

Four Months Later – Coronado Beach, San Diego, California, USA

Becky found herself cautiously watching her environment as Emma and Rosemarie played in the pool under the watchful eye of their grandfather. It was easy to see that Murphy was preparing to get in the pool himself.

Beautiful weather in San Diego. Now I know why people stay here...we got to get the girls back to school real soon, though. Who'd want to ever go to school here?

While Becky was grateful that Murphy had his own men scattered throughout the all-inclusive, secluded hotel, she was more appreciative that he agreed to find a couple of women to be part of his security team as well.

Where do you find women hitmen, anyway? You can't really put up an ad or look on the Internet. Actually, you really can. Her memories flooded back to her rogue years. She found everything a domestic terrorist needed on the Internet.

"It's a great country." She did her best to ostensibly relax poolside as the children and their grandfather played. While she appeared to be like any other vacationer clad in her slimming one-piece bathing suit, clutch, towels and wrap, her constant scanning and persistent feeling for her gun in her clutch deviated greatly from the average resort guest.

God, I wish I could turn this off. I wonder how Denise or Ana do it? They have to relax. Is it drinking? Dulling the senses?

Happy that she had taken an early morning run and hit the weight room, she felt as if she were more relaxed than if she didn't exercise. While her anti-anxiety medication really helped, she found it was the exercise that kept her edginess down and her thoughts less negative. Still, she had to thank David for convincing her to at least try medication. Her only complaint was her weight. It was going down. Feeling the need to eat was minimal and its enjoyment was less for her in the last two months. While hearing Burns talk about how he met and conversed with Samantha, David and a brief verbal exchange with Tony was nice, it reminded her of how much she missed them all. Her mind turned back to her medication.

It changed my life. That and Burns's training and exercise regimen, and the need to fight to survive. Why she smiled about those early days still surprised her. But then, everyone she loved was alive.

As she adjusted her sunglasses, she looked at her three-hour-old rum and Coke and actually thought about getting a refreshed drink.

You just can't relax, can you?

Just as she finished looking around, she caught sight of the hotel front desk hostess rounding the corner carrying a large plastic cooler and several bottles. Her immediate thought went into risk assessment mode. After seconds of analysis, Becky convinced herself that it would be easier to simply snipe her and Murphy rather than use explosives which she thought might be in the bottles the hostess carried.

If it was volatile, they would have exploded by now. Maybe it's just as it appears – cold drinks.

While wearing a very tight-fitting black hotel uniform, her dark tanned skin enhanced her presentation, as her shapely body and high heels made her movements look very sensual and alluring.

Not everyone could carry that off in such an ugly uniform so well. I don't think even Sam would have dared, she thought.

As the woman approached, Becky watched her looking at different guests as if she were looking for someone in particular. Becky got a little nervous when the woman focused on her and walked in her direction.

Now, I wonder what this could be about.

By now she had moved her gun from out of her clutch to her lap, concealed by a towel. Trying to look "casual" and relaxed, Becky feigned as if she just caught sight of the woman and addressed her before she came too close.

Okay. You're now within my ten-foot protection radius. Without much thought, she moved her concealed loaded gun in the woman's direction.

"Are you looking for me?" she asked.

Catching the woman off guard, she slowed to a stop, clearly surprised and uncomfortable with being addressed first.

"Ah, yes, I think. Are you Ms. Littleton?" she asked.

What the hell! No one knows that name here. She sat up straight with both bare feet on the ground. Murphy was in the deep end playing with both girls, and his men still on the perimeter. She decided to be ready. *I got this.*

"I'm sorry, but who wants to know?" Becky said. In seconds, she stood up and kept the towel draped across her stomach. Confused, the woman first backed away, and then assumed Becky was the person she was looking for. She still held the cooler of bottled drinks that glistened in the sunlight.

"Your brother, Tony, in Room 812 asked me to bring you suntan lotion and drinks for the kids. I took the liberty of bringing various sun blocking lotions as well as refreshments. While all the drinks are free, I find it more economical to simply fill a cooler with large bottles of water and juices rather than the small cups that are provided." The woman placed her bundle down and appeared to back up from Becky. For her part, Becky froze as she heard her deceased brother's name used as if he were alive. She scanned the pool area and the three buildings that surrounded it. Becky realized that whoever it was was able to see that sun tan lotion and drinks would be appropriate for being poolside.

Burns. Fucking Burns. Five months of peace and he needs to meet. What's going on now?

After years of practice, Becky put on a fake smile and surveyed the area again as nonchalantly as possible as she thought of a possible response. While still looking baffled by the whole interaction, the staff woman was about to depart but then turned to tell Becky something that Becky also was surprised to hear.

"Ah, before I forget, your brother asked me if you might be able to find his smartphone he had given you to hold when you were in New York. He says it had some important information on it and might assist him in looking for a USB flash drive. He's still upstairs looking for it," she said innocently.

A smile still cemented on her face, Becky was glad that the woman looked uncomfortable and not interested in reading social cues or micro-expressions.

"Oh, okay. And thank you for the drinks and lotion. I'm sorry. Where is Tony again?" Becky's causal presentation as she bent over to collect her wrap was perfect. Almost as perfect as how she effectively kept her gun concealed by the pool towel. Stopped in mid-stride from escaping, she looked back, puzzled but then reiterated his location.

"Room 812. He says he thought he had it with him but then he thinks he might have lost it at the Marriott Hotel."

Shit. Unbelievable. No wonder you can never relax. Burns is everywhere. Good thing I'm not on the toilet, though I'm sure he even knows my cycle, for Christ's sake.

Relaxed that it was undoubtedly Burns, a real smile emerged at the thought of seeing him again.

"Oh, okay. Thank you very much."

"You're welcome.

But, based on Burns' message, there was a problem. Becky was on the move. No longer comfortable lounging with Burns watching, she was glad to be focused on finding him and seeing what's up. There had to be a problem.

A very big problem.

As she entered the hotel lobby, she scrutinized every face as well as the placement of the exits and corners while keeping her clutch under her arm and towel covering her hand that concealed her gun. When the first elevator came up with two men, she motioned them to go even though there was plenty of room for her to share the ride. Even as three teenagers offered her room in the next one, she declined with a smile. Finally, as an empty elevator arrived, she looked around to make sure no one would suddenly be joining her.

Okay. The phone we got from Burns that was in New York not far from the Marriott Hotel was when all this shit got started years ago. The USB flash drive and asking me about it has to be about Albatross...yeah, there's some serious shit brewing. After years in the field, she held onto the memories of Tony, Samantha and David as a way of slowing her heart and calming her breathing. The technique always worked. As the elevator door opened, Becky peered to her left and right as she exited into the hotel hallway to get to Burns's room.

Is there shit going on here and I missed it? I hope not or I'll never hear the end of it from him.

As she found his room and then passed it, she waited a moment to make sure another hotel guest left the floor before she returned to the right room. She knocked quietly. It only took seconds for Burns to answer. Clad in a white t-shirt and dark bathing suit, Burns's physical appearance greatly departed from his usually nondescript dress of slacks, crew shirt, and light jacket.

But then, being in a bathing suit, flip-flops and t-shirt is nondescript at a resort. She followed him into the room to the bank of windows overlooking the hotel pool and two other surrounding buildings. As always, there was no discussion until they were securely in the room.

"You had to use Tony as a cover?" she asked.

"Best way to get you here without you coming in shooting," Burns said as he stopped in front of the window.

"Maybe I'm on vacation. Maybe I'm unarmed."

"And maybe monkeys will fly out of my ass. Revolver, semi-automatic or full automatic?"

"Semi-automatic, .45 caliber. I don't like how the automatic can get ahead of me." She moved the large caliber gun back into her large clutch.

"Very good stopping power."

"My days of screwing around with stopping power and enemies are over."

She was pleased to see that Burns was smiling. She took that moment to look around the well-appointed hotel room that was nearly devoid of anything personal except for a large duffel bag and a fully assembled, well-equipped Barrett sniper rifle sitting on the coffee table.

Flash guard, scope, suppressor, fully-stocked and ready.

Looking at the precision weapon, Becky smiled at immediately recognizing it and appreciating its power.

That brings back memories. It's like seeing my first love, my first high-powered experience. Becky shook off the odd but apt analogy and returned her attention to Burns.

"I suppose you already know how we all are doing," Becky said with a lopsided smile on her face.

"Yup. Emma has really gotten tall, almost as tall as Rosemarie."

"They are growing like weeds, and they get along like sisters."

"They love each other and fight a lot with as much intensity."

"You got it."

"David and Samantha would have loved to see it."

"They sure would have," Becky said. Burns nodded

approvingly as he handed her a second set of binoculars. She accepted them without question. She was impressed with his blond wig accessory along with perfectly flesh-colored tan to obscure his scars.

Hmm. The fake tan really covers the scars. Unless you're really looking, you wouldn't see them. Talk about blending in.

"I take it, it's spray on?" she said as she pointed at his skin.

"Of course. I don't have time to lie around drinking rum and Coke and get a real tan," he said sarcastically.

"You just couldn't let that go, could you Burns?"

"Nope, I couldn't."

She shook her head and looked out the window. She took in the panoramic view. The sun was high and probably reflected light off of his windows, obscuring them.

"You need a hobby, Burns."

"Probably, someday."

Burns smiled and redirected her to the windows as he pointed to the building right across from them.

"Three stories down, one o'clock, corner. Two men, military/law-enforcement type with binoculars. Three stories above them at eleven o'clock, two men who are non-military but watching two military types below at ground level with binoculars."

As Burns spoke, Becky targeted the areas to see exactly what Burns was describing.

"Building to the right, one floor above has a window that was opened with no screen and no curtains. I plan to visit there right after."

Great! Shit all around me and I'm sunning myself.

"Do you want me to clear downstairs or go with you?" Becky asked. She found it ironic that her tone was as if she were going to pick up food or laundry, though with an edge of annoyance.

Man, just like old times.

"No," Burns said as he pointed to the same building three floors down to the right. "I want you to check out those guys on the first floor. Military or law-enforcement types, man and woman, who are watching those two, non-military types, two stories above them in the middle of the building. I believe the woman's name is Ruth and the guy's name is John. Just let them know that I'll meet them at the bar at midnight."

Becky shook her head positively.

"Well, it's nice to see you're making friends. Back in the day I'd ask more questions but quite frankly, the less I know, the better. Does this affect the kids?" Becky asked.

What the hell is going on here?

"Not at all. I actually think it's more of a coincidence and logistics of me wanting to see you and the kids, and needing a meet with some contacts who apparently brought friends. Murphy's people are actually doing a good job though it would be even better if Cratty were running the team."

Yeah...I wonder how Denise is doing. Living with Cougar, no less.

"Is it true that Cougar and Cratty are living together?"

"Yup. Quite an odd couple."

"Jesus, Burns. Looks like a convention. Alright. I'll let Murphy know but on the down-low that you'll check out the one above to make sure it's not a shooter's perch while I contact your people over there," Becky said as she pointed to the military types.

Nodding with approval, Burns clarified missions.

Suddenly, Burns's demeanor changed and his voice seemed concerned.

"Sure you can handle it? Your skills might be dulled by the booze and you've been out of the field for a while...

"Shut up, Burns!"

Burns's smile was broad, probably his version of a belly laugh. He did shift back to business.

"Fact-finding only and deliver a message. No shooting involved. Tell Murphy but make sure there's no movement at the pool to spook the watchers. If it was a hit, I think they would wait until later. I just want him to know in case something goes wrong. If he does not hear from us in thirty minutes, collect everyone causally and go to dinner. If he doesn't hear from either one of us in one hour, he's to call Janeson and Andersen. Clear?" Burns asked.

Confused, Becky asked for clarification.

"Not Helms?"

"Retired."

"No such thing as a 'retired' Marine," Becky corrected.

"Absolutely. I'm sure Andersen will contact Helms and Welch. Clear on the plan?" Burns asked as they both put their binoculars down while still looking out the window.

"Clear. Do you think I should change or stay like this?" Becky asked. She remembered that her targets had poorly-tailored jackets that did not hide their high-caliber weapons at all.

"No. They will be less threatened by someone in a bathing suit, even if you're the potential target. But I think they're watching the other guys and waiting for me just like the other pair in the other building. Speaking of which, I'll look at the non-military people after I hear from you. I think you should go to the pool if all goes well and stay with Murphy in about forty-five minutes. You green?"

"Green," Becky said. She unconsciously rolled her shoulders to release the tension, and she was back to focusing on breathing.

Well...back into the shit.

As both Burns and Becky walked to the door, she retrieved her towel to cover her gun. She felt herself smiling even though she noticed her hands were sweating a bit.

"What?" Her smile was easy to catch.

"Just like old times," she said.

"It's probably the local Bureau watching Murphy's guys watch us," Burns offered.

Smiling more, Becky looked askance at him.

"It's not my first day on the job, Burns. It's something else. Nice try, though," Becky said as they cautiously entered the hallway.

"I know. I thought I would try anyway."

Becky looked closely at Burns. Other than his t-shirt, swim trunks and sandals, he was obviously without a weapon.

"Damn it, Burns," Becky hissed out. "Is this the way it's going to be? No weapons? Just your faith in people and dreams?"

Ever since he had those drug-induced dreams, he's been weird about weapons. In a good way except when I need him to use a gun. His description of Tony was eerie, she reflected as they rounded the corner to the elevators. Obviously still focused on his environs, Burns produced a shadow of a smile as he spoke next.

"My body is the weapon, Becky."

Becky rolled her eyes and sighed as she lifted the towel off her gun to make sure there was a bullet in the chamber and safety off.

Just in case.

"Fact finding, right? You're not planning on killing anyone, are you? I actually want to talk to these people."

"No. Just in case they think they can strong-arm me. I don't play well with bullies," she said without hesitation. But still her feelings did not support her words.

Ever since I killed those guys in the helicopter, I'm not sure I could kill again.

She changed the subject to get away from those depressing thoughts which led to another question.

"Does Rachael know? Sounds like you like her."

She remembered hearing from Burns that she was reportedly proficient in revolvers, full-automatic rifles and hand-to-hand combat that included edged weapons.

For a woman in law enforcement who's a friend and not a target, he seems to have lots of intelligence on her.

"Not yet. But she's a quick study. Once we clear this up, I'll bring her up to speed. Once I do that, she's all in. Are you okay with that?" Even as he spoke, she could see he was thoroughly scanning the immediate area for threats. It took a moment longer than Becky thought it would take but when she said it, it was heartfelt.

"Yes. I like her. From what little you told me about her and from our short time together, I'd like for her to be in," Becky said as she thought of Samantha and David.

"You still talk to her every week?"

"Sure do. Twice a week."

"That's good," Becky said. Out in the lobby, she reviewed her plan of action.

"Time to move."

"On the move," Becky said.

#

Helms found himself sitting on a park bench waiting for his wife, Ellen. The plan was to meet her at the Parker House for dinner in an hour. The Boston Commons was busy with people heading home as the evening rush hour was in full swing. Sitting quietly, he looked at his watch and saw it was 5:30 PM. He knew he wasn't far from Janeson's home on Beacon Street.

Alright. I'll see Ellen at 6:30 which gives me a half-hour to talk to Janeson.

He looked towards the south end of the Public Garden. After only one minute, among the commuters, came a cyclist that Helms knew as Davenport. He waved as he continued going approximately ten yards ahead before he stopped and spoke into his headset. Helms stood up and watched as he saw Janeson running at a very fast clip with a cyclist not far behind her and one giving her a wide berth on her left as well.

If it's Tuesday at 5:30, Janeson is just about here on her daily run, he thought. *Figures she has her team on bicycles. I bet no one can keep up with her.*

While she was still a ways down, he was impressed with how she looked very lean and muscular in her full, long-sleeved black running shirt with matching runner's pants and shoes. With her black hair tied up in a ponytail under her FBI hat, she looked like the poster child for joining the Bureau. Graceful, elegant and sleek, her movements were efficient yet expansive.

Still, you should change up your schedule. It would be easy to track you.

Helms nodded in approval at her security detail in front and behind her consisting of three cyclists. It took him just a minute to locate the Bureau car that had the other detail.

Well, at least you've increased your protection.

He shifted his focus back to Janeson as she approached. He was genuinely happy to see her after being gone only five months into his retirement. In an unusual display of emotion, Janeson smiled at him as she came to a gradual stop.

"Boss? How are you?" she said with more emotion that he had expected.

"I'm not the boss anymore, Acting Director Janeson. Anyway, I was in the neighborhood and just wanted to ask you something."

With her head tilted, it was clear that Helms lost her when he said he was "in the neighborhood."

"Ellen and I are having dinner in Boston, and I thought I would stop by and catch you on your run," Helms said as they both started to walk to the office. Even though she had been running at a very fast clip, Helms was impressed with how she had already brought her breathing under control. She nodded that she understood. They walked quietly for a moment as he formulated his question. One thing he loved about Janeson was that being blunt was the best thing he did and the best thing she was good with dealing with.

"Rachael, I'm going to be Chief Operating Officer at Welch's new firm, Allied Federation International, Inc. They have offices here in Boston, and one in London and Germany."

"That sounds great."

"While we already have contracts for security and protection with a number of firms and people right now, there is an investigative branch that might be of use to the FBI," Helms continued.

"As an armed law-enforcement federal agency in service to the American people and the US Government, we would not be able to provide any information on open and active cases."

"Of course. Are the Panelli case and Glenn file still active?" he said as he was already sure of the answer.

"Not now. Both cases are closed at the moment due to limited resources. As a result, I have asked Lieutenant Andersen to review a

number of case files associated with those very files including the
ones on Timothy Carter and Robert Wise," Janeson said without
skipping a beat.

"I see."

"Lieutenant Andersen has all the critical files for those closed,
inactive cases at the moment. However, the disappearance of Alica
Wise is an active case, and I may need an agency such as yours to
assist in some aspects of that search. Clearly on a need-to-know
basis," Janeson continued.

*For someone who can't read a room, you're very good in
communicating where we can go and what we can do, and where we
might be able to work directly.*

"Have Ramsey and Dillon's contracts expired?" Helms asked.

"Yes, as of 4:00 PM today. I have already informed Lieutenant
Andersen that they were working on the Glenn case and might be of
use to his investigation," Janeson said. She suddenly slowed her
pace down as she put a hand to her right ear.

Hmm. Must be a call coming in, Helms thought. He felt his
own phone vibrate. Taking a moment to look as Janeson listened to
her own call coming in, Helms read his text from Andersen.

**"Ruth is back. She knows about Wise. Ruth and Italian
intelligence say that Panelli is talking to crime families in Italy.
Also, something about Daniels having a cache of files that's
missing and Burns on some kind of mission. This could be real
bad. I already texted Welch – she's talking to all 'the girls.'"**

"Shit," Helms said as he put his phone away.

*How the hell did the Mossad and Italian Secret Service hear
about the mission? They must be tracking me or Welch or both...just
when you think the NSA is king of data collection...they must know
about Burns by now.*

Janeson came back with her own report.

"Regina Panelli has escaped from Danbury Federal Prison,
minimum security," she said as she gave her cycling team hand

movements to move out. She turned to the car where two of her men were already out waiting for her while simultaneously scanning for threats.

It looks like she's got this personal protection thing down. She had grown quite a bit.

"Just so you know, Andersen was contacted by Ruth and Italian intelligence about Panelli being in contact with crime families there too. They are also aware of Wise being MIA and are worried about that too." Janeson stopped in mid-stride and looked right at him.

"Thank you. I have a call waiting for me in the car from Murphy even as we speak. If you come across any more data, please let me know directly," Janeson said.

"Will do," Helms said.

"Janeson, your connection to Murphy and Burns, while valuable, may be misunderstood by other agencies and people who don't know you."

"Sir?"

"The NSA, Homeland Security, and CIA. They don't do well when high-level FBI directors have a mainline into organized crime and domestic terrorists, even if both have changed their ways. Flexible thinking is not their long suite."

"Should I resign? Would it be best for Gilmore and Johnson?"

Helms looked at her as if she were his daughter. Proud that she put others ahead of her, he was worried about her lack of reading the writing on the wall.

"Rachael, all I'm saying is that if the bullshit gets too high, you can walk away. I may be one of the few people who know you don't need the headaches or the money of the position."

"That is true."

"But just remember that in addition to Burns, you have me, Welch and Anderson on your side." Helms felt his eyes piercing Janeson's own deep blue eyes. If she could read the situation well, she would be able to see he wasn't worried about her abilities or the others; he was worried about what the assholes in the other agencies would do to her.

"Is that why you're taking a position at Allied Federation International? As a means of retreat, should I need it?"

Yes. She does get it.

"The pay is crazy good, the missions are of our choosing and the leadership is strong and driven in the direction I like. I also like having control over my own destiny, I want to know where my enemies are and I want my friends closer."

Helms was surprised at what he said. He was more surprised at the response. Without warning, Janeson crossed the distance between them, gave him a strong hug, and retreated almost as fast as she had moved in. Without further discussion, she was in the car, and it was moving at top speed back to the regional office.

"She has grown."

Helms looked at his watch and saw that he had more than enough time to walk to the Parker House. He knew that Ellen would be shocked at Janeson's reaction. Still, he was worried for her. It was hard for people to understand Janeson.

"So much for a pleasant, easy-going dinner," Helms said to himself.

Chapter 16

"The web of our life is of a mingled yarn, good and ill together."

Shakespeare, <u>All's Well That Ends Well</u>

Two Years Later...

Glenn took his time to catch his breath. Under other circumstances, he would have been impressed with his stalkers' abilities to track him this far. If his sister and niece weren't three blocks away, too close for his liking, he would have simply chalked it up to his evasive actions as just part of doing business. Four flights later he was looking over the roof line to the street below. He waited until there was movement. Though there were lots of commuters racing off to buses, cars and trains to work, the movements he was looking for would be those of trained law enforcement agents that stood out the more they tried to blend in. It only took him two minutes to catch his breath and ten minutes of waiting before his hunch paid off. Two women dressed in professional business clothes but they sported slacks as opposed to dresses most women were wearing. Their shoes were styled for running or rather chasing then showing off their legs. Even from a distance he could see that one of them was his Puerto Rican nemesis Ramsey, and the other was one of Cratty's friends.

"Damn."

Three men came from one end of the street and met them halfway down the block. After a minute of walking, four were now sixty feet directly below him while another moved across the street. He turned to make sure the door he barricaded in place was still secured and his alternative escape route, an eight foot leap to another roof was clear of obstacles. His gaze lingered on three midsized potted plants he didn't used to block the door. He felt his mouth form a smile as the thought of hurling down the pots to strike Ramsey filled his mind. His hand instinctively went to his scar, and then it traveled down to his holstered gun.

"I could just start shooting," he said. "But then that would really stir the hornet's nest. How did you find me, anyway?" By now he was looking back over the side of the building where he watched them talk, too far to hear but easy to see that they were scanning the area. He watched for another minute until Ramsey's gazes shifted skyward. Glenn pulled back quickly.

"Okay, enough of hiding."

He looked in the other direction to the distance between the two roofs, did his mental calculation, backed up another three feet before launching into his run. Clearing the eight or so feet was easy. Skidding to a stop on the gravel flat roof was not so easy. He moved quickly to the other side to more roofs heading in all directions, many with large roof exits blocking vision along the way.

"Good cover."

The choice was simple: move in the opposite direction of where his sister and niece were probably playing in the park. He had often watched them from a distance. That's when he noticed INTERPOL. He moved fast putting as much distance between him and his shadows.

"You'd think they would have other things to do than to look for me. Private sector's been good to Ramsey," he said as he cleared yet another gap between buildings. Even from a distance he could see that her clothes were more European tailored with matching sun glasses and sensible though classy shoes. Her wardrobe budget definitely more than her male counterparts that were easily

INTERPOL agents. He was three buildings away when he heard a distance crash of wood, pots and crates coming from behind. He moved quickly to put part of the roof's structure between him and the roof he left behind. He waited just sixty seconds before dropping to the roof top and carefully peered around to see if he was being pursued. It was easy to see that the three agents were looking around on the roof he vacated minutes earlier. He pulled back quickly, got to his feet and looked across the other roof tops to make sure that his escaped would be obscured by the large building structure that was the exit to the ground floor. Rather than taking a chance to hit the road, he decided that he would be able to dodge both the two agents on the street and the ones on the roof if he continued with his building hoping.

"Am I that high of a priority these days? Five agents looking for me? Probably flipping them finger back in Boston was not the best of ideas." He chuckled at the thought. Dumb but it felt good.

After three more roof tops, he turned to look behind him. There was no pursuit. He caught his breath as he looked across the next two buildings. Sweat poured down his face and salt stung his eyes. He had an overwhelming desire to stop and wipe his sweat off and apply suntan lotion. Even though it was overcast in the UK he still didn't trust the ultraviolet rays. His mind wandered as he thought of tanned skin which led him to think of Ruth's last update. The news was that Cratty, Ramsey and the entire crew were all now working for an international security firm under Welch and Helms. At the time, he was relieved in the hopes that they would focus on getting contracts, making money, get fat and forget about him. Over the course of nine months, he was able to duck them four times.

And they're getting closer too.

It didn't take him long to figure why Ruth looked so concerned at the time. He had been right all along with Daniels and Burns, but not so far with Cratty and her crew.

"These Ramsey and Dillon women are very Israeli, very Mossad, Mr. Glenn. They are not to be trifled with," she had said more seriously than he had ever seen her before.

Ruth, Cratty, Ramsey, Dillon…all cut from the same cloth.

"No rules about using taxpayers' dollars with no pesky jurisdictions issues, more money and women with long memories. You played that one well, you idiot." He may have killed Daniels, let Burns live and not pulled the trigger himself on Dr. Caulfield and the others, but they sure as shit didn't give the impression that all was forgiven and that they were going to leave him alone. Before he even knew it, he was on a staircase heading downward. Dimly lit but very clean, Glenn looked out the glass and mesh door window to see that the coast was clear. After just a moment more, he adjusted his attire along with his hair and walked out the door as if he were going to work like so many British citizens. As casual as he appeared, his mind raced to his next steps.

Time to move everyone out.

#

Ramsey was tired from all her traveling. Some of it was business, but her trip with Dillon to the UK was personal. She pushed the thoughts of missing Glenn out of her head and focused on her environment.

"So are you some kind of rich millionaire or something?" Ramsey asked Janeson. By now she was patiently waiting for the uniformed front gatekeeper and security officer to finish inspecting her corporate security identification and badge, license, car rental registration and car itself. With a mirror to check the car's undercarriage and a request to pop the trunk, Ramsey was sure she was going to be asked to step out of the car for a personal inspection. She sighed and waited. The azure blue sky, rose- and earth-colored villas and perfectly manicured grass made the older ocean-view gated community look perfectly charming. The Florida sun now at its zenith, the Spanish/Moorish architecture heralded an age of old money and well-built homes and compounds for the absurdly rich. Ramsey was impressed with the presence of now four security officers and gatekeeper in the "retirement" home development.

Wow! Janeson comes from money? You'd never know it. With time ticking away with their inspection coming to a close, she looked at Janeson, nose in a tablet, still wearing a long sweater and dark slacks and blouse even in the subtropical environment.

There's not much we really know about you, Ramsey thought as she continued to take in Janeson's librarian appearance. With the attire, presentation, and overall feel of an archivist, Janeson's physical features were attractive, refusing to be diminished or covered up.

"My father had very good sense in computer start-ups and my mother is a psychiatrist. Since my siblings are close in age..."

"You have siblings? What the hell, Rachael."

"I don't speak of them very often."

"You don't speak of them at all. What's the deal? Sibling rivalry shit?"

"Overprotection and fear of the unknown."

Ramsey turned back from watching the guards confer to look at Janeson.

"'Fear of the unknown?' Is there deep space exploration involved here or just family dynamics?"

Ramsey's questions were interrupted by the return of her identification forms and a reassuring nod from both the gatekeeper and the cluster of watchful officers. In classic Janeson lack-of-social-skills presentation, she continued to answer the question while still sifting through her "usual" tablet and what looked like a new one that was peeking through her large carry-on bag.

"My sister, Mary, is two years younger than me and is part of the local police. My brother is three years older than me and is a forensic behavioral psychologist for the FBI..."

"No way! You have two siblings in law enforcement and I'm hearing about it now? They could have been helpful back when we were looking for Burns."

"They inserted their way into the case for sure."

"And you kept them out? Is it a competition thing?"

"No. Not really. They would just lead us in the wrong direction.

They are conventional in their thinking. Logical but predictable. The closest target they ever got close to was Mr. Glenn, and that was because he was more focused on his loved ones than his cover."

"Glenn, that pale white bastard! We almost had him in the UK! I just know it...What other secrets are you keeping, Rachael?"

As she listened attentively, Ramsey drove well within the speed limit and watched the bumps so as to not damage her rental. Rachael was in her peripheral vision, and it was easy to see that she finally shifted her gaze from the tablet and was assessing the question as more than rhetorical.

"Many, but they would not be helpful in this line of conversation. But to get back to the previous subject: my siblings are pretty protective of me and as a result, I have needed to keep them at arm's length. That is why, when my projects, business and work require me to come to Florida, I will often not tell them and see my parents without them. Family dynamics have a way of resurfacing whenever we are all around. My father and I are very similar, and my mother...gets me."

"She gets you, as in she understands how you think and what you do, or is it more than that?"

Ramsey's thoughts jumped to her own mother's uncanny abilities to nearly read her mind and could catch her doing things that she was sure no one but God and the devil would know. She pulled back from her own thoughts as the silence persisted. She kept an eye out for the numbers and glanced to see Janeson reflective. A long pause seldom seen. Over the years, Ramsey had been able to work collaboratively with Janeson at the bureau while she worked for Welch and Helms at Allied Federation International, Inc. It was nice having the team together – Davis, Cratty, Dillon.

Fitzy, Witzy and Belben should be here. They would have loved it.

Still, over the past several months, she and others were worried about Janeson, as her directorship at the bureau came under scrutiny by the National Security Agency as a direct result of her relationship with Burns. While there was nothing concrete, there were surveillance, hearings and a whole lot of innuendos. Even with all of her supporters suggesting she should just walk away and work for Helms and Welch, she seemed almost oblivious to it, as expected. So when an opportunity came for her follow-up on a series of leads with three private agencies in Florida, just as Janeson was attending a weekend seminar, Ramsey thought she would take a shot in trying to convince her friend to join up. All arranged by "accident" via Gilmore and Johnson, as always. In the finest tradition of brotherly subterfuge and secrecy, both of them were on their way to her apartment on Beacon Hill to see if they could spot any NSA listening devices and spying equipment.

I'm not sure I would like them snooping around my personal stuff, even if they were like brothers to me. A flash of worry came over her face as she remembered where she hid the porn on her personal computer that she shared with Dillon sometimes. The file read "Tips on Physical Health."

The road came to an end in front of an impressive two-story home, perfectly maintained landscaping with bushes, small trees, boulders, and two benches overlooking the ocean. There was a parked police car in front of the open garage. She pulled up to see that the garage had a beautiful luxury SUV parked inside with a large number of shipping boxes and antique furniture wrapped for transport.

"Are your parents moving?

"Unlikely. They've been here for thirty years before this was a walled development."

"And the police car? Trouble or family?"

"As expected, my sister figured out my itinerary and has predicted my time of arrival. I must applaud her ability to deduce and speculate. Her skill-based competencies have improved. Still, I was hoping to see my parents without her," Janeson said. It was easy to see that her eyes and mouth expressed sadness, her drooping shoulders surrender and her tone was disappointment.

"She's good at being a pain in the ass?"

"Very. My brother is better. But no one beats my mother,"

Janeson said. As she spoke, she pulled her oversized bag together, filling them with other electronic pads, notebooks and other gadgets that were hidden in her pockets.

How do you carry all that stuff and not bulge out and look homeless?

Ramsey exited the car, stretched her back and looked around the lawn. To the far right of the open garage she saw a dozen plastic flamingos, all various sizes and stances but identical in color and details, carefully arranged in a group resembling a march towards the road. She stopped at the walk to the door, removed her sunglasses to take a better look at the family of flamingos. In a rare moment of reading social cues, Janeson must have seen that Ramsey was curious.

"My father has this thing with authenticity, birds and details when it comes to decorating. Why he insists on putting these out every late spring is beyond me." Without further discussion, Janeson marched straight to the door, head looking down, reminiscent of a prisoner heading to the gallows. Picking up her pace, Ramsey was right behind her when the door opened suddenly. Ramsey stopped quickly and went for her side arm that she realized was in her bag in the trunk.

Stupid, stupid, stupid...

After the initial shock of the door opening so quickly, Ramsey could now easily see that the person was an older man, wearing black shoes, socks, slacks, a white crisp shirt and a black tie. His appearance, facial expression and overall look was that of grave concern.

My God! Who's the funeral director? What the hell...

"Rachael! Thank God you're here. I need help with my servers. I've been able to hook them up wireless but I need to hard wire them for extra security and need help from someone who knows what they're doing. Mary is no help and your brother won't be here for another four hours." The man's tone was deadly serious and his situation sounded desperate, matched only by his determination to make things work. Without acknowledging her presence, Ramsey could see that Janeson had picked up her social skills from her father.

No one will ever believe this. There are two of them.

Without so much as a "hello", the man was off and Janeson was in pursuit. Ramsey was left on the front stairs, wide-eyed and not sure what to do next. She put her sunglasses in her breast pocket and really debated just waiting in the car.

Okay...Do I stay out here or head on in and make myself a sandwich, get a beer and re-arrange the furniture?

"You kind of get used to that," she heard a woman say from inside. Ramsey took a couple of steps closer to look in. She saw a more muscular, shorter version of Janeson dressed in full police uniform, with Glock, baton, cuffs, and stripes indicating she was a sergeant.

"Hi. I'm Rachael's sister, Mary. And who might you be?"

"Ah, I'm Ana Ramsey. I'm a friend of your sister..."

"Close friend as in Gilmore and Johnson, or co-worker/friend as in Martin?"

Ramsey took a moment to assess the subtle differences and to allow her eyes to adjust to the comparative darkness of the hallway.

"More like Davis, closer to Johnson but further than Martin."

"Close enough to have answers."

"Answers? Answers to what?"

"Want a beer? Come on back here and shut the door." The woman's tone was curt and her retreat to the back of the house swift. Surprised by the brusque response and how Mary just walked away, Ramsey came in, shut the door and headed in Mary's direction even though she heard Janeson talking to her father in a calm way in the other direction.

I think I might want to skip dinner here.

Deceptively larger in size than it appeared outside, Ramsey fell into a large, perfectly arranged kitchen with cherry wood cabinets, stainless steel appliances and perfectly matching marble and floor tile. With the kitchen facing the ocean, the windows overlooking the Atlantic were panoramic, floor-to-ceiling windows with sliding doors at both ends.

Jesus, Mary and Saint Joseph! Now what companies did her father invest in and where can I find some?

It was very hard to pull herself away from the view. She found herself taking a couple of steps to the island where a cold beer and Mary waited for her, no beer in her hand at all. *Well, it looks like I'm drinking alone.*

"So what's your name, again?"

"Are you having a beer too or are you on duty?"

"I had three already. So what's your name?"

"Ramsey."

She looked at her and found herself wanting to get in her face.

So no social skills and hearing issues...If I didn't know better I'd think you were a rude bitch.

Ramsey now felt her jawline tighten and the corners of her mouth and eyes grow taught. There was silence.

"Ana Ramsey. I'm a friend of Rachael's," she added.

"Well then, maybe you can help me out with getting a message to her other *friend*, Alex Burns. Can you let him know that he's screwing up my sister's life and I don't much like it? You think you can get that message to him?"

By now, Ramsey was not surprised by either the less friendly or the police-like, authoritative tone. Before she could even think, Ramsey's mouth shot off faster than she wanted.

"I'm sorry, and who the fuck are you and what the fuck do you want me to do?"

Well, that's not exactly friendly, Ana...

"I've got one sister, and she's getting a lot of shit from knowing this asshole..." Mary started with her finger pointing accusingly at her.

Alright! Here we go!

"And what makes you think I can control that? And why do you think I'm here? I want her to work with me and get away from that shit place..."

"The FBI is fine. It's her association with this asshole who's the problem. She had a pretty good thing going until that terrorist-spy showed up!"

"You think I asked him to show up? No one wanted Burns to show up, anywhere or any time. Why are you crawling up my ass? You're her sister and a *sergeant* - can't you do something?"

"She doesn't listen to me!"

"Now there's a shock!"

Ramsey felt she was ready for fists to fly, and she was sure that Mary was about to jump in until she heard a sharp rapping at the sliding door. Ramsey pulled her heated gaze beyond Mary, and saw a striking older woman, dressed in a white pencil skirt, matching blouse and tailored blazer. She was holding two bags of groceries. With the adrenalin flowing through her veins, Ramsey was startled by the woman's presence, and how she looked – stately, calm, focused and very familiar. As her fight instinct subsided and Mary's hostile presentation suddenly collapsed, she was impressed with how petite the older woman looked, and how her blonde and gray hair made her look much younger than she expected. But it was the stylish sunglasses placed on her head, tasteful jewelry and striking blue eyes that made her take another look before she was convinced that this had to be Janeson's mother, and how Janeson would look if she wore makeup and similar clothes.

Wow...is this mom?

Mary turned back to Ramsey as she walked to open the door. It was clear that Mary wanted the matter to remain private.

"This is just between us. My mother doesn't need to know," she hissed out as she turned back to open the slider.

"Yeah. Whatever."

Now this is really messed-up family dynamics. I guess Janeson was more than right on this one.

Ramsey did her best to pull herself together and put on her pleasant game face. Still, as hard as she tried, she still felt anger, adrenalin and the desire to hit Janeson's sister such that she picked up the beer and drank it quickly. She drank the majority of its contents by the time the woman moved from the sliding door, handed a bag to her daughter, and walked to the other side of the kitchen. It was evident that she noticed the urgency of her drinking her beer.

"Hi Mom. I was just stopping by to see dad when Rachael and her friend Ana stopped by. It looks like Dad is having issues with the servers and wireless again," Mary said casually. Mary's movements, tone and demeanor were totally altered to a calm, easygoing state as she started to pull out the contents of the bag.

Yeah...this is pretty messed up.

The mother ignored her daughter. It looked like the woman was going to say something but thought better of it. Instead, she turned to face her, pulled her sunglasses off her head and gave a warm smile as she extended her hand to Ramsey.

"Hello Ana. It's very nice to finally meet you. Rachael has spoken very highly about you, Christine, Jillian and everyone." Her handshake was firm and dry with a perfect squeeze. It was only then that Ramsey realized that her own hand was sweaty from the prior verbal altercation. Her thoughts didn't stay very long on her sweaty palms as she recognized that Janeson's mother knew all of their first names.

Finally...someone normal! And she knows our names too. I guess Rachael does have an outside life?

"Yes, Ma'am. It's very nice to finally meet you too," Ramsey said. Suddenly, her mind went blank as she tried to remember anything that Janeson had ever said about her mother, no matter how trivial.

Good God! I don't even know her name! Damn it, Rachael – what the hell!

"My name is Margaret, in case my Rachael spoke in vague terms of a family and parents, which she has been known to do," she said with a reassuring smile.

"Thank you," Ramsey said with too much emotion and relief to escape notice.

Why don't you stick with protection duty and investigation and steer clear from covert operations, Ana – you really suck at hiding emotions. Wonder why everyone can read you, dumb ass!

"Well, I thought as much. So what brings you here? Rachael tends to show up within an hour's notice and is typically alone," Margaret said. She backed up away from her, leaned against one of the cabinets and began watching her younger daughter Mary as she slowly and quietly started putting things away. While Ramsey started to talk about how she and Janeson were traveling together, it was obvious to her that Margaret was listening but was also assessing her daughter's behavior and state of mind. The scrutiny was palpable and it was finally evident when Mary put a quart of milk in the cabinet, and seemed more intent on listening than watching what she was doing.

Okay...this is really messed up.

Ramsey watched the interaction and began to hear slightly elevated voices from the other room, orders given about "codes" and routers.

"I'm sorry Ana, but I need to ask Mary something. Just stay there. Mary?" Margaret asked in a therapeutic voice, legs crossed at the ankles, hands folded in front of her as she addressed her daughter.

Oh shit! Looks like Mary is going to get called out.

"Yes, Mom," Mary said as she put a box of cereal in the cabinet the milk was in. It was then she noticed what she had done and undoubtedly what was next. The shoulders slouched and her hands fell away from the cabinet and landed on the granite counter.

And I thought I sucked at covert operations.

"How come you're here? It's Friday afternoon and you should be working. And Rachael called me two hours ago?"

The silence hung in the air. It was clear that Margaret's disposition and clinical training were playing themselves out as she patiently waited for an answer. By now, Ramsey just wanted to run to the car and wait. Sure that she would be halted in her steps by Margaret should she try, she felt like a witness to an execution.

"I...I was just stopping by..." Mary started but was immediately cut off by her mother. Margaret shook her head no and said as much as she looked at her daughter, who slowly turned to face her.

"No, no, no, Mary. Your sister is nearly forty years old, and you're not in middle school anymore."

"But Mom! She's messed up with…" Mary started with her hands akimbo and the sergeant voice starting up. In a flash, Ramsey's eyes widened as she watched mild-mannered, well-put-together Margaret move from a casual leaning posture to standing erect with her hands still folded but her voice firm and eyes piercing.

"Do not take that tone with me, Missy. I am your mother. And as I am the mother, you are not your sister's protector, and you are not going to push people around. And if your brother is on his way to 'visit' too, then you better call him right back and make sure he's bringing my grandchildren for the entire weekend. It would be nice to see all of you before our trip. Otherwise, he better not show up. And since you are here, you can put on civilian clothes, call Barry and have him bring Jennifer over for dinner. Do you understand me?"

As Margaret spoke in a clear, unyielding voice, Ramsey watched with barely concealable joy how Mary's entire posture and stance fell apart. She looked far more docile and tame than she had since she arrived.

"But Ma!"

"I didn't ask you to say anything, Mary. Am I clear?"

"Yes."

"And will I have to talk to you like this again?"

"No, mom."

"So we are done discussing this matter?"

"Yes, mom. Sorry, mom."

I really shouldn't have drunk that beer so fast, Ramsey thought suddenly. Even as her bladder filled, she felt a smile emerge, gratified with watching Mary's defeated look as she gazed at her feet while her hands dropped to her pockets. It was easy to see she was fishing around for her cell phone.

"I better call Barry."

"Yes. And make sure he knows what kind of mood I'm in."

"Yes, Mom. If he hasn't left, do you want him to bring the family and come over for dinner?"

"Yes, but make sure he leaves his law-enforcement persona at the door. And change your clothes."

"Yes, Mom," was all Mary said as she walked out of the kitchen. She was heading to where the voices were still coming from the back of the house. While still feeling a smile pulling at the corners of her mouth, Ramsey resisted the urge to stick her tongue out as Mary passed. Left alone, she suddenly felt as if she were in the presence of Denise Cratty and her mother when they were angry, and the smile evaporated for fear that she would be next. She was grateful and relieved to see the warm smile and calm demeanor of the woman return as she nonchalantly removed the milk from the cabinet to put it in the refrigerator. It was easy to see that she was preparing to make dinner as she collected fresh vegetables. Margaret pointed to a seat at the island for her to sit on and started to talk as she busied herself with pulling pans out. With beer in hand, Ramsey risked another gulp of beer even as her bladder felt full.

"I apologize if Mary was rude to you. She's worried about Rachael but she should know better than to be pushy with her friends."

"Yes, Ma'am," was all Ramsey said. She decided to nod, neither confirming nor denying anything.

It will be a whole lot safer if I just sit here and be quiet.

"I'm lucky that Rachael calls me three times a week, at the same time of course, and has grown over the years. But I can see why Mary would be nervous about what's happening to her. She doesn't see the growth and how Rachael has changed. She still sees her as her older sister being picked on at school."

The thought of Janeson being bullied and her younger sister needing to protect her made her feel sad and magnified her own concern for Janeson. But even as Margaret spoke, she didn't seem worried or concerned. Confused, and hoping to gather some of the woman's calm about Janeson, Ramsey was surprised at her question.

"Ah...well, Mrs. Janeson? Aren't you worried a little bit about her, too?"

If there was surprise, shock, or fear, Margaret was displaying none of it.

"Worried about Rachael and her relationship with Alex? No, not really. He's got issues but then we all do, some bigger than others. Unlike most, he knows he has them and seems invested in resolving them. My only worry is, is he ready for Rachael?" she said calmly.

Ramsey was clearly confused but grateful that she went on to elaborate.

"Rachael has been in love before but never like this. She's been obsessive before, and I do mean obsessive on a galactic scale, but there is a calmness I sense with her whenever she talks about Alex, a peace. Maybe she's getting older, or maybe she's just maturing. I do think that for whatever reason, she is ready for being with someone she feels something for romantically, not just sexually, but real intimacy," she said as she moved effortlessly around the kitchen. Her discussion about her daughter and the retired assassin was clinical, without judgment.

Damn...I wish I could talk to my mom about this shit. Kind of weird I guess, but then if you got a dad like she does and your mother is a psychiatrist...

"Mom! Mary's mimicking me again! Is she leaving?"

Ramsey's eyes widened at how Janeson's voice carried. She could see Margaret's eyes closing as if she were trying to shut out the impending argument.

"I am not mimicking you! And yes, I am staying! Mom said I could, 'Ms. Director!'" Mary's voice chimed in.

"It's 'Acting' Director, Mary!"

"No one cares, Rachael!"

"My friends and colleagues care, Mary!

"You don't have friends, Rachael!"

Jaw slackened, Ramsey had a clear vision of being eleven years old getting into a similar argument with her two younger brothers.

Unlike her own mother, who would have dropped everything and gone into the other room to "fix things," Margaret reopened her eyes and smiled.

"You see, Alex Burns will not only gain Rachael, but her family baggage. If he's lucky, she'll take some time and travel a bit and see the world so she can settle down and clear her mind. It would be best if she did it and better for him. I'm not really sure he knows what he's dealing with," she said quietly. Margaret put her cooking utensils down and moved with deliberate, measured determination to the source of the argument that continued to escalate. Ramsey was afraid she would pee her pants unless she found a bathroom soon, and looking around for the toilet seemed less daunting than asking Janeson's mom where it was.

"I'm sorry," she said. "But where is the bathroom?"

"Down the hall, last door on the right just after Rachael's bedroom."

"Thank you."

In less than a minute, Ramsey was going in the opposite direction away from the arguing siblings and was about to pass Janeson's bedroom when the sight of it surprised her. Rather than seeing a perfectly preserved little girl's bedroom or a young Janeson's teenage room, it was mostly filled with boxes and furniture that were wrapped in plastic for transport. She stepped in to take a look for anything personal such as a bed, posters, bureaus, desk, anything, but there was nothing. She was surprised at the absence of youth, childhood or anything lived in. Instead it was a room filled with neatly arranged, packed boxes. At first that was all she saw until she cleared the larger stacked boxes to see that not all the walls were bare. There was one lone picture centered perfectly on the wall with a small picture light carefully illuminating it as if it were a genuine masterpiece, or cherished heirloom. Conscious of her bladder but curious about the picture, Ramsey took a quick picture of it with her phone and retreated quickly to the bathroom. It took her seconds to undo her slacks and garments so she could find relief on the porcelain seat. She looked around the perfectly tiled bathroom with sparkling fixtures, clean pastel towels and frosted shower glass. The walls were a dark plum color in contrast with everything else in the spacious, spring scented bathroom.

"Does anyone ever use this thing?"

She turned quickly to make sure there was toilet paper and was happy that her fears about lack of use were not accurate. As she took a break away from the Janeson family, she took out her cell phone and did a search of the image she had snapped. It took mere seconds to find out what it was. The lone man with a cane clad in 19th century clothing was overlooking a very rough ocean. The man's back was turned but it looked as if he were deep in thought as he gazed into the sea.

"Caspar Friedrich's *Wanderer Above a Sea of Fog*? Of all the things to have hanging in a bedroom. Romantic period? 1818? This in a kid's bedroom? Did Janeson pick it?" She started a new search to see if the picture had meaning.

Images of her own parents' bedroom where Saints Mary and Joseph hung popped in her head. Davis's bedroom now sported original works of Ojibwe Native Americans in her bedroom and home.

Rather, Cratty's and Davis's home, she corrected. She smiled at the thought of how Cratty's influence had civilized Davis since she moved in. Relieved and curious, Ramsey took her time in cleaning up, and then summoned up the courage to leave the safety of the bathroom.

She took a deep breath and put her hand on the doorknob to leave. Her phone chirped indicating that there were a couple of search results for the painting. She took a moment to look at the first couple of entries. Ramsey was surprised to see that the picture was a well-known cover for Mary Shelley's book *Frankenstein: Or the Modern Prometheus*. She took in the multiple images of the masterpiece with cross-references to Shelley's work and influence.

"A masterpiece. No wonder I didn't know it."

Ramsey bookmarked the search, closed her phone and opened the door to get back into the family dynamics. It was quiet, too quiet for her liking. The cover of the "wanderer" got her thinking about what Margaret said about Janeson's wanting to travel.

Travel? Clear her head and see the world? Mother of God!

Chapter 17

"...Full circle. A new terror born in death, a new superstition entering the unassailable fortress of forever. I am legend."

—Richard Matheson, I am Legend and Other Stories

Eleven Months Later...

Christine Dillon pretended to listen as she navigated rush hour near Beacon Hill in Boston. Why Johnson and Gilmore had insisted that she and Ramsey come to the posh urban area for the elite was a mystery. An hour after the call, Dillon's love for mysteries was once again killed by Ramsey's insensate predictions and speculations of what it all might be. Originally, Dillon thought it had something to do with Rachael Janeson since the address was in her brownstone home but Ramsey pointed out the location was at least a half block away that emptied out on busy Charles Street while Janeson's apartment overlooked the Boston Gardens. Dillon had heard quite a lot about Ramsey's visit with the Janeson family for the past week since their return. Since then, Janeson had been out since her dog Roxie died.

"I bet it has something to do with Glenn," Ramsey said. Dillon risked shooting her a look while in traffic.

"Are you crazy? Why the hell would he look for Janeson? She

directs the FBI and she's been under watch from the NSA for months now. You'd think he'd keep away from both agencies that are looking for him."

"He's not Burns, Ana. He's good but he's not that good."

"Which means we suck since we missed him twice," Ramsey said as she looked out the window.

"You'll never let it go, will you?"

"Nope. He's my great white whale."

Dillon smirked at the reference. After years of being around Janeson, Anderson, Welch and Helms, they had both picked up a language of literary references and short phrases that aptly described most situations they experienced. Ramsey pointed down the street on the left-hand side where flashing blue lights from two Boston Police cruisers were parked with an all-too-familiar Johnson talking to someone on the phone.

"Finally, there's Johnson. Looks like he got a couple of units to get us some parking. Pretty nice," Ramsey said.

"Pretty nice since he called us down here during rush hour."

"He and Gilmore have been out here all day."

"How did you find that out?"

"Dispatch told me."

"Jesus, Ana. You'd think with all of your contacts you'd find Burns and Glenn by now," Dillon poked.

"I'm telling you, that white jack rabbit is here, probably watching us, laughing his pale ass off. Anyway, I did a search of Janeson's parents. There's a lot of stuff out there about her father, but did you know that her mother's maiden name was Marprapet Volkonoff."

Dillon's head whipped around to look at her. She had just finished a tight maneuver to park and couldn't believe Ramsey found out this Russian tidbit.

"Jesus! Do you think that's why the NSA is up Janeson's ass? Maybe it's not about Burns but her mother?"

"I've met Margaret. If there ever was a covert operative, it would be her."

"Janeson was in the navy, right? You'd think that connection would have been vetted."

"I think her father's brilliance and his work with the Defense Department probably let it slide. Anyway, I bet we're all being watched now."

Dillon was now out of the car. She watched out to make sure that a zealous driver heading home didn't take out her car door as she exited. Ramsey was right beside her.

"You really have to work on your paranoia."

"Whatever," Ramsey said.

Before Dillon was on the sidewalk and five feet from Johnson, he was still talking on his cell phone and handing Ramsey a tablet. He was standing under a sign "Public Alley 417" located behind exclusive Beacon Street not far from Newbury Street, Trinity Church, Prudential Center and just down the road from the State House. Dillon came along side of Ramsey and shifted her gaze to see images that looked like a live feed into Janeson's apartment. She was pacing around in a cluttered apartment. The black and white video captured laptops, desks with paper books and clothes in piles everywhere as she walked around in her classic long sweater and earth-colored, matching skirt and blouse as she looked at a tablet.

"Vintage Janeson," Dillon said.

"Ramsey nodded and made a shrug at Johnson. He accurately interpreted her non-verbal question. He covered the phone to speak directly to them.

"She's been under surveillance for at least a couple of months. We found the video feeds. Follow me. I found something interesting," he said as he went back to his conversation. The two sets of police officers split up with one set staying with the cars and the other following them. Johnson's pace was quick and Dillon looked at Ramsey who shook her head no.

"This is weird."

"Figures NSA would crawl up her ass. Don't they have anything better to do?"

"Guess not," Dillon said. She was now catching the end part of a heated argument that Johnson was wrapping up.

"I don't give a rat's ass what *Special* Agents Harper and Lee want. Forget about them. They're weird as snakes and I don't trust them."

By the time he finished, all three were at the rear of an alley just behind Beacon Hill. Johnson closed his phone unceremoniously and walked through a basement door. With few options, Dillon and Ramsey followed as the two police officers waited outside.

"Okay, Johnson, what's the deal?" Ramsey asked. Dillon was just glad that the lights were on in the basement. It made navigating the littered landscape easier. Dillon ducked and dodged the usual pipes, bikes, boxes and laundry machines that one would find in many basements.

"Back in the day, there was a fire not far from here. Someone illegally welded some rod iron and the sparks were carried to some debris in the adjacent apartment complex. When the firemen arrived, the place was not so bad until winds kicked up and the fire blazed into an inferno. There were a number of fireman that died as a result. They were trapped in the building's basement at the time."

"Okay," Dillon said. Confused, she was at the end of the basement where he opened an adjoining metal fire door that led into another basement, similarly filled and requiring the same level of effort to avoid falling.

"So there was a proposed ordinance that all brownstones in this area that were connected by a common wall have a fire escape, unlocked and free of debris to be put in place to make sure no one was ever trapped at the ground floor again."

"Are you kidding me? That must have been a miracle to pass," Dillon said. She was shocked that such a law would make it to fruition, especially if it meant the rich would have to spend money.

"It didn't. It was killed within twenty seconds. It never even made it to committee for review," Johnson said. He was now in front of yet another fire door. Dillon realized they were at number four. This one was different. There were two sets of crime scene technicians at this location. One was dusting the door handle and another was looking at a camera mounted at the far side of the door.

"Okay," Dillon said. "Then what the hell are these doors for?"

"Yeah, Johnson? I mean, who put them here?" Ramsey added.

"Now that's where it gets interesting. By the way, how's Janeson doing?" he said.

Ramsey looked at the tablet Johnson gave her. Dillon caught an image of Janeson sitting at her desk and looking at something on her monitor.

"Are you getting a feed on her monitor too?"

"Oh yeah. The NSA is really good at surveillance. Especially when it comes to potential threats like associating with Alex Burns if you're an acting director of an armed federal agency.

"That is such bullshit! Janeson is not a national threat," Ramsey interjected.

"I know that, Ana. Thanks for the update," Johnson said. The sarcasm was clear but devoid of anger. He was on the move again through yet another basement. This basement, however, was in much better shape. It was cleaner, far less cluttered and much more organized. As they proceeded, there were more technicians but they were easily identifiable as Boston Crime Scene Units working with the FBI teams.

"Could there be a Russian connection?" Ramsey asked. Dillon shot her a look. She was positive that had nothing to do with it.

"Oh, you mean Janeson's mom's brother? Dr. Volkov Volkonoff? You'd think that having a Russian secret service chief turned powerful oligarch as an uncle would have tripped some alarms before."

"Are you bullshitting me? Her uncle is some kind of warlord? No wonder the NSA is pissed. That's why she's never been a confirmed FBI director. What the hell was going on with vetting back in the day?" Dillon said. She was shocked that she was hearing all of this now. She was just glad that Ramsey gave her a heads up.

"Her father's connection to the Department of Defense, MITRE and all major computer companies made her processing in the armed forces easy. And her mother is a ghost. Never published, never in the public eye, just seeing patients and teaching," Johnson said. His attention was drawn to his caller ID. He ignored it.

"So what does this have to do with a law not passing about fire doors on Beacon Hill?" Ramsey asked.

"While there was no ordinance per se to enforce this safety measure, it was left as an option for landlords to consider. And on Beacon Hill where the blue bloods hate departing from their money, this was a joke. A joke to everyone except one couple that owned two four-story brownstone units and a foreign private investor who bought a couple more beside them at the very summit of the hill. Right next to the city's Capital."

"Wow! You mean someone actually paid to have this done? That's a lot of money," Dillon said. She had grown up poor and the amount of money she had seen the rich and wealthy spend often shocked her. But Boston's true wealthiest were known for not spending their money. It was difficult for her to believe that someone would spend the money, time and effort to put in a safety system that had no immediate or obvious effect.

"Yup. As it turns out, they did this about five years ago. It took about three years for the city building inspectors to make the connection that these doors were put here. It was only five months ago that all the buildings' plans in this area were modified to show these adjoining doors. I discovered that when the Boston Historical Board found out, they were really pissed and went to the Governor to change it all back. But it was a huge donation to the Gardner Museum that finally shut down the historical society's bid for the change."

"Shit. Money talks," Dillon muttered. She realized that she wasn't jumping over an obstacle course.

"Big money. Like God talking through a burning bush, kind of money."

Dillon let the loose comment go rather than figure out what Johnson was trying to say. She listened to the lengthy story in earnest as she watched how the presence of crime scene units and investigators was increasing with every step they took through each unit. Finally, Johnson stopped at one basement, a tiled floored unit with a stainless-steel washer and dryer, with a very clean furnace and hot water heater. What was really surprising was the fact that in addition to the terracotta tiles, the walls that were not exposed brick were painted a dark plum color and the stairs going to the first floor were worn though well maintained oak. Dillon turned to say something to Ramsey but was surprised by her expression.

"What's wrong, Ana?"

"This color. I've seen this color before. Recently. Damn it! I can't remember where though. Florida? No way!"

"How's our girl doing?" Johnson asked, pointing at the tablet. Ramsey pulled out of her reflection to see that Janeson was still at her desk.

"Johnson! What the hell is going on here?" Dillon was getting annoyed. She was open to many things, especially when it came to Johnson and Gilmore's melodrama of building their point through the art of demonstration. One had to be in the mood for it. Her patience was running thin.

"Dillon, calm yourself. There's a pretty big point here. Ana, look at the far left corner behind Janeson. It's really hard to see but look at the floor by the door way back and expand the image," Johnson instructed as he ascended the stairs. Dillon followed behind Ramsey and watched intensely as she followed his instruction. By now, all three had to step aside the various authorities and people with scanners, tablets and some small boxes. As Ramsey manipulated the screen, Dillon began to see a sight that would have been all but expected if it weren't for the timing of it all.

"Is this a *live* feed?" Dillon asked as she adjusted her eyes to make sure she was seeing what she thought she was seeing.

"That's, that's Roxy..."

"Son of a bitch! Rachael! What the hell, man" Ramsey said. Her grip on the tablet was tight as Dillon moved the image to get a better look.

"Yeah...it's alive, alright." Johnson's voice was lower and sounded tired.

Dillon looked carefully and saw a small white dog, a small poodle or rather a cockapoo that she had come to know as Roxie, was sleeping.

"No way! No way! I thought Roxie died last week," Dillon said.

"Rachael called out this week to get her head together from her visit and losing Roxie," Ramsey added.

"And she called out every day she was sick for the whole week. She used both phone and computer to do it each day," Johnson confirmed.

All three were now standing on the third-floor landing. There was standing room only. An apartment door was open and the source of the activities was evidently the apartment. Johnson took the tablet from Ramsey who did not want to give it up. He held it for a moment and opened up another window. It was broken up into eight smaller windows of surveillance footage. All areas looked familiar, empty and were readily identifiable as all the places they had just traveled through to get to where they were now standing. Johnson handed the tablet back to Ramsey and Dillon. They looked closely at it again to make sure they were not hallucinating. The plum-colored basement, the ultra-clean basements they had passed through, and the hallway they were presently standing in together with all the others, were empty.

"And just for the record, this is a 'live feed' too. As you can see, we're not here," Johnson said with his hands now planted on his hips. Dillon felt her mouth slacken and go dry. Ramsey's eyes darted up and down from the tablet to Johnson, her expression one of shock. Gilmore's voice startled them from the sudden realization that the live feed was an elaborate visual recording.

"Did you tell them who owns the adjacent units? You know just one of these things costs four million dollars?"

"Nope. I thought I would leave that one for you," Johnson said. An old-fashioned ring came in on his cell phone and Johnson moved off to take it. Gilmore waved them both into the apartment that sounded as if it were teaming with hushed activity.

"Just so you know, Janeson's family has more money than God. Janeson's uncle, on her mother's side, has more than them. So Paul and Margaret Janeson own this unit and the two units adjacent to this one on the Charles Street side, and her uncle owns the two flanking them. It's been in the family for more than twenty years. Our little girl Janeson never had to work but she was dedicated to serving the public," Gilmore said.

Dillon looked into the near-empty apartment. There was no furniture, just empty bookcases and open cabinet doors indicating no food or dishes. The hardwood floors sparkled in spite of the foot traffic. Dillon walked around everyone to investigate empty room after empty room. The reality of the empty suite was a startling contrast to the false feed of Janeson living in a fully furnished home. She heard bits and pieces of Gilmore's assessment of how Janeson's belongings and herself presumably, disappeared. The only indicator of life was one desktop computer. There was a technician who was looking at the rear ports and monitor. The screen was active and its presence was reminiscent of old crime scene pictures of the server Burns had used during the Merrimack Valley Crisis to launch the *Albatross* virus.

Really? She pulled the same stunt?

"About two months ago, the only other occupants on this side of the unit moved out. So the big moving truck didn't bring much worry since the NSA had eyes on her and what they thought was every escape route."

"All those boxes and furniture I saw at her parents' house were hers. Jesus. Her mother knew she did this. That's why she wasn't worried," she heard Ramsey say.

"Has anyone called Janeson's parents?"

"Sure did. Janeson's brother and sister confirm that their parents left for an extended vacation in Europe. The IRS who arrived to this party late found three corporate shells that all lead to Swiss bank accounts. And their US bank accounts have the bare minimum required to stay open. It took Martin one hour to see how they drained the account via investments in gold and other precious metals. Nothing like commodities and cash."

"They're gone, aren't they?" Ramsey said.

"Yup. But her kin don't think our Rachael is with them," Gilmore said.

"Where is she? And do the parents know?"

"I have no idea. And whatever her parents knew, it's clear that they and Janeson had been planning this one for months, maybe even years. The video footage for the last seven hours shows no repeats. The computer file called 'daily life' is massive. And the computer was programmed to do various searches at points so you would think she were home. It was also programmed to turn the lights on and off, and pay bills during the week. The only thing she couldn't account for was taking the dog out. That's why she had the dog 'die' and had her cremated at the Angel of Mercy Hospital."

Dillon's head snapped around at the thought of Janeson killing her beloved pet, a gift from Burns.

"And the cremation was for another pet. She altered the data and certificate. Janeson got into the hospital's records. She's unbelievable."

Dillon nodded. She was looking out the window and saw a couple of agents on the roof across the street. She was about to ask something when she heard a high-pitched whine, flashes of lights, sounds of sparking and burnt electric wires.

"Damn it!" The yell was from the technician who had been working on the computer. Every technician and agent in the apartment converged on the computer. Dillon, Ramsey and Gilmore didn't even bother to investigate.

"And I'm guessing that whatever little data that were on that computer are now gone," Gilmore said parenthetically.

"She's good. Very good," Ramsey said.

"As good as Burns," Gilmore said.

"She's better," Dillon said. Other than the colorful metaphors and expletives sounding off in the other room, she could tell that Ramsey and Gilmore were waiting for her rationale of how their little, adorable, naive Janeson was better than Burns. Dillon spoke next.

"Janeson probably planned this for at least a year even before the NSA starting climbing up her ass and the surveillance started. She put all of this material in place to give the illusion that she was living right here under the watchful eye of the NSA."

"And the only reason we noticed was because Johnson found the surveillance code and locations. If it wasn't for that and seeing the dog, we would be having this conversation a month from now," Gilmore said.

"Yup. Instead, she only has a week or so head start. She's managed to do all this while under the microscope. Burns always did his work from the shadows, hidden and obscured. Subterfuge and obfuscation; Rachael just predicted all of this and planned accordingly in front of all of us and moved on."

"The family knew, too. They all knew," Ramsey added.

"Does everyone know that Janeson's computer just flamed out? All the data, if any, are gone for sure," Johnson said as he entered the room. He was off the phone and moving to join the group who was still looking out the window at the buildings across the street from the Boston Gardens.

"Sounded and smelled like it. Are Janeson's bank accounts depleted or intact?" Gilmore asked.

"They're still there, untouched. Martin's accounting put it at five years of paychecks all direct-deposited. Nothing other than utilities, building maintenance and property taxes paid with it. Nothing else. No shopping patterns to give us any clue as to what she was doing," Johnson said. By the silence around her, she knew they were waiting.

"Her parents own this real estate, she comes from money and just for fun and laughs, she has a photographic memory of classified data and she has a thing for Burns...she doesn't need money. And then there's Uncle Volkonoff. If the NSA was worried before, they're going to go off the rails when they piece this all together. She's got everything covered. She's gone."

"Where?"

"I don't know," Dillon said.

"She's traveling," Ramsey said.

"What?" Gilmore asked. Dillon turned to look at her and could see that both men did the same thing.

"She's traveling the world. That's what her mother said she thought she should do to take a break," she explained. There was a comfortable silence in the room while the controlled chaos in the other rooms continued.

"The world is a pretty big place to search," Dillon said to herself.

Epilogue

"His very existence was improbable, inexplicable, and altogether bewildering. He was an insoluble problem. It was inconceivable how he had existed, how he had succeeded in getting so far, how he had managed to remain -- why he did not instantly disappear."

Joseph Conrad, <u>Heart of Darkness and the Congo Diary</u>

Two Months Later...

Davis was still trying to pay attention to the moon-like landscape as she continued to listen to what Cratty was saying on the phone. It was difficult as she watched neighborhood after neighborhood pass with boarded up, empty buildings in varying degrees of decay on sprawling acres of St. Louis' urban terrain.

"I said Linda and I are going to Vienna for a while," she said.

Wait a minute? What? What?

"What?! Why the sudden interest in heading to Austria?" she asked. After living with Cratty and her girlfriend for a while, Davis knew that neither had family there, or anywhere.

"I mean, if you told me Bahamas, I'd get that. But Austria? After nearly three years of living with you, you still zig when I expect you to zag. And Linda's okay with this?"

Davis thought of how Janeson just fell off the planet and now

Cratty and Linda were mysteriously taking off. To be fair, the analogy was not really apt. With Cratty, there was plenty of notice, as in the call she was on, however sudden. With Janeson, it was like the wind. She suddenly felt sad.

Man. I've really gotten attached to having them around. Even Martin loves it when they're home.

"You know, I have to tell Martin this. He's going to cry. Do you really want to make him cry?" Davis continued.

After a moment of silence, Cratty seemed to choose her words carefully just as she did when she told of her sudden vacation.

"Jill, you know me. I would only leave if there was a good reason. I'm not going to be gone too long, I think. No longer than three weeks I bet. I'm just going to be incommunicado for a while. Linda will be with me and I'll be with friends."

Narrowing her eyes to think, her question was out before she thought it through.

"What friends?"

Cringing as the words came out, she felt her eyes close tightly as her shoulders squeezed into her neck.

Oh that's nice! But after three years of living and working together with Welch and company, I would think I would know all of your friends.

Davis was surprised when the expected sarcastic response did not come.

"I know it's hard to imagine but I did have friends before I met you. But don't worry, Jill. I'll be safe and I'm sure you'll hear from me. I gotta run. Say hello to Burns for me and I'll see you in about a month," Cratty said. With no warning or allowance for any more discussion, Cratty went on to tell her one more thing. Davis was still stuck on why Cratty and Linda would be gone a month as she spoke.

"Oh yeah. There's a brown envelope from St. Louis waiting for you. And there's a small pan of lasagna in the freezer you should thaw out in the refrigerator first and then cook on 350 degrees for about an hour. But eat the spanakopita first in the fridge otherwise it will go bad," she listed out.

"You see Denise? How am I going to live without you in the kitchen? That's the only reason Martin comes over. He doesn't really come to see me... Wait a minute. Where's that package from?"

"St. Louis? Hey, I gotta run. See you soon, I'm sure," Cratty said.

"What the hell," Davis said as she closed the line.

"See you soon?" Three weeks? A package from St. Louis? Where am I right now? With Burns? Kind of suspicious if you ask me. And what's with this makeup he's wearing to cover his scars?

Still in shock by the turn of events and how Cratty ended the conversation without much of an explanation of what was going on, Davis carefully reviewed if there were any specific missions, assignments or projects that Welch or Helms were having her do.

They've been pretty close-lipped for the last three months. In fact, Cratty's not been her usual self, she thought.

Feeling the car slow down, Davis returned to looking at the urban setting and was truly impressed at the bareness of it all. As the car came to a stop, she exited it to see yet another three-story brick building which was formerly impressive but now also boarded up and clearly abandoned. She shook her head and looked at Burns as he exited the car and stood beside her.

"Not much to look at, I know, but it does have secrets. By the way, was that Cratty?" Burns asked.

"Did you send me a package?" Davis asked as casually as she could.

"Sure did. I sent a letter with a plane ticket and destination for our next meeting," he said. As he spoke casually about the package, ticket and other facts, he fished around a backpack for something.

Yeah, kind of over-prepared if you ask me. You ever take a break, Burns? A hobby maybe?

"I know it might seem a bit obsessive but I do like to be prepared," he said as he clearly found two flashlights. Davis nodded in agreement. Now that opportunity allowed, she turned to look at him more fully since she did not have much of a chance to do so when he picked her up at the airport. Without much fanfare, he immediately drove her through desolation to this location. Still, she easily noticed he was well groomed, his scars covered with makeup. As a further departure from his usual blend-into-the-woodwork look, he was sporting a very expensive dark suit. She couldn't help but notice just how different he looked, another person altogether.

Three years after Daniels's death, she and Welch's team had been on the search for missing files and more secrets that were allegedly "out there." She had been the field person to meet Burns about three times a year. The first two years were in California and then Wisconsin. Now they were in St. Louis, Missouri, and he was looking more "European" in dress and style, a fashion that she had never seen him in before. Throwing her a flashlight, he pointed to the side entrance of an aging, brick house with a slate roof. It seemed in worse shape than the other abandoned buildings in the entire landscape. Not wanting to talk about Cratty and her sudden departure, Davis jumped to the obvious questions.

"Burns - why the hell am I here? And what the hell happened to your clothes? Are you heading to a wake or something? I've never seen you this well-dressed, let alone in high fashion. What's going on?"

"Can't a man change his wardrobe once in a while?"

"A normal guy? Yeah, maybe, with a woman's help or a gay friend's advice. But you? You're far from normal."

"Well, that's kind of nice. Anything else?"

"Yeah. I hate the makeup. I like the scars. Makes you look more manly."

By now Burns was moving into the building, leaving her to complain. Davis stood in front of the building. She looked to her left and then right, and saw identical buildings about a half a mile away with dead grass between them. And there were no people.

My God, this place is empty. Where the hell are the people? Not even homeless people. Something about this place, though...Something I remember my dad talking about...

"Let me show you why," Burns said. He waited at the side of the building right next to a large entrance. Impressed with the building's grand entrance, Davis found herself truly wondering how a major city in America's heartland could be so empty. Not even the poorer sections of Massachusetts had such tracts of land that were so vacant. As far as she could tell, more than sixty percent of the buildings she saw on the way here were empty, dilapidated and decaying. Sprinkled throughout other nearby parts of the city were islands of well-maintained buildings, with swimming pools, manicured lawns and privacy fences. These islands stood out because there were so few of them and so different from the fallowed fields and empty landscapes. Once she was inside the building, her flashlight cut a swath of light in the empty rooms. In the darkness Davis followed Burns. She had not mentioned Janeson's disappearance to Burns but assumed he knew. While Cratty, Dillon and Helms were convinced he was in contact with her, she wondered, even hoped, that she left him as much as she left everyone else.

Nonetheless she was hesitant to bring up what she thought was a sore subject, especially since Burns looked so different.

Well, if I don't bring it up, Helms will have my ass. It will also be strange that I didn't.

"Burns? I'm sorry about Rachael. I'm guessing the inquiries, NSA and all the securities were making it difficult for her to do her job," she started. Much to her surprise, Burns's response was both brief and surprisingly professional as he continued to walk around without looking back.

"Well, when you refuse to end a relationship with a known terrorist, the FBI, NSA and Homeland Security are bound to take issue when you're the Acting Director of an armed federal agency."

Davis stopped in her tracks as if she were hit in the stomach. She found her grip tighten around the flashlight and quelled an image of smashing Burns's head with it and burying him in a shallow grave. Her anger boiled up fast at his callousness.

"Nice, Burns. Just nice. She loses her career, directorship and her entire standing in the intelligence community because she refused to stop her contact with you. If it weren't for Welch sticking her neck out to offer her a position, Rachael would be blacklisted. And this is how you talk about her as if she were a misguided idiot? Misguided to care for you, obviously." She hoped her words were as sharp as the daggers hurled at him in looks. Without waiting for a response, she moved aside and kept looking for anything other than him. To his credit, Burns remained silent.

What an asshole! Martin was right. He's bad news!

It was at that moment she nearly careened into a brick wall.

What the hell!

She backed off and looked around the sides to see if there was a doorway. Based on the other rooms, this room seemed much smaller than expected. She remembered she was now on the second floor, having gotten pissed at Burns at the bottom of the staircase.

Is this it? The end of the building? It seemed so much bigger outside.

While Davis's attention was totally shifted to the present, she recounted her steps that she and Burns had walked through the empty building. As they passed from room to room on the bottom floor again, she felt as if something about the building's design was not right. She thought the feeling would have corrected itself or she would have figured it out by the time she got to the second floor.

It really does seem so much bigger on the outside but small inside.

The thoughts of what the building looked like outside and the adjacent rooms just didn't seem right. Davis took her time and moved around the back room of the building again. This time she found herself drawn to a large, blank brick wall that deviated from the other faded walls. All the others were wallpapered with late 1980s patterns and it seemed consistent throughout the building. This was an exposed brick wall. Instead of staying on the second floor, she moved to the third floor where she traced her steps from below and saw the brick wall continuing up with no apparent openings beyond.

Three flights of this...

"Wait a minute," she said to herself. She moved closer to the wall. While the dark environment obscured her vision, she finally noticed that while the brick was old, it was much newer than the exterior walls. Littered floors, boarded-up windows, dark recesses: it was easy to miss at first but Davis made the connection sooner than she was sure she would have if she weren't with Burns, prince of "hiding in plain view."

The only one better is Daniels, and he's dead.

She turned to see Burns's smiling face. It was confirmation at the highest level.

"So Daniels's bunker is real. Where's the entrance? I'm assuming that this interior brick wall was put in place to hide a series of rooms behind it," she said. She pressed sections of the wall to see if there was a latch as she spoke.

"Yup. Downstairs. Second floor," he said as he walked ahead of her. The sudden mystery and new discovery made it easier for Davis to push aside Cratty's sudden departure and Burns's callousness about her friend. Her professional game face was on.

"So after nearly three years of searching, St. Louis, Missouri is where Daniels kept his secret files. His last line of defense," she said as she followed him.

"Actually, it's much more than that. The external hard drives I stole were only five years' worth. The files you extracted from the FIA servers held several years but not all of them. The real private files, hard and electronic, are here."

"You mean there's more?"

"A lot more. Daniels never did anything small. And like the Nazis, he kept thorough records of all the atrocities, names, locations, treasures, everything."

"He was a piece of work."

"You don't know the half of it," Burns said as he carefully pushed one brick which unlatched part of the brick wall to open for a person to walk through. Davis's jaw slackened in complete disbelief.

"Are you shitting me? A hidden door in a brick wall that leads to what? A secret laboratory? This is crazy."

"Crazy? No. Daniels doesn't do crazy or dumb or careless. He does simple and clean. Where do you hide a treasure in the 21st century?"

"In the middle of the last century. When the west was the new frontier. Abandoned neighborhoods that are too much money to tear down and too much to restore. So it sits in plain view," Davis answered. By now she was through the small space on the right behind Burns on a metal meshed landing. Their movement triggered a series of lights which illuminated everything above and below. While it was still mid afternoon, the boarded up building was dark. Now with the fluorescent lighting flooding the hidden stairwell, she had to cover her eyes for a minute to adjust to the brilliance. She found the railing and continued to follow Burns downstairs.

This must have taken him years to build! How does he get electricity here? He must be sapping it from the main lines. How did he get that by the municipal government?

It was Burns's voice that pulled her out of her speculation.

"I'm embarrassed to say that it took me this long to find it. I passed this place dozens of times. If it wasn't for an image of a picture with no name or reference, I never would have found it at all."

"I'm amazed you found it at all. And the other places?"

"Dead ends. They might have been something back in the day but they were now defunct. They were nothing of the scale and secrecy of this place."

"Almost as if Daniels knew this area would become this desolate."

· "Knowing Daniels, I'm sure he manipulated the local governments and local economies to spiral this area to this level of desolation."

"He was that good," Davis asked.

"He was better than good. Not a god like he thought, but he was good," Burns answered.

Finally they stood on the bottom floor of a well maintained, fully stocked high-tech room with what appeared to be sound-, X-ray-proof and/or radar-reflecting walls, or all of the above. Their voices had been absorbed the closer they got to the bottom floor. The air was stale but then air conditioning kicked in. Again, it must have been triggered by a motion detector. Still taking in the magnitude of the intelligence goldmine, Burns turned on one of eight monitors that displayed sixteen smaller pictures of various angles of the very building they were in. Davis looked around with her eyes since they were adjusted to the light. Davis caught sight of cases of meals ready to eat, weapons, file cabinets, and various luggage bags. As she looked through some of the bags, she noticed that one bag was neatly filled with thousands of dollars in cash. Next to it was a smaller computer case that had bearer bonds carefully packed with a small open pouch of uncut diamonds spilling on top of them. By the thickness of the bearer bonds, depending on denominations, there could have been millions in the small case. *And the diamonds? Millions more.*

"My God! There has to be millions here. I guess I was wrong to think that we had all of Daniels's assets frozen," she said.

Without a word, Davis watched Burns come up silently from behind, take the case with the bonds and gems from the shelf and then move it to the computer console where he repacked the fortune. He then fished through a small desk until he found and took out a smartphone and tablet and put them in the same bag. Finally he pulled out a relatively large laptop and put it in another compartment. He zipped up everything and slung the bag over his shoulder. This was all done silently and without hesitation or guilt. Motionless, Davis watched Burns meticulously pack up as if he were about to leave.

Unregistered bearer bonds, uncut diamonds - all untraceable, easy to carry millions of dollars in one case. What's happened to you? The suit? The makeup to cover your scars? You don't care about Janeson? What?

"Burns? Are you stealing evidence?" she asked. She was never good at hiding her feelings. She knew her face must have registered disappointment. If Burns was upset, he didn't show it.

"Yes," he said casually. He adjusted his bag and then looked at what appeared to be an expensive watch before he continued.

"Really?"

"Yes, really."

"And you see no problem with that?"

"No. Not really. Do you?"

Davis was stunned. He didn't seem to care about Rachael and he seemed completely focused on himself. Why she expected more was a surprise. She was about to say a couple of choice words when he looked back at her, motioned for her to follow and spoke as he led the way to somewhere else.

"I am leaving behind millions upon millions of dollars in bonds, cash, coins and jewels. More importantly, I am leaving behind more classified data that will take the intelligence community years to figure out and sort through. It's all yours, Welch's and Helms's to do with it what you want. I think after years of service and what this country cost me, I think a couple million dollars to ensure our future is a small price to pay."

He was just a little ahead of her and she was keeping pace to make sure she caught every word. Right before he ascended the stairs, he picked up a set of military-grade binoculars from the bottom of the stairs and motioned for her to follow.

Davis stood still as she replayed his entire response back in her head. While she might not have been good with hiding her feelings, she did hear well and could reason pretty quickly what was said, not said and implied.

"...ensure our future...?" That doesn't sound like a man flying solo. She followed Burns. There was more to come, she was sure.

What is going on now? He's definitely not himself. Welch and Helms are secretive, and Cratty and Linda decide to head to Austria? And Rachael's MIA. What the hell? Cratty went to Austria? What's in Austria of all places?

Davis was still swimming in her thoughts as she followed him silently up four flights of stairs to a securely locked, heavy metal hatch that led to the roof. Not completely free from her anger towards him, she refused to take Burns's hand for assistance. He acquiesced and let her hoist herself up through the hatch to a flat part of the roof. There were no obstructions which gave her an impressive view of the other buildings that were separated by vast tracts of empty and dried fields. There was just a small smattering of homes that looked inhabited. On a small wall, she saw very powerful telescope already mounted and securely placed. It sat above a bright orange painted arrow that was pointing due east, in the direction of a few, better maintained estates.

Stranger and stranger yet. What's he up to?

As odd as the entire encounter was, she was happy to feel a light wind coming from the east. It was cooler making it bearable on the hot, flat roof. The sun was lower in the horizon and the sky still blue with red highlights. Davis moved closer to the telescope to confirm that it was a powerful, spotter scope used to assist snipers in locating and pinpointing distant targets. She turned quickly to make sure Burns was not touting a high-powered sniper rifle. She was relieved to see him still only holding the binoculars along with the computer bag firmly over his shoulder.

Well, at least we're not up here to shoot someone, she thought while she took another reassuring breath. With her mind clear and her breathing back to normal from the climb and the anxiety, Burns handed

her the binoculars and pointed her due south to another abandoned building. She took the set and peered through just as he took out an old flip phone and pressed a speed dial. On the distant rooftop, she saw a dark-haired woman with sunglasses, a dark tan, and a brilliant smile. The woman waved to her as if she were on the beach holding a chair for her.

Oh, crap. Let me guess.

"It's for you. Her name is Ruth. She doesn't know about this place and its secrets. I wouldn't let her know about it until after you get your team here or the bureau, and the area is thoroughly secured. There's a satellite phone right beside the hatch that is secured," Burns warned. She pulled the binoculars from her eyes and stared at him. He handed her the headset and phone together. And then he produced a folded 8x10 envelope. She narrowed her eyes in suspicion. Davis took the envelope first and placed it under her armpit. She then put the headset on and spoke as she put the cell in her pocket. This freed up her hands for the binoculars again. Somehow, looking at someone as they spoke seemed to be the polite thing to do even if it were several hundred feet away.

"Good afternoon, Ms. Davis. I see Mr. Burns brought you to a vantage point for you to witness justice. After years of evasion, the truth will finally be revealed," the woman said.

Vantage point? Vantage point to see what? Damn it, Burns! What have you done now?

"Are you *the* Ruth that Lieutenant Andersen talks so highly of?" she asked. For now, Davis was buying time as she scanned just beyond the woman to see another figure on an elevated makeshift perch. It was easy to deduce that his prone position was to accommodate a high-powered rifle in his hand. Initially startled, she was relieved that it wasn't pointed at her but rather due east.

Due east. Just like the telescope. Shit...whom is she going to kill? Daniels is dead. Webber is gone. Wise? Who?

Davis put the binoculars down, walked to the telescope as she listened and tore open the envelope.

"The one and only."

"You are much prettier than I imagined. Lieutenant Andersen was very clear you were striking."

"He is too kind. Is he well?"

"Sure is," Davis said. She was struggling with the tear-resistant envelope.

Damn it, Burns. Really? Did you have to make opening the envelope so hard? Is this just to piss me off?

"Well, Ms. Davis, as you noticed, my colleague John is with me, and north of your position, my French colleague, James, is in a similar position just waiting for the word."

"I will take your word on that," Davis casually said. After a forceful pull, yank and turn, Davis was able to take a close look at the photographs, and blanched. She closed her eyes a couple of times just to make sure it was for real. Her gasp did not go unnoticed.

"Ah. You noticed," she heard Ruth say.

No way! This can't be!?

Davis dropped immediately to one knee to peer through the mounted telescope that sat above the big orange mark. She saw the two men that were in the picture. They were sitting in sun chairs, smoking poolside. They were surrounded by both security types in civilian dress and some scantily dressed women in bathing suits in high heels.

"Please tell me this is not what I'm seeing?" Davis said in disbelief. She stood up to look at the photographs again and then back through the lens just to confirm.

"Oh it's true, Ms. Davis. It's true. Two very unusual bedfellows indeed. Colonel Timothy Carter of the Republican Civilian Army, and the supposedly deceased Oman Sharif Sudani, who was supposed to join his terrorist friend, Osama bin Laden, on May 2, 2011. But there is no time like the present to right a wrong, wouldn't you say? I am certain that all our interests, personal and official, will be best served if we send these two individuals to their respective creators."

"No, wait. We just don't execute people here without due process."

There was silence for just a moment until she heard Ruth and a distant laugh break out. The wind was now more easterly. Making a shot at that distance with a head-on wind, no matter how slight, might throw off the bullet's grouping. It might even go wide and miss the target altogether.

"Due process? That is funny," Ruth said.

"Yeah, I know it sounds lame," Davis started as she looked back at the photographs. She was about to do her best to argue to keep both bastards alive but the entire argument was sounding hollow. Ruth didn't let her finish.

"While I respect your government's ideals of trial by jury to save the innocent, I prefer to forgo your justice system and take care of the matter. The way Mr. Burns had originally prescribed so many years ago."

"No wait! Really, we should bring them in. Sudani has intelligence we might be able to use."

"Yes. I heard that from Daniels before. He is undoubtedly waiting for these two in hell."

"No, Ruth! Seriously! We can take them and bring them to justice."

"That is what I am doing, Ms. Davis. Justice. Late but finally here."

My God! I want them dead too but this ain't right.

Davis turned to confront Burns, enlist his support and have him stop this madness. She first turned to her left, then right and looked all around her. He was nowhere to be found. He made his point clear - action by omission and not commission.

"Damn it, Burns! What have you done?! This isn't a game!"

"I think he is carrying out his original mission with a bonus of eliminating a domestic terrorist," the disembodied female voice answered. Davis knew Ruth was just waiting for the wind to shift before giving the order. There was still time but she ran out of things to say and arguments to try. Her weapon could never hit her target from that distance. At first the breeze seemed to die down but then it picked up as hotter wind shifted just from the west.

, *Damn you, Burns!*

"I like your Mr. Burns. He is almost Mossad - a man who likes the closure of a full circle. But enough of talk. *Sparare,*" Ruth said quietly. Davis could tell it was a command. She looked through the telescope to see two men still smoking cigars. They looked as if they didn't have a care in the world. Suddenly, each one convulsed violently backwards as at least two bullets hit their torsos at nearly the same time. With no audible gunshots heard, Davis could see the chaos break out at the pool. From her distance, the screams were barely audible as the targets were at least a mile away.

Suppressed weapons. Two well-grouped shots each...Jesus! These guys are as good as Ice and Nine.

Davis watched helplessly. All the while a warm wind from the west picked up, cooling her sweating body.

"Oh and Ms. Davis? If you have any control over Ms. Janeson, could you please tell her to stop stalking Mr. Glenn? He and his family are under Mossad protection for his assistance in the Daniels matter. And while Ms. Janeson is well-protected by Volkonoff Industries, there are a few rogue Israelis that would like to test that protection. Shalom."

"Rachael? What about Rachael? What does she have to do with it?" Davis heard Ruth sign off without answering the question.

"What does Janeson have to do with this!?" She said again to a dead line. She put the phone down and looked back through her binoculars and watched Ruth and her companion casually walk away from their positions. She sighed and looked at her watch. She really couldn't believe everything that had happened in the last fifty-five minutes. She took a moment to look back through the telescope where she took in the entire chaotic scene. Two bodies. One foreign and the other an alleged patriot.

One reviled and one under investigation.

Davis stood back up and looked once more at the lifeless, desolate urban desert. Absently, she thought of what it was her father had said that was significant about St. Louis. She remembered her dad talking about his father or grandfather attending the World's Fair there in early 1900's.

He used words such as "grand," "filled with life," and "spectacular." Somehow these words did not describe the St. Louis she was now looking at, more than a century later. She finally heard distant sirens and felt the wind pick up. She returned to the present to conduct an immediate threat assessment. There was none. Ruth and her team were gone. Now for the next steps.

"Should he get a medal for killing evil or be arrested for conspiracy and accomplice to murders before the fact? Jesus, Burns! Why do you have to make things so complicated all the time?"

She really didn't expect an answer from the heated wind. Instead, she turned around and headed back to the open hatch, still clutching the photographs of the now-deceased targets.

"I better find that secured phone."

#

One Week Later...

Burns sat quietly in plain view in his new Armani suit in a busy cafe just across the street from a busy hotel. He was taking his time admiring a picture Rachael sent to him. Oddly enough, she had not taken the picture though it was of her. It was very different from the pictures she had sent to him over the course of several months. They tended to be artistic, black and white, and all scenic. This picture was of her back turned away from the camera as she looked out over a valley. She was wearing a close-fitting dark running outfit cradling Roxie in her arms as they both took in a grand view of mountains, trees, blue sky and some fair weather clouds. Her long silhouette was striking even though her face and front were not visible. In fact the only face that was clear was Roxie intently looking at the person taking the picture. Rachael explained that the tourist was so struck by Janeson's image overlooking the grand scene while holding the dog that the woman felt compelled to snap the picture and share it with her. He had already made a copy of it and was manipulating it to reduce it half its size so he could snap another picture to appear beside it. Even with people milling about, he was able to focus on the task while keeping an eye on the activities across the street. He must have looked like many professionals fiddling with his smartphone with the local Austrian paper and a cup of espresso cooling on the table beside him while the noontime throng of both workers and tourists ate lunch. It was easy for him to quietly edit his picture and watch how Cratty and her friends were in complete laughing fits as Ramsey was clearly re-enacting something. Even though it was just barely noon in Vienna, it was clear that Cratty's friend Dillon and Ramsey were pretty close to drunk while Cratty, still laughing, was evidently not inebriated. In the hustle and bustle of passersby going to and fro, Burns felt his smartphone vibrate. He suspended his operation and looked at the caller ID. He answered the cell and smiled.

"Becky. It's about time. Your guests are waiting for you at the *Hotel Das Tyrol*. I'd get here fast before they start falling down drunk," he said quietly. The group across the street was animated in front of the hotel bearing huge red and white banners in the colors of the national flag. The banners went from the ground floor spanning three flights, gently billowing in the wind. The ground floor had an ornate array of red and white outside tables and chairs, and huge gold-colored pots by the grand doors. There were also small manicured trees lining the walkway with still more red and white ribbons on their branches. *Talk about national pride.*

"I assume you can see everything they're doing," he heard Becky ask.

"Sure can. By the way, Cratty looks like she's not drunk but I have to say she's having a good time without it."

"She's been dry from alcohol for years now."

"Was it the blast and leg rehab?"

"No. History of alcohol abuse, being in love and making up for lost time."

"Whoa."

"Word on the street is the last time she was three sheets to the wind was in a dive called the *Purple Sierras* just before you went MIA with Daniels. I guess people change."

"People sure can change," Burns said. "Did you find your new apartment in the city? There is more than enough room for you, Murphy and the kids?"

"My God, Burns. It's all gorgeous. Did you rob a bank or something? The landlord treated us like royalty. But then, I guess having an apartment paid for in full for the next two years is quite a windfall. Even Murphy was speechless, and that's hard to do."

"Is he really a chatterbox? It doesn't fit with a retired Irish mafia type."

"He's not your average former gangland leader. He's such a softy when it comes to his grandkids. Anything the girls want, he's all over it like it's the last act he'll ever do."

"Must be the guilt."

"Must be. How you doing?"

"I'm in good shape for the shape I'm in."

"Well, that's a whole lot better than the last time I picked you up. Are you going to see Janeson at some point?"

"Probably. She's traveling a bit but I talk to her every day and get updates on Roxie and the sites they see. Apparently she talks to me after she talks to her mother," Burns replied.

"Now that is serious," Becky said.

"You don't have to tell me."

"Especially Rachael's mom. I guess the siblings don't care much for you but mom is supportive of her daughter. Understanding woman."

"Can you blame the siblings for not liking me very much?"

"From what you told me about Tony, sounds like you pull that from people. All but one sibling, that is." Becky's voice sounded sad.

"Yeah. I was lucky there." It didn't matter how long it was, he would always love Samantha.

"I'm glad he didn't kill you though, Burns. You were lucky. It was close." The voice seemed to be a little lighter. Burns felt a little better.

"It was close."

Burns shook his head to clear his thoughts. It helped. He moved his head to see around a couple that was kissing to look up the street. They were perfect cover for him to use as camouflage. From his vantage point he could see a very tall Emma and Rosemarie walking with their grandfather. Just a few feet behind was Becky talking to him on the phone. Her eyes were everywhere. He switched his phone to Bluetooth, placed his phone back on the table and went back to his editing.

"So will Davis get her invite too? I'm guessing that Cratty and the girls don't know about their own apartments above and below us. How is Welch going to feel about her team relocating to Austria?"

"I'm guessing Davis will visit. The ticket is round-trip with no date stamp for arrival and departure. She's got a boyfriend at home and the house is her mother's. I think she's attached to it. Anyway, I'm going to be around but will probably be on the move. I think Janeson has a couple of missions she's running. She found Glenn and pulled INTERPOL in the loop but he was on the move before they got there."

"That's like the fifth time in about a year, right?"

"Yup. Time before that was the UK. Ramsey and Dillon swear they smelled his skin lotion on a roof in London."

"He's still pretty good at evasion," Burns commented.

"Glenn? That bastard. If you get a chance to plug him, take it."

"It won't bring David back."

"I know. It's not about that. I just want to hurt him. I got issues."

"We all do."

Memories of all the people he had killed for flag, country and vengeance still haunted him. He was doing his best not to add to the list.

"So I take it you'll be joining Rachael and Roxie soon?"

"Yup. I got a couple of things to clear up in Tangiers and then I have to head to Moscow, too. I'm following Rachael's lead and we'll figure it out."

"Word on the street is that your girlfriend has some pretty powerful Russian family members. I'm guessing that's one reason for the visit to Moscow?"

"Yup," Burns said. "You going to be alright with me gone?"

"Sure will. I've got Murphy and now Cratty and the girls. It's like we got the band back together again." Burns smiled at the comment. He also saw that Emma had spotted Cratty, Ramsey and Dillon and was in a full-tilt run towards them. It was truly a wonderful sight. He was also happy that he was nearly complete with his editing and now needed to take the perfect self-portrait to make the picture perfect. Burns quickly returned his gaze back to Cratty and the entire group of women standing up to embrace Emma and greet Rosemarie and Murphy. He felt a wave of peace come over him. His only concern was how thin Becky looked. She was thin several months ago but she looked like she loss more weight.

"Well, I gotta go, Burns. They spotted me. Thank you for everything and come see us soon," Becky said. Her voice was far warmer than he had heard in the longest time.

"Already am," he said as he tapped his Bluetooth off. He watched Becky look at the phone and then close it. He was sure she would have scanned the area but instead she was suddenly surrounded by Cratty and Ramsey before she could find him. He shifted his attention to his camera and made more adjustments that would make sure to snap his image but at the same time place Janeson's picture beside his with the background behind him. This way, whoever received the digital recording would be able to see not just him and her in the foreground but also be able to see who was in the background.

"You have to love this technology. It's great when it works."

He fiddled a little more and then he peered across the street to see if everyone was finally sitting down. He noticed that Cratty walked with a noticeable limp. After a few minutes more, he timed the passing tourists until he was sure he could snap a series of pictures that captured himself and the entire family reunion in the background with the red and white banners, trees and gold pots. It took seconds to take the pictures. Three minutes more to pick the best, splice them, and call up a quote he remembered hearing from Samantha to add to the text.

"Nothing like a little mystery."

After a moment more, he smiled at his work. He made sure to save it to his screen and crafted a brief text. It was from him with the picture attached and the quote in the narrative. Before he sent it, he stood up to collect his belongings, left money for his bill and walked away. As much as he would have loved to have seen the reaction, he focused on his next mission as soon as he sent it. By then he was already a city block away, deep in thought like so many other professionals on their way to work.

Glen is already out of the UK, I bet. The Panellis are in Naples,

and Wise is still state-side. I bet Janeson and I could find them all.
"Who will find them first?"

#

Denise Cratty was trying to hold back the flood of tears as she held a very tall Emma on her lap and listened to every word she, Rosemarie and Becky were saying about their times "off-grid."

I just can't believe it! Emma's so grown up! And Becky actually looks relaxed. Too thin but relaxed.

Cratty looked at Linda and caught her warm, caring smile as she looked on at this family reunion of sorts. She felt more tears threatening to break through. She just couldn't believe how lucky she was to find Linda, to be with friends and to be so alive.

It's like a dream.

She felt her phone vibrating. She thought about ignoring it but realized that a very short list of people had her number and that it might be important.

It might be Davis. I gotta get her and Martin here. I bet she found out she has tickets to get here.

Careful not to dislodge Emma from her lap while favoring her weak, aching leg, Cratty sighed with relief when she finally located and opened her phone for an incoming text.

"'All's well that ends well.'" was all the text said.

What the hell? Is this one of Andersen's famous mystery quotes? I hate it when he does this! Who the hell reads anyway?

Cratty was about to close the text when she realized there was a picture that somehow looked familiar at the bottom of the text. White and red banners, gold pots, trees with ribbons and a whole bunch of tables with people at them. Ten full seconds passed before it was clear to her that she was looking at a picture of the reunion.

"You've got to be shitting me! That bastard did it again!" Cratty's head shot up and she looked all around her. Memories suddenly surged of Burns snapping a series of pictures from within and outside a public event that was allegedly secure from intrusion, proving how he penetrated three levels of armed protection at Emma's First Communion in Torrox Costa, Spain, several years ago.

"That bastard! He did it again! He really does piss me off!'

"What's wrong?" Emma asked as she obviously felt Cratty's body jolt with surprise.

"Something wrong, Boss?" Ramsey asked. Without prompting, she too started to look around for anything out of place. Cratty was still scanning the area as she answered Linda squeezing her hand for the unasked question.

"I can't believe he did it again! He does this all the time!"

she continued, looking all around until her eyes settled on Becky who was smiling.

"When did he send it?" Becky asked calmly.

Cratty looked at the text receipt. She had to break away from a split picture merged together. It showed a smirking Burns in one half and in the other was Janeson's backside overlooking some mountains with Roxie's face peering at her. She had no clue where Janeson and the dog were but it was clear that Burns was just across the street to take a picture of them all.

"Less than two minutes. What balls! And Janeson's there too, and boy, does she look different. I guess we can still list her as MIA but she's alive." Cratty heard resignation in her own voice. She handed her phone to Ramsey to see and pass along.

It might as well have been two hours ago, she lamented.

Ramsey looked at the picture and then looked behind her as she clearly figured out the point of view and handed the phone to Dillon.

"I'm sorry...did I miss something?" Cratty heard Rosemarie ask.

"It's Uncle Alex, isn't it? Let me see," Emma asked excitedly.

"Oh yeah! He's the guy who saved us. He was shot in the butt!"

"You saw that?"

"It was gross."

It was Dillon's turn to stare at the picture and look around as she handed the phone to Becky, who didn't even bother to look as she passed it along to Murphy.

"Wow! Ms. Janeson looks beautiful! I'm so happy Uncle Alex

and Ms. Janeson met. Hey Mom? I bet Pappa would have liked them together," Emma said as she passed the picture along.

"He sure would have, hun."

"Well, at least it's not a picture of my ass," Dillon added. As if to convince herself, she looked behind her to make sure no one was there.

"Denise? What did you expect? He's always there and on the move. It's his way. He's a ghost...a legend," Becky said. Her tone was far more philosophical than usual. With little more than that, she resumed sipping a glass of red wine. Cratty needed to take a moment to try to emulate Becky's acceptance of the situation. The Alcoholics Anonymous saying of finding the higher power that will help you control the things you can and let go of the things you can't fluttered for just a moment within her grasp. But it slipped just out of reach as professional competition came to bear.

I expected to be able to spot him at least! I thought I would be able to relax but still be able to see someone I know taking a picture of me! You know – like a trained agent. Jesus!

She shifted her thoughts back to Alcoholics Anonymous and the saying of "One day at a time." She shrugged her shoulders, smiled and looked at Linda who touched her hand reassuringly. The feeling reminded her of how Janeson and Burns might someday be with each other.

"Yeah...I'm just glad he found someone, too."

#

Helms sat patiently thumbing through more files and tablets that were sprawled out over a large mahogany conference room table. He was trying to piece together the full meaning of the half of the phone conversation he was hearing. Watching Welch sitting back in a large, leather-backed business chair, he noted that the chic corporate office didn't come close to diminishing her command.

He smirked while he readjusted the font on one of the tablets. Pakistan and Afghanistan came to mind in complete contrast to their present setting. He remembered the first time he met her in the field so many years ago.

Ah yes. Before you became a legend. You haven't changed much, though.

He looked over at Steve Andersen who was looking at his own smartphone. At the moment, Andersen was smiling as he was obviously adjusting his own screen. Curious but not enough to interrupt him, Helms wondered how long Welch was going to be talking to Tombs so Andersen could go on with his report.

I wonder what it's like for him to see her after all these years? See her as a friend of your kid sister back in the neighborhood, and now CEO of a company? It has to be weird but nice.

"So what do you want me to do? Apologize to the Israelis, French and Italians for handing over Daniels's cache of records and secrets to our own Homeland Security team rather than letting them go through it like it was a yard sale?"

Helms felt his grip tighten on the tablet. He was pissed that everyone else was upset with Burns turning Daniels's bunker over to them and Homeland Security.

"Burns is many things but he seems to draw the line at not sharing national secrets when it doesn't directly affect him. Anyway, as much as I hated Sudani and Carter, I still have issue with these assholes feeling entitled to simply walk into my country and execute people they deemed the enemy. They should be happy we're giving them a pass, again." Helms was happy to hear the anger in Welch's tone. She articulated clearly how he felt.

Damn right! When does this shit end? And if we did that to the Israelis? They'd be up our asses with microscopes looking for every international law to hit us with.

After a few moments of silence, Welch seemed to soften. He looked up to see if her facial expression gave anything away. Welch rolled her eyes before she continued her half of the discussion.

I wonder what he said?

"Don't worry about it, Bob. It looks like Daniels's ghosts and legacy are finally at an end. We're still looking into the Panellis's

locations and we got a lead on Alica Wise. Steve Andersen and FBI
Special Agent Martin just came back. Still though, I really won't be
happy until we tie up those loose ends," she said. It was silent for
just a minute when he heard Welch's voice increase as if surprised.

"No! What was that? 'Black Swan'? You're calling her *Black
Swan*? That's what you guys are calling Janeson now?!" Helms
shook his head in disbelief. Whenever a person went rogue and had
classified information, they got a code name or number. He pressed
the search button to find out what kind of bird a black swan was,
apart from the obvious. He was surprised that Andersen was not
chiming in.

Maybe ornithological science is something he doesn't know.

As he read various sites' brief definitions, he heard Welch's
voice return to its level pitch.

"Yeah, well, the Navy could have done better with vetting her
but that's water over the dam. Janeson didn't need to take files. She's
a walking computer. That said, she could become a walking
command and control center, financed by her rich uncle or parents,
for that matter. CIA and NSA could have handled this better."

Helms came across a number of metaphors and meanings
attributed to the black swan other than an actual bird.

*An unexpected event or something unusual at the time. Huh. An
outlier...something out of the ordinary that has extraordinary effects.
Jesus H. Christ. Janeson.*

Helms felt a hand swatting his arm. He turned to see Andersen
leaning over to show him a picture on his phone. Helms's eyes
widened in disbelief and then motioned for Andersen to make the
picture larger.

*This is unbelievable. Black Swan? Looks like the guys who gave
her the name got something right. Wait till Ellen hears about this.*

It took him milliseconds to identify Janeson's backside, her dog,
Burns's face in the foreground and a whole bunch of activity behind
him.

"Burns and Janeson? Are they in the same place?"

"Nope," Andersen said quickly. "I think he edited that part but that's not the important piece."

Helms narrowed his eyes to see if that would help with identifying more details. The only thing that really stood out was red and white banners and big gold pots in the background at a distance. After looking in vain, Andersen adjusted the focus and brought the background into view to see beyond Burns to a group of people in front of some fancy-looking cafe.

"Are you shitting me?"

"Nope. Classic Burns.

"He's right in the middle of a family reunion."

"Makes sense. He organized it."

"He never gets tired of busting our balls, does he?"

"Nope," Andersen said.

Cratty, Ramsey, Dillon, Littleton, Murphy...everybody.

"For the love of God..." Helms uttered. Andersen pointed to two texts below. One was a quote of some sort and the other was a message.

"His very existence was improbable, inexplicable, and altogether bewildering. He was an insoluble problem. It was inconceivable how he had existed, how he had succeeded in getting so far, how he had managed to remain -- why he did not instantly disappear."

Helms re-read the quote. He found it fitting to both Burns, his situation in life, and the very nature of the situation.

"It's from *Heart of Darkness.*"

Helms looked at his friend askance. Once again, the Reading Detective knew a literary quote.

"Is that all you do when you're not working? Read classics? You're pretty well-educated and well-rounded for a constable."

"I'm not just a pretty face. And I looked it up," Andersen said as he pointed to the text that was forwarded with the pictures and quote. The note was from Jillian Davis.

"I guess I was wrong about Burns. He's not such an asshole. But a romantic?! I got a pair of round-trip tickets to Austria. I'll check in at our German location before I catch up with Cratty and all. Let me know what you think. I'm leaving tonight for Logan at 10:00 for a midnight flight."

"Unbelievable," Helms said quietly. It was evident that Welch was finishing her conversation.

"Well, I'm not worried about uncle Dmitri. The NSA's screw up with Rachael, on the other hand, is a real FUBAR of a situation. She's off-grid now, maybe disillusioned, and a walking encyclopedia of special operations, classified information and raw intelligence. They should have treated her better. They should have come to me or Helms. We would have figured it out. We can only hope she's at some museum or something. And if she's really in love with Burns and they get together, that is a potential security breach." There was more silence as Welch listened. Her tone when she spoke seemed to increase in intensity.

"So what were they thinking, acting like dicks to her!? Questioning her loyalty? Janeson of all people! *Black Swan? Really?*"

Helms looked back down at the phone's picture and then at Andersen. He knew that his timing might be bad but necessary. He waved to Welch, turned the phone over, he showed Welch. It took her a minute to take in all the data. It was easy to see that as each second ticked by, her jaw tightened. Eventually she covered the phone so she could speak.

"Are you two just screwing with me or is this for real?"

"Sorry, Diane. I just got it from Davis a minute ago, who just got it from Cratty five minutes ago...'Once more unto the breach, dear friends, once more...'" Andersen said. Helms looked back at Andersen as he retracted the phone and handed it back to him.

"Do you have a 'Quote of the Day' calendar or something?" Helms asked. He never heard the answer. His focus was back on Welch. It was rhetorical anyway.

"Bob? I gotta go. I think I might need to get ahead of a shit-fest that might come our way if someone reasonable doesn't step in. Tell Jacobson and all the other Homeland team to back off, and put the NSA on the shelf so that the adults can handle the Janeson situation, otherwise it could get a lot worse instead of better. And also remind them that Janeson and Burns found Daniels's shit and they could have given it to the highest bidder, you know, like her Russian uncle maybe. For all we know, Burns could have a whole bag of secrets he could unleash. And if I learned anything about him, he gets really pissed off when you betray him. If we screw with Janeson, that just might be enough to put him on the other side, again. The last time we did that, a civilian was killed with a whole lot of agents, and a whole lot of secrets got out. Talk to you later."

Welch hung up the phone and rubbed her temples. Helms didn't have to struggle too hard to pull up memories of Samantha Littleton being gunned down in Boston Plaza. And the secrets that flooded the Internet? He really didn't want to go back there.

A set-up from the start. And me and my team used like a tool.

Helms recounted for the millionth time if there was anything he could have done differently that day.

"Jesus H. Christ! Please tell me there's no warning or threats with that picture," Welch asked as she motioned to hold the phone for closer inspection.

"Nope," Andersen responded quickly. "Just another message in Burns's usually cryptic though literate self. Clearly the influence of Dr. Caulfield made an indelible impact."

"Hmm. Joseph Conrad, *Heart of Darkness*. I guess he sees himself as Colonel Walter Kurtz," Welch said. The fact that she was familiar with the quote, author and title impressed Helms. More shock than surprise, his expression was easily interpreted.

"Come on, Helms. The book was a classic. Soldiers, darkness, good versus evil, a soldier gone rogue. Fitting for Burns. And now Janeson. You'd love it."

Helms thought about surprising them with how applicable "black swan" was for Janeson. He decided to keep up his appearance of illiteracy. Fewer expectations, he thought.

"Alright. I'll take your word for it," Helms said. His smile faded as he assessed the situation. "You're right about Janeson and Burns getting together," he continued.

"It could be a real problem, especially if our government feels the need to do something," Andersen chimed in.

"Or the French, Italians..."

"Or Israelis. Of all of them, it's them I worry about," he said. The room was quiet for a moment as the gravity of the situation set in.

"And if Dr. Volkov Volkonoff is as tied in as we think, then Janeson and Burns have some off-the-charts resources, as if they needed any more," Helms said.

"What do we call him? It's an animal,right," Andersen asked.

"'Wolf.' His first name translate loosely into Wolf," Welch answered.

"For some reason, that figures," Helms said.

The room was quiet for a moment. Between Wolf and the Black Swan, it looked as if things were going to get worse rather than better.

"Alright, one thing at a time," Welch said. She handed the phone back to Andersen and picked up an orange case file. It was thick and well-worn. Helms put his tablet down to pick up his pad and pen again to continue with his notes. He planned to read more about the Black Swan Theory later.

"So, Steve? How do you know it was Alica Wise who was the 'Angel of Mercy'?" Helms asked. He found the spot in his notes where he left off just when Tombs called. Andersen picked up the story again.

"Well, when Martin and I had finally found the animal hospital in the middle of 'nowhere' North Dakota, they were surprised that a Massachusetts detective and an FBI agent were interested in how a stranger brought a severely beaten dog to the hospital."

"Well, that makes sense."

"They originally thought it was the woman who had hurt the dog but when she stayed there until they came out of surgery and paid them in cash, they were pleasantly surprised but didn't know what to make of how she paid. The surgery was about two hours long with an additional two hours of prep and post operation. She stayed through all of it."

"How much money did she spend?" Helms asked. He was already sure it would be in the thousands.

Animal care is just as expensive as human. Well worth it, too.

"Three thousand for the urgent care and then she put another two thousand for medicine, room and board."

"Not cheap. She sure has issues," Welch commented.

"They were also surprised when she left the truck she drove in with. They saw another guy pick her up and they left together. After a couple of hours in the sun, the smell from the truck started to really come through. It wasn't long after that they found the dog's owner's body in his truck," Andersen continued.

"Not exactly covert, is she?"

"Nope. Local authorities identified the pet and truck owner as a guy who spent a lot of time in front of judges for domestic violence, assault and battery, DUI's, and, worse of all apparently, multiple reports of cruelty to animals. He posted some of his killings on the Internet. A real charmer," Andersen said.

"Sounds like she was doing society a favor with this one," Helms said. "Dare I ask cause of death?" He picked up another tablet that showed a body on an autopsy table.

"He was shot close range four times in the chest and once in the head."

"I guess that is the first murder in this town in a while," Welch said.

"Yup. The town's on edge. It probably didn't help that me and Martin were out there six hours after they found the body."

"Witness reports?"

"The staff at the hospital remember she was a 'pretty little thing,' in a very 'hip and stylish' outfit and boots, but covered with blood splatter. They initially thought the blood was from the dog's injuries. There were no prints on the vehicle but there were two strands of hair on the dog's collar. It might be a match, should we ever catch her again. This crime scene is all consistent with Officer Tate's murder in Connecticut and how the cat seemed well cared for while everyone else around it was killed with conviction," Andersen said. By the end of his report, he was shaking his head.

Fact is stranger than fiction. A killer with a soft spot for animals, a rogue, covert spy taking his own picture for worldwide distribution, and the mild-mannered, logical Janeson off across the ocean to be with the same former spy-turned-terrorist-turned-nice-guy. Black Swan. Falcon. You just can't make this shit up.

Helms sat silently in his own thoughts. He looked at Welch for her thoughts.

"Well...it looks like we still have our hands full with the Wise siblings and the Panellis still at large. Jeffery Glenn is also off-grid with his family. And our girl Rachael has earned the code name Black Swan. And the only thing that might be on the quiet side is Alexander Burns," Welch said. Her eyes narrowed suspiciously at her own statements.

"For now, Diane, for now," Helms said. He took Andersen's phone again and looked back at the picture of Janeson, Burns and the dog.

I hope we don't screw this up like last time.

List of Characters

Alexander J. Burns – aka "**Falcon 5.**" First seen in *Albatross,* Burns survives a helicopter crash while en route to a black-ops mission to kill the terrorist leader, Oman Sharif Sudani. Brain-injured, he gets treatment that helps him regain his memory, and realizes he is a logistics field operative for the Foreign Intelligence Agency, FIA.

Samantha Littleton – aka "**Raven.**" Introduced in *Albatross* and carries into *Raven*. She is the first to find Burns being sedated in the hospital and facilitates his transfer to an outside psychologist who specializes in assisting trauma victims regain their memories.

Dr. David Caulfield – aka "**Samuel Coleridge.**" First seen in *Albatross* and carried through to *Raven* and *Eagle,* he is the psychologist who treats Burns and helps him regain his memories. He is also the one who convinces his friends to take the fight to the Eric Daniels' organization, the FIA.

Eric I. Daniels – aka "**Eagle.**" Mentioned in *Albatross,* first seen in *Raven*, and fully elaborated on in *Eagle,* he is the Chairman of the FIA, a privately held, clandestine intelligence agency that will work on behalf of the United States government when it aligns with its own interests and objectives.

Becky Littleton – aka "**Tiny.**" Introduced in *Albatross* as Samantha's older foster sister as well as Emma Littleton's primary caretaker after her brother, Tony, is killed by the mob. In *Raven*, her lethal skills grow exponentially, as does her role as mother, sister and wife.

Steve Andersen – Lieutenant, North Reading Police Department, MA, is the first to interview the witness "Samuel Coleridge" in *Albatross*. Additionally, he was on the team of Army Intelligence at Guantanamo that connected the dots to locate Oman Sharif Sudani. He is also best friends with Diane Welch who grew up in the same South Boston neighborhood.

John Helms – FBI Director, Boston Regional Office, he is the first to detect the diversions and covert plan in *Albatross,* as well as attempting a negotiation for peace with Burns in *Raven*. He was also Diane Welch's CO briefly in Afghanistan.

Rachael Janeson – aka "**Black Swan.**" Specialist at the FBI Boston Regional Office in *Albatross*, she becomes lead specialist in *Raven* where she exposes a plot to thwart the FBI's attempt to bring Burns into custody, and promoted to Deputy FBI Director in *Eagle* where she manages a rescue operation in Spain and a manhunt in Tangiers.

Diane Welch – Commandant, Massachusetts State Troopers, first mentioned in *Albatross* as Steve Andersen's close friend. In *Raven*, we discover she was a Warrant Officer of a Marine Air Ground Task Force on a covert operation to stem the flow of arms from the Swat Valley, Pakistan. Betrayed by Thomas Webber, member of Daniels' FIA team in *Raven*, her role continues in *Eagle* with her in hot pursuit of Eric Daniels.

Thomas "Steel" Webber – First seen in *Raven* as the "face" of FIA, and Eric Daniels's top man, we learn in *Eagle* that he was the team leader responsible for keeping Burns sedated and monitored in *Albatross*.

Jillian T. Davis – aka **"Cougar."** First seen in *Albatross*, she is an off-duty manager of the FIA's Operations Center who is recruited to courier top-secret, external hard drives to a secure location. In *Raven*, Davis leaves the FIA and teams up with the FBI to negotiate with Burns, while in *Eagle*, she is lead field specialist with Thomas "Nine" Williams and Daniel "Ice" Maddox, to disrupt Daniels' plans and take down one of his key players.

Denise Cratty – Introduced in *Albatross*, she is the on-duty manager of the FIA's Operations Center when it is compromised. In *Raven*, Cratty is on probation in the new Operations Center where she is the unlikely peacekeeper to end a dangerous standoff and then becomes lead agent on a VIP protection team in Spain. In *Eagle*, after tragedy strikes, she vows to bring her team back to the US and find the people responsible.

Jeffery Glenn – Seen first in *Raven* as mild-mannered Operations Center boss of Cratty and her team stationed in New York. In *Eagle*, after he is discharged from the FIA, he is paid for one last assignment that puts him on a path that will alter Cratty's and Burns's lives forever.

Emma Littleton – Introduced as a baby in *Albatross*, she is under the care of Becky Littleton and David Caulfield. She is introduced to her half-sister, Rosemarie, in *Eagle*. Their shared biological father is the son of South Boston mob leader, John David Murphy.

Alica Wise – Introduced in *Eagle*, she is a former Foreign Intelligence Agent specialist recruited for the top-secret, deep-cover "Intimate Contact" Branch. Still aligned with Daniels, she plans to carry out her orders no matter what.

Christine Dillon & Ana Ramsey – First seen as part of Cratty's Operations Center team in *Raven*, they later become leaders in their own right in *Eagle*. They are close friends of Cratty and her team members Cindy Belben, Kelly Fitzgerald and Molly Horowitz.

John Daniel Murphy – Leader of organized crime in South Boston, he is the paternal grandfather of both Emma Littleton and her half-sister, Rosemarie Flores. His character is hinted at in *Albatross* and *Raven* as the father of the man who kills Tony Littleton.

Dr. Volkov Volkonoff – aka **"Wolf."** First mentioned in Falcon, his late appearance reflects the cloak of mystery that surrounds Rachael Janeson's maternal uncle. His involvement in the Russian intelligence community is well documented though unclear in details. With the sole exception of watching out for his niece, his motivations remain unknown.

A Note from the Author

If you enjoyed this book please feel free to let your friends know about it. I would also appreciate it if you could leave a review. For more information on my other stories, please feel free to stop by my websites: www.jmericksonindiewriter.com

About the Author

In addition to the *Birds of Flight* series, J. M. Erickson has written the science fiction novellas *Future Prometheus I & II* series and *Intelligent Design: Revelations*. Erickson earned his bachelor's degree from Boston College in psychology and sociology, a master's degree in psychiatric social work from Simmons School of Social Work, and post-graduate certification in psychological trauma, clinical assessment and treatment from Boston University School of Social Work. He is senior instructor of psychology and counseling at Cambridge College, and senior therapist in a clinical group practice in the Merrimack Valley, Massachusetts, USA.